INVASION

HEARTLAND ALIENS
BOOK 1

JOSHUA JAMES

GET FREE BOOKS!

Building a relationship with readers is my favorite thing about writing.

My regular newsletter, *The Reader Crew,* is the best way to stay up-to-date on new releases, special offers, and all kinds of cool stuff about science fiction past and present.

Just for joining the fun, I'll send you 3 free books.

Join The Reader Crew (it's free) today!

—*Joshua James*

HEARTLAND ALIENS SERIES

Surprise! Meteor shower shocks astronomers

————

WASHINGTON D.C.: *A never-before-seen meteor shower will sprinkle tiny pieces of interstellar rock above virtually all of the continental United States later this week.*

"Perhaps what is most interesting is how unpredictable it is," said Diego Hanchey, a research astrophysicist at NASA's Goddard Space Flight Center.

It's unclear which constellation the shower will emanate from; its exact radiant — the point from which the meteors appear to originate — is uncertain because it's a brand-new event.

The source asteroid was apparently identified by NASA's Planetary Protection Coordination Office months ago, but because it broke up before it entered the solar system, it posed no threat to Earth and wasn't flagged. As a result, the cluster of tiny objects wasn't spotted by land-based telescopes until this week.

In addition to the late identification, the speed of the incoming particles is unusual.

"This isn't something that is orbiting the sun on a long elliptical," said Hanchey. "This is an extremely fast-moving group of interlopers that will pass through our solar system in a matter of days."

Astronomers across the northern hemisphere are quickly gearing up for what is likely to be the surprise event of the year, if not the decade.

"It's going to be quite a spectacle," Hanchey said.

PROLOGUE

Artemis SLS IV Mars Mission Transit Repair Test
15 million miles from Earth

———

MISSION LOG TIME: APRIL 25, 2026 // 15:43:54 GMT

SPACEWALK MISSION PARTICIPANTS:
MAC MICHALSKI, mission commander
DR. SARAH COHN, engineer
DR. VINOD AGARWAL, engineer
GENE HILL, Artemis (internal) capsule commander

--// TRANSCRIPT BEGINS //--

HILL (ARTEMIS ACTUAL): Um, please verify that the A-1 OBD removal of stringer one is complete.
AGARWAL: Confirm, OBD A-1 and A-2 are complete.

ARTEMIS ACTUAL: Okay. Copy that.

COHN: Can I get a tether check? I'm switching handholds.

MICHALSKI: Standby... Tether looks good. You won't be floating away on my watch. Say, Artemis, are we still going to get a good show from that meteor shower?

ARTEMIS ACTUAL: Well, PDCO is tracking a close trajectory. But, uh, unless you plan to go home to watch the lights in the sky, you won't see a thing. And, for the record, Mac, we just call them meteoroids up here. But I think you knew that.

COHN: Don't go explaining the science, Artemis. He's a simple man.

MICHALSKI: You know, back in my day, we didn't do spacewalks when there were rocks flying around.

COHN: Lemme guess, back in your day you had to go uphill in the snow to astronaut school.

MICHALSKI: Both ways.

COHN: You realize you're only 8 years older than me, right, Mac?

MICHALSKI: But in space years...

AGARWAL: Diagnostics are green. Link to communications card ready for data reception.

ARTEMIS ACTUAL: Copy that. Link in progress.

COHN: Those meteoroids will be going one-hundredth of a percent of lightspeed. Hitch a ride and you'll be back home in a few hours, Mac.

MICHALSKI: Are you telling me to take a hike, doctor?

COHN: No comment.

MICHALSKI: Vinod, you have any thoughts on this?

AGARWAL: Don't drag me into this.

MICHALSKI: You're no fun. These kids are no fun, Artemis.

ARTEMIS ACTUAL: Not like back in your day, eh, Mac? Vinod, what's your status?

AGARWAL: System is ready to reactivate.

ARTEMIS ACTUAL: Upgrade fully functional. Nice job, Vinod.

AGARWAL: Just a walk in the park, Artemis. Or a hike, right, Mac?

COHN: Nice.

MICHALSKI: Funny guy.

ARTEMIS ACTUAL: Update from PDCO, uh, well, it seems the tracking on our interstellar visitors has changed. Current path does not overlap with our trajectory but ... it's closer.

MICHALSKI: Copy that, Artemis. Define closer.

ARTEMIS ACTUAL: Too close. Vinod, start buttoning it up.

AGARWAL: Copy, Artemis.

COHN: A tracking update? On meteoroids? How did they mess up the tracking? It's not like those rocks changed course.

MICHALSKI: You know, back in my day, NASA didn't make mistakes like that.

COHN: Well, it was PDCO, so I guess NASA still does it as good as it did all those many years ago, Mac.

AGARWAL: Mac, can you join me?

MICHALSKI: On my way—

COHN: Whoa!

AGARWAL: What was that?

MICHALSKI: [indecipherable] ... contact was close. I say again, Artemis. [indecipherable] ... had a near miss with something. It came out of nowhere.

COHN: There's more! What the hell are those?

MICHALSKI: Artemis, we are aborting. Repeat, I am ordering a mission abort. Vinod, get off SLS structure and over to Artemis now.

AGARWAL: Copy.

MICHALSKI: Artemis, prep airlock.

ARTEMIS ACTUAL: Airlock engaged, ready to receive.

COHN: Those aren't rocks! Do you see this? Those aren't meteoroids.

MICHALSKI: Doctor, I'm not going to tell you again. Get back to—oh shit.

[indecipherable]

--// Medical data loss on DR. VINOD AGARWAL //--

COHN: Oh God!

MICHALSKI: Man down, man down! Artemis, confirming we are getting hit with debris and... something else.

COHN: Did you see that? They're changing course. They're coming—

MICHALSKI: Doctor, get back to Artemis actual now.

COHN: The propulsion tank! It's venting. [indecipherable]

MICHALSKI: Move it. If it breaches the fuel ring, it's going to—

--// Medical data loss on DR. SARAH COHN //--

--// Medical data loss on MAC MICHALSKI //--

ARTEMIS ACTUAL: Artemis to — oh! [indecipherable] no! [indecipherable]

--// Medical data loss on GENE HILL //--

Artemis status update incomplete.

Artemis status update incomplete.

Artemis status update incomplete.

--// END TRANSCRIPT //--

INVASION

PART 1

1
PAMMY MAE

PAMELA MAE JOHNSON stood on the steps of the Heartland County High School scrolling through socials — not that there was anything much to see. The only thing worth talking about, at least in Little Creek, was the party planned for Friday.

There was supposed to be a meteor shower Friday night, and someone had come up with the idea of hosting a rager in the woods near the old Sutton place. It was just an excuse to get drunk and make out under the stars. Pammy had no problem with that—in her estimation, it sounded like a pretty good Friday night. They had plenty to celebrate, after all. Graduation was right around the corner. They *deserved* to party.

She was still scrolling when a loud cluster of boys came tumbling around the side of the building, elbowing each other and pulling one another into headlocks. Pammy tucked her phone away, then pulled her backpack up onto one shoulder.

One of the boys broke away from the pack. Even after three years together, Pammy Mae still smiled every time she laid eyes on him. Objectively, she wasn't sure that she believed in true love, but Nate Lutz was enough to make her wonder.

Nate wrapped her in a bear hug and planted a long, deep kiss on her mouth. The other boys hooted and hollered, catcalling them.

"Hey, Beauty Queen!" one of the linemen shouted. "Call me when you're done dating Meathead here and want to see what it's like with a *real* man!"

Pammy pulled away for a moment, smiling serenely over Nate's shoulder. "Why, Sam, do you know one?"

The other boys laughed, and Sam waved her away. Nate threw one arm around her and pulled her toward the lot. "We still on for this afternoon?" he asked.

Pammy nodded, and let Nate lead her back to his Jeep, blowing kisses over her shoulder to the other boys. A few of them whistled, but mostly they just waved back. They'd all been in school together since their elementary school days.

"Bo and Logan are meeting us there. Is that okay?" Nate threw the jeep into reverse.

"You know I don't get intimidated by boys," Pammy told him. "They're welcome to come, as long as they know they won't win."

Nate hit the brakes just long enough to turn and plant a kiss on her forehead. "That's my girl," he said.

PAMMY MAE'S mother had always told her that she had a 'big fighting spirit.' Mostly, this meant that she was competitive, and that she didn't take no for an answer.

Emma Jean Johnson had been absolutely right.

"Hold onto your hats, boys!" Nate hollered as they tore through the woods on their four-wheelers. Nate and Pammy were neck-and-neck, sending a spray of mulch and loam up behind them. Bo was a little way ahead, and Logan was right on their tail, revving his engine like the nitwit he was. *What's the point of putting the machine through her paces like that, if you're not actually pushing her any harder?* Pammy wondered. Some guys were all about making as much noise as they possibly could. Pammy Mae was more interested in results.

Pammy knew the woods around Little Creek by heart: she'd memorized the topography, and she knew every slope and divot in the landscape, every creek that cut through the forest, every gulch and hill and dry riverbed. She hadn't made any particular effort to learn it, but in all the years of ATV-riding and hiking and back-woods partying, she'd picked up on a thing or two. She hadn't earned the title of Butter Queen based on good looks alone.

Pammy revved her engine, pulling up alongside Bo. "Want to race?" she asked.

"We've been racing!" he replied.

With a wicked grin that was hidden behind her helmet, Pammy Mae really laid on the gas.

She could hear the boys hollering behind her, but she didn't bother to look back. Before long, she couldn't hear them over the roar of the ATVs.

As she pulled ahead, Pammy leaned in. She could lose herself in these rides, out here in the woods where there was nobody watching. She didn't have to impress judges or lead a cheer routine; she didn't have to set an example or please anyone but herself. She was utterly free to do just as she liked.

And, truth be told, Pammy—the golden girl in so many other respects—liked a thrill.

As she shot up the ridge, Logan pulled up beside her and waved cheekily. He was always rebuilding his equipment, and his newly upgraded dirt bike was the only thing that could keep up with her. He shot to the top of the hill, then braked, pulling off his helmet so that she could see him laughing. He thought he'd won.

I guess he didn't get the memo, Pammy thought. Instead of braking, she fixed her eyes on the treeline.

Logan realized that she wasn't stopping, and his mouth dropped open. Pointing out along the trail, he shook his head frantically, then drew a finger across her throat. Pammy ignored him. She'd have to time it just right, but that was the beauty of this: the knowledge that there were consequences. Other people made the safe choice, but Pammy Mae never shied away from a challenge.

She hit the top of the ridge, and time seemed to slow. Logan was gaping at her, the four-wheeler left the ground, and Pammy banked sideways as the ATV sailed out over empty air. She'd known that the gulch lay below, and why Logan had stopped at the ridge.

Eighteen feet wide, she reckoned, *and I can make twenty on a bad day. Never mind the rocks below, or the forty-foot drop. It won't matter, because I know I can make it.*

Logan's screams followed her out through the air, and she saw Nate and Bo pull up short as she flew over the ravine, over the far lip of the gulch, and landed on the other side so heavily that every bone in her body rattled.

She killed the engine and yanked the helmet free, letting her blonde hair spill out around her shoulders. All three boys were staring at her open-mouthed.

"Looks like I win, doesn't it?" she hollered.

"Dude, your girlfriend is *nuts,*" Logan said.

Nate nodded, looking genuinely shaken. "Yeah," he said. "I know."

"See you back at the trailhead," Pammy called. She mashed the helmet back on her head, then took off through the woods.

There was nothing better than life in Little Creek. Everything she needed to be happy was right here.

2

GUPPIE

"HOW'S IT GOIN', Guppie?" asked Sean Hawes, looking up from his newspaper.

Guppie Martin waved to the older man and approached the porch. "Just getting my steps in. You know, the doctor says I've got to keep moving—stay active, drink water, take my vitamins..."

Sean snorted, leaning forward on his rocker. Guppie could remember back when the house was new, but in recent years a green moss had begun to take hold in the boards, rotting the wood and causing the whole structure to slant more and more with each passing summer.

"Buncha bullshit if you ask me," Sean grumbled. "Big pharmaceuticals want you taking that crap, you know, so that you come to depend on 'em. My Nana drank rye whiskey and smoked cigarettes like it was her job, right up until the end. Died in her bed at ninety-eight. You didn't see *her* counting her steps or turning her nose up at a hunk of red meat, now did you?"

Guppie, happy for an excuse to stop walking, ambled up to the porch and leaned against the rickety railing. Like the rest of the house, the paint on the railing was slowly peeling away from the posts, and when Guppie adjusted his grip, a flake of white paint stuck to his skin.

"House is just like the rest of us," Sean grumbled. "Falling apart." He reached into the soft-sided cooler and fished out a beer. "You want a drink, Guppie?"

"No," Guppie said morosely. "Doc says I gotta cut back on my drinking, too. My pops was on dialysis at the end, so I'm just trying to keep an eye on my health while there's hope."

"It's light beer," Sean argued. "It's practically water."

Guppie patted his gut. "Thanks anyway."

"Shoot," Sean said, shaking his head. "You eating kale, too? Five servings of veggies?"

Guppie nodded amiably and changed the topic. No point in arguing. Once Sean got going, nothing would stop him. "Anything interesting in the paper?"

Sean's ire immediately shifted tracks, and he slapped the back of his hand against the paper. "Oh, heck, you know how it is. Everybody's talking about this meteor shower. Just one more sign that the world's ending, if you ask me. They want you focused on something over here... *Look at those pretty lights in the sky!* But really, it's just something shiny to keep people's attention away from what's *really* going on."

"Don't disagree with you," Guppie said. And he mostly didn't. "Sorry, Sean, I gotta keep moving."

"Get your steps in!" Sean hooted, waving his can in the air. He took a deep swig of it, smacking his lips for dramatic effect. "As far as I'm concerned, if you can't eat anything good and you can't drink beer, what's the point of living? None of that rabbit food for me, boy, no siree..."

Waving over his shoulder, Guppie set off. He'd laughed at his doctor, too, when he'd first brought up the issue. There'd been a time not so long ago when he could run a marathon in under three hours, and he vividly remembered slogging through the desert carrying a pack that weighed more than a hundred pounds, back in the Gulf War.

Turned out, that had all happened a lot longer ago than he'd realized. Now, his five-mile round-trip walk through town was enough to leave him winded. He still wasn't sure that he *needed* to make the walk every day. At this point, Guppie was just doing it to prove that he could.

There wasn't much to Little Creek: a couple of restaurants, the bookstore, the Country Duke, the gas station that was also, more or less, the grocery store... and that new upscale boutique garden center run by the young woman with the headscarf. Guppie could never remember her name, but she was all right. Like the rest of the folks in town, he'd been wary of her at first. Sean was still boycotting her shop—possibly for political reasons, but it wasn't like he was gardening much these days anyway—but Guppie had gone in one time and found the shop oddly charming. It wasn't as expensive as it looked from the outside, either.

On a whim, he decided to stop in and see if they had a bird feeder. He'd started putting them out, first to feed the birds, but he found that the squirrels liked them, too. He liked watching them through the window, but he'd forgotten to bring his old one inside the other night, and the bear had gotten it again.

Guppie pushed through the door. The garden center was empty, but he could hear strange noises coming from the back room.

"Hello?" he called.

"Hello?" a thin and breathless voice replied from the back.

Guppie went back to investigate and found the owner in the stock room, struggling to lift a large bag of mulch up onto one of the shelves. He hurried over and took it from her.

"Where do you want this?" he asked.

She pointed, and before she could say a word, Guppie lifted it into place.

"You made that look easy," she said. Guppie hadn't seen her smile often, but her lips turned up into something like one.

"A lovely lady like you needs to find a man to do this heavy lifting," Guppie said.

The gardener's smile disappeared. People could be so sensitive these days.

"What can I get for you, Mr. Martin?" she asked.

"You can call me Guppie," he assured her. "Everybody does."

She nodded politely but said nothing. Fair enough, he thought. Small things shouldn't come between folk.

She listened thoughtfully as he explained his predicament, asking questions about his yard and setup. With her help, Guppie selected a suitable replacement for the downed feeder, paid in cash, and then set out for home.

Another quiet day, just the way he liked them.

He was halfway home before it occurred to him that, once again, he'd forgotten to ask the woman's name.

3

VERA

BY THE TIME she closed up for the day, Vera Khan was nursing a headache. Once she had the new shipment of plants priced and out on display, she'd struggled to keep them in stock. Little Creek might be small, but business was booming, and people often drove in from the surrounding counties to view her famously wide variety of unusual perennials and hardy fruit trees.

At six o'clock on the dot, Vera locked the door, then headed into the back room, finally letting herself relax.

"Now it's just you and me, my beauties," she crooned to the plants. They were the real reason she'd wanted to open a garden center in the first place. She loved to watch things grow.

She had just fired up the sticker gun when her cell phone rang. Only a few people ever called, which meant it was either a supplier, her mother, or one of her aunties calling to tell her that someone had died. When she saw the number, Vera sighed.

Just what I need, she thought.

There was no good in dodging the call, though, so Vera put on her sweetest Good Daughter voice and answered.

"Hello, Mummy!" she chirped. "I'm putting you on speaker... my hands are full!"

"What, you don't have time to talk to your mother?" Burcu Khan demanded.

"We're speaking right now, Mummy," Vera pointed out.

Burcu muttered something in Turkish in a deeply aggrieved tone, but Vera had never had a keen ear for the language, and her parents had raised her and her brother to speak what they called 'unaccented English.'

Whatever that means, Vera thought. *It's not as if I sound like the natives of Little Creek...*

"Maybe if you had a man in your life, he could help you in the shop, and you would have more free time."

She and Mr. Martin should team up. That was one topic that Vera wasn't touching with a ten-foot pole. "I'm doing just fine for myself, thank you. How are you today, Mummy?" Vera asked, still trying to sound upbeat. She ran her fingers over the leaves of the closest rhododendron, and immediately felt a deep sense of calm wash over her.

"I'm well, but I'm lonely. My only daughter never calls..."

I wonder why? Vera had learned long ago that arguing got her nowhere, so she'd given up trying to appease her mother. It was usually easier to distract her instead. "I've been so busy, you know. The garden center is doing well."

"That little hobby-shop, you mean?" Burcu clicked her tongue. "It's so hard to think of it, Vera, how you threw away a perfectly good future to play gardener."

Vera rubbed her fingers over the soft leaves of a pineapple sage plant, then breathed in the sweet aroma. "I'm happier here than I was before, Mummy. Why did you call?"

"Just to talk," Burcu said. "I miss you."

Vera bit her lip and stared down at the tag printer. This, she knew, was the absolute truth. She secretly hoped that she and her mother might be able to reconcile one day, but Vera had spent most of her life trying to please her family, and she had never been really happy until she put all that pressure aside and struck out on her own.

"I miss you, too," Vera admitted. *The way we used to be.*

"You are so stubborn, şekerim," Burcu said fondly. "And so am I. Will you be home for Eid?"

"Not this time," Vera said. "I don't have help, and I can't close the shop right now... "

"Then for the Fourth of July?" Burcu asked hopefully. "The shops will close in your town for the Fourth, won't they? Alfie and his wife will be here with their boys. You could come, even if it's only for a couple of days?"

Vera tagged a small pot of rosemary for $2.99 and said, "Let me think about it."

"That's a maybe?" Burcu asked hopefully.

"It's a maybe." Unable to bring herself to make a more specific commitment, Vera detoured once more. "By the way, did you see the news about that meteor shower? It's supposed to be beautiful, especially out here. No light pollution this far out in the country, you know?"

"Well, at least there's *one* good thing about living there," Burcu said, but even her complaints sounded happier now.

It took Vera another twenty minutes to wheedle her way off the phone, and when she finally hung up, she was exhausted.

"Never mind," she told the plants. "I'll go on the Fourth, if I think I can manage it. Otherwise, I'll beg off until her birthday." Her mother would be so happy to see her, and the drive wasn't *that* bad, not when she only went to see her family three or four times a year.

Left alone with her plants at last, Vera finished her tagging, then began hauling them out to the front.

Sometimes, she felt, it would be easier if every human on Earth just disappeared, and Vera could spend every day tending to her plants.

4

COOPER

COOPER LUTZ WOKE to the sound of his alarm and brought his hand down on the snooze button. He felt as if he'd been beaten over the head with a claw hammer. It took him a few moments to remember why he felt like death incarnate, but the empty bottle labeled *Pinnacle Whipped* brought it back all at once.

He'd been chatting with @onebiggurl last night, and then Cooper just *had* to go and ask if she wanted to meet up for the sky-watching party in the woods that weekend, and she'd ghosted. After half an hour of total silence, he'd decided to start drinking, and he hadn't stopped until he hit the bottom of the bottle.

Cooper rolled over on his back and ran his hands through his hair, trying to tame the mess. As his hand passed his face, he frowned, then examined his fingernails. Apparently, sometime during his one-man pity party, he'd decided to paint his nails black. *Interesting.*

With a sense of deep dread, Cooper reached for his phone and opened the chat. There were three new messages, all from @onebiggurl.

You seem like a nice guy, @revmyengine, but I'm not ready to meet in real life. And I don't think I'll ever be ready for a goth metal band. :P

It just doesn't seem like it would work out. I'm a conformist, you know? I don't have the guts to stand out. I'm sorry.

[@onebiggurl has blocked you from the chat.]

Cooper dropped his phone onto the bed with a groan, then mashed his palms into his eyelids until he saw stars. "Stupid," he muttered. "Stupid. Why'd you have to push her? It was going so well."

The alarm blared again, and this time Cooper ripped the cord of the clock right out of its socket and threw the whole device across the room. Feeling incredibly sorry for himself, and more than a little hungover, he swung his feet out of the bed and staggered over toward his bathroom.

"Cooper?" his mom's voice called from below. "Are you okay?"

"Yeah," he called back. "I just tripped on something." A moment later, his bare foot landed on the empty vodka bottle, and he actually did trip, catching himself against the wall just in time.

"From your lips to God's ears," Cooper muttered. It was the kind of thing his mother said at every opportunity, and if she'd been watching him, she'd have said it first.

Cooper finally made it to the bathroom, where he slumped against the edge of the vanity, staring at the sallow, green-haired, obese sucker trapped behind the glass. His mohawk was completely wasted. The fact that he'd fallen asleep in his jacket didn't help in the sweaty face department.

"You look like hell," Cooper informed his reflection.

After a moment's consideration, the fat guy in the mirror gave Cooper the middle finger.

"Yeah," Cooper told himself. "You've got that right."

He brushed his teeth, tried to tame his chin-length hair, and washed his face. At least his acne had cleared up since high school.

"Looking better," Cooper told his reflection. "But listen up, buddy, you've got to get out of this town."

"Cooper?" his father's voice came from the hallway. "You up and flying yet, buddy?"

"Up, up, and away."

His dad was a pilot, so the dad jokes ended up being plane jokes. The old man used to fly commuter puddle jumpers with BlueAir, but then he'd been diagnosed with epilepsy. Even though he'd never had a seizure, they'd revoked his commercial license. Now he sold appliances at the Home Depot two towns over.

He'd tried to get Cooper interested in flying when he was younger. Even set him up with some lessons from a family friend. But once Cooper realized his dad wanted him to get a license and follow in his footsteps, he'd dropped it fast.

Cooper retrieved his clock from the far side of the room, then pulled on a gray t-shirt and navy canvas coveralls that constituted his work uniform. His second day on the job, Cooper had ditched his official *Country Duke* cap, and nobody had said a word.

Kathy Lutz already had eggs and bacon on the table, and English muffins in the toaster. Nate was slathering his with a healthy serving of butter.

"Good morning, Cooper!" Kathy said cheerily. "Ready for another beautiful day?"

"Born ready," Cooper said, dropping heavily into his chair.

"Did you hear the good news?" his father asked. David Lutz's bushy mustache bristled with pride. When Cooper stared blankly at him, he flicked his eyes toward Nate.

"Let me guess," Cooper said. "You got into Penn State?"

"Better than that," Nate said, slapping two strips of bacon onto his muffin. "They offered me a scholarship."

"Wow," Cooper said, shifting to make room as his mom set a glass of orange juice in front of him. "How does Pammy Mae feel about that?"

Nate's smile slipped. "I haven't told her yet. I just got the letter last night."

"Uh oh," said Cooper, unable to suppress a smile. "I guess there's trouble in paradise, huh? I don't think the Rural Queen is going to like it when she finds out you're headed way up there."

"Butter Queen," Nate corrected defensively. "And it's not 'way up there.' It's a couple hours north of the state line. Who knows? Maybe she'll come with me."

"I smell a shotgun wedding," Cooper sing-songed.

Nate jabbed his fork at Cooper. "You don't have to be a dick just because you can't find anyone willing to put up with you."

"Nate," Kathy said sternly. "No language at the table. Cooper, leave your brother alone."

"I was just going," Cooper said, swigging his orange juice and getting up from the table. The smell of food made his stomach clench. "I've got tractors to fix. Not all of us could get a scholarship. Some of us have to work for a living."

"That's your fault," Nate grumbled. "Not mine."

"Aren't you hungry?" Kathy asked.

Cooper shook his head. "Thanks, but I don't want to be late."

"Have a good day, sweetheart!" Kathy called after him.

Cooper slammed the door behind him.

5

LEN

"INTO YOUR CRATES, BOYS," Len Bonaparte said.

The dogs obeyed instantly, and Len tossed each of them a treat before grabbing his pack, retrieving his empty gas can, and heading for town.

These days, he only went into town every two or three weeks. Come summer, it would drop to once a month. The garden was looking good, and he was already harvesting plenty of greens, not to mention the groundhogs and rabbits he regularly trapped. Skunks he let go for the obvious reasons; besides, having a skunk around usually meant that he was less likely to get other critters messing with the garden. Opossums got a free pass, too, since they kept the ticks in check. Foxes were usually smart enough to avoid the traps, but when he caught them, he took the males to the other side of the valley. Females got to stay, in case there were pups.

After all the time he'd spent out here, Len had a system. He was almost entirely self-sufficient.

Sometimes, though, nothing would do but a Cheez-It.

As he made his way down the mountainside—more like a hill,

really, but the locals called them mountains, even if they lacked the majesty of the larger ranges—Len steeled himself for yet another encounter with the locals. Any outsider would have drawn attention, but Len stuck out like a sore thumb.

When he and his wife first married, she used to joke that they couldn't take a photo on the beach together. It was impossible to get the exposure right. Either her pale Irish skin made for a white splotch, or his dark Nigerian skin made for a black patch. "The tech hasn't caught up with us," she used to joke. She was so funny. She was tough, too. Her mother called her a firecracker. She called him a gentle giant. He wasn't so sure about that one. Nobody here would call him that. Then again, nobody in Little Creek had ever met his wife.

As he headed into town, he passed an older man with a potbelly and a fishing hat headed the opposite direction.

"Morning, Mister Len!" he called. "Nice day for a walk, isn't it?"

Len nodded, "Sure enough," but didn't slow his pace. Being in town made him twitchy. He wasn't used to being around people, even nice-enough people like the one he'd just passed. He made straight for the gas station.

"How's it going, Mister Len?" asked the man behind the counter.

Skipping the niceties, Len jerked his thumb toward the pumps. "I'm going to fill my canister on two, if you don't mind, and then come back in for the rest. Mind if I pay all together?" He always asked, and the man behind the counter always gave him the same answer.

"Sure thing. I'll ring 'er up when you're done."

Len filled the canister right to the five-gallon mark, then headed back inside for supplies. Most of what he bought was practical: a bag of flour, a sack of sugar, a box of iodized salt. He picked up a couple of other things, too, snacks and treats, small luxuries to make his time on the mountain more bearable. He brought them all to the counter, then stood there as the man rung him up.

His eyes were wandering at random when he happened to glance up at the muted TV just as they were running the weather.

"Meteor showers?" he asked, cocking his head. "Any idea what that's about?"

The attendant looked up from his scanner, then nodded. "Oh, yeah, people can't stop talking about it. It made national news... Although I guess you aren't much for that, huh? It's in the newspaper, too." He gestured to the metal rack by the door.

With a rising sense of dread, Len crossed to the stand, then lifted out a copy of the *Heartland County Gazette*. Sure enough, the story had made headlines.

As he scanned the article, the attendant chuckled. "Seems like the media will talk about anything these days. Don't we have anything better to talk about? Must be pretty slow times if that's all the news that's fit to print..."

Len didn't wait for him to finish. He tossed the paper back into the rack, turned on his heel, and went back to the shelves. With shaking hands, he grabbed two of each item on the medicine shelves, then darted over to the pantry items and grabbed two more sacks of flour and a large bag of rice. As he walked, he was already counting out supplies in his mind: *There's water in the cistern, and the rain barrels are almost full... I just restocked the ammo, and the MREs are in the cellar. I've got dog food, fertilizer...*

"You okay?" asked the attendant nervously.

Len nodded. There was no point in trying to explain. Very possibly, there was no point in stockpiling supplies, either, but it was worth a shot. Better than doing nothing, anyway. He returned to the counter and added to his first pile. After looking everything over, he went back for another box of crackers.

"This is an awful lot of stuff to be carrying back on foot," the attendant observed. "You gonna be okay? I bet there's ninety pounds of stuff here, plus the canister."

"I've got it," Len assured him. "Thanks for asking."

The man chuckled, sizing him up. "Yeah, I reckon you do."

Len filled his pack, then tossed the rice over one shoulder and lifted the gas can in his free hand. He could only imagine what he looked like as he set off for home, but despite all the weight he was carrying, Len found himself practically sprinting.

Maybe being alone in the woods so long had made him paranoid, but if he'd understood the subtext of that article, tonight was the night. He broke into a run.

It was starting.

FIVE YEARS EARLIER
WASHINGTON, D.C.

NASA's Advanced Technology Research Lab (ATRL-East)

———

"We're missing *something*."

Carla braced her fingers against her temples and scowled at the screen, as if concentration alone would glean anything from the radio wave transmission that the *Stark* probe had relayed back to them. The series of tones played on a loop, totaling only three minutes in length.

"It has to be a natural phenomenon," Nathan muttered.

"It's *not* natural, Nutty." Stew drummed his fingers on the desk and fixed his eyes unblinkingly on the screen. "I'm telling you, it's a message."

"Stop," Nathan groaned. "Just stop. We already tried binary pattern algos even though I *told* you that was a waste of time."

"We can run it through every supercomputer on the planet,

but if it's a ciphertext then we aren't getting anything out of it without a cryptovariable. And if it's a stream cipher, well..." Stew shrugged and trailed off.

Jeremy Steward, like Carla and Nathan, was a PhD candidate from MIT. They'd all been thrown together by Carla's doctoral advisor, who had close ties with NASA. Carla's sole focus had been astrophysics until recently. Nathan, too, had a life before data analysis. But Stew was a pure theoretical mathematician — and had been since birth, according to him.

"A cryptovariable?" Carla said. "Like a key?"

"Right, because it has to be a *hidden message*." Nathan squeezed his eyes shut. "Haven't we had enough crazy lately, Steward?"

Right after they'd arrived for their research stint, the three of them had joined a host of theoretical simulations from somebody up the chain in Space Force. In most of them, an alien species violently invaded the planet for reasons unknown. Space Force wanted to know how early and in what fashion they could detect their arrival — if at all.

"What if the crazy wasn't crazy?" Stew hissed.

The three of them had spent several weeks working on the project. The scenarios were specific, right down to the name of the hypothetical alien species: *homoptera invadendae*.

That had sent Stew into a tizzy, because apparently it was a popular catchall name in the weird forums he hung out in. Carla just figured Space Force was trolling them. In the end, nothing had come of it beyond fueling Stew's imagination.

Just the kind of ludicrous thing that military people fetishized.

But this was different. This message was pulling directly from the *Stark*. It couldn't be spoofed, and the header data was unambiguous. The source was extrasolar.

"Seriously, guys, can we focus, please?" Carla sat back. "Let's go back to our top-line assumptions."

"It's radio waves bouncing back to us from objects in space," Nathan said dismissively.

Evidently realizing that Stew wasn't going to engage with him, he turned to Carla. "You remember back when Cassini was scanning Kraken Mare out on Titan? And we were able to explore the lake just by bouncing radio signals off the surface? That's all this is. At best, we might be able to map a distant star by triangulating the source—or rather, the *midpoint* of the messages. God knows we've blasted enough radio signals out into space over the years."

Carla shook her head without glancing up from the RFS chart of the transmission. "I understand what you're saying, but wouldn't you expect a radio wave to be warped by the gravitational field of whatever's feeding it back to us? This is so *regular*."

"Like a kid flicking a flashlight in the woods so that his friend can see it from next door," Stew mumbled. "Look at it, Nutty. There's a pattern."

"A pattern we made," Nathan insisted. "Like... like flicking your flashlight in front of a *mirror*. Your weird internet friends can say whatever they like on their blogs, but this is man-made."

"Yeah?" Stew dropped his voice an octave and tipped his head toward the door of the lab. "Then why's *he* here?"

All three swiveled their chairs toward the man in black sitting by the door. He was reading a paperback, as he had been ever since *Stark*'s transmission had come in. Carla had yet to see the man take a lunch break, although he drank coffee like it was his job, ignoring the sign on the door that said *No Food or Beverages in the Lab*.

He was an agent, Carla reckoned. FBI, CIA, NSA. One of those 3-letter ones. And they wouldn't send a guy in unless they had a reason.

Since when do you buy into this Area 51 garbage? Carla forced herself to take a long, slow breath. *Nathan's right. It's probably just signals bouncing back to us from an object in deep space, or some unrecognized natural phenomenon.* They were all going to feel like real idiots when they realized that it was just some old Soviet transmission warped by the gravitational fields of a hundred stars...

Stew sat up abruptly and began to type. A moment later, a message popped up through the encrypted chat feature on Carla's screen.

All it said was, *ARECIBO.*

Nathan was included in the chat, and he made a small, skeptical noise at the back of his throat. His fingers flew over the keys, and his response populated within a matter of seconds. *Drake's Arecibo?*

Carla returned her attention to *Stark's* transmission. It had been well over a decade since Carla had been an undergrad, but they'd covered the Arecibo transmission her junior year: Drake, a professor at Cornell, had drafted a message meant to describe the most basic aspects of life on Earth to any potential inhabitants of the M13 star cluster, where their transmission had been sent. He'd used binary to depict images representing human beings, the chemical building blocks of life on Earth, the planet's position with the solar system, and more.

Carla returned to chat after making sure that the guy posted by the door was still engrossed in his mystery novel. *You sure about that, Stew?*

Stew snorted. *I'm resetting the binary sequence right now, using Drake's parameters to generate an image. I'll send the results when I'm done.*

"Hey, Nutty," Carla said, spinning toward her colleague. She never used Stew's nicknames, and hoped he'd catch on. "Here's another theory. You know how when black holes form they send out massive radio signals? Maybe we're getting some kind of weird feedback from a similar phenomenon."

Nathan nodded with understanding. If they suddenly fell silent and communicated *only* over text, they were going to arouse the guy's suspicions. Maybe Stew's paranoia was rubbing off on her, but the whole situation was odd.

"I don't know." Nathan tapped one knuckle against his jaw. "I still think that we're just getting cosmic echoes, if you will."

Carla shrugged. "Say what you guys like, I believe you're limiting yourselves by not considering the fact that it might be... might be..." She'd been hoping to keep the agent distracted by continuing their squabble about the origin of the signal, but the image Stew had just sent over the chat caught her full attention.

So much for apophenia. There was no way this was a coincidence.

The original Arecibo message had featured the image of a human centered over a representation of the solar system, wherein Earth had been set a row above the rest of the planets. Stew's image showed the same man, but with the line of pixels connecting the two halves of his body removed, as if the simple figure had been split in half from his head to his groin, and while it stood over a series of planets that was in every other way identical to Drake's original, Earth was not included in the sequence.

The rest of the message was entirely different. Carla squinted at the strange, misshapen figure at the top of the graph. It reminded her of an octopus, or an insect of some kind.

The other portions of the image didn't make sense at first glance, but Carla had a feeling that it contained more information about the bisected man and the absence of Earth in the solar system.

Carla's skin prickled, and not only as a result of the picture. A reflection in her screen shifted, and she glanced over her shoulder to find the Fed standing there, watching the monitor with hawklike intensity. He raised a bulky phone to his ear. She guessed it was military-grade, because the lab was underground and essentially a Faraday cage.

"Yes, sir," he said. "They've got something. You're going to want to see what they've come up with."

"Hey, phones aren't allowed in here, buddy," Nathan said, sounding genuinely offended.

The guy ignored him. "You got it. I'll keep them here until you arrive." He lowered the phone and backed up a pace so that he could see all three of them. "I'll need the three of you to stay right where you are for the next fifteen minutes, and then you'll be getting some answers about the work you've been doing."

His tone was perfectly calm, but something about his demeanor set Carla's teeth on edge. She pushed back from her desk.

"Is this legit?" she asked, motioning to the monitor. "Like for real?"

The agent shook his head. "The answers are coming—"

Stew spun around abruptly. "Does this have anything to do with *invadendae*?"

The agent's eyes darted away. "I don't know details."

Carla glanced at Stew and knew he found the guy as unconvincing as she did. She suddenly felt very cold.

"Will we get to go home tonight?" Carla asked quietly.

The agent shook his head. "We'll need at least another day to debrief you. We'll be keeping you on-site until then."

At least another day. The strange, stilted expression on his face told Carla everything she needed to know: this was a party line. A crock of crap.

"We don't work for NASA, you get that, right?" Stew asked.

Carla got to her feet. "I'm going to go call my husband. I want to let him know that I won't be home tonight." She took a step toward the door, but the agent moved to block her, his calm smile never wavering.

"I'm afraid that I can't allow that," he said.

Carla shook her head. "All due respect, but I'm still not clear who you are. If you're going to detain me, I'm either going to need to see a warrant of some kind, or I'm going to require an explanation from the director."

The agent's hand moved toward his hip and his eyes turned cold. "You might want to reconsider that stance."

He's got a gun.

The idea that the man was armed had occurred to Carla, but she hadn't worked out what to do in that case.

She was still standing there, trying to decide how to respond, when Stew launched out of his chair. The agent reached for his gun, but Stew came in swinging, tackling the man with such force that they both fell to the ground. The gun skittered away across the floor.

"Steward!" Nathan exclaimed. "What are you *doing*?"

"*It's a cover-up!*" Stew bellowed. "This is the new Roswell. It's Holloman Air Force Base all over again. Look at the evidence!" He dug his knee into the guy's back. "The hypotheticals were *real*. They *know*."

Carla glanced toward the monitor. She wasn't big on conspiracies, not like Stew. *What normal person is?* But the strange creature in the image, the bisected man, the missing planet Earth... she could have laughed it all off if it wasn't for the fact that both NASA and the feds were taking this all so seriously.

If it's true, I have to warn Len.

She bolted for the door at the same moment that the agent brought his elbow slamming back into Stew's gut. "Everyone stay put!" he snarled. "Backup's on the way."

But backup's not here yet.

Stew curled into a ball and whimpered, while Carla dove for the gun. She snatched it up and aimed it at the agent with trembling hands.

The agent rose to one knee, sneering at her. "You gonna shoot me?"

Carla's brow crinkled. "You know, I think I might."

She didn't mean it, but then Nathan shuffled toward the door and the agent lunged for him. Before Carla could think, she aimed low and pulled the trigger; this was followed by a soft *pfft* and a spray of blood. The agent cursed and collapsed onto the floor, covering the fresh wound in his thigh with both hands.

Carla stared down at the gun in her hand, then across the room to where the agent lay, palms pressed against the bullet hole in his flesh. *What the hell is going on?* Her first impulse was to drop the gun, to get as far away from it as possible, but her fingerprints were all over it now.

Why are you worried about fingerprints? You shot *someone.* The guy just wanted you to stay put and you shot him. Surely, in the grand scheme of things, that was the bigger problem?

No. She forced her hands to stop trembling and kept a tight grip on the weapon. *The problem is that I just shot a guy who would shoot me first.*

Nathan's eyes widened as he examined the gun in Carla's hand. "He's got a *silencer* on that thing. That's not right. Is it?"

"Damn well isn't." Stew uncurled and stood quickly. "If he's got people coming, we don't have much time." He ran back to the console and pulled out an ancient-looking flip phone.

"Hey!" Nathan said. "Not cool."

"Seriously, Nutty?" Stew said as he plugged in a cord to the back of the computer. "You're worried about my phone?"

"We have to get out of here," Carla said urgently. She looked down at the gun. *What do I do with this?*

"Just one second ... Got it." Stew ripped the cord out of the phone and spun around. He headed for the door. "Let's see how far we can make it before the Roswell squad catch up to us. Bring the gun, Carla."

The agent scowled, but the sheen of sweat on his brow and the ashen pallor of his face suggest that he wouldn't be giving chase anytime soon.

"You want the gun, you take it," Carla said shoving it into Stew's hand. With her other hand, she plucked the flip phone out of his hand. "I'm calling my husband."

With one last glance around, she rushed into the hall. Stew and Nathan followed.

The phone was heavier than it looked. She dialed as she ran, but when she held the phone to her ear, she didn't hear a dial tone.

"Does this thing even work, Stew?" she shouted over her shoulder.

"Not like that," he called back. "You won't get a signal down here anyways. We need to go up top for that. But the phone doesn't make voice calls. It's shielded and needs an authentication token. But you can leave a voice message. Just dial and talk. It will convert it into an untraceable attachment as soon as it gets a signal."

"Chrissake, Stew."

"What, you think the NSA is using that huge budget and every specialist in the world *not* to listen to all your phone calls?"

Carla made for the main stairs, still gripping the phone, but Stew came up next to her and shook his head. "Take the rear exit," he said. "Even if they're watching it, they'll have fewer guys back there."

"You watch too many spy movies," Nathan muttered.

"Yeah." Stew jogged toward the research facility's rear stairs, which were on the opposite end from where they were. "You're welcome. It's what's going to keep you alive today."

Carla stopped listening as she dialed again. She didn't know what she would say, but the words just tumbled out in one long stream. Len surely would think she was crazy. Maybe she was. She finished just as they reached the rear exit and burst into the stairwell. The echo inside was disorienting.

"I'm finished," she said. "Now what?"

"Now just hang up. I built an application on the computer in my mom's basement to do all the conversion work there."

"Your mom's basement?" *Dear God, what have I done?*

"I know you two think I'm off my rocker," Stew said, taking stairs two at a time. "But this is a *warning*. About a hostile alien invasion that will threaten the lives of every human on Earth."

"How can you be so *confident?*" Nathan asked, sticking close to Stew's heels.

"We're not the first to work this out. Just the latest. The truth is out there. People are talking."

For all Carla knew, Stew had finally cracked, but as they reached the top landing, she kept imagining the bisected man in the message.

Stew stopped at the fire door just long enough to take the flip phone back from Carla and look down at it. "Yours is sent. Now to send mine," he said with a smile. "Time to let the cat out of the bag."

He elbowed open the door as he dialed. Carla was the first through the door. Even in late afternoon, the summer sun reflected brightly off the concrete pavement and she was blinded for a moment.

"Freeze!" a deep voice bellowed. "Stop where you are and put your hands up. Do it *now!*"

Carla saw soldiers in body armor pointing guns at her and she threw her hands up instantly.

"Gun!" another voice screamed.

She panicked. She didn't have the gun. She'd given it to — *Oh no! Stew, don't do it!*

She turned to look behind her, arms still raised. But Stew looked as bewildered as she did. He had both his hands raised. Then she saw it. The phone was in his outstretched arm.

"No, wait—"

The phone exploded in Stew's hand. He screamed out and blood splattered across his head and shoulders. He fell to the ground and rolled around, clutching his hand.

Nathan stood above him, staring down dumbly in shock.

"Hold your fire," said a thin, reedy voice. "Hold your fire!"

A small man in a uniform walked briskly past the soldiers. He was a Space Force officer, but Carla wasn't sure about the rank. She couldn't make out the name, either.

A soldier rushed past him with a medical kit and dropped down on the ground next to Stew. At least Carla could see all his fingers.

The officer watched the medic work for a moment, before his piercing blue eyes swept over Carla and the rest of the scene. Then he broke into a smile. "I'm afraid there won't be a field trip today, ladies and gentlemen." His smile grew wider. "Or any day for a long, long time."

6

COOPER

"YOU LOOKING FORWARD TO TONIGHT?" Kat asked, sliding out from under the tractor they were fixing.

Cooper shrugged. "What, the rager? Yeah, I might not go."

"Aw, come on," Kat said, sitting up and wiping a streak of commingled grease and sweat off her forehead. "The view's supposed to be amazing. Don't you want to see that light show everyone's been talking about?"

"Not really," Cooper muttered. He actually *had* been looking forward to it, until he'd asked @onebiggurl to come. That disaster still left a bitter taste in his mouth.

Or maybe that was the flavored vodka.

"Come on, man," Kat urged. "It's graduation. Don't you want to celebrate your brother?"

"Everybody in town celebrates him," Cooper argued. "What does he need me for?"

"Party pooper," Kat said. "Hand me a wrench."

Cooper complied, and Kat slid back under the tractor. While she was at it, Cooper checked the hydraulic lines and checked the oil. He didn't mind this routine maintenance stuff, but it didn't take much thinking.

Which at least left plenty of time for talking.

"What other big plans have you got for your Friday night?" Kat asked from under the tractor.

Cooper shrugged, forgetting that Kat couldn't see him. "I'm old and boring. I'll just stay home."

Kat laughed. "Come on, dude, you're what, three years older than us?"

"Four," Cooper said. "I turned twenty-two in January. I'm practically a fossil."

"I would have sworn you were a senior when I was a freshman," Kat said.

"Yeah." Cooper said bitterly. "I got held back a year."

"For reckless behavior?" Kat teased.

"No." Cooper cleared his throat, debating whether he wanted to get into it, then sighed. *What the hell? Not like today can get any worse.* "For bullying."

"Ah." Kat reemerged and lay on her back, looking up at Cooper with a thoughtful frown. "Cause of the goth thing?"

"Yup," Cooper said. "For the goth thing." And the overweight thing. And the social awkwardness thing. He just wanted to smoke, play MMORPG games, and listen to *The Birthday Massacre*. Was that such a crime? OK, fine. Smoking weed behind the gym was a little wrong.

Kat nodded sympathetically. "That sucks, man. People are sheep sometimes. They just want to conform or whatever."

Cooper liked Kat. He was sure she had her share of troubles — like Cooper, she wasn't what anyone would call conventionally attractive — but if the next words out of her mouth were something like, *I know how hard it can be to feel like an outsider, I had to wear braces until I was sixteen,* Cooper was going to blow his lid.

Instead, Kat got up, wiping her hands on the dropcloth. "It takes a lot of guts to stand out."

Cooper froze. Could it be a coincidence? @onebiggurl had used that exact phrase.

"You two almost done back there?" their manager, Dick Ansel, called from the doorway.

"Just finishing up," Kat assured him. She set the cloth aside, then turned back to Cooper. "You got this? I can get started on the paperwork."

Cooper felt like his heart might very well crawl up out of his throat. He had no proof, but the way Kat was looking at him, he could feel the truth of it right down to his bones.

Kat is @onebiggurl!

"Yeah," he squeaked at last. "I've got it."

Kat nodded, then turned to go. She stopped in the doorway, then turned back, smiling. "It would be nice to see you at the party tonight. Just think about it."

"I'll be there," Cooper said instantly.

WHAT DO *you wear to a meteor shower keg stand in the woods?* It sounded like a riddle, and Cooper had no answer to it. He settled for a fresh t-shirt and dark jeans. No point in drawing more attention to himself tonight. All he really wanted was a chance to talk to Kat. If that meant toning down his look, so be it.

Cooper arrived fashionably late, mostly because he didn't want to have to hitch a ride with Nate.

By the time Cooper reached the party, half of the kids were already hammered. A shirtless dude-bro he didn't recognize tackled him as he approached the main bonfire and yelled, "Gonna see some wild stars tonight, man. Want to see a full moon, too?"

"Not yours," Cooper said, extracting himself from the kid's grasp and shuffling away.

It took him a while to track down Kat, and he was on the verge of giving up when he spotted her in a cluster of people, alongside Nate and Pammy Mae.

I guess it'll be a good cover, at least. Cooper approached, dropping down onto a large blanket between Nate and Kat, hoping that it seemed like no big deal.

"Hey," Nate said coolly. Apparently he was still salty about their argument over breakfast.

"Hey yourself," Cooper said.

Nate glowered at him for a moment before taking Pammy Mae's hand. "Come on, baby, let's find a better spot." The two of them got up and headed off, while their friends watched them go.

"I'll bet you twenty bucks he knocks her up tonight," said Logan, waving a beer bottle after them.

"Nah, not Pammy Mae," said Kat. "I'll bet you twenty bucks he proposes." She turned to Cooper, acknowledging him for the first time. "What do you think?"

Cooper shrugged. "My twenty says he dumps her."

"No way," Logan scoffed. "If you had a girl like that, you'd never let her go. Trust me." He finished his beer, then got up to get another. "You losers want anything?"

Kat shook her head. "I'm good."

Logan stumbled away, and Kat shifted closer. "We haven't seen any shooting stars yet," she said in a low voice. "Want to watch with me? It's supposed to be quite the show."

Cooper nodded, then lay back on the blanket to watch the sky. Kat lay next to him, just far enough away that nobody would question it, and just close enough that Cooper's heart beat double-time.

What does this mean? he wanted to ask. *Why did you change your mind?*

He was so focused on his own thoughts that when Kat gasped and pointed upward, Cooper jumped.

"There was one!" Kat cried. "Did you see that?"

Cooper's eyes refocused, and he found himself squinting into the night sky. The moon was barely a sliver, which meant that he had an excellent view of the two or three bright pinpricks of light streaking across the heavens.

"Wow," he said. "It's so *clear*."

Kat shifted. "Look, there are more."

He was right. More and more bright streaks filled the sky, and the other partiers—at least, those sober enough to be paying attention—gasped in delight.

"Incredible!" someone said loudly. "Did you see that?"

To Cooper, it seemed like a miracle. A sign, maybe, that tonight was the start of something that would change his life forever.

"Kat," he said. "I was wondering..."

Cooper was cut off by a sound from the woods. It had all the sharpness of a gunshot, but deeper, so deep that it seemed to rattle the earth beneath him, and it was accompanied by a blinding flash of light. The ground was still shaking when Cooper realized that the air was full of a smell like burning metal.

"What the hell was that?" Kat asked, sitting upright and looking around in alarm.

"I don't know." Cooper got up and peered into the woods in the direction he thought the sound had come from. "Some narcos blowing up a hidden meth lab, maybe?"

"It sounded... big." Kat rose to stand next to him, and Cooper could feel her tension as a physical presence in the air.

"Should we check it out?" Cooper asked.

Other people were already headed toward the source of the

noise, some of them shouting in wild, drunken voices. They all seemed to think it was part of the show.

"No," Kat said. "I think we should get out of here."

Cooper looked over his shoulder. Kat was serious.

"Yeah," Cooper said. He didn't feel so hot about the incident either. There seemed to be some connection between the lights in the sky and the noise on the ground, even if it made no sense. He began to back toward the bonfire. "Did you drive?"

Kat nodded. "Yeah. Come on."

That was when Cooper heard the first scream, and once they started, they didn't stop.

"Come on," Kat said, plucking at the sleeve of his hoodie.

Cooper stumbled a few steps after her, then stopped. "You go," he said.

"What?"

"Nate's out here somewhere," Cooper said. "I just need to get him. Okay? But he has a car, so if you want to go, I get it. I just need to make sure he's okay. Mom will kill me if I leave him here and something happens."

He expected Kat to bolt for the car, but she didn't. "I get it," she said. "I'll come with you."

7

PAMMY MAE

"WHERE ARE WE GOING?" Pammy Mae asked as Nate led her deeper into the woods. "Is something going on with you and Coop?"

"This isn't about him," Nate said. "This is about us."

Pammy clamped her hand around his. "Nate..." she began.

He stopped so abruptly that she bumped into him. "Look up," he said. She could barely see him in the dim light, but when she did as he asked, her mouth fell open.

"*Oh*," she gasped. The sky was alive with falling stars. "Look at that. It's spectacular."

Nate wrapped his arm around her waist, pulling her close as they both stared up. They watched in mutual wonder, with her back pressed to his chest.

And then the sky fell apart.

Pammy saw the object rocketing toward her just in time. She threw herself backward, knocking Nate over, too, as a hunk of metal the size of a tank came crashing to earth. A wave of intense heat washed over her. The object skidded past them, striking the ground with tremendous force, accompanied by such a loud noise and bright light that for a moment Pammy thought she had been struck deaf and blind.

She wasn't sure how long it took for her head to clear, but when she sat up, Nate was groaning beside her.

"What *was* that?"

Pammy Mae reached into the pocket of her capris and fished out her cell phone. Turning on the flashlight, she aimed it at the ground.

A tremendous gouge marred the land now. Whatever had come through had been powerful enough to reduce the surrounding trees to matchsticks. Pammy traced the light down the track, then gaped at what she saw.

It wasn't just a meteor. It was a *ship*.

"Geeze," Nate murmured. "Take a look at that. It's huge."

Pammy had almost forgotten he was there. She reached for his hand, then took a few steps toward the giant object.

It had to be a spaceship, although it looked nothing like a flying saucer. It was clearly manufactured. It was cylindrical in shape, with deep grooves and accompanying seams, along with clear evidence of panels held together by rivet-like fasteners.

"I bet one of those meteors knocked a satellite out of orbit," Nate said confidently.

Pammy Mae wasn't so sure. Whatever it was, it didn't seem to be badly damaged. It must have somehow slowed at the last second, which might explain the wave of heat she'd felt, but certainly wouldn't be a feature of any satellite falling back to earth.

A few of their classmates were emerging from the woods now, lights and phones held aloft.

"Check this out!" someone slurred. "There's a door!"

Sure enough, a small round port on the top of the cylindrical object was partially open.

"Holy crap, dude!" The drunk guy staggered forward, arms held in the air. She recognized Sam, one of the linemen from the football team. "This is wicked! First contact, baby!"

Nate moved to follow him, but Pammy clung to his hand, rooting him in place.

"Come on," Nate hissed. "Don't you want to check this out?"

She shook her head, digging in her heels. "Not yet. Let's just wait and see what happens, okay?"

Nate scoffed. "You'll jump a gap blind in an ATV, but you don't want to check this out? Where's the infamously brave Pammy Mae I know so well?"

There's a difference, she thought, *between brave and stupid.* When she'd jumped the gulch, she had known what was waiting on the other side. Right now?

Right now she had no clue what was going to happen next.

Nate was straining against her grip, trying to approach Sam. The big lineman had stopped a dozen feet in front of the opening and was leaned over, peering in.

Pammy sensed more than saw a flicker of movement.

Somebody gasped.

Then a long, thin dark limb reached up out of the opening.

Even with all the lights trained on it, Pammy Mae could barely make out the shape. At first, she thought it might be a human arm, dressed in some glossy black material. But the arm seemed to keep coming, and there were too many joints.

Her classmates cheered and whistled, as though they were celebrating a touchdown in a home game. Pammy found herself looking around at the others as though they were strangers.

A second limb joined the first, and slowly pressed upwards, bringing a large and ill-defined body along with it. It was like a dog, almost. A dog with confusing legs, no neck, and a long prehensile tail.

"We come in peace!" Sam shouted.

The creature shivered, as though shaking water off its back. A low clicking noise emanated from an unseen mouth. The sound might have passed for that of crackling twigs underfoot in the forest, or a distant radio transmission lost to static.

I hope it was hurt in the crash. It wasn't a very Christian thought, as her mother would have said, but did you have to have a Christian spirit toward something that didn't belong on Earth? Pammy didn't doubt for a second that it was real. She had never been afraid of ghosts, or of scary movies, or monsters under the bed, but this creature sparked a nameless terror in her belly. She had only ever experienced that a handful of other times in her life.

"We are not worthy!" Sam called, miming a deep bow.

Pammy Mae couldn't see the creature's eyes. Still, she could feel that it was looking at Sam.

So apparently she was the only one who wasn't surprised when it jumped.

One moment, Sam was gyrating drunkenly. The next, there was a spray of something dark and wet across the clearing; when it hit Pammy's face, she thought at first that it was blood, but when she lifted her shaking hand to wipe it away she could feel that it wasn't as *smooth* as blood. There were chunks in it, and something that felt like human hair.

"Sam!" Nate's hand tightened around Pammy's until she felt her knuckles crack.

The creature looked up, and beneath it, Pammy Mae could just make out a glistening smear that looked like raspberry jelly or fresh scrapple. One of the girls started screaming, and within seconds, the cluster of people around the strange ship devolved into scrambling chaos.

Nate stood immobile, and Pammy could empathize, but now wasn't the time to panic. In her training for the Butter Queen competition, she had learned that even a moment of poorly-timed panic could cost her the crown. She yanked on Nate's arm, and when he didn't move, she grabbed his shoulder.

"Come on," she snapped. "We've got to go."

"Sam...?" Nate said. He seemed to be lost in a trance. Out of the corner of her eye, Pammy saw the enormous creature move. It had already proven how fast it could be, and how ruthless.

She yanked harder, and this time when she pulled on his arm, he followed her.

Most people were scattering, acting purely out of panic, but Pammy's brain was already in overdrive. Instead of picking a random direction, she headed for the cars.

A cluster of sophomore girls was headed that way, too. Pammy ran for them; they were wearing shoes that were totally unsuitable for the forest, and they were tripping all over each other.

Good, she thought. *If we can get ahead of them, we'll be able to outrun them. It's like Mom always says: 'I don't have to outrun the bear, I just have to outrun you.'*

Now that Nate was moving, he seemed focused, and soon he was outpacing her. Pammy let go of his hand; if he could make it to the car, they could sort the rest out later.

One step at a time.

They passed the cluster of shrieking girls, weaving between the trees toward the bonfire. Pammy didn't look back.

They were halfway to the cars when she heard another *thud*, this time from the direction of town. The blowback it created was strong enough to send her sprawling forward into the dirt. She tasted loam and pine needles, and the sharp tang of copper from where she'd bitten the inside of her cheek. Pammy lay there for a few seconds, stunned, before she forced herself back to her feet.

There were more of them.

As she spat the dirt out of her mouth, Pammy looked up at the sky. The meteor shower was still going strong, and as she stood still, she could feel more impacts echoing through the ground like drumbeats.

How many of them are there? she wondered. *How many of them would it take to turn the whole world upside down?*

8

VERA

IT WAS ALMOST nine o'clock when Vera opened her freezer and discovered that she was out of ice cream.

"Maybe it's a sign," she said aloud. The last time that she'd gone home, her mother had gotten on her case about her expanding waistline. Perhaps tonight, she should just skip the dessert. In the spirit of general self-improvement, maybe she should skip her Netflix binge, too. She could take a bubble bath, read a book, and go to bed early. She had work tomorrow, after all, and Saturday was usually one of her busiest days.

Yeah, and maybe I should move back home and start dating friends of the family like a good girl, Vera thought. She closed the disappointing freezer, reached for her purse, tied on her hijab, and set out for the gas station.

It was a warm night, and cicadas were buzzing in the trees above her. She often wondered what the people who had grown up in Little Creek thought of their town. Vera had chosen the place somewhat arbitrarily. It wasn't like she'd always dreamed of living in West Virginia. The agent said the county was called

Heartland because it was the 'Gateway to America's Heartland,'
which struck her as something you said when you weren't actually
in America's Heartland. But she'd gotten a good deal on the shop,
which was her main reason for moving here. There had been a few
other requirements: she wanted to live in a quiet town without a
lot of pressure, and she wanted to be close to public lands so that
she could spend time learning more about the native plants in the
area. It helped that, even with the lights coming from the restaurants and the gas station, she could see the stars from her back
porch on a clear night.

One of the downsides of living in a small town like Little
Creek was the lack of adequate grocery stores. In D.C., Vera had
been within walking distance of half a dozen bodegas, markets,
and international grocers. Now, unless she wanted to drive forty
minutes to the Walmart just over the county line, she was stuck
with whatever the gas station offered. If she wanted fresh fruit, she
was lucky to find a banana; if she wanted vegetables, she often had
to settle for a V8. The one thing she could guarantee, however,
was ready access to an unrivaled array of junk food.

The attendant looked over as she walked in, gave her a
distracted smile, and then turned back to the TV. Vera glanced up
as she strolled past. It was more coverage of that meteor shower.
No doubt half the town was out in the woods tonight with beers
and telescopes, marveling at the sight. Vera had never been particularly interested in stargazing. Then again, according to the subti-
tles on the screen, this was a once-in-a-lifetime event.

Vera made her way over to the frozen food section. This
consisted of three doors: two for microwaveable meals, and one
entire bay for ice cream. She had only just reached the door when
the bell from up front sounded again. Guppie Martin strolled in,
nodded to the attendant, and began making his way back to where
Vera stood.

Vera quickly turned back to the ice cream display. She should just grab something while she still had a chance to get away. Technically, there was nothing *wrong* with Mr. Martin. He'd never seemed to begrudge her, not the way some had when she first arrived. He was *nice,* which was almost as bad. You couldn't tell *nice* people off, even when *nice* people said things that were belittling.

Vera impulsively reached for a tub of Groundhog Tracks ice cream—whatever *that* was—and tried to make her getaway, but it was too late.

"Hello again!" Martin said, grinning at her. "What've you got there? Oh, *ice cream.*" He nodded. "Understandable. Can't eat the stuff myself, according to the doctor." He patted his gut. "I'm watching my diet."

"Mhmm," Vera said, because how was she supposed to respond to that? *I'm* not *watching my diet?* Besides, she was certain that he was about to reach for the frozen waffles or something equally unhealthy and want to talk about that, too. Mr. Martin was a talker, perennially looking for even the smallest scrap of congenial interaction.

Sure enough, he reached for a plastic-trayed meatloaf meal and held it up with a smile. "As for me, I'm here for what I like to think of as my Lonely Man dinners. You gonna watch the sky tonight? I figured I'd sit out on the porch with my meal and see what I can see. It's supposed to be the event of a lifetime."

"No," Vera said, forcing a smile. "I plan to go home and eat ice cream and watch British people frantically baking meat pies. I hope you enjoy your evening, Mr. Martin."

As he always did, the man shook his head. "You know you can call me Guppie—"

"*Holy crap.*" The attendant slammed both palms down on the counter. "Get over here, you've *got* to see this." He pointed up at the TV with a shaking finger. "This has got to be a fake, right?"

Vera lifted one eyebrow, and Guppie chuckled. "Kids these days," he stage-whispered. "They'll believe anything they see on TV." They both turned to look at the screen, but Vera couldn't make out the screen from this angle. She took a few steps to her left, craning her neck to see what had the attendant so shaken.

Just as the screen came into view, however, the power went out.

The attendant screamed, and Guppie chuckled again.

"Settle down, Hoyt. The way you're carrying on, you'd think the world was ending. It's just the power going out. Happens all the time."

"You didn't see!" Hoyt cried. "You didn't see what they were saying—"

The entire store had been thrown into darkness when the lights went out, and the ambient sounds of the refrigeration units had died. Vera was suddenly aware of a distant series of thuds that rattled the walls of the gas station and shook the floor.

"What is that?" she murmured, more to herself than either of the men.

"Dunno," Guppie said. She heard his shuffling steps behind her, and then his shoulder bumped hers. "Ah, there you are. Don't worry, it's probably just a storm rolling in. Or maybe some kid got distracted by the meteor shower and drove off the road into a pole, that kind of thing happens all the time..."

A light flashed outside, and Vera turned toward the window. Most likely, it was a car pulling off the road to use the gas station. Too bad for the driver. Without power, the pumps would probably be down. They'd most likely be stranded in Little Creek until the power was restored.

Hoyt whimpered.

"Aw, Hoyt, it's all right," Guppie said. He took a step forward; Vera could just make out his silhouette by the light of the approaching high-beams.

The lights were getting too close. *Maybe they can't see us in the dark,* Vera thought. *It wouldn't be the first time someone drove through the front of the store—didn't someone do that about four months ago? Right after the ice storm, they lost control of their car and took out some of the front windows.*

Guppie seemed to have the same thought, because as the lights grew brighter, he tackled Vera, knocking her away from the windows. A second later, the safety glass exploded.

Hoyt screamed, and Vera made an echoing noise of alarm, although it was much fainter. Guppie was heavier than he looked; he knocked the breath out of her as his momentum carried them forward. They collided with a rack of chips and packaged cookies, which collapsed under their combined weight. Glass rained down on them, but they were blocked from the worst of it by other display shelves.

At least a car hadn't come barreling into the store, so there was that. But what exactly had happened to blow out the glass?

Vera caught her breath and tried to wiggle out from under Guppie.

"Sorry," Guppie said, sounding genuinely contrite. "I didn't want you to get hurt."

"So much for—"

She stopped abruptly, cut off by a rattle from outside. It sounded like a lawn mower, or a chain saw coming to life. *Oh, lovely. Mummy is going to have a fit when she hears that I was attacked by a chainsaw-murderer. That was one of the things she was worried about when she heard that I was moving to the country...*

Vera took a deep breath and tried to calm herself. What were the odds, really, that a power-tool-wielding madman had chosen to attack a gas station? She was only on edge because of the darkness, and Hoyt's panic, and the fact that Guppie had tackled her while she was trying to buy ice cream.

Guppie, for his part, went rigid at the noise.

"Will you please—" she began.

The sound repeated, and Guppie clapped a hand over her mouth. The light outside diffused across the walls and ceiling above them, and Vera could only just make out the look on Guppie's face: terror.

Long ago, Vera had learned that some people had to move through the world with more fear than others. People like her—brown-skinned women with immigrant parents, to be precise—had to be cautious. Fear was an instinct, an ever-present voice at the back of her mind. She didn't like this truth, but there was no denying it.

Guppie's fear, however, stopped her cold.

She took a short, shuddering breath, watching his profile. He was looking sideways, toward the next metal rack. He couldn't see anything, of course, just as she couldn't, but Vera was certain that he was listening. Something moved beyond them, and her eyes flicked toward the ceiling. A long, misshapen shadow moved across the ceiling. Whatever it was had moved in front of the lights outside.

Her heart pounded in her ears.

"Oh, God," Hoyt wailed. "No, no, get back, don't—*oh, God*—"

There came a slurp, and a wordless scream that was abruptly cut short. Something dark splattered against the ceiling near the register. Vera could feel herself trembling, but aside from the slight tremor in her limbs, her body was paralyzed with fear. There was no other sound from Hoyt, but that revving noise repeated periodically.

Then came the worst of it all: an echo that reminded Vera of something being unzipped. The smell of offal and warm meat washed over her, and her stomach turned.

Guppie didn't move. He stayed stock-still, hand over her mouth, one arm braced against the floor, still listening.

What if whoever it is realizes that we're here, Vera wondered. *What did they do to Hoyt? How badly did it hurt?*

Before she'd left for Little Creek, Vera had trained as a PA. She'd studied the intricacies of human anatomy. She was intimately familiar with nerves, muscle, tissue, and bone. She knew what she was smelling, and the source of the cracks that echoed through the blown-out room. She'd heard bones break before.

She did not move. She barely breathed. The two of them lay in silence, not making so much as a sound as Hoyt was taken apart by someone or something unseen.

And strangely, all that Vera could think was how smug her mother was going to be when all her fears about the nature of country life were proven right.

9

LEN

BY THE TIME he reached the house, it was nearly dark, and Len's arms ached with the effort of carrying all of his spoils back up the mountainside. The adrenaline had worn off a few miles back, and Len had spent the latter part of the climb making plans.

He reached the house just before sunset. This time, he didn't stash the gas can in the shed where he usually kept it. The dangers of it igniting inside the house would soon be outweighed by the threat of not being able to reach it at all.

When Len had first pitched the idea of using a modified shipping container as a home out here, the county commissioner had laughed in his face. Len had stood his ground: he knew what he wanted, and he was more stubborn than the Heartland County Council of Governments by a long way. In the end, he'd not only been given permission to place the steel structure on his land, but also to pour the concrete foundation on which it stood, including the bunker beneath.

When he threw open the shipping container door, Phobos and Deimos looked up at him with their ears perked. Len loved his dogs like crazy, but he'd chosen the pair of them for more than companionship. Phobos, the German Shepherd, had received police training before Len acquired him. Deimos, the bloodhound, was a rescue, but he had a natural talent for tracking, one that Len had honed extensively over the last five years.

He didn't pause to greet them. Instead, he made straight for the reinforced panel in the floor. He flung it open and descended into the darkness below, where his emergency supply stash was stored in the underground bunker.

The few people who knew the extent of Len's preparations had told him, point-blank, that he was crazy. He could see their perspective. There were nutjobs out there, he knew *that* all too well, but Len wasn't basing his life on a conspiracy theory. He knew what was coming, even if he didn't know when.

He dumped the canister in a spot along the far wall, then dropped his backpack beside it. It took him a moment to find the cord for the lights, but when he did, a bank of LEDs flickered on, illuminating his stash.

Over the course of the last five years, Len had managed to accumulate hundreds of MREs, a dozen or so military-grade medical kits, and even a few higher-tech items: the self-cooling deep freezers that could last without power for as many as a hundred days, the satellite link that would keep his internet connection going even if the grid went down, the fumeless generator, and even a shower stall. There was no head for the shower, but Len had rigged up a bucket system that worked pretty well, and the drain was functional. There was even a composting toilet for when his other needs became pressing.

He let out a short, sharp breath of relief. He'd made it home in time.

As he'd assembled his supplies, Len had wondered once or twice about whether there was any point to all this. With everything he had down here, he could easily survive a few years off the grid. If he could keep tending the garden, so much the better. If he couldn't, then it would be easier to ration his supplies; the less work he did, the fewer nutrients he needed. He could always split the MREs into thirds, or even quarters. If he couldn't use the well, he would simply ration himself to half a water bottle a day.

Even now, when the proof of the danger had yet to arrive, one question burned in Len's mind. It was the same question that had troubled him even as he was building the house: what was the point of living like this when the world had already ended?

When he finally mounted the stairs with his empty pack in tow, Len wanted nothing more than to collapse into bed and fall asleep. His sprint home from the gas station had left him drained and weary. He closed the hatch again, and the sound got both dogs looking up at him a second time.

"Hey, boys," Len sighed, hanging his pack on its peg by the door of the shipping container. "Need to go out?"

Both of them got to their feet and trotted over to him. Phobos waved his tail.

"All right, then." Len threw open the door, and the dogs rushed outside. It was fully dark by then. The sky was clear. Sometimes, on a good night, Len could see the Milky Way from up here. The Crag's Head Gamelands weren't officially a dark sky park, but the view had been one of the things that sold Len on moving here. The couple who'd sold him the acreage thought that this was romantic.

Len knew better. He hadn't wanted to see the stars because they were beautiful. He'd wanted to know what was coming.

Both dogs rushed out to mark the yard, while Len leaned against the side of the shipping container and stared up at the sky. It was possible, of course, that nothing would happen. If only he could convince himself that it was a false alarm, that would be a blessing.

Even as he stood there, a silver streak slipped across the sky. It was soon followed by another, and another.

"Just meteors," he said aloud, crossing his arms to ward off the evening chill. "There's no reason to be afraid."

Deimos finished his business and trotted back over to him. He looked up with a question in his eyes, wagging his tail in that slow, uncertain way he did when he wasn't sure of his mood. Len reached down to scratch his ears.

That was when he heard the first impact.

It echoed through the ground, shaking the very Earth. Len squeezed his eyes closed as both dogs turned toward the noise. Phobos growled.

"Quiet," Len snapped, making the hand gesture that accompanied the sound even though Phobos was facing the other way. The German Shepherd immediately fell silent. That was one of the first commands he'd taught them.

More dull thuds, clustered around the bottom of the mountain, reverberated through the house.

You should go inside, Len told himself. *You have a plan. You have supplies. You can hold out indefinitely if you have to.* He would stay here, and the people of Little Creek would die one by one.

Dammit, he didn't know those people. He didn't owe them a thing. But it would take a special kind of monster to know what was coming and walk away.

With a growl, Len turned back to the house. The dogs followed, but Phobos kept looking back toward the base of the hill, and Deimos walked with his nose in the air, sniffing the breeze.

There was an extensive arsenal in the basement, but for now, he would use the emergency kit. His training vest and rifle were in the gun safe by the door, on standby for this very occasion. The e-collars and earpiece he used in the dogs' training sessions were still attached to the charger. The moment he picked them up, both dogs sat and watched him intently; even Deimos, usually the lazier of the two, was on high alert by then.

"This isn't a drill, boys," Len said, buckling the collars into place. "Remember what I've taught you."

They didn't understand, of course, but Len knew by now that tone was more important than words most of the time. As long as he sounded confident, the dogs would know they could trust him to have the situation in hand. Trust was one of the most important elements of training.

When he was ready, Len gestured for the dogs to heel, strode out the door, and activated the lock behind him. Then he swung his rifle into position.

It was time to go hunting.

10

GUPPIE

IN THE YEARS since Guppie had left the military, he'd continued to think of himself as being in fighting shape. It had been a rude awakening to discover that his self-image had failed to keep up with his expectations, and vice versa. Back in the day, he'd been able to carry two 50-pound ammo cans across a battlefield, run nine-minute miles wearing a full set of SAPI plates, and do a hundred push-ups at a clip—*real* push-ups, unlike the half-assed flailing of those pansies in the 'Chair Force.' After his last visit to the doctor, he'd come home in a mood and done as many push-ups in a row as possible, just to prove he could.

The final tally? Thirty-three. Thirty-three lousy push-ups, and even those were so sloppy his old drill sergeant would have sent him to the sand pit for a circuit of lunges as punishment.

As he crouched there, practically crushing the pleasant lady who owned the garden center, he discovered that not *all* of his training had fallen by the wayside. His body might not have kept up, but his instincts were still on-point.

The thing beyond the chip rack, whatever it was, let out

another rattle. Hoyt had been silent for far too long. Guppie hadn't seen *exactly* what happened to him, but he had enough situational awareness to know the poor kid was gone.

Fight, or flight? Guppie wondered, holding his breath. His natural instinct was to scope out the situation better and meet the problem head-on, but realistically, that wasn't a sound plan. The garden-lady wasn't trained, and Guppie was well past his prime.

The woman he'd pinned to the ground stared up at him with wide eyes. She was shaking, as well she should have been. *She's a civilian. Nothing in her life has prepared her for this. Your job, Gup, is to keep her alive.*

Guppie leaned closer, until his mouth was almost against her ear. "Be quiet, okay?" he whispered. "Don't move. I'm not leaving you here."

She nodded, and her eyes flickered in the direction of the counter.

Slowly, carefully, Guppie sat up. The chip bags scattered around them presented a problem; even brushing against them could alert the enemy as to their location with an ill-timed crinkle. Guppie slid sideways, holding his finger to his lips. The woman didn't move, but she watched him as he went. He nodded, trying to exude confidence he didn't feel. If she panicked, whoever was out there would come after both of them. Guppie didn't like the odds of a fair fight.

With one last steadying exhalation, he forced himself to peek around the corner of the rack. One glance should be enough to give him the lay of the land. Two seconds.

As it happened, those were two of the worst seconds of his life.

Hoyt lay splayed over the counter, belly-up and arms flopping down to the floor. His feet were still on the other side of the register, and his spine was curved at an impossible angle. His mouth was open, his eyes bloodshot. He was staring directly at Guppie, but his eyes were blank and glassy in the bright light still shining through the now-empty windowpanes.

That, Guppie could make sense of. It was awful, but he'd seen worse, like the time Jimmy Payne had stepped on a landmine. The thing that Guppie could *not* reconcile was worse than the sight of a man he'd just known reduced to mere meat. It was the thing on *top* of him that was going to haunt Guppie's nightmares.

It reminded him of one of those zillion-leggers that sometimes got into the house, the kind that fell to pieces when you tried to scoop them up and deposit them on the porch, but with the body of a bear and a head like a Wheelbug. Its proboscis dipped into Hoyt's open belly, and its glistening black body undulated in the light as it fed.

Guppie pulled back and leaned against the rack, gripping it with a shaking hand. The instant that he stopped looking at it, his brain tried to convince himself that he'd imagined it. People often got confused in the face of violence. The mind played tricks on you, adrenaline heightened everything... all this talk of meteors, paired with Hoyt's panic, the darkness, the sight of a murder, it was all too much.

He closed his eyes, steeled his nerves, and forced himself to look again. The sight was exactly the same as it had been. This time, though, Guppie put his horror aside. He shut down his emotions, and his confusion, and his disbelief. Maybe he was going mad, but if a man couldn't believe the truth of his own eyes and ears, what *could* he believe?

These, then, were the facts as far as he could see them: Hoyt was dead. Something was eating him. Guppie and the gardener were currently in the same room as the hungry thing, unarmed, ill-prepared, and defenseless.

This time, when he pulled back, Guppie let his instincts take over. The windows were blown out, and the hungry thing had come from the front of the building, where the lights were. If they went that way, they'd be easy to see. Their best bet was to escape out the back if they could manage it. The thing *might* leave once it had fed, but Guppie wasn't going to bank on that.

There was a door at the back of the room, just down the aisle past the frozen foods. It was the only other door Guppie could see from where he sat. At the end of the chip aisle, which ran perpendicular to the chilled items, there was only a bank of coffee machines. The bathroom, if he recalled correctly, was in the far left corner, and the register stood to the far right. If they stayed low and moved quietly, the thing at the register would have no line of sight on them.

Guppie scooched back toward the gardener. He hoped that his face was blank. He lifted one hand and pointed toward the door in the nearest corner. The woman nodded.

She was clearly prepared to follow his lead, so Guppie went first, sliding back toward the far wall. He watched the gardener, just in case she went rogue on him, but to his relief she sat up and followed suit, sliding on her butt rather than risk stepping on a chip bag in the dark, or standing up so high that the hungry thing at the front of the door could see her.

When he reached the door, he waited for her; there was no reason to alert the enemy to their presence even a second before it was necessary. Only when the gardener was next to him did Guppie reach up and turn the metal handle. To his relief, it didn't squeak. He leaned his back against the door, pressing it open, then motioned for the gardener to scoot through. She did so, and all the while Guppie prayed that the hungry thing was so distracted by its meal that it wouldn't see the movement of the door over the racks.

Once the woman got through, Guppie followed. He was halfway through when that rattling sound came again, and then a metallic clatter. A spindly leg appeared over the top of the nearest rack, followed by the body, and Guppie found himself staring up into the face of—well, he didn't know *what* it was. That proboscis-like appendage extended toward him, and Guppie whimpered.

Then a hand closed on the back of his jacket, and the woman tugged him. For all the times Guppie had offered to help her with the heavy lifting in her store, he'd underestimated her strength. She pulled him back with enough force that he hit the storage rack behind them. She flung her whole weight against the door. It snapped shut just as the hungry thing collided with the other side.

Guppie scrambled to his feet and rushed to add his considerably greater weight to the door. Just as he reached it, the thing struck again, and only their combined efforts kept the door from being flung wide open. But it was still ajar.

The woman's feet slid, and Guppie's knees almost buckled under the force of the onslaught. He let out a growl of fury, but they were losing ground as the thing outside pushed against the door with relentless intent. At this rate, they were only delaying the inevitable.

Will it kill us before it starts feeding? Guppie wondered. *Or will it take its time?*

"Go," he told the woman. "I'll hold it off."

As he spoke, a long, spindly limb appeared around the edge of the door, grabbing blindly at her. It managed to catch the corner of her headscarf, only inches from her face.

Guppie watched in resignation as the woman let out a horrified breath and took a step back, leaving him the only thing standing in the way of the hungry thing.

Good. At least she would get away.

To his surprise, however, she did not flee. She took two paces back and then, with a guttural cry, she threw her whole weight against the door. There was a snap, and then another sound from the creature outside, a rattling scream that made Guppie's hair stand on end. Something clattered to the floor, and Guppie managed to slam the door shut. This time he found the door handle and locked it.

Neither of them stepped away as the beast outside threw itself at the door again and again, but the door was a big steel affair and the lock held, and the hinges bent but did not break. After another agonizing moment, silence descended except for their frantic breathing. The object on the floor scrabbled uselessly against the tiles; the creature's grasping limb had broken under the force of the gardener's blow.

The woman leaned both hands against the door, breathing hard. "What," she gasped at last, "*is* that?"

"You know as much as I do," Guppie panted. "Come on, we need to get out of here. The longer we can't hear it, the farther away it can get. For all we know, it's coming around back to meet us."

The woman nodded and straightened up. There was only a little light in this room, the source of which Guppie could not yet make out. "All right, Mr. Martin. You take the lead."

He wiped his palms on the thighs of his khakis, rolled his aching shoulders, and turned to the far wall, expecting to find an exit.

There was none, only row upon row of storage: cases of Oreos, pallets of chips, bottles of soft drinks and cold-brew coffee, all the overstock that Hoyt would use to fill the shelves when supplies got low.

They hadn't reached the back exit. They'd only managed to find the supply room.

They were trapped.

BEYOND LITTLE CREEK

The South African Large Telescope
Sutherland, South Africa

———

Kwame Moloi examined the most recent images from the telescope.

His colleague, Josef Vogel, was sitting next to him and reading from the emergency broadcast they'd just gotten over the ANET. "This is unreal," he said, his voice growing more incredulous. "They say we're going to lose all access to the satellites. They say it's not just one unlucky strike from one of the meteoroids. It sounds like dozens of hits. And it's a full blown cascading Kessler event. NASA thinks ISS is ... already gone? How can that be?"

Moloi barely heard him. He had a mystery of his own. "This cannot be right, can it?" he asked.

Vogel pulled his eyes away from his screen to peer over Moloi's shoulder. "Is she picking up traces of the meteor shower, or...? Wait, what *is* that?"

The two men stared at the readouts in silent confusion. Over the last few days, the researchers at SALT had been buzzing with excitement over the incoming display. It didn't match the cycles of any of the known showers, but it'd been easy enough to spot the objects moving in a cluster across the cosmos. Observing them presented a tremendous opportunity. The researchers had theorized that the objects were big enough that the shower would be visible even in daylight.

Except now that the objects were passing through the atmosphere, they weren't burning up. What's more, they were multiplying. And most impossibly of all, they were changing course. There were reports of showers happening all over the globe, which couldn't happen all at the same time. It would take a full day of the Earth rotating through an enormous field of debris for that to happen.

Dr. Moloi had managed to capture a clear picture of one just before it hit the atmosphere, and he didn't understand what he was seeing. The meteor wasn't a chunk of ice or cosmic debris. It was...

A ship?

Vogel stared at Moloi. "This is from the main array?"

He nodded.

"What's the time delay?"

"About four minutes."

Both men were still staring at the screen in bewilderment when the first echoing boom shook SALT. Vogel was thrown off his feet, and Moloi had to grip the edge of the desk.

The second impact came a moment later. This time, the ceiling gave way, and an enormous, nearly cylindrical object crashed through the equipment and burst through the floor to ground level. A flash of blinding light and a wave of intense heat blasted him off his feet. For a stunned moment, all Moloi could think was, *The telescope. It destroyed the telescope. That's going to cost a fortune to replace.*

Vogel struggled to his feet and peered over the lip of the newly-formed crater. "What *is* it?" he asked, clutching the side of his head. A thin trickle of blood dripped from his temple.

In answer, Moloi lifted his eyes to the sky, where the roof of the building had once been. A huge portion of the wall had been shorn away as well, leaving him a clear view of the veldt. There were only a few wisps of cloud to mar the pale blue of the Northern Cape sky. Streaks of orange and gold raced across the heavens—dozens of them. Hundreds. He could still *feel* them falling to earth; plumes of russet dust erupted from the landscape as they made contact.

"We called it a meteor shower," Moloi breathed. "But the sky is falling. Vogel, what is happening?"

Vogel moaned and lifted one shaking hand to point into the depths of the hole. No one beneath them had cried out. Moloi assumed that everyone else in the building was dead, and the thought occurred to him with such dispassion that it seemed to have come from someone else.

And yet, in the area below him, something stirred. The object that had destroyed the telescope shifted.

Vogel started screaming, but Moloi watched with only distant interest as the enormous, many-legged shape emerged below him.

You are panicking. This is an emergency. You should do... something.

Only Moloi could not think what.

Run, you fool. Run.

Instead, he turned his head toward the grasslands, where dark shadows moved across the land, closing in on the telescope in a gathering swarm.

There was nowhere to run. If each of the so-called meteorites carried these monsters, then they were all over the world by now.

Moloi began to laugh.

"What is wrong with you?" Vogel screamed. He hammered Moloi with his fists, as if he could beat sense back into his friend. "Say something! *Do something!* What *is* that thing?"

There was nothing to do. All his life, Moloi had been a witness. An observer. His job had been to watch and study and catalog the goings-on of the stellar expanse. He had studied dying stars, tried to quantify the gradual expansion of the universe, had mapped the course of meteors. It was all theoretical.

As it turned out, Kwame Moloi's final act was to witness the beginning of the end.

11

COOPER

IT WAS impossible to tell what was happening. People were running as fast as they could, most of them in the opposite direction of the one in which Cooper and Kat were headed. Girls were screaming, and most of the guys were, too.

"What's going on?" Cooper called, trying to stop people as they passed. "Have you seen my brother? Nate Lutz—where is he? Is he okay?"

A girl Cooper barely recognized collided with him, and he caught her before she fell. It took him a moment to figure out who she was: Cindy Beeling, one of Pammy Mae's cheerleader friends. Her makeup was streaked down her cheeks, and she was sobbing.

"Hey, hey." Cooper rubbed her back. "What happened back there?"

"It was a monster," Cindy wailed. "It got Sam..."

"Football Sam?" Cooper asked, realizing as he said it that this might not make any sense to her.

She nodded, clutching the sleeve of his shirt. "It killed him."

Sam's dead? Cooper shook his head. No way, that was impossible, he'd just seen the guy staggering around with a Solo cup in hand.

"Cindy, look at me: was my brother there?"

She hiccupped. "I—I don't know, I think so…"

Cooper got to his feet and started running again, with Kat on his heels.

"No!" Cindy screeched. "Don't leave me!"

Cooper didn't stop to answer. Most of these kids had spent his whole life either ignoring him or being shitty to him. Heck, Nate was pretty awful most of the time, but Cooper cared about him more than anyone else in town. Sure, they'd tried to kill each other growing up, but didn't *everyone* have a beef with their kid brother?

He spotted a flash of blonde hair in the trees and stopped so suddenly that Kat ran into him. "Pam?" he called. "Nate?"

"*Cooper!*" Nate changed course and bolted toward them. "Go, go, go, we've gotta move."

"What's going on?" Kat asked. "They're saying Sam's dead."

"Sam's gone," Pammy Mae said as she reached them. There was a wild, almost bloodthirsty look in her eyes, and her hair was full of twigs and leaves. That, more than anything, drove home the fact that something was terribly wrong. Pammy Mae was always sleek, always cheerful, always *perfect*. Now, she reminded him more of a wild animal than a Barbie Doll.

"Head for the car," Nate ordered. "We've got to get out of here before—"

"*What the hell is that!*" Kat pointed up toward the canopy.

Cooper followed the angle of her finger, and when he saw what Kat was pointing at, his heart almost stopped. He'd spent most of his teenage years watching bad horror films, and he'd even tried his hand at stop-motion animation a few times. The thing moving in the branches above reminded him of the spider monsters in *Web of Nightmares* and *Swarm From Beyond the Stars!*, only bigger.

Much bigger.

Also, *real*.

"Christ on a cracker," Cooper muttered. "Is that..."

"It's what got Sam." Pammy Mae grabbed Nate's arm. "Now keep moving, or we're going to leave you behind."

Cooper couldn't tear his eyes away from the thing undulating through the trees above him until Kat grabbed his elbow.

"Come on," she hissed. "We gotta go. *Now*."

Cooper stumbled backward, nearly tripping on a fallen branch. He had the horrible sensation that if he looked away, the thing in the trees would somehow catch up to them in an instant.

He was still moving backward when it dropped, landing directly on top of two girls who were limping along arm-in-arm. They screamed, but the sound was cut short by an echoing squelch.

Cooper turned his back, grabbed Kat's hand, and began to run.

He had never been as fast as Nate, and his brother was in a lot better shape these days, but Cooper had never run so fast in his life. He and Kat pelted through the woods, gasping for air. Cooper's lungs were on fire.

"Don't look back," Kat barked. "Whatever you do, don't look back."

Cooper had no plans to do any such thing. They soon passed Cindy, who reached for them as they shot by. Cooper didn't so much as stumble as they passed. Nate was just ahead of them, and Pammy Mae's blonde hair streamed behind her like a golden pennant. Cooper focused on it, telling himself that as long as he kept pace with her, he and Nate would end up in the same place.

At first, Cooper wasn't aware of a new sound. Between the screams and the crackle of feet pounding over last year's leaves and the rush of his pulse in his ears, there wasn't room for anything else. Only as the sound grew closer did he realize that it didn't fit the rest. It reminded him of a handful of D20s rolling across a wood table, or an engine trying and failing to turn over.

He was still trying to place it when Kat's hand was ripped out of his own. Cooper pulled to a stop a few paces ahead of her.

Kat lay on the ground, one arm outstretched toward him. She groaned as she tried to sit up.

Cooper backtracked to her side. "What happened?" he asked.

"Ankle," Kat gasped. They both looked down to the old tree root that had snagged Kat's foot. "Oh, God, that hurts."

"We've got to keep moving," Cooper said. "Can you stand on it?"

"Coop!" Nate screamed from somewhere up ahead.

Kat reached down to touch it and let out a hiss of pain. "I don't think so."

"*Cooper!*"

"Maybe I can carry you," Cooper suggested. "That thing looked pretty busy back there."

"You should go," Kat said. "I'll be dead weight, and that thing could be anywhere. Hurry up, get out of here. You don't owe me shit."

Cooper wiped one palm across his cheek and grabbed Kat's hand with the other. "Come on, Kat, this is stupid. Let me help you."

"*Cooper, look up!*" Nate screamed.

Both of them turned their faces skyward at the exact same moment that the thing above them dropped from the branches.

Cooper had a lifetime of videogames and tabletop role playing under his belt. He loved all of them, but his favorite stories were the ones where he got to play the hero. As a chubby, awkward kid who never fit in anywhere, it was wonderful to believe, even for a moment, that all the things that set him apart from his schoolmates were things that might make him The Chosen One in some fantasy version of his life.

In his real life, there were no quests. There had been no real danger. As the shimmering creature plunged through the air above them, Cooper was faced with the first true monster of his life. His instinct was undeniable, and in that moment, Cooper learned who he truly was.

He let go of Kat's hand, lurched to his feet, and fled.

Nate was reaching for him, but Cooper couldn't bring himself to look his brother, the golden boy of Little Creek, in the eye. Faced with a true test of mettle, Nate had come back for him.

And Cooper?

Cooper had run away.

He kept running all the way to the car, hoping to outrun Kat's final screams. As it turned out, he wasn't fast enough.

12

VERA

VERA STARED at the back wall of the gas station and took a deep breath. She still didn't quite believe what had happened with the thing outside. There was no rational way to explain it to herself. Still, she could feel the reality of it in her aching muscles, and the bruise that was already blooming on her shoulder from where she'd struck the door that last time.

Which meant, logically speaking, that whatever was happening was real enough to present a danger. It would be easier to focus on that than to try to make sense of the many-jointed creature that looked like something out of a late-night B-movie rerun.

"All right," she said aloud, shaking her head as if to clear it. "There's no door. We need to find another way."

The last thing she wanted to do was go back through that door, but if it came to that, they would at least need to be armed. Her eyes landed on the cleaning supplies stacked in the corner. The thing outside looked as much like a bug as anything, and Vera had plenty of experience dealing with garden pests.

"Any ideas, Mr. Martin?" Vera picked up a bottle of bleach

and examined it. That wasn't ideal; with no way to aim it, she would be as likely to spill it on herself as on their attacker. On the other hand, it might be the best weapon she could find back here. She set it aside just in case.

"You can call me Guppie, you know..."

Vera whirled toward him with a spray bottle of Lysol held aloft. "Now is *not* the time."

"If we're going to get our guts sucked out by a giant bug, you can at least tell me why you won't call me by my name."

Vera snorted. "How many times have you called me by mine?"

"Well, I don't know yours."

"Exactly. I hope that answers your *exceedingly* ill-timed question, Mr. Martin." She turned back to the supplies. The little spray bottle wouldn't be useful; it was too small and the range was too short. She had no intention of sticking her arm that close to the creature's face to guarantee a hit. What she needed was something she could use from a distance, preferably something she wouldn't need to hold onto afterward. The creature had been strong, and from the way its arm had splintered, she was certain that the rest of its exoskeleton could withstand a blow. She could think of a dozen useful supplies back at the garden center, but cheese puffs and pork rinds were hardly ideal ammunition...

"Where do you think he keeps the fire extinguisher?" Guppie asked.

Vera suppressed a sigh before his words sank in. "A fire extinguisher," she mumbled. "That would be perfect. It's probably... Oh!" She pointed to the corner near the source of the diffused light. As she did, she realized that the narrow window in that corner was more than that. It was set into a heavy door covered in the same material as the wall. With a gasp of excitement, Vera rushed over to it.

Her thrill was short-lived. The door didn't lead to an exit. It looked back into the coolers. The light from the narrow window was coming from the front of the gas station by way of the glass doors. In between stood row upon row of ice creams and beer cans and yogurt cups.

Vera craned her neck, trying to get a view of the creature. She couldn't see the beast itself, but she could make out the slender shadows it threw across the walls over the register.

She jumped when something snapped next to her, but it was only Guppie unclasping the metal band which held the fire extinguisher in place.

"I know it's a bad time," he said, "but we're in this together now. What *is* your name?"

"Vera," she sighed. "Vera Khan."

He chuckled. "Any relation to Genghis? Because we could use that fighting spirit now."

She didn't bother correcting his geography. He was trying to make small-talk. Vera understood the impulse; her heart was hammering again, and she needed to calm down, to stop her hands from trembling while they tried to make a plan. Right now, they were relatively safe.

"Maybe we should wait here," she suggested. "We can hold out for a while, as long as it doesn't break the door down. We've got food. Drinks. If we wait, maybe it will go away—or someone will come for us." She smacked her palm against her forehead. "Of course, what am I thinking? We should call the police."

"I don't have a phone," Guppie admitted. "I prefer a good old-fashioned landline."

"Fortunately for you, I live in the twenty-first century." Vera fished her cell phone out of her pocket and powered on the screen. The light was blinding in the dim room, and she quickly ducked away from the window so that the creature outside wouldn't see it and come their way.

Her wifi connection was down, but Vera was used to that out here. According to the icon on the screen, she still had two bars of cell service. She punched in 911 and lifted the phone to her ear.

"It's ringing," she murmured, feeling herself automatically relax. She'd been afraid that it wouldn't, that the line would be dead or her reception in this insulated room so poor that the phone would be unable to connect.

Only the ringing didn't stop. No one picked up, even though the line was clear. Vera collapsed back against the wall and slid to the floor as her shaking resumed. Even out here in the boondocks, 911 was supposed to be the one number you could always call for help. It was what people *did* in an emergency.

"No answer?" Guppie asked around the twentieth ring.

Vera lowered the phone from her ear and ended the call. "Nothing."

A hundred awful possibilities sprang to mind, each one more terrible than the last, but no matter what the cause of the missed call, one fact was inescapable.

No one was coming for them.

Guppie knelt beside her, one hand pressed against the door. "You've got a point about our supplies," he murmured. "But I don't think we can stay here."

"Why not?" Her voice came out louder than she intended, and Guppie pressed a finger to his lips, then pointed to the frame of the door over her shoulder. Vera looked up, although it took her a moment to understand his meaning.

There was no bolt on this door. No lock. It might be a physical barrier between them and the thing in the gas station, but if it tried to attack them, the door would barely slow it down.

"We need a plan," Guppie pressed on.

Vera nodded. She was already trying to chart an escape route and a defense plan using what little they had. It was hard to think clearly, however, over the suspicion that was growing at the back of her mind.

That thing, whatever it may be, isn't alone.

13

PAMMY MAE

PAMMY MAE CLICKED the unlock button on the car keys and yanked open the driver's side door in a single motion. She dropped behind the wheel. She didn't even wait for the boys to close the door behind them before throwing the car into reverse.

Cooper sobbed like a baby.

"Coop, man, are you hurt?" Nate asked.

"I left her," Cooper was wailing. "I left her—"

"You had to, man." Nate rubbed his back. "It was too late, there was nothing you could do." He glanced forward and met Pammy Mae's eyes in the rearview mirror. "I've never seen anything like that. What were they?"

"Your guess is as good as mine," she said. Her eyes flicked back to the road just in time to see another car backing out ahead of them. She had to brake so hard that all three of them were thrown forward.

Her eyes were already scanning the landscape. Most cars were sticking to the road, but given how erratically people were driving, it was only a matter of time before there was a pileup or a traffic jam. *Anyone in a compact car is gonna be toast... these low-to-the-ground sports cars and Priuses don't stand a chance if they have to go off-road.* Everyone stood the best chance of surviving if Pammy Mae pulled around the other cars—not that she particularly cared about their occupants; she'd ramp off the sides of the other vehicles if that was what she had to do to keep herself and Nate safe, but there was no reason to risk other people's lives if it made everyone safer.

With that thought in mind, she whipped around the MINI Cooper in front of them, spanning the pine needle-lined bed of the ditch at the side of the paved road. As she did, a few of the other off-road vehicles followed suit, chasing her tail.

It's fine if they follow, but if anyone tries to cut me off, I swear to God...

Breaking into two lanes meant that all the cars could move faster, and before long a few of the smaller cars were zipping past them on the tarmac.

"Should we get back on the road, babe?" Nate asked.

"I'm watching for an opening." Her voice came out sharp with fear, which wasn't a good look. Playing it cool was all part of her Butter Queen training.

She was aware, on some distant level, that this was much more serious than anything she'd gone through before. As much as the pageant had seemed like a life-and-death affair, she had been well aware that it wasn't. If she'd failed back then, nothing bad would happen to her other than a hit to her self-confidence and her social standing. If she failed now...

Pammy Mae didn't let herself consider it. Nate and Cooper were depending on her to stay calm and think clearly. Her own life depended on it. So Pammy Mae didn't let herself think in terms of survival. She focused on winning and let her well-honed instincts take over.

Her headlights picked out a large boulder jutting up out of the ditch with just enough time to spare. There was a Civic just shy of her tailpipe, and Pammy Mae had to gun it in order to pass the smaller car. She whipped over into the road just in time to keep the Jeep from bottoming out on the large rock, missing the front bumper of the Civic by a hair's breadth.

The SUV behind her wasn't so lucky. The driver lay on the horn, swerving to the right and colliding broadside with the compact car. Pammy Mae watched in her rearview mirror as both cars spun around; the Civic ran off the far side of the road and spun out into a tree. The SUV ended up on its side, and the car behind it collided head-on with its undercarriage, pushing it a few dozen yards in their direction before coming to a halt. By then, they were too far away to tell if anyone rear-ended them, but the damage was done: between the rock, the downed SUV, and the totaled Civic, the access road was now totally blocked off.

Pammy Mae took a few shuddering breaths and gripped the wheel so hard her knuckles ached. The woods around them were thick; she wasn't sure that anyone would be able to find a path through the trees.

"Shit, that was close," Nate said unhelpfully.

"They're screwed," Cooper moaned. "Those things are going to catch up with them, and they're all going to be completely and totally fu—"

"There's nothing we can do about it," Pammy Mae said. "So just forget about it."

The blare of horns followed them for another half mile, until the only other car lights they could see were ahead of them.

"Oh my God," Nate groaned. "What are we gonna do now?"

"We need a plan," Pammy Mae said automatically.

"Right." Nate swallowed hard. "A strategy. Gameplay tactics." She heard him sigh from the back seat. When he spoke again, his voice was more solid, more confident. "All right, so we get back to town, we call the police, the emergency services... we get someone out there as soon as possible. They'll send in the National Guard or something. In fact, I bet people are already on their way. In the meantime, we get our ATVs and a couple of my dad's guns and we go back out there. See who we can save."

Pammy Mae nodded, already feeling a little of the tension leaving her. It helped to have a plan. A checklist. Preparation was key.

"What if they don't believe us?" Cooper whined. "Hell, I saw those things, and *I* barely believe it."

Pammy Mae resisted the urge to roll her eyes. She had never been particularly close to Cooper. She didn't have anything against him, per se, except that he was the kind of person who always ran away from a fight. She could understand, on some level; Nate had told her how much Cooper had been bullied back in the day, especially as his weight ballooned and he started getting weirder and weirder, but what *he* didn't seem to register was that if he'd just stood up for himself and put a couple of the worst kids on their asses in a fight, they'd have backed off.

He just watched someone die, she reminded herself, but that seemed like a weak excuse now. They had *all* seen people die tonight.

Nate gestured at the cars ahead of them. "I think there are plenty of people who will back us up."

Cooper nodded and met Pammy Mae's eyes in the rearview. Then his jaw dropped open. "Dear. *Dear.*"

"What?" She frowned at him, not understanding.

"*Hit the brakes!*" he screamed. "*Deer!*" He leaned up between the seats and yanked on the steering wheel.

Fortunately, her foot moved before her brain caught up with her. They spun ninety degrees before coming to a stop just as hundreds of white-tails leapt out into the road. Pammy Mae had hit plenty of them in her day, especially when she first got her license, but usually there were only a few of them in one place at a time. She'd never seen them like this, fleeing in one enormous herd. There were so many of them that she actually lost sight of the car ahead of them for a moment.

For their part, the deer didn't appear to acknowledge the cars. They were so intent on their flight that they bypassed the Jeep entirely. Pammy Mae was aware of dozens of eyes flashing in the midst of the leaping, roiling mass before them. Then, just as suddenly as they had appeared, they were gone, with only a few stragglers leaping in the wake of the herd, their white tails flashing behind them.

"Sorry," Cooper panted, as if the three of *them* had been running while the rest of the world held still.

"Don't apologize," Nate replied. He pointed up ahead, to where the car in front of them hadn't been as lucky. It was dented and battered, with dozens of hoof-shaped pockmarks in its hood and roof. "The canvas top would have taken a beating."

"Thanks, Cooper," Pammy Mae added, with real feeling this time. She backed up to get them re-aligned with the road.

When her headlights hit the other car, however, she could see that they weren't going anywhere fast. A coil of smoke billowed up from the hood, where a mangled buck lay splayed across the windshield. A spiderweb of cracks radiated out from the passenger side of the glass.

The driver's side door opened, and Brandon Locke—a junior—stumbled out. He rolled his shoulders a few times as he limped around the front of the car and began to tug on the dead animal.

"We should help," Nate said, already reaching for the handle of his door.

"*No!*" Pammy Mae said. "*Stay here.*" With both sets of headlights aimed forward, the road was clear enough, but the woods were dark.

Nate ignored her and opened his door. "If we help him get moving, then we'll be able to get to town faster," he said as he stepped out.

Pammy Mae didn't hear him. She was staring out the window of the Jeep in the direction that the deer had come from. There wasn't enough light to see by, but she was still aware of something out there: a silhouette that didn't belong among the branches, and the flash of a pair of eyes.

The shadow moved, and Pammy Mae let out a soft breath of relief as the five-foot wingspan of a great horned owl spread wide, and the bird took to the sky, heading back into the woods away from the road.

"I'll be right back," Nate said.

Everything seemed to happen at once. Nate took a step away from the Jeep, something on Pammy Mae's side moved, and in front of his own car, Brandon went rigid. An instant later, he was gone.

She felt a scream rising in her throat, but didn't give it voice. There was no time to cry out, and no purpose in it. Brandon had already vanished, yanked backward along an unseen line with his limbs as loose and jointless as a doll's. There was no blood. It was as if he'd never been there.

"What the hell what the hell what the hell!" Cooper screeched, until the words became one indistinguishable sound.

Nate spun around and jumped back in at once, slamming the door behind him. Pammy Mae didn't wait to see what emerged from the undergrowth on the left side of the road where Brandon had vanished. Instead, she spun the wheel to the right and dropped her foot on the gas with all the force left in her body. The tires squealed, and the stench of burning rubber wafted through the vents as they whipped around the damaged car.

Cooper was still muttering oaths like a prayer. Nate was silent. Pammy Mae, for her part, was too. She kept seeing Brandon's boneless body being whipped back into the darkness as if he'd been sucked into a black hole from which there was no escape. He hadn't opened his mouth. He hadn't had time.

She was certain that he was dead already.

Whatever those things are, they're fast and they're ruthless. We've got nothing to fight them with and no way to defend ourselves. Nate's right: we need help.

Once they passed Brandon's car, Pammy Mae swerved back onto the road and kept her foot on the gas. The pale trunks of trees whipped by, and the moon shone overhead. Once or twice, she lifted her eyes to the sky. The moon and the stars glimmered above them, but from the looks of things, the meteor shower was over. She tried to remember how many there had been.

How many of those monsters are out there in the hills, hunting my friends? How much damage would they be able to do before help arrived?

Pammy Mae's resolve to stand firm in the face of terror had begun to waver. Nate had been trying to help Brandon. If he'd gotten all the way out of the car, it could have been *him* getting tugged off into the night.

The potholed tarmac of the access road soon smoothed out as they approached town. The parking lot for the party spot was at least five miles behind them now. The posted speed limit was twenty-five, but Pammy Mae had easily doubled, if not tripled, that.

A drainage pipe ran beneath the access near where it joined the narrow two-lane highway leading back to town. Over the years, it had buckled the tarmac above it, forming a deep dip in the pavement. The last few times the county had repaired it, they'd failed to fill the dip up to the height of the rest of the road, treating it as a speedbump for the kids who came out this way, a reminder to slow down before they reached the intersection. Pammy Mae knew it was coming and tapped the brakes, although she had no intention of stopping.

The Jeep had other plans. When she'd slammed the brakes to avoid the deer, she must have damaged the mechanism somehow or stripped the brakes entirely. The Jeep shuddered but didn't slow, and they hit the dip so fast that she was afraid that the Jeep would overbalance. Instead, it took flight for a moment before shooting out across the main road and it kept going, crashing into the metal barrier on the far side with such force that Pammy Mae's chest was driven into the steering wheel and something popped painfully in her neck.

"Sorry!" she gasped. "Is everyone okay?"

"Yeah," Cooper said thinly. "I mean, given the circumstances. You all right?"

"Hmm-hmm. Nate?"

When he didn't answer immediately, she thought her heart would stop.

"Yeah," he said at last. "Seatbelt's gonna leave a bruise, though."

She almost sobbed with relief and despair. "You're worried about a *bruise?*"

Nate snorted. "Yeah. Pretty dumb, isn't it? Is the Jeep still working?"

She had been too afraid to check, but she tried to back up when he suggested it. The engine growled, but the Jeep didn't move.

The three of them sat in silence for a long moment as the conditions of their circumstance sank in. For once, Cooper didn't pitch a fit. Instead, he nibbled one of his black-painted nails. Nate had gone terribly pale.

"I think we know what needs to happen," Cooper said at last.

Pammy Mae shifted around in her seat to look at him. "Do we?"

"Only one of us knows cars, am I right? Nate doesn't know shit about an engine, and you... did your Butter Princess camp teach you about car repair?"

"Not on this scale," she said, letting the jab slide without comment. "But you're not getting out of the car."

"What? Why not?"

"You *saw* what happened to Brandon."

"Yeah, and I saw what happened to Kat." Cooper's eyes blazed. "You think any of us are safe?"

"We're safer in here than out there," Pammy Mae argued. "Nate, tell your brother to keep his butt in that seat until we make a plan."

"Nate, tell your pushy girlfriend that I don't want to get eaten by giant *space bugs*," Cooper retorted.

"Will you both knock it off?" Nate barked. "Cooper, sit still and shut up. Babe, do you have your phone?"

Pammy Mae whipped her cell out of her back pocket and powered the screen on. "No service out here," she said. There were no bars, but she stared at the screen all the same. Only two hours had passed since she and Nate arrived at the party. Now, she wasn't sure how many of their friends were still alive. How could so much have happened in so little time? It didn't seem right.

"Okay, then." Nate crossed his arms and frowned down at the floor of the car with that intense expression he always got when he was thinking about a game. "We're on the road now. Someone could come by. If they do, we'll flag them down. Until then, we're safer inside the car than out there."

"You're making a mistake, man," Cooper told him. "A car's not going to stop one of those things."

"I know that you don't have any tools with you, and you're going to be easy as hell to pick off if you go out there," Nate argued. "I don't want you to end up like Kat."

"Don't talk about her," Cooper growled. "Don't. I can't think about that right now."

"Exactly. I can't think about you getting killed in some dumb daredevil rescue stunt. Pammy Mae is right. We stay in the car."

"Whatever."

Nate closed his eyes, shook his head once, and turned to Pammy Mae. "Okay, okay. Let's just stop and think for a minute. Can you try the engine again?"

Like that's going to do any good, she almost retorted, but that was the fear speaking. Nate was right: they had to think smart if they wanted to get out of this in one piece. She turned the car off, waited a few seconds, and tried again. The engine rumbled to life, but the Jeep didn't move when she tried to back up. Instead, the whole vehicle rumbled, the way it did when she was stuck in mud or deep snow but the tires couldn't find purchase.

"It's no good," she said, taking her foot off the gas. The rattling sound continued.

"Stop giving her juice," Cooper said.

"I'm not."

"I can *hear* it," he said.

He was right, but the rumbling no longer came from beneath her feet. Now it came from the night around them, a clattering, clanking echo. It seemed to circle behind them, coming around to the driver's side. The Jeep rocked, and all three of them looked up in tandem to see half a dozen dimples appear in the canvas moonroof.

Cooper swore under his breath, and Pammy Mae bit the inside of her cheek.

When she had been a little girl, she'd been afraid that a giant tarantula lived under her bed, and that if she got out of bed in the night it would grab at her ankles with its hairy limbs, snap her up in its mouth, and jerk her beneath the wooden frame so that it could wrap her up in its web and suck her dry. For months, she would lie awake at night, caught between her need to use her bathroom and her fear of the unseen beast that she was *certain* waited below. If she wrapped herself in her blanket and stayed very still, she convinced herself that it couldn't hurt her.

As the many-legged creature prowled above them, rattling as it went, that old instinct returned. *If I am very good and very quiet and perfectly still, nothing bad will happen.*

That logic had worked in childhood.

It did not work now.

The rattling increased, and a long, narrow object pierced the canvas above them. Cooper screamed long and loud.

If it has to be one of us, I'm glad it's him. Pammy Mae didn't mean to think it, but the words came to her mind unbidden, and they were cruelly honest. Of the three of them in the car, he was the only one she viewed as disposable.

"Nate!" he was screaming. "Nate! *Nate!*"

Pammy Mae twisted in her seat, expecting to find Cooper grabbing at his brother, begging for help before the thing—whatever it was—killed him. Instead, she found Cooper grappling with the narrow object, clutching it in both hands and trying to snap it in two. Nate sat in his seat, an expression of dull surprise on his handsome features.

Her eyes traced the long, narrow object down to the hole in his shirt, where bright blood welled around the wound. He was pinned to the seat, with the object piercing the center of his chest around his solar plexus.

Nate lifted his eyes to hers and frowned. "Pammy?" he asked. "Babe?" His mouth was too red, and a trail of foamy spittle dripped from the corner of his mouth as he spoke.

Pammy Mae reached for him at the same moment that he was jerked upwards with a terrible force. His chest hit the metal struts of the moon roof, spanning them so that his head hit the back of the structure and his feet dangled over the passenger seat at the front, weakly kicking against the dash and leaving a smear of dirt where they hit. She grabbed onto his leg while Cooper tried to anchor him by an arm. He lowered slightly, and she thought that they must be pulling him back down until he hit the roof again with a jolt that shook the whole vehicle. Somehow, the creature out there had grabbed him and was trying to pull him up and out, yanking him the way a toddler might, unwilling to acknowledge that he wouldn't fit through the hole.

"Give him back!" Pammy Mae screamed, bracing her feet against the underside of the dashboard as she tried to pull Nate down into her arms. *"Give him back!"*

Nate groaned as he was slammed against the roof a third time, followed by a fourth. On the last attempt, a prolonged *crack* echoed through the car, until his spine bent backward too far, accordioning in on itself as the canvas tore to allow him through. Pammy Mae's grip was no match for the force of that colossal tug, and she made one last grab at him as his fingers slipped through hers.

The rattling noise retreated, leaving Pammy Mae and Cooper alone in the car with the starry sky visible above them, a hole in the leather of the seat Nate had occupied the only proof that he had ever been there at all.

14

GUPPIE

"ARE YOU READY?" Guppie whispered.

Vera nodded. She was trembling, bless her. Any fool could see that she was terrified, but from her pursed lips to the set of her jaw, she was clearly poised for battle.

"I'll go first," he told her. "Stay close."

Their plan, such as it was, didn't involve a great deal of fore-thought. Vera was holding the bottle of bleach she'd found earlier, while Guppie wielded the fire extinguisher. Neither of them made for terrific weapons, but other than a few cases of soft drinks and snacks, they didn't have much else to choose from. The refriger-ated unit ran from one end of the store to the other. If by some miracle they could make it to the far end without being seen, they would make a break through the drink display at the end closest to the windows and make a mad dash for freedom.

Just stay here, Guppie's mind whispered. *Bunker down. It's an animal of some kind, it'll get bored eventually and leave once it's done with Hoyt.*

All that sounded nice enough until Guppie remembered the

other folks living down the street. Sean Hawes was a tough old bastard, but if the hungry thing made its way through the town, it would leave nothing but ruin in its wake.

Somebody had to warn the neighbors what was coming.

Guppie pushed the door of the refrigerated unit open and took a hesitant step through. The doors weren't all that well insulated, and the power had been down for at least half an hour by now—it was still cool inside, but not as chilly as it would have been if the unit was still up and running.

Until that moment, they had been afforded some cover, but the moment Guppie stepped out into the fridge, he was exposed. True, the items on display stood between him and the creature that had killed Hoyt, but it would still be able to see them through the gaps between the rows of sports drinks and bottled water.

Guppie paused just outside the door and looked around. The lights from outside were still blazing, but even though it was bright enough to make out the ruins of the display knocked over earlier, and the blank and sunken face of the corpse up front, there was no sign of the creature. He even leaned forward to check the ceiling. Creepy-crawlies were usually climbers, and he wouldn't put it past that thing to be watching them from the ceiling like a spider waiting for the flies to pluck a strand in its web. There was, however, no sign of it.

Guppie glanced back, and Vera placed her hand on the door, holding it open as he shuffled forward. It was tempting to make a run for it, but Guppie knew that he didn't stand a chance of outpacing that thing. He'd rather see it coming and have a chance to react than get tackled from behind and fall without a fighting chance.

With each step, Guppie was sure that something more was going to happen. When nothing did, rather than relaxing, his nerves only wound tighter.

"Any sign of it?" Vera whispered.

Guppie shook his head. He was still scanning the vicinity for any sign of movement. "No," he hissed. "So, here's the plan... I pull the racks out of the way at the back, and you head for the windows. I'll cover you."

Vera nodded, clutching the bottle of bleach to her chest.

They were only a few paces away, and once they were out, they needed to be ready to move. Setting the fire extinguisher aside, Guppie reached for the middle shelf and tugged.

Most of the other shelves included tracks that gravity-fed the bottles downward toward the display doors, so that the racks always looked full. The shelves on the end, however, held two-liter bottles, which were placed loose on the wire racks. When Guppie pulled on the shelf, the bottles wobbled, and one fell to the ground at his feet.

Guppie froze, listening. He hoped against hope that the hungry thing hadn't heard them. It might be out in the parking lot by now, getting the lay of the land. Heck, for all he knew, the darn things didn't have ears at all.

Silence returned.

"It's okay," he whispered, "I think it's gone—"

Even as he said it, the creature shot over the top of the shelves toward them and threw itself at the unit door. Vera squeaked as the beast collided with the clear surface; Guppie had assumed that it was glass, but judging by the way it warped without breaking, it must have been some sort of durable plastic. The creature stopped, shook itself, and then reached up with two limbs to grab the top corners of the door. With a single sharp movement, it pulled the door right off of its hinges.

"Get back!" Guppie cried to Vera, just as one of the creature's legs shot forward, plunging into the meaty flesh of his upper arm. Guppie glanced down at the injury in shock. The leg went clear through the soft tissue, exiting through the back. On the far side, the narrow limb twisted and expanded, forming a three-headed talon reminiscent of a grappling hook. It didn't even *hurt,* at least not yet.

Then it yanked him forward, and the pain set in. It didn't stop with the burning agony of the hole in his arm. When he hit the shelves, the creature pulled Guppie with such force that the wire shelving shot out the other side into the main room of the store, sending bottles of Mountain Dew and Diet Coke flying. At least the resistance of the shelves pulled Guppie free of the creature's limb. He hit the floor hard and rolled into the side of the candy rack.

He'd lost track of Vera, and the fire extinguisher was still standing inside the cooler where he'd left it. Guppie tried to pull himself to his feet in search of a weapon, but he could barely think through the pain in his arm.

Come on, old man, you've been through worse, he scolded himself. That had been his pep talk for himself these last few years, but in this particular instance, he wasn't sure that he still believed it. What could be worse than this?

The creature made that rattling sound again, and lunged toward him. It was only a few paces away.

Something white sailed through the air, directly on course for the creature's thorax: the bottle of bleach Vera had been carrying. It hit the creature's side, splattering the caustic liquid against the monster's exoskeleton. The creature hissed and spun toward her.

"Get the fire extinguisher!" Guppie hollered. He tried again to get to his feet and only succeeded in pulling down a rack of candy. As it hit the floor, Guppie blinked.

It was a stupid idea, and they were short on time. Then again, they only had seconds to spare, and it wasn't like he had any other tricks up his sleeve.

As the creature moved toward the fridge again, Guppie grabbed a roll of Mentos from the floor, and a bottle of soda in the other. "Hey, you big ugly sonofabitch!" he yelled. "Look over here!" He twisted the cap off the soda with one hand even as he tore the wrapper apart with his teeth, dropping the whole roll of candies into the bottle at once.

The effect was almost instantaneous: a geyser of pressurized foam jetted out of the mouth of the bottle, spraying the monster in the back. It immediately rounded on Guppie, rattling as it approached. Its long, narrow proboscis extended toward him at lightning speed, and he dropped to the floor a second before it could spear him, still aiming his makeshift weapon at the creature.

Almost instantly, it was on top of him, caging him in with its insectoid limbs, preparing for a deadly strike. Guppie squeezed his eyes shut and dropped the now-empty bottle. *We all gotta go sometime. Didn't think it was gonna end like this, but here we are.*

"Over here!" A loud popping noise sounded through the room, so sharp that Guppie thought it was a gun at first. He looked down toward his feet where the noise had come from and saw Vera, fire extinguisher in hand, just as she brought her heel down on another bag of chips with such force that it burst like a balloon. "I'm the one you want to worry about."

The sound was apparently enough to draw the creature's attention too, because it swung its head in her direction. Vera swung the hose up to face it and pulled the handle of the fire extinguisher.

Nothing happened.

"Pull the pin!" Guppie howled as the creature turned its segmented body back to face her. Vera swore and fumbled with the pin for one precious second. The metal tinkled against the floor, and just as the creature prepared to strike again, she tried again.

Between the strange lighting and his general state of confusion, Guppie hadn't been able to get a good look at the creature's face. He wasn't certain that it had *eyes,* not in the usual sense. Even so, he was sure it didn't like the effects of the fire extinguisher. Its pained cries echoed through the gas station, reverberating off the walls. It backed up, scraping at its face with its forelegs, chattering in disoriented pain.

Vera dropped the canister and swept toward Guppie, hauling him to his feet. He had to put more of his weight on her than he wanted, but he managed to get up and running toward the door. With each passing moment, though, he was becoming more and more lightheaded, and his feet didn't want to obey him anymore.

"Thanks," he slurred. "Good shootin'."

"I never thought I'd be put in a position where I'd need to weaponize snack foods and safety equipment," she panted. "Come now, Mr. Martin, stay with me."

As they stumbled through the parking lot, Guppie pointed to his car, the beat-up old pickup truck he'd been driving for the last two decades.

"Key's're in the ignition," he told her. "Gotta go. Gotta get... help..."

They passed the source of the light, but Guppie's eyes didn't seem interested in focusing anymore. It almost looked like a space-craft or a satellite of some kind, but the harder he squinted, the more that light smeared across his corneas into a meaningless blur.

"Stay with me," Vera repeated. At the truck, she paused to prop him against the side of the vehicle while she opened the door. It was all Guppie could do to drag himself into the passenger seat. A moment later, she climbed into the driver's side, turned the key, and revved the engine. "Talk to me, Guppie."

"Hey. You said my name. An' I know you, you're *Vera.*" He let his head roll to one side so that he could smile at her. The pain wasn't so bad now. In fact, he was starting to feel almost comfortable. Warm. Like he was floating in the ocean on some quiet, sun-drenched bay, buoyed by the saltwater as the tide ebbed and rose.

"That's good, Guppie," she said, pulling out of the spot. "I need you to keep talking. We'll get you somewhere safe and take a look at that wound of yours."

"My wound?" He glanced down at the puncture where the beast had speared him, then giggled. "Look, Vera, I'm *holy*. Get it? On account of the hole?" He chuckled to himself, settling back against the seat. As his eyes roamed over the scene around them, he sighed dreamily. "Look at all the lights."

Vera let out a choked sob. That didn't seem right. The lights were lovely, illuminating the town from end to end, some of them brilliant white and others flickering in shades of yellow and orange.

He blinked twice and squinted, trying to make out the source of the illumination. Fireworks, perhaps? Sparklers? It was months until the Fourth of July, but maybe people were celebrating early. There was a lot of patriotic pride in Little Creek. He wouldn't put it past them to show off their American spirit just for the hell of it.

Then his vision came into focus and the laugh died on his lips. It wasn't a festival that had the town so bright.

Little Creek was burning.

15
LEN

LEN HEARD the scream of metal on metal from half a mile off.

"Heel," he snapped into the mic, and took off running.

When he'd started training, Len had focused on running in short bursts at tremendous speed, but these days he was more interested in long-distance mileage. If something really wanted a piece of him, he was unlikely to outrun it, but if the grid went down, he might need to travel on foot. The ability to run one six-minute mile wouldn't be nearly as useful as the ability to run a hundred consecutive ten-minute miles, and he'd kept in shape with this principle in mind.

It took him almost five minutes to reach the source of the sound; it wasn't hard to pinpoint, since the car had collided with a shoulder barrier and all the lights were on. He listened as the engine revved uselessly.

"Wait," he told the dogs. Phobos immediately dropped to the ground, but his ears kept swiveling around. Deimos sat and sniffed the breeze.

Len was about to step out when the sound of the Jeep's engine died and something else took its place: a rattle, like a box of ball-bearings being shaken at a steady pace. He lifted his rifle to his shoulder but didn't put his eye to the sight.

Something moved in the road alongside the crashed Jeep.

Len saw the vehicle rock and heard the screams, but he still couldn't make out what was happening. The one thing he'd never been able to picture in all these years was exactly what the incoming aliens would *look* like. It was, he had told himself, better that way, or he would have lain awake at night *knowing* rather than simply wondering.

The Jeep rocked a few more times, and Phobos stirred, tense for an attack.

"Can you see it, boy?" he whispered.

Phobos let out a breath that stopped short of a whine and cocked his head. Len had trained him to be silent while hunting, and of the two dogs he was usually more interested in following orders, but whatever he could see or smell now was so compelling that it tried even his patience.

"*Wait,*" he repeated. It wouldn't do anyone any good to fire directly at the car. He could kill the occupants shooting blind like that.

Something emerged from the top of the vehicle, and it shook again. Len watched as a pale and misshapen object was dragged over the far side of the Jeep and disappeared. He waited ten seconds before moving forward; he'd have liked to wait longer, but the keening from inside the Jeep was too terrible to ignore.

Without giving the dogs another command, he jogged out into the open, sweeping the area just in case the alien returned. The Jeep's lights were still on, and as he approached the car he saw that there were two people inside. Kids, practically. Not small children, but not adults, either.

He pounded on the door, and the guy in the back seat jumped.

"It's back!" he yelped in a muffled voice.

"It's *not*," Len told him. "Open up. I'm getting you out of here."

The door popped ajar, and a young man's tear-streaked face poked out, capped with a wild mop of bright green hair. "We don't need to get out of here," he said. "What we *need* to do is get my brother back."

Len gritted his teeth. It was unreasonable to expect ordinary people to understand what they were up against. The government had gone to great lengths to cover up everything that they knew, and as far as Len could tell from his lurking and prodding online, he was one of the few persons outside of NASA who had the slightest idea what to expect from this 'once-in-a-lifetime' meteor shower. Surely there must be other world powers who had worked the details out on their own, but he doubted that anyone had a widespread system in place for dealing with the invasion.

"Hurry up," he told the kid, picking words that the dogs wouldn't mistake for commands. "Let's get to safety and then you can tell me where your brother is."

"He was just here!" The kid pointed to the far side of the car, the direction in which the pale object had disappeared. "We gotta get him before..."

"He's dead," said the driver.

Len peered up front. A girl with bleached blonde hair was in the front seat. When she turned toward Len, her eyes were blank and glassy. Something had switched off inside of her.

Len knew that look all too well.

"What are you talking about?" the boy said, waving his arms. "He was just here."

The girl shook her head and didn't break eye contact with Len. "Cooper's in denial. Nate's dead. People don't *bend* like that. Do you know what these things are?"

The matter-of-fact way she spoke made goosebumps prickle on the back of Len's neck, but for the moment, he'd take emptiness over hysterical tears. "I have an idea."

"And you've got a weapon." The girl's eyes dropped to Len's rifle. "Any chance you carry a spare? I know how to shoot."

"You're not getting out of the car," the boy, Cooper, argued. "The last thing Nate said was—"

"*He's dead.*" The girl whipped toward him at last and bared her teeth. "You've been useless all night, Cooper. Nothing you've done has helped even *slightly*. You're the reason Kat's gone, you're the reason the brakes were shot, *you're* the reason Nate got *broken in half* and carried off. So how about you shut up and let the adults talk for a minute?"

Cooper recoiled, and Len took the opportunity to scan the area again.

"We need to move," he said. "We're in the open."

The girl immediately slid across to the passenger side and opened the car door, joining Len on the road.

"Hurry up, Cooper," she snapped in a voice dripping with sarcasm. "Or we'll leave you behind."

The green-haired boy gulped and slid out of the back seat without another word of protest.

"Follow me," Len said, waving to the pair of them. He could only imagine the extent of what they'd been through that night, but he was certain that it was bad, and equally certain that it was only the beginning of what awaited them.

This time, both kids kept close and quiet as they crossed the road again and entered the woods in the direction of Len's home.

They were about six miles out. Len could cover that distance in an hour, but he doubted the kids could manage it. The girl, maybe, on a good day with the right shoes and a clear head. As it was, they were both in shock. The return trip would take their group twice as long as if Len was running alone, if not more.

Unless we go toward town. We're halfway there already. Maybe we should keep heading that way and see if we run into anyone else?

Caught between two options that both sounded less than ideal, Len chose to hunker down in the ditch alongside the road, just below where he'd left the dogs.

"How many of them are there?" he asked without preamble.

"We don't know," the girl said. In the lights of the car, her clothing and makeup had struck Len as fussy and self-absorbed; she was a teenager, after all. Len didn't expect her to be ready for battle. In reality, however, it was obvious which of the two survivors was the more dominant.

"What are they?" Cooper asked.

"Aliens," Len said. "I know how it sounds, but…"

"That makes sense." The girl pulled her blonde hair away from her face. By moonlight, she looked more like a warrior than a cheerleader. "We saw them come out of the ships. How do we kill them?"

Len cocked his head. "Do you really know how to shoot?"

"Rifle and pistol," the girl responded at once. "And crossbow, but only the compound kind, and only with a stand. My family's big on hunting."

"What about you?" Len asked, turning to the boy.

Cooper grunted. "No." He didn't elaborate, and Len didn't press him. If he wasn't confident about using a gun, he wasn't interested in arming him.

"Listen," he said in a low voice. His personal training regimen had never factored in comforting traumatized survivors of the invasion, mostly because he was *supposed* to be hiding out in his bunker at the moment, getting cozy while the world fell apart around him. His instinct was to keep moving. He knew how to keep *himself* alive, but other people?

Lately, other people seemed like a total mystery.

He intended to continue speaking, but Len had forgotten the dogs. Phobos took his word as a command and jumped to his feet a few yards away. Cooper flinched and raised his arms to cover his head.

Len turned to his dog. His quiet snuffling echoed in his mic. "What do you hear, boy?" he whispered.

The growl started low in his throat, and Deimos joined in. Len couldn't see them clearly from here, but he could tell that they were pointing at something, prepared to strike if he gave the command.

He didn't. Until he knew exactly what they were up against, he wasn't about to send his boys into danger.

Len unholstered his pistol and shoved it into the girl's hands. "If you don't have a clear line of sight, don't shoot. This is for self-defense. *Don't be a hero.*"

The girl nodded and accepted the gun, immediately checking for the safety. *Good. She really does know what she's doing.*

Len stood up, holding his rifle at the ready.

"They're in the trees," Cooper hissed up at him. "They like to attack from above."

"Thank you," Len said, and he meant it. "Stay low. I'll be back if I can." He didn't bother to explain himself. Those kids had seen enough to understand what he meant. It was entirely possible that they would take off toward town the moment he was gone—honestly, that might be the best outcome for all of them. At least they were armed, now. If they ran into trouble, Len wouldn't need to blame himself.

"Deimos, *lead*," he said.

Immediately, the hound dropped his nose to the earth and padded off in the direction of the intersection.

"Phobos, *heel*," he added. Leaves crackled under the German Shepherd's paws as he rushed to his side. He kept one shoulder against his knee as they followed the hound toward the intersection.

Len could see where Deimos was headed even before he arrived. The metal pipe running under the road was almost three feet in diameter and at least ten feet long. Deimos stood on the pavement above the opening, sniffed twice, then looked to Len for confirmation.

"Wait," he told the dogs. Deimos immediately sat, but Phobos followed him for another pace until he growled, "*Wait*." He dropped to the ground beside him and let out a disapproving grumble.

One of the few luxuries Len afforded himself was a satellite TV. He didn't use it much this time of year, but on long, frigid winter nights, he piled into the couch with the dogs and watched movies. Ever since building the bunker, he'd had a special affinity for apocalyptic and horror films. In a twisted way, watching them was another form of training, often a lesson in what not to do. More than once, he'd chuckled grimly over the fact that, in a town of rednecks, a black man and his two dogs would likely be the first to go.

He had no intention of letting life imitate art. He was going to get these bastards before one of them got him.

A damp, meaty odor emanated from the tunnel. Len stopped a few feet away and crouched down. Still gripping his rifle in his right hand, he reached for the little flashlight dangling from his vest. Bracing for an attack, he flicked it on.

There was a teenage boy in the tunnel, or what was *left* of a boy. He was wearing a white t-shirt and khaki shorts, now smeared with mud and gore. His face, mercifully, faced away from Len, but there was no doubt in his mind that this was the pale thing he'd seen pulled through the roof of the car. He wasn't just dead. He was *shattered*.

There was clearly nothing he could do for him, so Len didn't dwell on his fate. He flicked the beam of light around inside the tunnel, hoping to get a view of the thing that had killed him. Cooper had warned him that the aliens liked to drop on their prey, so if he didn't spot it soon, he would retreat and head for cover...

Then his light caught the gleaming reflection of a pearlescent sheen on a dark object. It was pressed to the roof of the tunnel, flattened against the ribbed lining of the drainpipe. Len's brain took a moment to process what he was seeing, beyond the softly pulsing figure.

Only when it darted toward him did Len realize that the creature was upside-down, clinging to the ceiling like a monstrous silverfish. It skittered toward him in a whirling maelstrom of legs that were much too long and too slender, a glittering obsidian mass.

Len whipped to one side and dropped to the ground as the creature leapt toward him, right through the spot where he'd crouched. The creature hit the ground, emitting that ball-bearing rattle as it did.

Phobos didn't wait for a command; he was only a few feet away from the alien, and instinct overrode training. With a snarl, he jumped up toward where Len assumed the creature's head would be, although he still couldn't quite tell which parts were which; he had yet to get a good view of its body. Phobos snapped at its underbelly, weaving between its jabbing limbs, until he could get a good grip with his jaws. When he did, something splintered and cracked, and the creature let out an otherworldly scream.

Len didn't fire his weapon. For one thing, he didn't want to hit his dog; for another, he didn't want to waste his ammo. He let the rifle hang from its strap over his shoulders and grabbed the hunting knife hanging from his utility belt.

"*Hunt,*" he cried.

Phobos redoubled his efforts as Deimos came pelting down the slope. The usually placid hound grabbed one of the creature's hind legs in its jaws and twisted, splintering it off. He'd trained them to hunt deer with the intent of bringing the animal down as quickly and cleanly as possible, but the tactics here were equally effective on aliens, apparently. Deimos went for the legs while Phobos aimed for the throat. Len's part in these operations was simple: sever the spinal cord and put the thing out of its misery.

He darted forward as Phobos pulled the creature to the ground with his own weight. Len wasn't exactly clear on alien anatomy, but he'd eaten enough lobsters in his life to have a rough idea of what he was doing. He reached up to the creature's back and drove the tip of his knife between the lapped plates of its exoskeleton, then threw himself across its body. Not only did his weight help to bring it down, but the knife slid to the peak of the creature's back, snagged, and then severed whatever was beneath it. A thick, foul-smelling liquid erupted from the wound, and the creature screamed again, shuddering as it collapsed. Len yanked his knife back and scrabbled away on all fours while the dogs stayed on top of the beast.

It took a long time to die, or at least for him to be sure that it was dead. It continued to shudder and rattle long after it rolled onto its side. Until then, it had reminded him more of an oversized bug, but as it went limp, he could see that there was more to it than that, although even when he trained his flashlight beam on it again, he couldn't tell exactly what he was looking at.

I'll need to come back in the daylight, or kill another one and take it back to the bunker. The prospect of doing an informal autopsy on one of these critters was compelling. He'd love to see what made them tick when he got the chance.

"*Heel,*" he told the dogs, and they both immediately let go of the dead creature, trotting back to his side. He ran his hands along their backs and legs, checking for injuries, but found none. "Good boys," he said, and got back to his feet, taking careful steps toward their downed quarry, in case it wasn't *really* dead, but it didn't rise again. Just to be sure, he drove his knife into its belly, splitting it open. He was damned if he was going to have to face one of these bastards twice.

To his surprise, the kids were waiting where he'd left them. Phobos eyed them warily, and Deimos wagged his tail once as he sniffed them.

"We heard... noises." Cooper swallowed hard. "Did you get it? Is it dead?"

"One of them is," Len said. "Although I'm sure there are more." He wiped the knife on the leg of his pants before tucking it back into its sheath. "You should know, I found your brother."

"And?" Cooper's voice was full of undeserved hope.

"And your friend is right," Len said. "He's gone."

Cooper moaned, and the girl let out a muffled sob.

"I'm sorry," Len said. "We can come back for him later, if we make it through the night." The words were already out before he realized that they probably weren't the most tactful ones he could have chosen. "I'm sorry," he added, both because he'd spoken without thinking, and because... well, all of it. He was sorry for what had happened to the boy in the tunnel, and the night, and the kids' future. He was sorry that they couldn't go back in time to the world before.

Above all, he was sorry that there were people who had known all this time what was coming, and they had done nothing to ensure these kids' safety.

"Come on," he said, "let's get you home."

It was a mark of penance that, when Len started walking, he aimed for Little Creek rather than the safety of his bunker.

BEYOND LITTLE CREEK

Restricted Airspace
Washington, D.C.

———

Merry Clark's Boeing AH-64 Apache had seen its fair share of action through the years. She'd completed numerous missions overseas, and a few rescues in the states. She knew the ship inside and out. It was like an extension of her body.

What she *didn't* understand was what the hell was going on in Washington.

"*Clark, I need you to keep on course,*" her commander barked through her radio. "*We've got two other choppers following your lead. They'll cover you, but you're our main.*"

"Easier said than done, Greene," she snapped. "Are you seeing this?"

Below her, the city was burning. The Potomac, usually a dark strip across the land at night, reflected the flames that ravaged Georgetown. Deep pits left by the falling meteors marred the gutted neighborhood.

"*We've got visuals, Clark. Just stay on target.*"

"Roger that. I'm coming over Theodore Roosevelt Island now..."

Most of the time, on comparable missions, Merry was over unfamiliar territory. When she'd helped with the evacuations during the floods following Hurricane Cadence, she'd had to rely on maps of Southern Texas to guide her. It was obvious that the landscape had changed as the waters rose, but it wasn't *her* turf. The sight elicited more pity than pain. Seeing Washington go down?

It was different. This was home.

Who would do this? she wondered, knowing full well that every survivor fleeing a war zone asked the same damn question. *Who would do this to the place* I *call home?*

Someone had to be responsible. The notion that this was a random meteor shower was a crock of crap. Who was it? The Russians? The Chinese? And perhaps more importantly, why hadn't anyone seemed to see this coming?

She had eyes on the White House now. "Should I be expecting to take fire?" Merry asked.

There was more candor than usual in Greene's voice when he told her, "*Frankly, Clark? You should be ready for anything.*"

That didn't exactly inspire confidence.

Merry brought the Boeing low over the White House lawn. There were more people out there than she'd expected, most of them dressed in black or camo, forming a protective ring about the President and his family.

"*Your backup is going to cover you from the air,*" Greene said. "*Get the First Family and get out. Is that clear?*"

"Roger," Merry barked. She brought the Boeing in to land. Before she touched down, the group of people was already moving toward her.

Viewing the city from the air had been bad enough, but it was worse on the ground in the thick of things. When she couldn't *see* what was happening, she could only imagine.

The other two choppers hovered above them while the President and his family climbed aboard. His youngest daughter was crying, and the First Lady clung to the little girl, uttering nonsensical words of comfort.

The President, however, wore no expression at all.

Two members of the security team piled in last, and Merry started up the rotors again, preparing for takeoff. As she did, something moving across the lawn caught her eye: dark shapes that moved like animals with far too many legs.

Drones, maybe. Some kind of remote weapon. They descended on the group of special ops and security still gathered on the lawn. The sharp report of gunfire was audible even over the thrum of the blades, but Merry didn't stick around to see what would happen. Within moments, they were in the air.

"I'm out," Merry said. "Awaiting new coordinates."

"*37.807342 north by -76.111492 west*," Greene said at once.

Merry frowned as the White House shrank to the size of a dollhouse beneath them, bone-white amidst the flaming wreckage of the city. "That's in the middle of the Chesapeake, sir."

"*I'll meet you there, Clark.*"

She'd learned a long time ago not to ask questions, but as Merry Clark navigated toward the sea, she realized just how widespread the damage was. Fires burned all along the coast, not just in D.C., but in the nearest parts of Virginia and Delaware as well.

How far does this go? she wondered.

She glanced over her shoulder for another look at the President. He might as well have been carved from stone.

Everywhere, she thought. *What if it's* everywhere?

The three helicopters passed over the dark waters of the Chesapeake, leaving the burning coastline behind.

16

COOPER

MY PARENTS ARE GOING *to kill me,* Cooper thought, before remembering what had happened to Nate. He'd watched Nate's body hit the supports of the moonroof, limp as a ragdoll, with the same sort of detachment he felt when he drank. What had happened to Nate might as well have happened to a stranger, for all that Cooper could make sense of it. One minute, he'd been there giving orders like he was calling plays for the football team. The next—

He was supposed to go away to college this fall. He was supposed to be some pain-in-my-ass hotshot football player. He was supposed to be the one that made Mom smile, the one Dad liked, the success.

He was supposed to make up for me.

Everything Pammy Mae had said hurt, but that didn't mean she was wrong. Cooper had spent the whole night screwing up. As he trudged along behind the stranger with the dogs and Pammy Mae, his mood sank lower and lower with each passing step.

If he'd stayed home tonight, Nate might still be alive. And Kat.

He should have insisted that Kat leave without him. Better yet, he should have left Little Creek behind years ago. He and Nate argued a lot, but when it came down to it, his brother had been the only person who really wanted him around.

You're broken.

You're a screwup.

It's your fault that they're dead.

Cooper stumbled on a branch and almost fell, but he managed to catch himself just in time. Pammy Mae glanced back over her shoulder at him, her scowl accentuated by the harsh angle of the moonlight. He quickly righted himself. Pammy Mae had been a badass when she was driving, and their savior had actually *killed* one of those things. He wasn't going to need rescuing again tonight, dammit.

"Who are you?" Cooper asked.

The man kept scanning the woods around them as he walked, with his two giant dogs walking close on either side of him. "Name's Len."

"Len?" Cooper stared at him and almost tripped again. "Len Bonaparte?" He almost added, *The Devil of Crag's Head?* but stopped himself in time. There were all kinds of stories about the crazy prepper dude who lived in the woods, but Len wasn't what he'd pictured. He'd imagined some old white man with no teeth and an American flag tattoo who wouldn't shut up about the second amendment. Now that he thought about it, he'd simply remembered the man who lived next to his grandmother, the one who cussed him out the first time he'd seen him. He'd just smelled weakness on Cooper, and he'd become synonymous in his mind with the type of person who thought the end times were right around the corner. He'd died the year before his grandmother had.

"And you're Cooper," Len said, dragging him back to the present. His thoughts weren't linear right now, which was for the best, because any time he reeled himself in, all he could think was, *Nate's dead. And for some shitty reason, I'm still alive.* "Cooper and...?"

"Pammy Mae Johnson. And don't lump us into the same group. We're not friends." Pammy Mae spat the words.

"To be honest," Len said, "I don't really care. No offense, but you kids can work your crap out once you get home."

Home. It should have sounded safe, but Cooper was already dreading walking in the door alone. He was dreading the inevitable question, *Where's Nate? Where's your little brother?*

What did you do?

Worst of all would be the expression on his parents' faces, the one that would tell him flat-out that the wrong son had died.

Len stopped suddenly and lifted one hand in the air, forming a fist. "Wait." His voice came out as a sharp command, and both of his dogs froze.

"What is it?" Cooper hissed, shuffling closer. The eerie silence that had pervaded the woods when Len killed their attacker had faded. The usual night noises had returned, and Cooper had unconsciously allowed himself to relax a little. He was tired and heartsick and he ached all over. With Len's gesture, however, all of his earlier tension returned in a rush of adrenaline.

"Look at the sky," Len said.

Cooper and Pammy Mae looked up. The sky had been clear all night, but now a dim orange haze hung over the horizon, almost like...

Smoke.

"No," Cooper breathed. The light came from the direction of town, and he knew in his gut where it had originated. His aching feet were suddenly light, and he lurched into an awkward run. He'd never been particularly athletic, even before he was over-weight. His classmates had never wanted to pick him for teams, and he was more interested in working on cars and farm equipment than jogging, but now he needed to get closer, to see for himself.

"Cooper!" Len called after him.

He expected Pammy Mae to spit some curse at his back, but to his surprise she ran with him, keeping pace. She could have pushed on ahead, but Cooper had the feeling that she didn't want to go alone. She didn't want to confirm her fears any more than he did, but they had to know.

They reached an overlook not far from the road. Cooper had hiked to that very spot dozens of times when things got too tense at home and he had to get out of the house and let off some steam. He liked getting up high and looking out over the town. All of his problems seemed smaller up here, faraway and remote, shrunk into miniature. The combined elementary and middle school where he'd been taunted mercilessly was the size of a dollhouse from that height, and the high school lay even further away, almost lost on the far edge of town. From the gas station on the west end of the main drag all the way down to the Country Duke on the east, tiny cars that looked like children's toys zipped past night and day. People didn't stop to think about Little Creek. Why should he?

Now, Cooper stood on the gravel turnoff and gaped down at the chaos. Dozens of fires blazed throughout the town, most of them coming from houses. At the small Heartland County Municipal airport just outside town, every single hangar was burning. His dad's POS Piper would have been in there, not that the thing was flightworthy. But other planes would have been, at least before they all went up in flames. Could his parents have made it to a plane and gotten out?

Craters made by the fallen ships had marred lawns and punched holes in the sides of buildings, and in the hazy light cast by the flames, Cooper could make out dozens more of those rippling, insectoid figures darting among the ruins. There were people down there, too, but Cooper could barely distinguish between the makes and models of cars on the road, never mind identifying the individuals moving along the streets.

"Mom," Pammy Mae breathed.

Cooper gulped. He could see his house as 1014 Maple Street; it wasn't on fire, but the lights were out, and his dad's car was still in the driveway. Unless they'd left on foot or hitched a ride with a neighbor, they were probably inside.

"We've got to go down there," Pammy Mae said.

Len jogged up behind them and took in the scene. "What we *ought* to do is go back to the bunker. We should wait out the night. Come back tomorrow."

Pammy Mae whirled toward him. "Are you *crazy?* My *mother* is down there."

Len held up his hands, and the dogs stiffened, clearly waiting for instructions. "Listen, I know it sounds awful, but what are we going to do? The smart thing is to regroup, arm ourselves, and come back stronger."

His words made sense, but Cooper kept staring at his silent house amid the ruins of Little Creek. He'd already turned his back on one person that night, and failed to save another.

"Pam's right," he said. "We can't just leave them."

"I'm confident that your family would want you to find your way to safety," Len said.

"Maybe," Pammy Mae admitted, "but I'm not leaving until I know she's okay."

Or dead. Cooper heard the unspoken fear in Pammy Mae's voice. Her home was in Cloverleaf out near the high school. There were no fires back there, at least not yet, but the mayhem was spreading. It was only a matter of time before the whole town was overrun.

"We should get going," he said.

Pammy Mae widened her stance and stared defiantly at Len. "Are you coming with us? Or are we on our own?"

Len shook his head. He didn't *want* to agree, that much was obvious, but between Pammy Mae's determination and the night-marish landscape below them, he was clearly at a loss.

"Fine," he said. "But if you want my help, you're going to need to listen when I tell you what to do. Otherwise, I'm taking my dogs and I'm going."

Pammy Mae nodded.

"Come on, then." Len turned to the deer trail that led down the side of the hill toward town with his dogs in tow. Pammy Mae followed, and Cooper brought up the rear as they descended into what was quickly becoming a war zone.

17

VERA

GUPPIE'S HEAD lolled back against the headrest of the
passenger seat as the pickup rattled over the road. Vera had never
quite gotten used to how poorly these little roads were maintained
even at the best of times; if anyone at the county commission could
see them now, they'd throw a fit. Chunks of pavement had been
knocked free of the road, and she had to drive on the center line to
avoid the worst of it.

"You remember what I said?" she asked Guppie. "I need you
to listen to my voice and focus on me. You're going to be fine, okay?
We're going to get you to a first aid kit and fix you right up." It was
the sort of soothing babble she'd perfected during her six-week ER
rotation. The words weren't important. What mattered was
sounding like she had the whole situation in hand and keeping the
patient calm and alert.

"What's the matter, Vera?" Guppie giggled. "Something
bugging you? Get it? Cuz it was a bug that got me."

"That's very funny," Vera said in the exact same tone she'd

used ever since they pulled away from the wreckage of the gas station. "You like puns, Guppie?"

"Always had a gift for 'em. Used to drive my dad crazy with 'em." Guppie closed his eyes and sighed. "What would daddy say about all this?"

Vera couldn't imagine what any rational person would say or do when confronted with the creature that had attacked them only minutes before. Every time she blinked, her mind replayed tiny snippets of their battle in the gas station, and she still couldn't work out what that creature had been. It moved like an insect, and parts of its anatomy were reminiscent of a scorpion or a truebug, but if anything that big existed, Vera was certain that she would have heard about it well before tonight.

One thing *was* certain. If Guppie hadn't willingly taken the lead, it could just as easily have been Vera slumped in the pickup's bench seat. She owed him all the help she could muster.

Too many conflicting thoughts were running through her mind at once. She needed weapons, she needed medical supplies, and she needed to keep Guppie talking. She couldn't yet think how she was going to do all of it at once, especially not considering how scattered she was.

Back in the storage room, she had assumed that there was only one of those things, but her failed call to emergency services had placed the first seed of doubt in her mind. Seeing the fires that raged through Little Creek proved just how wrong she'd been. The town looked as if a bomb had gone off within its limits—several bombs, in fact. Some of the houses were ablaze; when Vera peered toward the homes, she saw that the power lines had been knocked down across the roofs, which was probably how the fires had gotten started in the first place.

I just wanted some damn ice cream, she thought irritably. *If I'd*

*known this was coming, I wouldn't have worried so much what
Mummy thought of my waistline.*

Vera felt strangely disconnected from the world around her.
Adrenaline certainly played a part, but one of the things she'd
learned while in the ER was that if she had a single task to focus
on, she could drown out the madness of the world around her.
Guppie Martin had become that project now, and for the first time
since she'd met him, he was the one thing keeping her *sane.*

"What do you think that creature was, Guppie?" she asked.

He rolled his head toward her and frowned. "Dunno. Is it a
cicada year?"

"Cicadas?" She choked on a laugh. That creature in the gas
station had *certainly* not been a cicada.

"Yeah." Guppie nodded, misinterpreting her response. "Don't
you have them where you're from? They live in the ground? Hatch
every, dunno, twenty years or something?"

She swerved to avoid a box truck lying on its side in the
opposing lane. There was a dark smear across the driver's side
door. *Don't look,* she told herself. *You need to keep Guppie alive.
There's no time to worry about anyone else.*

"I'm certain that it wasn't a cicada, Mr. Ma—Guppie."

"Huh." Guppie frowned at the roof of the car. "Maybe they
came over on a boat from Asia, then?"

"Excuse me?"

"You know, like those big wasps." He held up a thumb and
forefinger about an inch apart. "Got some in my garden last year.
They girdled my lilacs."

"Asian hornets." She nodded and gripped the steering wheel
tighter.

"Yeah, but like the bees." Guppie's words were becoming more
slurred by the moment. "You know, the Africanized bees, the ones
that'll sting for hell of it. Although it didn't just sting Hoyt..."

He continued to babble about infectious pests, but his comment about hornets had sparked something in Vera's mind. No, the creature in the gas station had certainly *not* been a hornet, but it *did* have a similar body type.

"You got quiet there, Vera," Guppie mumbled.

"I have an idea." It wouldn't protect them from the fires, but it might solve two of their problems in one go.

Until that moment, Vera's main intention had been to put as much distance between herself and the creature as possible and get Guppie to the nearest hospital, which was two towns over in Millersgrove. Given the level of destruction that had occurred in Little Creek, going to the hospital now seemed like a poor plan. It would likely be flooded with other patients. Guppie could end up lying in a bed for hours before anyone could see him.

He didn't need a hospital. He needed Vera.

With a renewed sense of purpose, Vera swerved off Main Street. Her house was a few blocks behind them, but there was nothing there that could help them. She kept a better medical kit at the shop, mostly for insurance purposes.

That was also where she planned to load up on her *other* supplies.

Years before Vera had moved to Little Creek, the local business owners had put in for a government grant to have the power lines in town buried. According to the paperwork Vera had reviewed, they'd cited health reasons as their primary concern, but it was an open secret that what they'd *really* wanted was to increase the town's quaint, open feel.

It was a good thing they had. Unlike some of the residential areas on the outskirts of town, there were no downed lines in the town center, and the fires hadn't spread this far. The top had been scraped off the drugstore, however, and all that was left of the

Dollar Tree was a smoking crater. An unfamiliar metal object sat deep in the pit. She didn't see a single person outside.

Vera pulled around back to the loading bay where, once a week, her suppliers dropped off truckloads of live plants and bagged mulch and garden tools. Fortunately, she'd never gotten out of the habit of locking her doors—something most of the locals viewed as a 'city habit'—and she was able to unlock the rolling overhead doors.

"Stay here," she told Guppie.

"Not goin' anyplace," he assured her. His eyes were closed, and his breathing was becoming labored. With one last worried glance in his direction, she hopped out of the truck and hurried into the store.

Despite the mayhem in the streets, the inside of the Little Creek Garden Center had looked exactly as it had that morning when she walked in before sunrise to open the shop. In the dark, cool depths of the store, Vera could almost pretend that everything else had been a bad dream. The warm, slightly acidic smell of bagged peat and damp mulch and seedlings permeated the air.

Vera tried not to look at the plants as she walked past; there was no way that she was going to be able to rescue them all. If the building survived the night, maybe the plants would, too, but there was no chance that she was going to get all of them in the truck, and no time to waste on saving flowers as the town collapsed around them.

Instead, she grabbed a wheelbarrow from the display along the wall, steered it over the pest control display, and started filling it.

Some things, of course, weren't worth bothering with—flypaper, for example, would be totally ineffective. Likewise with some of the foaming sprays used to block off the exits of hornets' nests. Anything that could be used as a deterrent or a pesticide, however, was fair game.

In the beginning, when she'd first opened the shop, Vera had tried to avoid the worst of the pesticides. She preferred the more natural treatments, things that required more time and effort to work but left a smaller footprint: peppermint oil, lemon extract, and citronella were her weapons of choice. Early on, however, she'd learned that the people of Little Creek would drive all the way out to the big garden center on Route 47 if she didn't keep the more lethal options available. She loaded up on sprays of every size and composition; there was no way of knowing which, if any, would be the most effective if that *thing* came back. For good measure, she threw a few long-handled gardening tools on top. A tree-limber might be long enough to keep that *thing* at bay, but even if it wasn't, it might come in handy in other ways.

As she jogged back through the store, Vera grabbed anything that she thought might come in handy—better to bring things she didn't need than wish she'd thought of it later. In went a chainsaw, and a hand-held auger, and a whole mess of fuel. By the time Vera reached the truck again, the wheelbarrow was threatening to tip over. Fortunately, a lot of her customers drove trucks, and she'd gotten Jerry Peterson to build her a plywood loading ramp a few years ago in exchange for a discount on bulk-order grass seed. He lived out in Cloverleaf, and he often joked that his lawn was his religion. Judging by how much business he brought in, Vera wasn't sure he was kidding.

She opened the tailgate, drove the wheelbarrow up into the bed, then jogged around to where Guppie sat.

"You still with me, Guppie?" she asked.

"Mmhmm." He smiled drunkenly out at her. "You're a national treasure, Vera."

"Great." She slapped her palm on the door of the truck. "I'll be right back, just gotta get the med kit."

The emergency kit was in Vera's back office, and she hurried through, past the unopened boxes of peat pots and half-assembled trellises. Vera grabbed both of her kits—she kept an extra heavy-duty one on standby out of old habit—and turned to go.

As she did, her eyes snagged on a large cardboard box marked with strongly-worded warnings on every surface. It had come in with the last shipment on special-order for Jerry Peterson. It was the newest element of his anti-weed lawn arsenal.

Vera laughed aloud. "Well," she said, "that'll certainly do." Thank God for loyal customers.

They were lifesavers.

18

LEN

LEN FOLLOWED the kids down the road into town with an ever-growing sense of foreboding. Even on a good day, being this far away from the bunker left him anxious and twitchy, and today certainly didn't qualify as 'good.' It was going to be a real kick in the teeth if he couldn't even make use of the bunker he'd poured so much time and energy into, just because he'd gotten a bee in his bonnet about finding other survivors before it was too late to save them.

Deimos trotted along, placid as usual, but Phobos kept shooting him questioning glances.

"You were a good boy, Phobos," he assured him. "You remembered our training."

Phobos panted and stayed close to his side.

Little Creek was in ruins, and so far, there were no clear signs of survivors. From the hill, they'd been able to see a few cars, and the wildly-swinging beams of flashlights. On their descent, he'd been able to pick out the bark of dogs, a few shouts, and one particularly loud squeal of tires. When they finally reached the bottom and crossed Main Street, however, the town was quiet.

"Len, do you have the slightest idea what's happening?" Cooper asked.

"The invasion," he said. His grip automatically tightened on his rifle.

"You already knew they were coming, didn't you?" he pressed. "You know how to fight them."

"Only inasmuch as I know how to kill anything. I didn't know what to expect, only that *something* would be headed our way."

Cooper nodded, and the girl, Pammy Mae, made a low sound in her throat, one of simultaneous understanding and resignation.

Cooper was like a dog with a bone. "Why didn't you warn anyone?"

Len snorted and smiled grimly. After he'd learned the truth of what was coming from Carla, and then the fleeting rumors of a Steward Message, he'd had the strange sensation of being left on a train track in front of a runaway engine, but one that was making its way forward at incredibly slow speeds. It wasn't as if he'd been tied down, or even had his resources taken away; he simply wasn't allowed to leave. The same people who'd taken Carla would be looking for him, he knew that. He had to lie low and survive the oncoming train.

His panic had been relentless, his uncertainty maddening, and in the end his best hope had been to put his head down and brace for impact.

There was no time to explain all that now, so rather than argue with Cooper, he simply asked, "If I had, would you have listened? Would you have believed any of it before what you saw tonight?"

Cooper stopped talking.

The more out in the open they got, the more Len's nerves kicked in. Most people found the concept of being in town comforting, but the minute that they stepped away from the tree-line, Len felt exposed. He knew that it was irrational, that the creatures were just as dangerous in the woods as they were out here, but Little Creek proper wasn't his territory. In addition to the aliens, he now had to worry about people's response to the crisis. Fear made people act in unpredictable ways.

Phobos, too, raised his hackles and glared down every cross-street and alleyway they passed. Down here, the crackle of the downed power line was so loud that the very air seemed alive with electricity. At least the roads were dry, but Len still worried about the dangers of gas lines and transformers. The fires were bad enough, but at least they could avoid them. An explosion or another downed line, however, could significantly change the landscape.

Len became aware of a rattling thrum, a low clatter that echoed off the walls of the buildings around them. Cooper halted in his tracks.

Pammy Mae gripped the pistol and kept moving.

Len followed. He had to give the girl credit. She'd come to terms with the fact that fear did her no good in this instance. He couldn't say the same for her companion.

"Don't leave me!" Cooper hissed as he hurried after them.

They had yet to encounter another person since arriving in town. As they came around the side of the post office, however, they met the first. Len didn't recognize the middle-aged man pinned to the wall. His feet dangled well above the uneven squares of the sidewalk. He was held in place by the two front legs of a many-limbed, many-jointed creature, which had speared him to the wall through both shoulders.

Len wasn't sure if the man was alive or dead. The way his head and limbs moved might have been on his own volition, or the result of the movements of the alien. He sincerely hoped the latter,

especially when a long, thin whip of flexible tissue whipped out of
the alien's mouth, scored the man down the front of his torso, and
then plunged into his stomach. Len watched as the creature, illuminated by firelight, began to expand and contract, pulsating as
it fed.

Without hesitation, Len lifted his rifle to his shoulder, targeted
the center of the creature's mass, and pulled the trigger. The creature jerked and dropped its prey. If it hadn't been for the sharp
report of the pistol, Len wouldn't have realized that Pammy Mae
had fired as well. The girl was an excellent shot; her bullet hit
almost the same spot Len's did.

The alien screamed as dark liquid, thick and noxious as motor
oil, spilled down from its belly and spattered against the road. It
swayed on unsteady legs, attempting to use its forelimbs as
weapons, but too disoriented from its injuries to be effective. The
rattle increased, and it snapped twice at them with the mandible
that covered its spiral mouth before collapsing to the ground in a
heap.

"Nice shot," Len said as the rattling died.

Pammy Mae's eyes were fixed on the man's fallen form. When
the alien had dropped him, he'd fallen with his back to the wall, his
legs splayed in front of him.

"That's Mr. Cassidy," she mumbled. "The music teacher. I
used to catsit for him before he got remarried."

Len was more concerned about the downed alien. He strode
over and shot it again, just to make sure. Phobos growled at it.

Deimos still stood at Cooper's side, which was unusual.
Instead of watching Len for instructions, he kept his nose high,
sniffing the air.

"What is it, boy?" Len asked.

Deimos rumbled and raised his hackles. Phobos instantly
joined in, peering around at the rooftops. His ruff bristled, and he

put his ears back. He'd never seen him look more like a wild animal, and the change in his temperament was terrifying.

This is what's happening to all of us. We're all changing, learning who we truly are in a crisis.

"Uh, guys?" Cooper pointed to the rooftops with one shaking hand.

As Len watched, the rooftops seemed to come alive. Dozens of inhuman figures emerged over the corners of the buildings with the slow intensity of hunters moving in on their prey.

"We need to get out of here," Len said, rotating on the spot. There was no safe exit, but if they retreated, they'd stand a chance.

"Screw this," Pammy Mae barked. "I'm going to find my parents." She took off at a run, deeper into the rubble.

"Me, too!" Cooper called. "Wait up!" He pelted after her.

Len hissed a curse between his teeth. As the kids took off, a few of those shadows peeled away and began to chase them. *Dammit.* Pammy Mae might be a crack shot, but with only five bullets left, she wasn't going to be able to protect herself for long, and Cooper wasn't armed at all.

Len whistled, and both dogs flew to him as he made a break for it, continuing in the same direction that he and the kids had been going when they came across the man in the alley. At the very least, he could hope to divide and conquer for now, and reunite with the two of them at a later date.

Or you could just run for home. Honestly, you don't owe this town shit. You made a promise to lie low and stay safe if you could. Does a sense of obligation to two strangers truly matter more than the oath you made to her?

This certainly wasn't the right time to think about it. What he had to do now was stay low and get out of the open. At the bunker, he had the home-field advantage. Out here, in unfamiliar territory, he and the aliens were both on new soil.

He kept his left shoulder to the wall of the buildings as he ran, so close that his sleeve almost brushed it. Deimos ran beside him, with Phobos on their heels as the rear guard. When the skittering grew too loud above him, he stopped with his back pressed to the wall, steadied himself against the brickwork, and fired straight up. The alien had been climbing down the wall toward him, and when he hit it, the sound crescendoed as it fell. He had just enough time to dart to one side before it landed with a crunch beside him.

"Heel," he snapped, and ran for it.

Two streets later, they reached the street behind the shops lining the main square. There were no fires here, and no sound other than the rattle of the aliens, the dogs' panting, and the pounding of Len's heart.

Deimos suddenly darted right into an open bay door, and Len followed. The second that he was underneath, he grabbed the base of the garage door and slammed it behind him with such force that he almost overbalanced. He leaned against the metal panels and peeked out through the scratched Plexiglas windows that stood at eye level.

Seconds after the doors closed, half a dozen aliens rounded the corner of the street. There were probably more than that out of his line of sight. Len froze and held his breath as they skittered past, disappearing down the far end of the back alley.

They passed from his line of sight, and Len breathed a sigh of relief. He wasn't entirely sure how they hunted, but he had a feeling that they operated as much on sound as on sight. They weren't speaking in any human sense, but they could obviously communicate in some other manner. The rattling sound they made with their carapaces must be how they 'talked,' as it were. He would have to observe that in the long-term. Maybe there was a way to use that against them.

At his side, Phobos had begun to growl. Len turned to check

on him and found himself face-to-face with a glittering metal blade.

"Not another step," a woman's voice said. "Not until you tell me who you are and what you want."

Len blinked, looking from the metal object up into a woman's panicked face. She was wearing hijab, a common enough sight during his childhood in Nigeria, but the last thing he expected to see in Little Creek. Judging by the state of her clothes and the bruises already blossoming on her cheek, she had clearly been through the mill already.

Instead of answering the woman's questions, Len focused on the blade held to his neck. "Are you really threatening to decapitate me with a *nurseryman's shovel?*" he asked.

The woman's expression didn't soften. "I guess we'll see."

"Vera?" A man's thin voice trailed out of the darkness. "We got a problem?"

"Stay where you are, Guppie," the woman snapped.

"Vera, there's a dog! Where'd you get a dog from?"

The woman turned her head fractionally, and Len saw his opening. He whipped out one hand with as much force as he could muster, grabbed the shovel just below the seam between the metal head and its fiberglass handle, and jerked it away. Vera yelped as the shovel slipped out of her hands.

"I'm not your enemy, trust me," Len said. "Has your friend got a gun? I've had a shit night already, and I'm not looking to get shot."

Vera balled her hands into fists as the man sing-songed from the back of the garage. "*Shit, shot.* Almost rhymes, don't it?"

Len snorted and leaned on the handle of the shovel. "You've seen what's out there, right? The things that are swarming all over town?"

"Yes," Vera said. "If you're going to leave me unarmed, though,

I'd appreciate you putting your gun down. I don't fancy getting shot, either."

Len shook his head and passed the shovel back. "Take it, if you want. It's not going to help you much against those things."

"I've got other plans for them," Vera said. She took the shovel back, but the urge to fight seemed to have left her.

Phobos was still growling. Len laid a comforting hand on his back, and he stopped at once, dropping obediently into a sit.

"Mind if I stay here for a minute?" Len asked.

Vera shrugged and waved her hand to the store. "You're welcome to bunker down with us. Sorry about the shovel, by the way. I saw you come in, and I panicked."

"You're planning to hole up here?" Len asked. He stepped deeper into the loading bay. As he did, a pickup truck came into view. Deimos was standing by the open passenger door, where a man was sitting and petting the hound's long, floppy ears.

"Aren't you beautiful?" the man asked, and Deimos's tongue lolled. The stranger seemed totally out of touch with the danger around them.

"For the time being," Vera said. She leaned against the side of the truck bed. The woman was clearly exhausted, and Len felt another surge of sympathy for all these small-town folks who didn't know what was happening to them, or why. "At least until morning. Guppie got hurt, so I loaded us up on anti-bug supplies and then got to work on his injury. The trouble is, I'm not sure what to do next. Emergency services are down, and the roads are a nightmare. Where do we even go from here?"

Len approached the cab. He'd seen the old guy in the front seat wandering around town a few times, and the name Guppie rang a bell, although they were hardly friends. When he saw him, Guppie's face lit up.

"Hey, lookit that, it's Len!" He lifted one hand for a high-five. "Figures that you'd make it past the hungry things."

Len leaned his rifle against the door, out of Guppie's reach. If Vera really wanted to grab it, she probably could, but that was a risk Len would just have to take.

It wasn't hard to see where Guppie had taken a hit. A thickly-wound, bloodstained bandage covered his shoulder. Despite the red mark in the middle, the bandages were remarkably clean and well-wrapped.

"You a doctor by any chance, Vera?" Len asked. "This looks like professional care."

"I was in the medical field before I changed careers," Vera affirmed.

Len stood up and retrieved his rifle. "I could use a doctor. Listen, Vera, I don't want to alarm you, but this isn't going away overnight. There are dozens of those aliens out there. Hundreds, maybe. If they wanted to swarm your shop, they could do it, and good luck fighting them off with shovels."

Vera's lips pressed into a thin line. "Did you just say that those things are *aliens?*"

Len nodded. "The meteor shower? That was just the beginning."

"Ah." Vera rubbed her temples as she considered this. "Well, I guess that makes sense..."

"They're just cicadas," Guppie slurred.

"They're not—" Vera stopped herself and let out a short, sharp breath of barely-concealed annoyance. "Doesn't matter. All right, they're aliens, and they're happy to eat us. What do we do about that?"

Len cocked his head. "You're just going to accept that?"

"Do you have any idea how many hours I've spent in biology classes?" Vera asked. "I have no better explanation for what those *things* are, and I have even less of an idea of what to do about them. If we need to perform an emergency surgery, I would expect you to take my word for it and get out of my way. In this case, you're the one with the experience, so why wouldn't I extend you the same courtesy?"

"Fair enough." Len turned to the bay door and weighed their options. His last rescue attempt hadn't exactly gone according to plan, but Guppie was incapacitated, and Vera seemed like she had a good head on her shoulder. Plus, a medic could be invaluable in the coming days.

"Do you have people in the area?" he asked.

Vera shook her head. "My family's in D.C."

Len's smile felt grim. "Mine, too. If you want to take refuge for a while and combine forces, you can join me at the bunker. Him, too, unless you think he's likely to cause problems."

"He's..." Vera wrinkled her nose as she looked toward Guppie. "*Nice.*" It didn't sound entirely like a compliment, and Len had the feeling that he knew exactly what she meant.

"Aw, you're nice, too, Vee." Guppie giggled. He could only imagine what kind of pain meds Vera had dosed him with.

"How do we get there?" Vera asked. "The truck, I assume? We don't have any food supplies, but we'll barter with what I grabbed, if you like."

"Don't get me killed, and you're welcome to anything I've got," Len said. "Although... although there is one condition. I came into town with a couple of kids, and they took off. If we can find them, I'd like to help them."

Stupid sentimental impulses. Goddamn hero complex. It's going to be the death of me.

Vera nodded. "Any idea where they live?"

Len shook his head.

"You know their names?"

"Pammy Mae and Cooper. Don't know their last names."

Vera leaned away from the truck and spoke louder. "You hear that, Guppie? Do the names Cooper and Pammy Mae ring any bells?"

"Oh, sure, the Butter Queen and the weird Lutz kid," Guppie said at once. "Pammy Mae's a nice girl. She's dating the younger Lutz boy."

The boy from the tunnel. His limp form was going to haunt Len's nightmares, that was for damn sure.

"Where do they live, Guppie?" Vera asked.

"Lutzes are up on Maple, and the Johnsons live in Cloverleaf," Guppie said.

Vera waved her hand. "*Et voila.* Looks like you've got not only a doctor now, but the town gossip, too."

Len smirked. "So I see. Have you got anything more lethal than a shovel in here, Vera?"

Without a word, Vera led him around the bed of the truck to a large box. Len peered down at the side. "A landscaping torch?" he asked. "What does that even mean?"

"According to Jerry, it means no more dandelions in your turf." Vera patted the box. "It's a flamethrower backpack, essentially, and I'm only barely exaggerating."

"For *dandelions?*"

Vera shrugged. "Think you can figure out how to work it?"

"Sure." Len nodded, already skimming the instructions printed on the box. "Mind if the dogs ride in the cab?"

"As long as they don't bite."

"They're trained—" Len began.

From the far end of the building, out in the main part of the store, came the tinkling of glass. They both froze.

"Did you hear that?" Vera hissed.

Len nodded. "I'm going to ride in the bed. You know how to get to Maple Street?"

Vera nodded. "I'll make it happen. Be careful back here."

"Same to you," Len said.

As Vera let the dogs into the cab, then threw open the bay door, Len wondered if he'd made a miscalculation years ago. If he'd spent more time in town getting to know the Little Creek residents, would they have formed bonds? Would he have had Vera on his side since day one? If more people had believed him, they could have built more bunkers, and there would be more survivors—

No point in thinking like that, Len told himself. The only reason Vera had accepted his explanation so readily was the fact that she'd seen the damn things herself. There was no room for doubt.

Rather than looking toward the past, Len focused his attention in sorting out the controls of the landscaping torch. He could only hope that he'd reach Cooper and Pammy Mae in time.

Before they ended up like the boy in the tunnel.

19

PAMMY MAE

AS SHE WOVE between the buildings of town, Pammy Mae moved with single-minded purpose.

I'm not going to lose anyone else.

She didn't slow down, even when Cooper called out to her. He was falling behind.

It wasn't fair, she knew, to blame him for everything that had happened that night. If he hadn't pulled in the wheel when the deer crossed their path, then they would probably all be dead. It was easier, she supposed, to blame him for his incompetence than to admit her own shortcomings.

She'd failed Nate.

"Look out!" Cooper cried from just over her shoulder. A moment later, he collided with her, knocking her to the ground. As he did so, a glittering narrow object speared the vinyl siding right where her head would have been.

That was how they'd gotten Nate. She'd put it together when they'd seen Mr. Cassidy held up by the alien's legs. They speared a person to immobilize them. As for when Brandon had been sucked out of sight, that might well be the result of the weird, spiral tongue thing that had been used to feed on him.

She was glad, in a way, that Nate had been dead when he was pulled from the car. At least she knew what his last moments had been like, instead of having to wonder how much else he'd been forced to endure.

Pammy Mae lifted her pistol and fired point-blank into the chitinous bulk of the alien. She didn't have time to aim, and her first two shots blew off chunks of exoskeleton around the front limbs but didn't seem to penetrate. She kept firing until finally she saw the dark motor-oil blood coming out. Only when pulling the trigger resulted in nothing but a sharp click against her palm did she realize she'd unloaded the whole mag. At least the alien crumpled to the ground, shivering slightly as it died.

Cooper sat up and looked up at the roofline above them. "Uh, Pammy? Any chance you've got more ammo on you?"

Pammy felt a chill as she saw movement on top of the nearest building. She counted at least four of the giant insects. Then she saw movement on another roofline. Then another. They were all around them.

"No," she murmured to Cooper as she lurched to her feet. "But they don't know that." She planted her feet so that Cooper was behind her, then pointed the pistol upward and waited.

It was a bluff, and a mad bluff at that. But the aliens hadn't used anything like a gun on them so far, so it stood to reason they wouldn't know how one worked. Besides, in a choice between admitting defeat and bluffing like hell, Pammy Mae would make the same call every time.

God knew she'd done enough bluffing in front of the Butter Queen judges, and look what that had gotten her. Her Momma, who knew a thing or two about winning beauty contests, had called it her reservoir of bullshit. *You'll need a lot of it in this world*, she'd said. She wasn't wrong.

Pammy Mae dug deep, right where that old reserve was. She aimed her sight right at the nearest roofline where she could see movement. The pistol pulled left, and even though pulling the trigger would accomplish nothing, Pammy Mae adjusted her aim to account for it.

"Come on," she snarled. *"Try me."*

An alien in the general vicinity she was aiming began to rattle its carapace. A second alien took up the rattle, falling into perfect percussive harmony. The otherworldly sound of the pair was earsplitting. And still, she held her ground.

Then a third joined in. A fourth. Soon she lost count. A wave of percussive harmony began and spread all around them, bouncing off the building walls in a confusing crescendo of sound. There must have been dozens more of the creatures singing from the rooftops nearby. It became deafening and she began to wince involuntarily, the gun shaking in her hands. The sound throbbed like an out-of-whack subwoofer and she waited for a full-blown rush of the creatures. This was it. This was the end.

But the rush never came. Instead, the sound abruptly dissipated. The creatures along the rooflines retreated until Pammy Mae and Cooper were left in silence. The only thing Pammy could compare it to was watching the bustling hallways of the high school suddenly empty moments before the first bell.

"What the *hell* just happened?" Cooper wheezed. "Also, you're *insane*."

"Maybe." She lowered the pistol and listened for movement. She pulled Cooper to his feet and scanned the roofline again, still unsure of what she'd witnessed. She couldn't shake the feeling that they were still being watched. "Where did they go?"

"Who cares," Cooper said. "Let's not look a gift horse in the mouth."

"They'll be back." She'd hunted her whole life and she knew that animals that made that much sound were communicating *something* with each, one way or another. "Come on. We'll stop by your house first."

Maple Street was only a few streets away. By the time they made it, Pammy Mae was breathing hard and Cooper was gasping for breath and looked like he might throw up. Even so, he hadn't slowed her down.

The Lutz house was dark, but all the houses in the neighborhoods were dark by now, except those along the path of the fallen power lines. The stillness was pervasive; the grid must have been knocked out, because even the usual passive lights were extinguished. The glows of fridge displays and laptop cables and TV screens had all gone out. Only the moon illuminated the scene.

It could have been just another power outage, except for one disturbing fact.

The front door of the house was gone. Not open, not smashed, but completely removed. It lay beside Mr. Lutz's car. Aside from the splintered wood still clinging to its brass hinges, there was no sign of damage.

Pammy Mae couldn't imagine that a person had done that.

"Oh, God." Cooper sank into a crouch and cradled his head in his hands. "No, no, no..."

Pammy Mae squeezed his shoulder. "Do you want me to go in?"

"I don't wanna see," Cooper said.

Standing there, Pammy Mae made a little bargain with herself. There was no telling what had become of the Lutzes. There were clues, of course, but anyone who found her Jeep along the side of the road would likely make some assumptions, and they were

almost guaranteed to be wrong. If the Lutzes were inside, hiding in
the bathroom or barricaded behind their bedroom door, she would
go to Cloverleaf tonight and look for her mother.

If not...

"Come here, by the door." Pammy Mae approached the house
and squatted down beside the entryway with her back to the wall.
"Like this. That way, you can see if anything's coming and give me
a shout. Okay?"

Cooper sat and he scanned the street as she'd asked. "Okay."

Gripping her empty, borrowed pistol, Pammy Mae mounted
the stone steps toward the Lutzes' front door. She stepped across
the threshold and into the darkness.

That distinctive rattling was absent, which seemed like a good
sign. As far as she could tell, they didn't make that sound *all* the
time, but she had yet to work out the rules.

Moving quietly, she tiptoed down the entryway hall to the
living room. It was empty, although the blue corduroy couch in the
kitchen looked as if a dog had gotten to it. *One of those things was
in here,* she said. *It climbed over the couch with those clinging feet.*
There was no blood, however. That was a good sign.

The kitchen was tossed but similarly empty, and the den and
dining room were unoccupied. As she examined the ground floor—
the one that would be easiest to escape if Cooper started hollering
—she listened for any sounds coming from above. There was nothing, which could be either good or bad, depending on how she
looked at it. No monsters, but no sign of Cooper's parents, either.

At the bottom landing of the staircase to the second floor,
Pammy Mae gripped the handrail. She couldn't see the top step
from where she stood, and walking up to the second floor felt
about as clever as a mouse climbing a cat tree.

I could always tell Cooper that I looked, she thought. *He would
never know.*

But I would know.

With that, she began the ascent.

As she slipped from one step to the next, she all but held her breath. The sound Sam had made when that first alien leapt on him echoed loud in her ears, and every time she blinked she remembered Brandon being hauled off into the darkness too fast to scream.

She didn't allow herself to think of Nate at all. She had a feeling that her self-control would only last so long.

At the last step, she paused, listening. She was listening so hard for the rattling that she could almost hear it, but that was only her mind playing tricks on her. The house was as silent as a mausoleum.

The first room off the upstairs hallway was Nate's. Pammy Mae moved past it without glancing inside. Cooper's was next; the door was slightly ajar, but when she peeked inside, the moonlight threw shadows across an absolute mess within. Having been inside his room a few times, she was pretty sure that Cooper and not aliens were to blame.

The last door led to Mr. and Mrs. Lutz's room. It stood open, but the door was still on its hinges, at least. Pammy Mae's gorge rose, but she had to know.

It was worse than she'd imagined. Mr. Lutz's face, with his signature mustache, was barely recognizable, and Mrs. Lutz wasn't even whole. They had clearly fought back, or tried to. Pammy Mae didn't even remember moving. She simply blinked, and the next moment she was sitting on the top step, one hand pressed over her mouth and eyes squeezed shut.

No, she told herself. *You didn't see it. None of this is happening. Ma's fine, and this is a terrible dream, just like when you used to think there were spiders under the bed. It's not real.*

Monsters aren't real.

She was still sitting there when the roof creaked above her. Pammy Mae opened her eyes, but every other muscle in her body went still.

There was something in the eaves of the attic, moving above her with a mere few layers of insulation and subflooring between them.

Had she screamed when she saw the Lutzes? Not loudly, she was sure, but how loud would she have to be to draw that thing's attention?

For what felt like an eternity, Pammy Mae sat perfectly still, barely breathing, barely *blinking*. Every instinct inside her screamed for her to run, but if she did, it would surely hear her and come chasing after her. She would end up like the Lutzes, like Nate, like everyone in this town.

Every house on this street is like this one, she thought. *Every house in Cloverleaf, too. We've spent our whole lives trying to convince ourselves that we aren't in danger, that if we hide under the covers and stay away from the windows, we're safe. Nothing bad ever happens in Little Creek, until it does.*

She knew the names of every person on Maple Street. She knew what she would find in those houses.

And she knew, bone-deep, what was moving around in the crawlspace above her head.

So tell yourself another story, Pammy Mae. Tell yourself the story that will help you survive this. You shape the course of your own life, but only when you're in control of your actions. You can't change what happened here. You can't wish the creature above you out of existence. The only thing you can do is decide how you respond. Ask yourself how the best version of you would handle this moment, and do that.

Making that choice required a sort of mental fortitude that Pammy Mae had never experienced before. It required becoming two people at once, just for a moment. The Pammy Mae who had screamed when Nate was dragged out of the Jeep, who had yelled at Cooper when they first started walking, who had dashed out into the hall when she saw the Lutzes — that Pammy Mae had to go away. She had to become the Pammy Mae who won pageants, who made cuts to the cheer team, who jumped gorges on the ATV. And she had to remain that version of herself *exclusively*. If she didn't, she was going to go mad.

She shoved the screaming, terrified part of herself aside and locked it away. Then she got carefully to her feet, gripped the handrail, and descended the steps in total silence.

Cooper looked up as she stepped out of the front door. "What happened?" he asked.

Pammy Mae shook her head. "They weren't there."

Cooper scrambled to his feet. "They got out? Are you sure?"

The old Pammy Mae would have told him the truth. She'd have tried to comfort him and assure him that none of this was his fault.

If you do that, Cooper will break down. He'll slow you both down, and you'll end up dead.

So don't tell him.

"I went through the whole house," she said. "Come on." She set out for the shed at the side of the house at a steady clip.

"Oh, thank God," Cooper said. He trotted behind her. He was being much too loud, but she knew that if she told him to keep it down, they were both going to unravel. Instead, she reached for the lock of the shed and started to enter the combination, even though her fingers trembled so badly that she had to start over twice.

"Do you know how to drive these things?" she asked as she flung the door open. She'd gotten in the habit of stashing her ATV at Nate's place.

"I'll manage," Cooper said. "But don't you think we should take the car?"

Pammy Mae tossed him one of the helmets. "You saw how hard it was to use the cars off-road."

"Right, right. Besides, what if my parents need it, and it isn't here when they come back?" Cooper mashed the helmet onto his head and swung up onto Nate's four-wheeler. "Where are we headed? Cloverleaf? We should look for your mom..."

"No," Pammy Mae said at once. She already knew what she would find at her house, and if they didn't go, it would always be possible that she was wrong. She would never have to see the proof with her own eyes.

"Then where—?" Cooper began.

Before he could finish his question, a shadow moved across the lawn. Pammy Mae grabbed the door of the shed just in time to slam it shut before one of the aliens collided with the flimsy OSB door.

"Holy crap!" Cooper yelped. "Where did that come from?"

"Must have followed us," Pammy Mae said. *Most likely, it's the one from the attic. It must have seen us cross the lawn, or heard Cooper when he raised his voice.* At least he hadn't seen it emerge from his family home. He'd have realized, then, that she was a liar.

The thing bashed against the wall again and chittered at them. The door wouldn't hold for long, and Pammy Mae weighed her options.

"We need to find Len," she said. "He had a plan."

"Yeah, but how the hell are we gonna do that?"

An engine rumbled outside, and the pounding stopped. The rattling withdrew. Pammy Mae waited three seconds before pushing the door open a fraction.

"What are you doing?" Cooper hissed.

"If that thing's distracted, this could be our only chance to make a break for it," she hissed back. She pressed her eye to the opening and peered out.

A battered pickup had pulled onto Maple Street, an out-of-place blur of sound and light along the darkened road. As Pammy Mae watched, the alien skittered toward it.

"It's gonna get them," Cooper said from much too close to her ear. "Just like it got the Jeep."

Pammy Mae wasn't so sure. A dog barked from the cab of the truck as the alien approached.

Then a stream of fire sprang from the truckbed like one of those flamethrowers in an old war movie.

The alien shuddered and then burst into flames.

"I could be wrong," she said, "but I think they might have things under control."

20

GUPPIE

THE WORLD WAS STARTING to come back into focus. The pain in his shoulder was ever-present, but Guppie was on his third bottle of water and more painkillers than he could count. Sure, things were still fuzzy around the edges, but after spending the last few hours lost in a fog, he could finally tell which way was an improvement.

"This is Maple Street," he said, pointing to the turn. "The Lutzes are the fifth house on the left. Why are we here again? Did I already ask that?"

"One of them's a friend of Len's," Vera said. Her voice was electric with strained patience, but she'd yet to really go off on him. He was going to pay her back for that someday. For her patience and her medical know-how. He prodded the bandage with one finger and giggled to himself. *She has the patience, but I'm the patient.* He was pretty sure that there was a good pun in there, but it needed a punch-up.

"Almost there," he said, still trying to work his finger through a loose wrap in the bandages. "Next house."

He was forgetting something important... ah, yes, the source of the injury. Someone had shot him, probably one of the spies that kept trying to get past the guards and lob a grenade over the fences.

No, wait. It was that hungry thing.

Even through the contented blur of the drugs, he remembered to be afraid of the hungry thing. It was relentless. Monstrous. Frenzied.

"Say, Vera, what's the plan?" he asked.

Vera didn't answer. One of the big dogs in the back seat was growling; the mean one, not the nice one. It was the same kind of dog that had bitten him as a kid. He'd never liked that kind of dog, he still had scars on his leg...

The dog barked as something raced across the Lutzes' lawn toward the truck, and a moment later, a gout of fire exploded from the truckbed. The hungry thing was almost on them, but the flame not only sent it scrabbling away, it lit the whole dang critter on fire.

The wave of heat burned off a little more of Guppie's haze. He was suddenly and profoundly aware of the danger of being out in the open. He remembered, too, the man in the truck bed.

Leave no man behind.

When he unclipped his seatbelt, Vera turned to him. "Stop whatever you're doing. You stay in this car."

"Can't leave him in the lurch," Guppie insisted. Vera hit the child locks, but that didn't stop him. Instead, he leaned back between the seats and pressed himself between the two big dogs. The shepherd growled again.

"Gotta get to your boss," Guppie explained. That seemed like the right word for Len's relationship with the overgrown pups. He struggled with the back window until the latch released and he was able to swing aside.

"Guppie, *sit down*," Vera ordered.

Those commands might work on a dog, but Guppie's training ran deeper than mere commands. They were in a firefight now, and in a firefight it was imperative to protect the flank. He hauled himself through the window and landed with a grunt in the truck bed.

"What the hell—?" Len demanded. The alien he'd fired on —*get it, fire?* Guppie thought—was in its death throes on the lawn.

"You've got a gun," Guppie said, lifting the rifle he'd left on the bed of the truck, alongside all the shovels and saws and bottles of pesticide that Vera had brought along. A sharp pain climbed his neck and down his ribcage. Most likely, he'd reopened his wound as he flopped around in the truck, but that was probably for the best. Pain kept him focused. Grounded.

"You sure that you should be handling that?" he asked warily.

"I know my way around a rifle," Guppie assured him.

Len's once-over suggested Guppie was looking a little rough around the edges. *Aren't we all.* As Len opened his mouth to argue, the door of the shed alongside the Lutz house was flung wide, and two ATVs came barreling over the diamond-plate floor panel. They pulled up alongside the truck, mere feet away from the smoking remains of the hungry thing. It hadn't just died. Instead, it had half-melted into a greasy smear on the grass.

Guppie had known Pammy Mae Johnson since she was knee-high to a grasshopper. She'd grown up pretty, but he still thought of her as the kid who'd gone around town showing everyone her front tooth after it fell out. Now, when she lifted the visor, her eyes blazed from the shadow of her helmet.

"Are we getting out of here?" she asked.

"Hell yes we are," Len said. "Are you coming this time?"

Cooper nodded. "If you'll still have us."

Len nodded before sticking his face in the open back window of the truck. "You know where we're headed, Vera?"

Vera shook her head, and Guppie explained, "She's new."

"I know the way to your place," Pammy Mae said. "I've ridden by a few times. I'll lead the way." She dropped her helmet back into place, gunned her engine, and whipped around the side of the truck. Cooper followed, and Vera hit the gas.

Guppie was glad that he'd been able to ignore the damage to Little Creek on their first trip through. Now, however, the sight was enough to break his heart. He'd spent the best years of his life here. Every corner held memories, spread out over decades of small-town living. They passed the Dollar Tree that had previously been the department store that had replaced the old movie theater where he'd had his first kiss—and seen the first installment of *Star Wars*, although not on the same occasion—and it was gone. The laundromat that had been in the family for three generations was on fire.

Businesses, however, weren't what made a town. What made Little Creek so special was the people, but the only signs of them were grim and intermittent.

"Guppie!" Vera called from the front of the truck. "Up ahead!"

He peered over the top of the cab. One of those hungry things was standing in the road ahead, blocking their path. Guppie didn't have to think. The rifle was already at his shoulder, natural as breathing, and he was already aiming, already firing. The beast went down, and Pammy Mae didn't change course, just ran over the thing like it was a bump in the road.

"Damn," Len breathed. "Nice shooting, old timer."

"And you thought you couldn't trust me."

"*Get down!*" Len screamed. Guppie grabbed the brim of his hat and ducked low as one of the hungry things landed on the roof of the cab. Len whipped his arm up, taking aim with the hose of that handy little flamethrower.

As the hungry thing rattled, blazed, and began to melt, Guppie shouted over the rushing wind, "Man, I need to get me one of those."

Wherever the dark fluid of the creature's melting thorax dripped, it bubbled against the paint and took the whole layer clean off. Vera swerved, and the half-ruined corpse of the giant bug flew to one side and landed in the road behind them. Others of its kind gathered around it. Just before they turned onto the main road, all of them glanced up, and Guppie got his answer about whether or not the damn things had eyes. Thousands of mirrored fragments were suddenly turned on him, glowing silver-green like a cat's eyes in the dark.

Then they were gone.

"Nice going, partner!" Guppie held his hand up for a high-five as he sank down against the cab to get his head out of the wind. The truck picked up speed as they left the cramped and fractured streets of Little Creek behind.

"I'm not sure I want to high-five over this," Len said. He mirrored Guppie's movements until they both sat in the truck bed. The poor guy looked almost as tired as Guppie felt.

"Any day above ground is a good day," Guppie said. "Or would you rather be like Hoyt?"

"The guy from the gas station?" Len turned his face toward him. "They got him?"

"Yeah. Early on. You know what those things are?"

"Aliens," he said. He closed his eyes, smiling as a long pink tongue emerged from the still-open window to lick his cheek.

Guppie nodded. "You knew about this ahead of time, I take it?"

"Some."

"Ah." He settled the rifle beside him and crossed his arm. "And you've got a plan?"

"Survive," he said. "That's the only plan."

"Well, it's mighty nice of you to come back for us." Now that the adrenaline was fading the fog was gathering around the edges of the world again.

Down in the valley, from the place where Little Creek one stood, came a mighty hum. It was deeper than the rattle the creatures made when they attacked. Guppie had a vague memory of a few summers past when the cicadas had crawled out of the ground after their long sleep. One on its lonesome wasn't too bad, but once they got going, they could kick up a racket. He'd *told* Vera that these things were like locusts, and he was right.

"They're making a racket," he said.

"Yeah," Len said darkly. "They sure are. It means something. Need to figure out what."

As they drove, the song grew, until it no longer came from the town. It echoed off the mountains, across valley after valley.

Must be millions of 'em, he thought blearily. *Instead of coming up from the ground, they've come down from the sky—a plague of locusts. A sign that the end is coming.*

Or that the end has already come.

BEYOND LITTLE CREEK

Combined Force Space Command Survival Outpost
[Location Redacted]

————

Carla stared at the image on the projector in horror as video footage of the invasion scrolled across the screen. To her left, Nathan sat with one hand pressed over his mouth. To her right, Stew watched the screen with an expression of utter disbelief.

Around them, soldiers wearing matching full-body protective gear sat in folding chairs, their expressions mostly hard and inscrutable.

In the middle of a shot of the aliens descending upon a woman in the streets of Seattle, the screen went blank. One of the officers stepped forward, hands clasped behind her back.

"This ends the transmission from *Seattle Daily*. As of approximately thirty minutes ago, all of our satellites are down. The grid is shot. This, ladies and gentlemen, is not a drill. Outpost Alpha is officially under lockdown." She turned and began to pace, with her short blonde hair skimming her cheeks. Her eyes seemed to be focused on something far away.

She has a little of her humanity left, Carla thought, *and she is trying to squash it.*

"Our orders are unchanged," she said. "You are tasked with protecting the individuals who have been deemed indispensable. The President resides in this location. His cabinet is also under our protection. Humanity's most valuable members are protected here and in other armed outposts. You know what you are supposed to do, and we shall proceed... shall proceed... I'm sorry, is there a question?"

Carla swiveled her head and discovered to her dismay that Stew not only had his hand up but was completely standing up. His face was beet red.

"Yeah," Stew said. "I'm just wondering... what the *hell* have you been doing the last five years?"

"Excuse me?"

"Lady, the three of us have spent the last five years slowly losing our minds in this damn place trying to fully decode the message that warned us what was coming, *but it's not like we didn't know it was bad.* I was under the impression"—he waved vaguely at Carla and Nathan— "*we* were under the impression that you idiots with the big guns were actually *doing something to protect people.*"

Her expression hardened. "If you'd rather go out on the street, I'm sure that can be arranged."

"Are we seriously just going to let all these civilians die?" Stew bellowed. "*What was the point!?*"

A ripple went through the group. A shifting of feet and a turning of heads. Perhaps some of it was disapproval or curiosity, but it seemed to Carla that Stew was speaking to something that at least some in the room privately agreed with.

"The point is that humanity will survive." The officer lifted her chin and glared down her nose at Steward. She took a step forward, and Carla tensed. Over the last five years, her mistrust of authority figures had sharpened to a fine point.

The officer pointed to the blank screen and let her eyes sweep over the assembled crowd. "Scenes like this are playing out all over the *world*. There is no way to evacuate on that scale, so we've taken the steps to ensure the survival of our species, and—*yes*, what now?"

Nathan raised one quaking hand. "M-ma'am? How many cities *were* evacuated?"

The officer stared at him with her lips pressed into a thin, tight line. "This is not the only outpost."

Nathan nodded quickly. "Well sure, but I mean, even if they are all—"

The officer abruptly turned away. "Your shifts will begin in eight hours. You will receive more specific instructions at that time. For now, you will return to your quarters for lights-out. And fair warning: anyone who engages in *any* activity that compromises the security of this facility will be considered an enemy of the state and treated accordingly."

Carla glanced around; a few other people scattered around the auditorium looked as shell-shocked as she felt, but they had the good sense to keep their mouths shut.

"You're dismissed," she said. "Send in the next group."

The audience rose with military precision, and they streamed out the door at the back of the room, while the officer prepped for the next wave of individuals.

Stew led the way back to their quarters while the other two straggled behind. Nathan wasn't blinking, and Carla kept turning the words over and over in her mind. The officer's final warning had been clear, and it didn't take much imagination to work out that being treated as an enemy of the state during an alien invasion would end with a bullet... or worse.

The minute all three of them entered their quarters, Stew slammed the door. "What the *hell?*" he bellowed. "Where are the damn tanks? The bombs? Hell, nuke something. I don't care. Make a defensive line or whatever"—Stew waved his hands—"that kinda military stuff. I mean, what do they know that we don't know? What are they *waiting for?*"

Nathan sank down on the edge of his folding cot and ran his hands over his crew-cut. "Does that mean that they didn't evacuate *anyone?* Why not? We gave them ample warning."

Carla retreated to her bunk, but she couldn't bring herself to lie down. Instead, she paced back and forth beside it. She wanted to hit something. She wanted to scream.

"How far does it go, do you think?" Nathan murmured. "Did they tell other governments? Did they tell *anyone* what was coming?"

"They told the president," Carla spat.

Stew snorted. "Well, I didn't vote for the guy. Couldn't, since I was stuck in a *secret outpost* during the last election. Jesus, do you think any of our people are going to survive? You've both *got people*, right?"

Nathan stared down at his toes.

In all their years, this was the one thing they never talked about. It was an unspoken rule. Stew could bullshit all day long, but they didn't talk about the people they'd left behind.

Until now.

"I was single," Stew said. "And my ex-wife, well, she and whoever she's screwing these days are gonna make top-notch alien food, but my daughter was in college. She'd just gotten accepted to

Julliard when they... when they..." He trailed off and lifted his fingers in front of him, ticking off the years. "Aw, hell, my daughter has *graduated* from Julliard. And she's out *there,* with those things! What's she supposed to do, fight them off with a Stradivarius?"

"I had girls, too," Nathan murmured.

"Yeah?" Stew cocked his head. "How old?"

"Six and four," Nathan murmured. "When they took me away."

"Aw, screw it!" Stew kicked the wall.

Carla still couldn't believe it. She'd spent five years as a political prisoner, practically erased from existence by a government that had been terrified that she would leak their secrets. Five *years.* As they'd decoded more and more layers of the incredibly complex message below the simple binary one, they'd come to understand that on some faraway world, an alien race had reached out to offer a warning. Carla had begun to feel kinship with whoever had composed that message. Had they survived? Had they found a way to fight back? And now it seemed the higher-ups had used that warning to save themselves and leave the rest of the world to die.

The lights above them shut down, and Stew threw himself into his cot with a groan. "Right. 'Cuz we're gonna *sleep* now, knowing that those things are out there..."

Carla lowered herself into the bed and leaned back, but her heart was still hammering.

"What about you, Carla?" Stew asked in the darkness. "Who are you worrying about right now?"

"My husband," Carla murmured.

"You have kids?"

"Nah."

To her left, Nathan began crying so softly that Carla at first assumed that she was imagining it.

Stew snorted angrily. "This is such bullshit."

Carla knew why Stew was so upset, even more than the rest of them. After their initial attempt to escape, he'd confided in Carla that his message had gone out, just like hers. It only took a split-second connection. He said all his buddies on the dark web and in the weird forums and elsewhere now had the original transmission along with the key.

In the months he was healing from the surgery on his hand, he was even cocky. He kept expecting the program to get shut down at any moment. There was no reason for all the cloak and dagger stuff, he said. The truth was out there at last.

But that never happened.

Carla wasn't surprised. Direct, unaccountable violence could do a lot. Servers could be destroyed. Algorithms tweaked to relentlessly repress anything. The knowledgeable hunted down and silenced. Considering the magnitude of the coverup, she wouldn't be surprised if hundreds of people hadn't been murdered or detained to control it.

But not her Len. He was too smart and too strong for that.

And so was she.

What do they know that we don't know? Stew had asked. *What are they waiting for?*

He was right. There was more going on here than they knew—maybe than anyone knew—and she was going to find out what it was. And then she was going to make those responsible pay.

PART 2

THREE WEEKS LATER

21

PAMMY MAE

IN THE THREE weeks since the world had ended, Pammy Mae had spent most of her time on the ATV.

First, she'd gone out to the site of the star party, the one where it all began. She found the cars piled up, much as she'd left them. There were signs of their previous occupants, all of them disheartening: a dropped shoe, a purse with a broken shoulder-strap, a t-shirt dragged through pine needles and smeared with something dark and crusty. That afternoon, she'd found what was left of Nate in the tunnel under the road. It wasn't really Nate, though. She told herself that as she lifted him onto her shoulders and carried him out of that stinking tunnel. Not sure what else to do with him, she laid his body on the corpse of the alien who had killed him, the one Len had brought down while she and Cooper listened. She lit the damn thing on fire and watched them both go up like a torch.

Ever since Invasion Day, she'd been circling town. She'd kept one of Len's rifles at the ready everywhere she went, but she'd seldom needed to use it. For the most part, the aliens remained in town. They seemed to have decided to leave the little outpost in the bunker alone. They were too busy doing *something* in town, but Pammy Mae couldn't determine what that might be.

They could communicate with each other, Pammy Mae was sure of that. But were they biding their time in order to hatch a plan, or had they simply decided that the humans in the bunker weren't worth the trouble?

It depends on how smart they are, she thought.

It was a disconcerting notion, because nobody *knew*.

Their little enclave took turns watching the night sky. As far as they could tell, no new alien ships had arrived since that first night, and none of the aliens had returned to wherever they had come from. They'd seen a few military jets fly high above, and Guppie said they were taking images of the whole area. He said if the military saw them, they might come get them. But then the planes stopped flying overhead. Whatever the military was doing to stay busy, it didn't involve saving them.

Just like whatever the aliens were doing in the ruins of Little Creek was keeping them busy. Observing them hadn't revealed their secrets, and Pammy was getting tired of sitting around twiddling her thumbs and waiting to go on the defensive again. It was time to make a move.

Noon had long since come and gone by the time Pammy Mae rode her ATV back up to the bunker. There was no place to store it inside, but there was a shed out front. The doors locked, and Vera had put pest-deterrent around the outer perimeter, just as she had around the bunker itself. That was as safe as it was going to get.

But what happens when the aliens realize that they can cut me off from my wheels? she wondered, and once again, the answer was nothing but question marks.

Vera was weeding in the garden, and when Pammy Mae

emerged from the shed, she looked up with a smile. "You're back," she said. "That's a relief."

It doesn't matter if I come back, Pammy Mae thought. *All this is temporary.* If she said those words aloud, though, Vera would figure out the secret. She'd realize that Pammy Mae had found a way to turn herself off, and when people realized things like that, they always assumed that the solution was to turn them back on. Pammy Mae wanted no part of that. If she rewired her brain back to how she *had* been, she'd be forced to think about Nate, and the Lutzes, and her own mother.

Better to leave the switch turned off, thank you very much.

"In one piece, too." Pammy Mae shook out her hair. "Nothing new, though."

"They're still just hanging around down there?" Vera asked. Her brow puckered in confusion. "I suppose that might make sense, if they're like hornets. Some of those hive insects are territorial, but..."

"But?" Pammy Mae asked when the older woman trailed off.

Vera blocked the sun with her hand and squinted at Pammy. "But they're an invasive species," she said. "And this isn't their territory."

That brought a real smile to Pammy Mae's lips. "No. It's mine."

Something crunched behind them, and Pammy Mae whirled, but it was just Guppie jogging up to the house.

"Hey, ladies," he puffed, coming to a halt at the end of the lower garden bed. "How are you? Anything new down there?"

"No, Mr. Martin," Pammy Mae said.

Guppie fanned himself with one hand and rested the other on his waist. "Figures." He looked up at the sky in irritation, like the warmth of the day was his biggest problem.

From the emotional distance offered by the shift in her mind-set, Pammy Mae could understand the new normal. After a day of shell-shock and horrified disbelief, everyone in their little colony had decided on their purpose. Len's was organization; Vera's was gardening; Guppie's was training; Cooper's was planning; and Pammy Mae circled the carcass of Little Creek like a vulture, hoping for a sign that had yet to come. They'd fallen into a routine, and part of that routine relied on pretending that everything was *fine*. The others hadn't taken that level of play-pretend as far as Pammy Mae had, inasmuch as she could tell, but as long as they all said their lines and smiled on cue, they were going to be fine.

Or at least, fine enough. It was all relative.

"I'm going inside. I need a shower." Pammy Mae turned toward the shipping container and made for the door.

"How's the gardening, Vera?" Guppie asked. Pammy Mae reached the door before she could hear the answer.

The shipping container made for close quarters, which was one of the reasons Pammy Mae spent so much time on the ATV. Len had done an astonishing amount of work preparing for the invasion, but although he'd never said as much, he clearly hadn't been planning to play host.

Cooper sat at the kitchen table poring over maps of town. When she stepped into the room, he beamed up at her.

"Hey, Pams!" he said cheerfully. "I've been looking at the map. Think the ATVs could get us to Mount Heron and back?"

"Not on one tank," she said. "Why do you ask?"

"It's the closest town." Cooper rumpled his hair. It was becoming ever shaggier around his ears, and the once-bright green had faded to an almost white bleached base, while the roots grew in dark. "That's closer to the hospital, and their police force is better up there. You think people might have headed that way?"

Pammy Mae crossed her arms and stared down at the map. "They might."

"Then we need to figure out a way to get there. Or maybe radio them." Cooper knocked his fist against the table. Deimos, who'd been napping on the couch, opened one eye. "There's an idea—satellites might not be working but it's possible that we can still use radios. We'd just need to tune into the right frequency..."

Pammy Mae nodded and kept moving. When Cooper got like this, it was almost impossible to talk to him. His relentless optimism could be smothering.

The hatch down into the underground bunker was already open. Len and Phobos were down there. Len was constantly taking stock of their supplies, scribbling his results into a notebook.

"Calculating how much longer we can hold out?" Pammy Mae asked as she reached the bottom of the steps.

"Not exactly," Len muttered, making another note. "The thing is, we're using things up at different rates than I'd expected."

"If there's anything you want me to pick up while I'm out, let me know," Pammy Mae said. "I've been refilling the fuel tanks as I use them up."

"I'm not sure it's worth the risk." Len tapped his pen on the paper, and Phobos stared up at him. The dog made Pammy Mae nervous. It was so attentive, so focused on the movements of the people around it. She had a feeling that the dog could tell that something was wrong with her and might decide to act on it.

"What kinds of stuff are we running low on?" Pammy Mae asked.

"Dumb things," Len said. "Snacks, mostly. The thing is, they're part of what's keeping us sane, and once we run out of them..." He shook his head.

"We'll start to lose equilibrium." Pammy Mae leaned against the racks of emergency supplies.

Len shot her a look over the top of the paper. Like Phobos, he seemed to be able to see under Pammy Mae's skin, down to the secret dark heart of her. Pammy Mae wasn't afraid of Len seeing that part; Len, too, had switched parts of himself off long ago. He seemed to recognize the necessity of it.

"What happens next?" Pammy Mae waved to the concrete walls of the bunker. "What's the plan?"

"This was the plan," Len admitted.

Pammy Mae lowered her voice. "Look, Len, that might work for the two of us, but them?" She tipped her chin toward the ceiling. "They need more. They need something to hope for."

Len searched her eyes. "And what about you?"

"One of these days," Pammy Mae said, "I'm going to start needing something, too. And I'm not sure it's going to be compatible with your plan to hunker down and survive."

Len flipped his pen back and forth against his thumbnail. "It's not going to be enough for me, either. I thought it would, but..." He shook his head. "I knew that something was coming, but as far as what those things are going to do now that they're here, your guess is as good as mine."

"I have an idea," Pammy Mae said. She was almost whispering now. "The thing is, we run the risk of kicking the hornets' nest. Right now, they're leaving us alone."

Len scoffed. "That can't last."

"I know." Pammy closed her eyes and took a deep breath. "This plan of mine, should we run it past the others?"

Len licked his lips and let his eyes roam over their stores once more.

"This is your home," Pammy Mae said. "You're the boss. You saved them, and you get to call the shots."

"I'm not sure it's that simple," Len said. "What did you have in mind?"

"I want to figure out how they work. What they *are*. I want to figure out their weaknesses."

Len nodded. "Do what you have to do. But don't take the ATV. I don't want them to follow the sound of it back here, okay?"

Pammy Mae smiled, baring her teeth in a bitter grin. "I'll do my best."

Time to stop waiting around for a rescue that would never come, or for death to creep up on them slowly. Time to stop being at someone else's mercy.

Pammy Mae was ready to go hunting.

22
GUPPIE

WHEN HE'D SERVED in the Marines, Guppie Martin had learned a few things about himself. For one thing, he was tougher than he'd assumed—not just physically, but mentally. It was possible to push himself to never-before-imagined feats of prowess that made his limbs ache and left his lungs burning, and to lie perfectly still for hours while shells went off around him. He learned that he could shoot another person while making every protest lodged by his brain perfectly quiet. He still thought of himself as that person, even though he no longer *had* to be. Beneath the beer gut and the stiff joints lay a man of action.

As it happened, he'd been right.

Who knew what that little slip of a girl, Pammy Mae, spent her days doing. Sometimes, when Guppie was running through his self-imposed training regimen, he would reach a break in the trees and spot her zipping down the roads toward town on the ATV. More than once he was tempted to follow her, but he had other plans, and he had no intention of getting distracted.

Guppie had seen how those leggy bastards climbed, and he

wasn't having any of that. Len was a smart cookie and a good tacti-
cian; the guy had a mission; as for Cooper and Vera, well, they had
their uses, but they weren't fighters at heart. Someone needed to
make sure that nothing happened to them.

The wound in his shoulder still hurt like a bitch, but after a
week of healing, Guppie had gotten back on his feet, and he hadn't
stopped moving since.

Three weeks and one day after the end of the world, Guppie
sat everyone down at the table for dinner. Pammy Mae had left
early that morning, but she kept odd hours, so there was no telling
when she'd be back.

After their meal of powdered eggs, white rice, and canned
stewed tomatoes, Guppie laid out the topographic map of the
game lands that he had borrowed from Cooper, alongside the
hand-drawn diagram he'd spent the last few days putting together.

"All right, everyone." He slapped one palm on the table so
hard that the dogs jumped. "I've been thinking about how to
fortify our base camp. Len's done an excellent job with the
building itself, and Vera's taken over the gardens, but if we're going
to make a stand here, we're going to need to upgrade our defenses.
I've already placed the solar-powered pest-repellents that Vera
brought from the garden center at strategic intervals around the
perimeter."

"What about the chemical repellents?" Vera asked.

Guppie nodded in acknowledgement and held up one hand,
ticking his points off with his fingers. "I've put out some, and I've
rigged some up in the trees, like bear traps. It's not enough, though.
We've seen how they climb, and they're a hell of a lot smarter and
more deadly than the average hornet. We're gonna need to bring
out the big guns sooner or later. I propose a trench, cut from here
to here." He dragged one finger along the outline of the property.
"We should cut down any trees within a hundred feet of the

house. That way, if they come at us, they'll have to charge at us directly. None of this dropping from above nonsense. Then, we lay a circle of the chemical pest repellant around us. The garden will be inside the perimeter, and all our supplies."

"You're assuming that the repellent works on them," Len pointed out.

"Not especially. I'm simply treating it as an added precaution." Guppie referred back to his drawing. "When that's done, we take all the trees and limbs we've cut, and we build a barricade wall. Before you ask, no, I don't expect it to stop them, only to slow them down. Every second we can buy ourselves is another chance at survival."

Vera shook her head. "I appreciate what you've come up with, Guppie, but that's a short-term solution. How are five people going to make it through the winter here? The garden can only produce so long, and when the nights get longer..." She shivered.

Guppie had an inkling of what was on her mind. He remembered the hungry thing charging into the gas station unseen, and the way it had turned Hoyt into a snack, easy as breathin'— assuming the damned things even needed to breathe. He always got cabin fever over the winters, and this one promised to be the worst of them all.

Although, to be fair, you're probably being too optimistic. It'll be a miracle if you all survive the fall.

Cooper shook his head. "Listen, I get where you're going with this, but I don't think we should be digging in our heels. There have to be other survivors out there. We should be looking for them."

Guppie was of two minds on this topic. On one hand, he wanted to believe that there were still people in town, and in the world outside of Little Creek, who had managed to survive, just as they had. Surely, they couldn't be the *only* ones to get lucky.

Then again, what if they were? Sure, there were folks like Sean Hawes who knew a thing or two about the world, but the town was overrun. There had been a lot of those lights in the sky.

Which meant a lot of those aliens on Earth.

"And what do we do if we find more?" Len asked. "Do we bring them back here? Because Vera's right, I didn't build this place with the idea of running a boarding house."

"My *parents* are out there," Cooper insisted.

Vera nibbled her thumbnail. "If there are other survivors, I think it best to team up... although I agree that it wouldn't make sense to house them here. Is there somewhere else we could go? Somewhere outside of Little Creek?"

"How would you plan to *get* anywhere?" Len asked. "Setting out without a goal would be suicide. Even if you can find gas to refill the truck's tank, that doesn't mean it's wise to go out on your own. What happens at night? Where do you hole up? We already know that hiding in the truck itself isn't safe."

Cooper let out a soft, pained cry. "Damn right," he murmured.

"Besides, we can't speak for the rest of the world, but we can make one assumption about the aliens in Little Creek." Len waved his hand in the vague direction of town. "They're gonna be hungry. Their food supply won't last long as they pick people off. Even if there are a few folks left alive in town, they won't last."

"All the more reason to try," Vera insisted. "What do you think happens when they decide to start sniffing around up here? They must have some sense of where we are, and not *just* because Pammy Mae rides her four-wheeler around like it's her job. I'm sure they can hear her, and it wouldn't be hard to keep track of us if they follow her." She gestured upward to the lights. "We know they're out there, but we have no idea what they are, or how they tick. You all saw how they pulled away from us when we fled town. They didn't follow us, but they watched us. They're clever.

Calculating. If a hundred of them put their minds to it, I'm sure they could get in here."

"Which is why we should come up with a plan to leave," Cooper said.

Len waved to the door. "You're welcome to go any time..."

Before he could finish, something slammed into the door from the outside. The dogs sat up, ears pricked, and the shepherd growled.

Len reached for his gun, Cooper snatched up a fork, Vera's shoulders hunched, and Guppie raised his fists. The door thumped again and flew open. It was night outside of the shipping container, and only the silhouette of the figure beyond was visible. Too many legs, glistening with a black fluid as thick as motor oil, stood splayed in the door, with Pammy Mae's head clutched between its legs.

Guppie's stomach lurched before the figure took a step, and he realized that it *was* Pammy Mae. More of the black fluid stained her face and her clothes, and she had one of the creatures slung over her shoulders, the joints of its abundant legs clutched in both hands.

"Pammy?" Cooper rocketed to her feet. "What happened? Are you hurt?"

The girl shook her head, lifting the creature over her head and dropping it to the floor with a thump. It was dead, but the dogs still bared their teeth, and Cooper flinched back from it.

"Somebody wanna give me a hand with this? It was the smallest one I could find, but it's still a pain in the ass to drag around."

Len calmly grabbed one of the thing's limbs. He seemed to be the only one of them who wasn't in shock. In fact, he was smiling. Together, he and Pammy Mae got it all the way inside before Guppie remembered that he could have helped, too.

"I had a feeling you had this in mind," Len said. "Did you have any trouble?"

"Honestly, I think they're getting lazy. This one didn't have any others around. I'd blown a couple holes in that soft underbelly before he even seemed to realize what was happening. I was only worried about his friends coming back, but I guess he was alone."

"Maybe he's young?"

"Could be. He's small. But hell, what does it say if they got young here and they've been here all of three weeks?"

"Nothing good," Len said.

Guppie cleared his throat and Len and Pammy Mae looked up, realizing the rest of them were staring at them.

Pammy Mae nodded and rubbed her shoulder, then said, "Now I know you guys laugh every time I mention the Butter Queen pageant," as if there was nothing unusual at all about her arrival. "But when I was training for it, one of the first things I learned was to spot my rivals' weaknesses. Once you figure that out, it's easy to figure out how to stop the competition in their tracks. You gotta learn what makes the other girls go, figure out their flaws, and use it against them." She nudged the dead monster with her foot, then looked up at Vera. "So I brought you the competition, Doc. Figure out what makes it go so that *we* can figure out how to beat them."

Vera stared at the corpse for a long moment, her full lips parted in stunned surprise. Out of all of them, Guppie figured that she was the least equipped to fight the invaders, but he'd seen her reaction in the gas station; her instincts were good, and she played to win.

After a few seconds' hesitation, she turned to Len.

"I'm going to need a tarp," she said. "And some gloves. And a *very* sharp knife."

23

VERA

IT HAD BEEN years since Vera had anyone under the knife, and gutting an alien was like nothing she'd ever done before. There were scientists, surely, who would kill for an opportunity like this, for the chance to dissect an entirely new species of intergalactic life. Vera was not one of them.

She insisted on working outside, which meant waiting until morning. None of them could sleep with the body in the main part of the house. Cooper had suggested locking it in the basement, but Len refused to leave it downstairs with their supplies. Setting it outside in the open seemed unwise. In the end, they rolled it in a tarp and carried it out to the shed for safekeeping.

Which was how, after a breakfast of instant oatmeal and watered-down coffee, Vera found herself standing in front of an alien while the survivors of their little compound watched her, waiting to see what she'd learn.

"You do understand that this kind of thing isn't my specialty, right?" she asked.

Len passed her a pair of bright yellow cleaning gloves. "There aren't many people on Earth who could claim to be prepared for this."

Vera pulled the gloves on. She'd have preferred latex, but the ones included in the medical kits only came up to her wrist. She wasn't thrilled with the idea of getting alien blood—or whatever it was—all over her sleeves, especially given that she was wearing the only set of clothes she currently owned.

The knives she had collected from the house came in a wide array of sizes, but now that they were all laid out on the folding table Len had provided, Vera felt less confident than ever about using them. She adjusted the gloves more than was strictly necessary.

"We could tie it up," Guppie suggested. "Gut it like a deer."

Cooper shook his head. "Maybe if we intended to eat the thing, that'd make sense, but when we did dissections in bio, we had to label the organs as we removed them. The point isn't to clean it out. She's trying to see how it works."

Pammy Mae leaned against the wall of the shipping container. "Crazy idea, guys: why don't we let the professional handle this?"

Vera chuckled. "Let's not get carried away."

She had to admit that this wouldn't have been the group she chose to spend the end of the world with, but she liked Pammy Mae a lot more than she'd have guessed.

Vera leaned over the folding table with the biggest knife Len had on offer, rolled the corpse on its back so that its belly was exposed, and drove the tip of the knife into a joint where the thick chitinous armor gave way to a more pliable material that reminded Vera of the underside of a lobster tail. It gave beneath the tip of the knife, but the blade failed to pierce the flexible substance. Vera had to lean a substantial amount of her weight on the knife before it scored the shell deeply enough that a well of black fluid bubbled up through the puncture.

"Ugly stuff, innit?" Guppie asked cheerfully.

Vera set the knife aside and reached for a pair of garden shears. They were sharp enough to clip through the underbelly, and she split it open from the first joint all the way to its tail in one long slice. When she did, she gagged so violently that she nearly dropped the shears.

"Lord, that stinks." Guppie waved one hand in front of his face. "The thing looks like a wheelbug from Hell, but it smells even worse."

"A wheelbug?" Cooper echoed, waving the smell away.

"Aw, yeah, those weird-looking critters you see in your garden sometimes," Guppie said. "They don't usually have anywhere near that many legs, of course, but they're not so wildly different. Got a big hump up top that looks like a wheel sticking out of it."

"They're also about two inches long," Len observed drily.

"This one *is* a lot smaller than the one we fought in the gas station, Vera," Guppie said. He rubbed his chin. "I'm not sure I've seen any as big as that sucker, come to think of it."

"Hard to say." She had been so frightened that first night, so riddled with terror and disbelief. That first one had indeed seemed bigger, but more than the physical dimensions of the beast, she remembered how large it had *felt*. It had seemed to take up the whole room, even though it couldn't have been much larger than a man, realistically speaking. Could Pammy have carried a beast of that size on her shoulders?

Vera took a few gulps of fresh air before returning to her task. The liquid had bubbled over and spilled across the tarp, offering a better view of the creature's organs, although they still glistened with oily residue.

"Cooper," she asked, "can you draw?"

"Pretty well," he said.

"Good. Get your notebook. We're going to do this as properly as we can."

He jogged back to the house, doing a body-block on the door to keep the dogs from darting out to investigate. A few minutes later, he came back with a stack of paper and a ballpoint pen.

"Got it," he said, kneeling down beside her and using his leg to support the notebook. "Where do we start?"

"General notes should do, I would think." Vera steeled herself against the rank odor and got back to work. "Specimen 001..."

"There are going to be more?" Cooper asked.

Vera gestured to their little group. "Let's assume, for a moment, that a non-human species stumbled across this group. What assumptions would they make about our overall species from examining *one* of us that could easily be disproved by examining *two*? We have no way to account for issues like sexual dimorphism, age, injury, or mutations. For the moment, we're going to assume that every single one of them is different, until proven otherwise."

Pammy Mae snorted. "Told you she was the pro."

Cooper nodded. "No argument here. Okay, specimen one it is."

Vera nodded and turned back to the corpse. "All right, S-001. Let's see what you've got for us."

She circled the table to the creature's head and examined it closely. Guppie was right; at first glance, the thing did bear a certain resemblance to a wheelbug, with its folding, spearlike mouth. It took her three tries to force her hands toward the creature's face and pry the folded mouth out to its full length, which was a few inches longer than her whole arm. When she did, a slender sable tongue made of some much softer material peeked out from the creature's head beneath the serrated tube. Gingerly, Vera took it between two fingers and pulled.

And pulled.

And *pulled.*

Guppie whistled as she fed out another arm's length of tongue. "Christ Almighty, you musta pulled out fifteen feet of that stuff. It's like a magician's trick, or one of those extendo leash doohickeys that Carol uses to walk her Pomeranian."

Cooper glanced up from his paper. "Er, should I be writing down the stuff he says, too?"

"It's not as if my observations are going to be particularly accurate," Vera said. "I never bothered with the study of etymology, except inasmuch as it can be used in conjunction with the study of medicine. If you feel that Mr. Martin's analogies are helpful, you may as well make note of them." As she spoke, she let go of the tongue, which whipped back into place at such tremendous speeds that it struck her as it retracted. Vera yelped and jumped away, releasing the folding beak. It closed with a snap so loud that her ears popped.

All five of them stared at the creature in stunned silence. Vera was filled with a terrible dread, a conviction that the creature would sit up and take a deadly interest in her. When it didn't move, she remained frozen in place, heart pounding. It had been all too easy to distance herself from the horrors of that first night by keeping herself busy. Working the land kept her mind busy during the day, and left her so exhausted at night that she fell asleep the moment her head hit the couch cushions. Now, forced to confront the fact that the invasion had been more than a distant dream, her blood turned to ice.

It must be almost Eid by now. Alfie, Sarna, the boys... Mummy and Daddy... what has become of them?

Vera took a deep breath and steadied herself. She was always more effective when she narrowed her focus down to a pinpoint. S-001 was the patient, and therefore all that mattered.

"That is their first weapon," she said. "Their mouths. We know that they use them to feed, and as part of their hunting strategy."

"Bloodthirsty sons of—" Guppie began.

Vera held up one black-and-yellow gloved finger. "Not necessarily. We know that they kill and eat people, but we can't rule out the possibility that they're omnivorous."

Cooper scribbled something, and Vera continued her exam. She crouched down to put the creature at eye-level. "Their eyes are segmented, like those of a fly, although..." She prodded one of the orbs. "We can't know what they've developed to see. Cooper, make a note on another page: *Theories.* Most creatures' eyes are developed in ways that help them identify optimal food sources. We have no idea of these creatures—" She trailed off, then turned to Len. "What do we call them?"

Len's eyes widened as he looked around the little group. "How would I know?"

"You're the one who has the best idea of what we're up against," Cooper pointed out. "You knew to make this..." He gestured to the shipping container.

"Plus, you know how to kill 'em," Guppie added. "You know more than you say, that's for sure."

"I knew that *something* was coming. It's not like I had a name for them." Their host shrugged. "I was too busy getting ready for the end times to worry about the nomenclature."

"We should come up with one, then," Vera suggested. "A way to talk about them."

Pammy Mae hummed. "Things aren't as scary when they have names."

"That," Vera said, "but also simply for expedience. We can discuss it later. For the moment, Cooper, please note that we're not sure if the species to which S-001 belongs sees heat, color, or some other marker to help ID their prey. It would be nice to know that, but some further experimentation may be required."

"Nice." Guppie nodded. "I like where your head's at, Vera. We need to know how to put these little bastards on the defensive."

"I'd settle for knowing how to survive another wave of them," Cooper said. "Maybe when we understand that, we'll be able to plan a way to leave and look for other survivors."

"Is that the plan?" Pammy Mae asked.

Vera held up her hands. "One thing at a time. Cooper, please go back to your primary page. S-001 has thirty-six legs, six segments in its thorax, and six corresponding ridges on its back. In each segment, there's a small external organ that, as far as I can tell, looks like..." She rolled her eyes where Guppie couldn't see. "The tymbal of a cicada. I think that's how they produce that sound we've been hearing."

"Ha!" Guppie pumped his arms in the air. "What'd I say? Big old space cicadas."

Cooper groaned. "We are *not* calling them that."

"You can laugh, but it means that they're doing more than rattling when they attack," Vera pointed out. "They're signaling, and likely not to us. I expect that this is how they let other members of their species know where they are and what they're experiencing."

The smile on Guppie's face died. "You think they can talk to one another?"

Vera nodded. "Almost certainly. From what we've seen, they hunt in groups."

"And they're smart," Pammy Mae added. She shook her head and pushed away from the metal wall of the shipping container. "They're not just feeding down there in Little Creek. They're coming up with something."

Vera opened her mouth to respond when a movement at the corner of her vision caught her eye. Something was wriggling in the exposed meat of the alien's belly. Her stomach lurched—she shouldn't be shocked to learn that the aliens carried parasites, but the idea of some new invasive species piggybacking on the monsters that had destroyed the town left her nauseated. *They could bring other illnesses, too, like colonists bringing smallpox to the New World.* She'd done enough reading in her epidemiology class to have a sense of how high fatalities from a secondary plague could climb.

Nevertheless, drawn by an impulse she could not explain, Vera took a step toward the wriggling object. It was almost perfectly round, with a transparent casing filled with a dark fluid much like the one that had spilled out of the creature's body. Something moved within the black liquid; if the morning sunlight hadn't slanted through at just the right angle, she wouldn't have understood what she was looking at.

Vera's gorge rose, and she took a few steps back, covering her mouth with her elbow. The thin, acidic coffee from breakfast burned at the back of her throat, and her eyes watered with the effort of swallowing.

"What?" Len asked, taking a step toward her. "What's wrong?"

"Eggs," Vera choked. "It's full of eggs."

Len made an incredulous noise and strode over. He grasped the split sides of the thorax in each hand and yanked it in two. Hundreds of eggs spilled out, dropping to the ground and rolling across the loam, among the twigs and pine needles shed by the trees last fall.

"Dammit," Len breathed.

"That's what they're doing in Little Creek," Vera choked. "They're *nesting.*"

The five of them stared in horror at the masses of eggs. Even if this was the only female in the entire group, she could have tripled or quadrupled the number of aliens living in the town.

Now, thought Vera, *multiply that with the assumption that approximately half of them are female, and Little Creek isn't the only town that's been overrun. These creatures have no natural predators.*

In one generation, they could overrun the whole planet, and whatever survivors are out there will be wiped out.

Including us.

24

LEN

LEN AND GUPPIE built a bonfire in silence, almost half a mile from the cabin. Then they dragged down the tarp on which the body of the dead alien still lay. Len did most of the dragging and Guppie did most of the directing, but he wasn't in the mood to quibble.

If Len's childhood taught him anything, it was that mental fortitude was at least as important as physical strength.

In a village where even the most basic supplies were scarce, it was easy to get desperate and take risks. Even clever and strong people would do it. It was a mental illusion, he realized, one that would make people vulnerable to impulses.

After his brother was beaten to death for stealing from a market, Len vowed to never give in to desperation. No matter how sick he was, or hungry or thirsty, he wouldn't allow his mind to go to some dark place that gave credence to those destructive impulses.

Right now, though, he felt like a little boy all over again. He felt weak of mind.

He felt desperate.

They hadn't bothered to finish the autopsy; whatever sense of adventure they had felt when Vera first put her knife to the creature's belly was long gone, smothered by the new knowledge they had unwittingly unearthed in the process.

While Len stoked the fire, Guppie held the pistol, watching the trees and the sky.

"You know something," he said at length. "More than you're letting on."

He broke a few more twigs and tossed them onto the growing blaze. "So everyone keeps telling me."

"Come on, Len." The older man clicked his tongue. "Enough of that nonsense. You're the only one who saw this coming."

Len shook his head. "Not the only one."

The creature's eggs sizzled and burst, melting away to reveal the beast's half-formed larvae. He watched in silence as they died. His mother had raised him to believe that wishing death on another living thing was a terrible unkindness—not a religious transgression exactly, but a spiritual one. Len had gotten over that a long time ago.

"It doesn't matter what I know," he murmured. "It can't fix anything. I can't turn back time. We're trapped here, Guppie, all of us. What good would the details do?"

"You owe them answers," Guppie told him.

He spat in the loam by his boot. "I don't owe anyone a damn thing. They're in my house, eating my rations, living under my roof. I'm keeping them alive."

"Yeah, but who the hell wants to *be alive?* To survive? For a while, it's good enough, but not forever. A divide's coming. You can see it, can't you? Folks want to leave. Telling them the truth might change their minds."

"I said that I saved their lives, not that I own them." Len stood and knocked dirt and soot off his jeans. "If they want to go their own way? Let 'em go."

"Doesn't work like that, I'm afraid." Guppie sniffed and twitched his nose. "Back when I was in the Marines, this guy in my unit got hit in a skirmish. Took a bullet right between his ribs. The poor bastard lost a lot of blood. Fellow's name was Leonard. Leonard Riggs. We had the same blood type, so the camp doctor had me sit by his bed for a direct transfusion. By the end of the night, we both felt like death warmed over, but Leonard Riggs was aboveground, so we called it a win."

Len dug a furrow around the burning corpse with the toe of his boot. He wanted to ask Guppie if his story had a point, but he deserved more respect than that, so he merely nodded and waited patiently for him to continue. Some childhood lessons still clung doggedly to him. Respect for elders was one of them.

"See, after that, things were different between us. You save a guy's life, you know, you start to feel responsible for him. We looked out for one another. Shared our care packages, shared our smokes, that kinda thing. One day, we're marching across the desert along with the tanks, when Leonard stops. He had this crazy look in his eyes, and he wouldn't move a muscle. So I stopped, you know, to ask him what was up." Guppie wrinkled his nose and let out a deep sigh. "The poor bugger stepped on a mine. He'd felt the give, heard the click. He knew that the second he took his foot off that thing, he was gonna get blown sky-high. He waited until everyone else was through. Told us to leave him and just hope the landmine was a dud. I wanted to make myself stay with him, but I didn't, so in the end I watched his last moments from far off with the rest of the guys." Guppie shook his head, an expression of long-studied bewilderment etched on his features.

"Of all of the guys, why'd it have to be him? I saw the smoke, saw some other guys go back for whatever was left for the body, and I kept thinking, *What a waste*. I'd saved his life, and for what? To watch him die less than six months later?"

"And you think I'd feel the same way about Cooper and the rest of them, if they took off and didn't even make it out of town?" Len asked.

"Well? Wouldn't you?"

Len closed his eyes and tried to picture it; not that it was hard. He'd seen the dead boy in the tunnel, and the remains of his almost-neighbors in the streets of Little Creek. He never saw his brother's battered body, but his mother had, and he never forgot the hollow look in her eyes. It was always shocking, how a person could transform into nothing but meat and bone in an instant. When he and his mother moved to America with his uncle, he'd watched his mother take the long road, witnessed her slow slide into oblivion, mind-first. That had been its own kind of horror, but at least she'd had time to prepare. Forced to choose between the creeping terror of prolonged illness and the violent shock of being felled by one of the invaders, Len might have chosen the former for his loved ones... but the latter for himself.

Selfish, isn't it, to be glad that you'll most likely face death head-on with all your senses still intact?

"I don't know what I would feel," he said at last. "Can't predict something like that with any accuracy until it's already happened. Still, I'm sure you're right—I'd hate to watch any of you die, but I'm not doing this for my own karma or out of guilt or whatever you want to call it. I'm doing it because it's what my wife would have done. She was the one that warned me about all this, before she..." He choked on the next words. Every time he thought about it, he wanted to knock someone out. "Out of the two of us, she was the good one. She would have done more, if she'd had time."

Guppie shot him a sorrowful look. "Ah," he said, and didn't ask any more questions.

"I understand wanting answers, Guppie, trust me. I wish that I had more of them. All I can tell you is this: the government saw this coming from a long way off." Len rubbed one temple with his index finger. The scorched remains of the alien lay at his feet, smoldering among the ashes. "And look at what happened? Clearly, the folks at the top came to a decision about what to do and who to save." He looked pointedly at Guppie. "We didn't make the cut. So if you think someone's coming to save us, don't hold your breath."

"Wish I could say that surprised me." Guppie kicked at the burned-out carapace of the alien. "This'll burn itself out within the hour. We should get back to the bunker."

Len kicked dirt over the edges of the fire, retrieved his tarp, and began the walk back home.

"Have you thought any more about my suggestion?" Guppie asked. "About fortifications, I mean?"

"Wouldn't hurt to have them," Len said. "I can't speak for everyone—and frankly, I don't want to—but I have no intention of leaving. I plan to hold my ground for as long as I can, and take as many of them as possible down with me when I go."

"That's your call," Guppie said. "Personally speaking, I was never one to accept defeat. While there's life, there's hope. I'll get Cooper to help me tomorrow. Maybe that'll get his mind off this fantasy of running off."

Don't bother, he almost said. He'd planned to be able to bunker down for at least four years on his own, but the rations were being taxed. He'd been worried about that before, but today, when he'd seen that mass of eggs in the alien's ovipositor, he'd seen the writing on the wall.

They wouldn't last a year up here, not with those creatures

breeding in the valley, laying their eggs in the battered walls of Little Creek. Sooner or later, they'd be overrun.

It was only a matter of time.

25

COOPER

"WHAT ARE YOU LOOKING AT NOW?" Vera asked, peering over Cooper's shoulder.

He'd retrieved the map from Guppie, and was engaged once again in the seemingly endless task of calculating and re-calculating all the places where the other survivors might have fled.

"I'm thinking about distances... where can we check without running out of gas?" Cooper tapped one finger against his lips. "We'd need to be able to make a round trip on one tank, or find a place to refuel along the route." He shook his head. "I wish we could fly."

"You fly?"

"Sort of. I mean, I don't have a license or anything, but I got pretty decent in a Cessna."

"Huh." Vera pulled up another chair. "What about the airport? Could we find a plane?"

"Hangars were burned to the ground. I mean flat to the ground. We saw it when we first came into town with Len. The whole area over there was scorched. I think those alien ships had, like, thrusters on the front of them. Something to slow them down at the last second, make the impact survivable. Probably what caused so many of the fires." He was babbling now, but it was hard to stop. "Anyways, all the planes are gone. My dad knew a few guys doing home builds, but if they were still in a garage somewhere, they weren't finished. If they were ready to fly, they were in the hangers. So ... yeah. Driving it is."

"Well. We have fuel tanks here, you know."

"Yeah, but if we burn through Len's whole supply, he'll have our heads."

Vera ran her palm over the map. "I understand that the pumps at gas stations might not be working, but there are other fuel supplies out there. Plenty of folks in town kept canisters on-hand."

Cooper shivered. "You wanna go back into town?"

"Everyone talks about it like we have an option, but we don't. I don't mean that we'll have to go to Little Creek, but we'll have to go somewhere." Vera's eyes roamed over the map. "Len doesn't like to let on, but we can't stay here forever. At least, not *all* of us can."

"You want to leave." Cooper sat back in his chair. "Not just for the day, but for good."

Vera waved to the map. "If you didn't have us here, but you'd survived that first night with a car... where would you go? Where would you have headed if you were trying to flee?"

The thought of running away turned Cooper's stomach. He'd let so many people down already. He hadn't been able to force himself back to the multi-car pileup they'd left in their wake when leaving the party, and he had nothing to indicate that any of the people who'd fled first were all right. But Logan had run for his car rather than following the rest of them into the woods, hadn't he? Which meant he'd had a chance to get out before the shit hit the fan. If Logan had come down the mountain and seen the town on fire, where would he have gone?

Cooper's eyelids fluttered closed as he tried to picture his next course of action. He didn't like Logan. He'd picked on Cooper a lot, and would have a lot more if he wasn't Nate's brother. But he could imagine what he'd do. What he'd probably *done*. "People would go for help... right? They'd go to the cops, the hospital, maybe even the military. Or churches, I guess? They'd be clueless about what to do, so they'd head for the people who might be prepared."

"That was certainly my first impulse," Vera agreed. "And if the cops were as baffled as they were? If the hospital closed its doors and the church burned down?"

"They'd go for the woods. They'd try to get away."

For the first time, Vera shook her head. "I see what you're saying, but I think you're wrong. Most folks in Little Creek might think they know back-country living, but they don't know how to survive in the wilderness. They don't know plants, they're terrified of even *little* insects, and if a snake comes into their yard, they'll throw a fit." Vera shook her head. "Trust me on this one. I talked to a lot of them at the store. If their safe havens didn't offer protection, they wouldn't run for the hills... and if they did, most of them wouldn't last long." She reached across the table to trace her finger east along the highway. "The smart ones would try to congregate. Find weapons, shelter, *food*. They'd look for a safe place." She reached the edge of the map and stopped, looking up at Cooper with a question painted on her features.

"You think they went to D.C.?" Cooper ran his hands through his messy hair. "That's a long way."

"And a one-way trip, if I'm wrong." Vera folded her arms and leaned her elbows on the table. "It's possible that the cities are even worse."

"So let me get this straight." Cooper held up his right hand. "We can either bunker down here until a zillion more of these critters hatch out and wait for our supplies to run out..." He held up his right hand. "*Or we can head off into the great outdoors and risk dying horribly and/or finding out that everyone else is also dead.* Gee, what a couple of great options."

"Let me tell you something." Vera lowered her voice and stared straight into Cooper's eyes. "It's possible that neither option is good. When I worked in the ER, I had to make life-and-death calls in a matter of seconds, and sometimes the person would die. I would beat myself up over it, but the truth is, they might have died even if I made a different choice. I'll never know. And sometimes, someone would come in, and I'd think they were destined to die, that anything I did would be a waste of time... and then they'd live. You truly never know, but there's one thing I always kept in mind: I had to do *something*. Even if it was the wrong choice, I still had to make *a* choice."

"And you choose D.C.?" Cooper asked.

"My family's there. Or rather, they were there." Vera swallowed hard. "I'm not going to try to trick you or mislead you, but sooner or later, I'm going to have to know. Even if the only good thing that comes of this is one less person eating through Len's supplies, so be it."

Cooper hadn't heard Pammy come in, so her derisive laugh startled him.

"Are you two serious?" she demanded. "You think you're going to go on a road trip through enemy territory in a pickup truck? Or a stolen beater? Get real, Cooper." She shook her head at Vera as she cracked open the lid of a water bottle. "Him I get, but I expected better of you."

Cooper set his jaw and twisted around in his chair to scowl at her. "I've gotta know what happened to my family, Pammy. When this all started, I just ran. I didn't do anything. You said yourself that I could have done more to help Nate. I'm done running away."

"So you've decided to run headlong into danger instead?" Pammy took a swig of her water and leaned one skinny hip against the kitchen counter. She was losing weight like crazy. They all were, to some extent or another, but she seemed to have aged a decade in the weeks since Nate's death.

Nate never told her that he planned to leave. In their first days in the bunker, Cooper had probed around this topic with delicate questions, and she'd unwittingly confirmed his suspicions. In her mind, she'd lost the love of her life, not some shitty ex who broke her heart at graduation. He'd considered telling her the truth in the hopes of setting her free on some level, but he was pretty sure that it would only make things worse. He'd kept his mouth shut.

There were some stories you had to tell yourself to keep sane, and if Pammy needed to believe that Nate had been unquestioningly loyal and devoted, so be it.

"I'm not running into danger," Cooper countered. "I'm looking out for the people I love. My family's out there somewhere, and for all we know, your mom is, too. Don't you want to know for sure?"

Pammy's jaw clenched the way it did anytime he mentioned his family. He knew that she was remembering the sound of Nate's body cracking apart as it hit the top of the Jeep. Sometimes, in the night, Cooper dreamed about it: not the sight, just the sound.

"I'm not sure what we could do for them, even if we found them." Pammy's voice was gentler now.

Cooper gripped the back of his chair. "I don't, either, but like Vera said, I have to try."

Pammy looked back and forth between them, then cut her eyes away, poking her finger through a hole near the hem of her ragged shirt. "Are you going to tell Len and Guppie about your plans?"

"Of course." Vera cocked her head. "We're in this together. If they want to come, we should invite them, at the very least, and we'll need to discuss any supplies we might want to take."

"Great." Pammy finished her bottle of water, closed the cap, and set it aside. They'd been collecting empties to refill during rainstorms. "Let me know what they say."

Cooper swiveled to watch her as she stalked past. The rifle was leaning by the door, and she slung the strap over her shoulder as she went.

"Where are you going?" Cooper asked.

Pammy Mae didn't bother to turn and face him. "Out." She closed the door without another word.

"Is she okay?" Vera asked.

"Are any of us?" Cooper asked.

The gardener clicked her tongue. "That's not what I mean. She's a wild card."

"Maybe so." Cooper pushed his chair back and got to his feet. "But you didn't see her that first night. She's unpredictable, but that means *they* can't predict her either."

"The Rattlers?" Vera asked.

Cooper paused. "The aliens, you mean?"

"I thought I'd try something out." Vera shrugged. "But I don't love it. Sounds like a high school football team."

"We'll keep trying." Cooper stretched his arms over his head until his shoulder popped. "In the meantime, we should make a list of what we'll need and plan our route."

Every time Cooper had tried to bring up the idea of leaving, the others had pushed back. It was a relief to know that Vera, at least, would be along for the ride.

If he had to go alone, however, he would. He was done with running and hiding. It was time for the aliens to learn that they'd messed with the wrong town. Cooper hated Little Creek, but that didn't give them the right to ruin the good parts.

26
PAMMY MAE

SHE KNEW BETTER than to let Cooper's words get under her skin. She *knew*.

And yet, here she was, storming out of their safe haven with a burning question at the back of her mind: *What happened to my mother?*

What happened to all of them?

She had seen no definitive signs of human habitation in the town below, but Cooper seemed so *sure*. It was probably a result of his ignorance—after all, she'd planted a seed of false hope in his mind when she'd told him that there was no sign of his parents in their home. She was wise enough not to hold out hope when the reality of the situation could crush her. Anger was a better weapon. It kept her sharp.

But whenever she leaned into her rage, it was accompanied by doubts. Because what if she was wrong?

Pammy had left the ATV near the road when she went hunting for that specimen for Vera. She hadn't wanted the creatures to hear her coming, and once she'd killed her quarry, she'd been closer to the bunker than the vehicle anyway. As she made her way down the mountain, she passed its hiding spot. She'd covered it with tree limbs so that anyone, or any*thing*, passing by would be hard-pressed to recognize it. The keys were still in the ignition; she'd been worried about losing them during a hunt.

She stopped for a moment to consider taking it the rest of the way to town, but the vehicle was too loud. If she rode it toward town, the aliens would hear her coming. She would be safer on foot.

With that in mind, she set out for town, leaving the ATV where it sat. She might not make it back by nightfall, but so be it.

Pammy had to know the truth, whatever the cost.

The aliens could climb, but even knowing that, Pammy Mae felt safer beneath the trees. She'd gotten used to the cover, especially in broad daylight. For all she knew, the aliens still hunted by daylight, but it *felt* safer.

Although, technically speaking, that kind of thinking could take her off her guard, and Pammy had no intention of getting lax.

At any rate, she knew the landscape of the Gamelands better than the town now that most of Little Creek had been razed. It took an effort of will to step out of the trees and onto the road running from the south end of town up toward Cloverleaf. Pammy clutched the rifle strap in both hands as she inched her toe out into the open. When nothing happened, she took another step.

She didn't see a single alien as she strode through town, but that wasn't for lack of trying. When something moved in the window of one of the houses she passed, Pammy yanked her rifle to her shoulder without a moment's thought. She stared through the scope until her brain caught up with her; one of the upstairs windows was shattered, and a stained curtain was blowing in the breeze.

"Deep breaths," she murmured, hearing the words in her Momma's voice. "Steady steps. Don't let them see your fear."

She turned in a slow circle in the street, poised to find one of those leggy, shimmering bodies clinging to a wall or peering over the peak of a roof. When she found nothing, Pammy began to walk again, although she didn't lower the rifle.

Little Creek as she knew it was gone. Most of the houses were burnt-out husks. Once-sagging porches had now collapsed, and the charming air of nostalgia that the locals were so proud of had been erased.

It was a good thing she'd come alone, she reckoned. Cooper's fragile dreams of finding other survivors would have been crushed underfoot. She'd only had a vague sense of how bad things were when she'd seen the town from afar on her recon missions. Out there, things looked bad. Up close, they were goddamn heartbreaking.

Pammy stuck to the ruined parts of town. The aliens had to be hiding somewhere, she figured, and since she couldn't see them, they were probably inside. The more distance she put between herself and any buildings that still stood, the better. She passed the ruins of the Dollar Tree and the foundations of the pizza parlor before heading up the road toward the high school on the north side of town. The building was intact, as far as she could see; but why would the aliens have bothered with it, after all? It would have been empty that time of night, and if Vera was right about their hunting instincts, they would have had no reason to gravitate to an abandoned building.

The road into Cloverleaf was barred by a gate with mechanical arms that raised and lowered with the swipe of a card or the entrance of a password. At least a couple of times a year, some idiot drove straight through the arms, splintering them off to stubs until they could be replaced. When Pammy approached the gate, the arms were intact, and the metal fence surrounding the community was undamaged.

We thought this made us safe. We thought a fence would keep the whole world at bay. Pammy shook her head as she slipped under the flimsy barrier. *We were idiots.*

On any other night, Pammy would have been home studying, or baking with her mother, or planning for her post-high-school future. She'd have been in their living room when the world fell apart. She and her mother would probably have taken refuge in the basement if they had any idea what was coming; if they'd been asleep, they might have died in their beds like the Lutzes.

Unlike the rest of town, Cloverleaf was virtually untouched. Doors stood open, either thrown wide by their occupants or beaten in by the aliens. Pammy wasn't sure which was true, and she reckoned that it didn't matter much. One way or another, there was nobody alive in those houses.

As she approached her home in the middle of Cloverleaf, her hands started to shake. *Don't do this*, she begged her nerves. This wasn't the time to lose control. If she was going to enter the house, she'd need her wits about her.

The front door of the Johnson house, unlike so many others, was intact. The garage bay door was halfway raised, and her mother's car still sat inside. Pammy forced herself to slip beneath the partially open barrier. There was no sign of bloodshed, and the door into the house was still on its hinges.

Walking through the Lutz house at night had played on Pammy Mae's oldest fears. Now, in her childhood home with summer sunlight streaming through the windows, she couldn't muster the same rigid strength. Rather than surreal dissociation, she felt... comfortable. The house was just as she remembered it, with no sign of having been ravaged by invaders.

She kept the rifle at the ready as she walked through the house.

A mug of tea stood on the table, with the string and paper tag still dangling over the lip. The chair was pushed aside, as if Emma Jean Johnson had just stood up in a hurry.

Pammy sighed and ran her fingers over the back of the chair. *Where are you, Ma?*

The rest of the split-level ranch was equally empty. Pammy peered through the doors, scanning each room from floor to ceiling. Her room, at the far end of the hall, was the last one she glanced into. Standing in the doorway, she could tell that it was just as she'd left it when she'd stepped out that night before the star party; her makeup bag still sat on the counter of her vanity, and the closet was thrown open, revealing all her clothes.

Pammy stepped inside and shut the door behind her. She upended her bookbag which she'd left on the foot of her bed, opened her dresser, and began tossing things inside.

In the Time Before—as she'd begun to delineate the passage of days prior to the invasion—she had worried about her hair, her clothes, her makeup, her *reputation*. Now, she didn't give a damn, and there was no one to impress. She packed her bag with her most rugged jeans, with tank tops and sweatshirts, with socks and underwear. This was her last visit. There was no coming back, and her mother had always warned her that she wouldn't want to die in dirty underwear. Johnsons had *standards*.

She stuffed her most comfortable pair of sneakers in the top of the bag, zipped it up, and pulled it on. As she turned toward the door, her eyes snagged on the poster she had made as part of her Butter Queen training. Her mentor had called it a Vision Board, but it was wish fulfillment as much as anything. Pammy had cataloged the things that mattered to her alongside her hopes for the future. There was a photo of her and Nate, a drawing of the Butter Queen trophy, and a color-coded list of her hopes for the next five, ten, twenty, and thirty years. She'd spent so long on that poster. If she made one now, she wouldn't be able to think beyond tomorrow, and her only goal would be, *Stay Alive.*

She yanked the door open, brought her rifle to bear, and stepped out into the hall.

Cooper was right. It was time to leave this town behind.

Her steps echoed down the hallway with renewed purpose. As she passed by the front door, however, she paused. Her mother's shoes, which usually stood on the mat in the entryway, were gone.

Pammy crouched down beside the mat and let her palm rest on the empty space, just to make sure that she hadn't imagined it. Someone had taken those shoes, and it was hard to imagine that aliens were to blame.

With a renewed sense of purpose, she got to her feet and traced her mother's steps through the house. She must have been sitting at the kitchen table when something tipped her off to the fact that the lights in the sky weren't meteors. Perhaps the power had gone down when the lines in town were damaged, or the first of the fires across town had been lit. Or maybe someone had called. The car keys were still hanging on the peg by the door. She snatched them up, clutching them tight in her fist, reveling in the cold, sharp sensation of them.

With a mounting sense of excitement, Pammy bolted back to the garage. If her mother had made it out in one piece, she *must* have left a message for her. She wouldn't have left without leaving some sort of clue, not if she'd gone under her own power. Pammy all but skidded back through the man-door into the garage. Her breath caught in her throat as she took in the inside of the garage bay door. In a clumsy hand, someone had used a tube of lipstick to scrawl the word, *KEYSTONE.*

Pammy stumbled toward the door and pressed her palm against the segmented barrier. She knew that shade. L'Oreal Paris Number 254: Everbloom. Her mother's color.

"Mom." Pammy closed her eyes and let her forehead rest against the aluminum. "You got out."

She knew Keystone. It was a few hours' drive away at the Maryland border, at the Army base where Uncle Kevin was stationed. She and her mother went out that way every six months or so to visit him.

Of course that was where she would go. Perhaps her uncle had even *been* here. If anyone knew what was coming, it would be the Army, right? He could have come for both of them. Maybe he'd even been in a helicopter. If they'd been ordered to evacuate everyone, and Pammy was unaccounted for, they wouldn't have stuck around.

For the first time in weeks, hope sprouted in Pammy Mae's chest. There might be something waiting for her beyond tomorrow. There might be a destination. Other survivors.

There might be a reason to keep going, beyond the fact that her heart was still beating and her lungs drew breath.

Hope.

She'd forgotten the feeling.

Pammy put one hand beneath the bottom lip of the garage door and raised it up, pushing it over her head so that she could clearly see the street outside. The door rattled as it rose.

The rattling didn't stop when the door reached its apex. Pammy froze as the tableau before her came into view.

A half-dozen of the creatures stood in the untended garden at the center of Cloverleaf. They formed a semi-circle around the largest one Pammy had seen. It was the source of the ongoing rattle.

Vera had been right; now that she could see them clearly, it was obvious that no two of the aliens looked exactly alike, but the one standing closest to her was a full foot taller than the rest, bringing its ungainly body almost to Pammy's eye-level. One of the front legs was splintered off at the end, and a silvery scar covered both of its segmented eyes.

They're smart, she reminded herself, *Which means they can be scared. And bargained with.*

Before she even realized what she was doing, the butt of the rifle was pressed against her shoulder, and the scope was trained on the alien at the center of the circle. Its silver scar flashed in the sunlight.

"Stay back!" she bellowed.

The rattling didn't stop as the creature took another step toward her. She could see it moving, rubbing its legs along the tymbals that Vera had identified during her autopsy. The pitch shifted subtly, and the ring of aliens drew closer, encircling her.

In Bio III, Ms. Ellis had shown the class a video about Cape Hunting Dogs, explaining the complexity of their communication system and the way the lead hunter could command her pack. At the time, she'd watched in astonishment as a group of dogs no bigger than her neighbor's golden retriever had taken down a wildebeest, as if the pack of dogs were one beast ruled by a single mind. Now, Pammy could understand how the wildebeest felt.

"Stay *back,*" she snarled again, but the alien only advanced. Pammy's hand shook as her eyes darted between the beasts. If she shot one of them, the pack might scatter—or they might decide that enough was enough. The tongue that Vera had fed out of the mouth of that one she autopsied could span the distance between her and the pack leader. If that had been what got Brandon on the road that first night, she wasn't safe even if they stayed at this distance.

Adrenaline flooded her brain, stretching each second to the breaking point. A trickle of sweat slipped down her hairline. Her finger twitched on the trigger.

She saw the long proboscis lift, exposing the orifice from which that awful tongue protruded. In the split second between when it moved and the attack came, Pammy stepped to one side and dropped her supporting arm from beneath the rifle. As the tongue whipped past her, Pammy flung one arm out, wrapped it around the long, narrow appendage, and gripped it tight in her fist. She tugged with all of her might, firing wildly with her other hand as she did so.

A line of bullets swept across the beast's face and it let out a high-pitched whine that left her eardrums aching. The tongue came away in her hands. Black blood spattered the driveway where a younger version of Pammy Mae had spent her afternoons drawing elaborate sidewalk art. She screamed an unintelligible oath as the other aliens descended on her. Even the wounded leader of the pack was still moving, approaching her with its serrated proboscis raised. Pammy lifted the rifle to her shoulder and emptied her magazine, picking off the uninjured ones as she backed toward the car. The second she was inside, she slammed the garage door down. Less than a second later, three deep dents appeared in the aluminum.

How the hell am I supposed to get out of here? she wondered. She had been holding the car keys, but in the madness of the moment, she'd dropped them. There was no sign of them on the floor of the garage, which meant that they were still outside.

"Shit, shit, *shit!*" She opened the car door and tossed the useless rifle inside. "Where the hell am I supposed to—"

"*Get down!*" someone outside screamed. Pammy didn't stop to think. The voice was obviously human, which meant that whoever it belonged to was on *her* side in every way that mattered. She dropped to the concrete, belly-first, scraping her palms against the rough surface when she landed.

In the driveway outside, something exploded, peppering the garage door with dings and dents from shrapnel. Pammy threw her arms over her head and bit back a scream. The rattling receded, leaving nothing but silence in its wake.

She lay there for a few moments, breathing hard. When she finally lifted her head, she saw the message again: *KEYSTONE*. The formerly pristine door was now punctured with what looked like carpenter's nails.

The whining in her ears faded, and Pammy rolled to one side, pushing herself to her feet. She was only halfway up when the door shuddered and rolled upward.

In the past few weeks, Pammy Mae had seen a lot of unbelievable things, but even with a month of nightmares under her belt, she wasn't prepared for the figure standing in the driveway amid a handful of bent nails and shards of ridged aluminum. An old man with wild eyes and an unkempt beard stood outside, wearing flip-flops, cargo shorts, a beer-and-sweat-stained wifebeater, and a tinfoil hat over his scraggly hair shaped like an oversized Hershey's kiss. He bent down to pick up the car keys, then tossed them to Pammy, who caught them without taking her eyes off of the strange apparition that seemed to have emerged from nowhere.

"You okay?" he asked. Dozens of tin cans were tied to a sagging belt that encircled his waist, and a grill lighter hung around his neck on a rough piece of twine.

"Are those homemade bombs?" she asked.

The man nodded. "Smart cookie. You're that pageant girl, aren't you? You got a hidey-hole up in the mountains? A safehouse?"

Pammy nodded, and the man pushed past her, grabbing the leaf blower that her mother kept in the garage. He turned it on high and returned to the driveway, scattering the shrapnel across the pavement and into the grass. The disembodied, whiplike tongue of the injured alien tumbled away like so much discarded string. When he was done, he moved to return the leaf blower to

its original spot, but stopped short. After a few seconds' consideration, he opened the back door of the car and tossed it inside.

"Well, don't just stand there with your mouth hanging open."
The man trotted over to the passenger door and yanked it open. "I
saved you from King Clanker just now, but I doubt I killed a single
one of them." He glanced over his shoulder to the middle of the
cul-de-sac and grinned, revealing his uneven teeth. "Although it
looks like you got two of them all on your lonesome. Not bad for a
little whippersnapper like you. Come on, get in, little lady. You've
pissed off the King something fierce, and now that he's got your
scent, he won't let you go."

Pammy opened the driver's side door and slid behind the
wheel of her mother's silver SUV, tossing her backpack between
the seats to join the rifle and the leaf blower. She put on her seat
belt in one automatic motion.

ATVs were one thing, but on the road, Pammy was a careful
driver. Or she *had* been. She backed out of the garage at full speed,
running over anything and everything as she went, then floored it
out of Cloverleaf. The lightweight gate at the limits of the little
community didn't even slow her down. The old man hooted and
hollered, slapping his palms on the dashboard as she drove out of
town as fast as the car would take her.

In the distance, she could hear the hum of the aliens, that
echoing song that had signaled their departure from town on that
first night. They were talking to each other, informing their fellows
of the girl who had come and gone, leaving death in her wake.

When they passed beyond the town limits, Pammy Mae bared
her teeth in triumph.

Keystone. There was hope in Keystone.

Now that she had something to aim for, nothing was going to
get in her way.

BEYOND LITTLE CREEK

Qaitbay Citadel
Alexandria, Egypt

———

Abbas abn La 'Ahad and the Army of Orphans ruled the streets of Alexandria. Only a few weeks before, Abbas had been a nobody, a throwaway kid with no future in a city where he had no place to lay his head.

Then the sky had fallen, and the world had turned upside down, and all of a sudden, Abbas *mattered*. The city had toppled, and the street rats were all that were left. A lifetime of scrambling to survive meant that Abbas knew the ins and outs of the city as intimately as those who had built it. He knew where to hide, where to find food, how to move from place to place without getting caught. Other survivors found him, and Abbas had become a king. He made the rules, and those who didn't follow became outcasts, left to face the bugs on their own.

The bugs had overrun the city at first, but in the weeks that followed, Abbas and his army had begun to push them back. They took the Citadel of Qaitbay, which had become the seat of Abbas's rule. He was only sixteen, but even the older children deferred to him. Unlike the rest of them, Abbas had a plan.

That morning had dawned cloudy and cool, at least for that time of year. Abbas had noticed that the insects were more irritable on warm days, although he was still testing this theory. It would be a good day to head to the mainland for more supplies.

The Citadel stood in the water at the mouth of the Eastern Harbor. The bugs did not like saltwater, and the fortress was built on an island surrounded by the sea. This made it easier to defend, not only from the bugs, but from other invaders. There were other factions within the city, and Abbas did not trust them. They had not been on his side before the invasion. He saw no reason why things should be different now that resources were dwindling.

Rabbel and Yara stayed close to his side as they left the citadel, barking commands to the others. Rabbel was eighteen, two years Abbas's senior; Yara was only twelve, but she had survived the worst of the attacks, and she had killed more of the bugs than any other soldier in the orphan's army.

"Where are we going today, boss?" Rabbel asked.

"We'll follow El-Gaish road," Abbas told him. The Army had already collected several dozen rowboats, and they brought in plenty of fish. Abbas was more worried about fresh water; it had not rained for a week, and their cisterns were running dry. Anything else they could scrounge up would be a blessing. "We'll keep the sea to our left so that the bugs cannot attack us from that direction."

The concrete husks of modern buildings lined the beach, and Abbas watched them, wary of anyone—or any*thing*—that might be lurking inside. His soldiers had been attacked before. Yara clutched her rifle to her chest and glared at the buildings. The knives she carried on her belt were for more than show. Some boys might be ashamed to treat a younger girl as their bodyguard. More fool them. Those boys were long since dead.

"King Abbas!" From further down the beach, a little boy of eight came sprinting back his way. "King Abbas! Come see what we've found!"

Yara bared her teeth, but Abbas laid one hand on her shoulder. "Let's see what he has found."

The other children had already begun to gather around a black cylinder that had washed up on the beach. It was not old, but it was crusted with barnacles and calcification and green slime.

Yara immediately raised her gun. "That's one of their ships," she snarled.

Abbas had seen them, too. Some of the ships must have fallen into the ocean on their descent. He had not seen them in the sky since that first night. Now that they had taken over the city, the aliens seemed content to make their nests and hunt for food. It had never occurred to Abbas that they might be able to fly again, but as he examined this one, he wondered... if they could take off once, might they not be able to do the same again? If the Orphan's Army could make use of rowboats, how much more could they do with a flying ship?

He moved between the other children, who parted for him, and approached the side of the alien craft. It lay on its side, with its hatch facing the sea.

"Cover us," he told Yara.

Rabbel followed him toward the hatch, while the rest of the children retreated, muttering under the breaths and quaking with fear.

"Are you sure we should do this here, boss?" Rabbel asked under his breath.

Abbas nodded. "I want to take the ship back to the fortress, but I don't want to risk letting one of the bugs loose within the walls. Besides, it's been a few days since we've killed one. I wouldn't want them to think we're getting weak, would you?" He grinned at Rabbel and gripped the handles of the kataras that one of the boys in the citadel had helped him make. "Open the door. Let's see if the demon inside has survived."

Rabbel frowned, but he did as Abbas asked and tugged on the hatch. The older boy was smart, but his real advantage lay in his strength. Abbas was agile and lean, small for his age, while his second-in-command was as sturdy as the walls of the Citadel.

The hatch didn't move at first, and Rabbel pulled again. His cheeks puffed out with effort and the muscles in his neck bulged. At last, with a terrific roar, he tore the hatch open wide, revealing the compartment within.

"Good work, Rabbel!" one of the onlookers shouted.

Abbas did not move to congratulate his second-in-command. From what little he could see of the ship's interior, it did not appear to be flooded. It might have been at sea for weeks, but if the bugs could survive the journey between worlds, it stood to reason that they could survive in the sea. Abbas had no schooling, but some of the other children had, and his advisors at the Citadel had explained their theories on where the bugs came from.

He waited, staring into the darkness, braced for an attack.

"Maybe it is empty," Rabbel said. "Maybe it's dead."

"We have time," Abbas assured him, still staring into the darkness. "Wait a moment, just in case—"

The words were still on his lips when the creature lunged out of the darkness. Rabbel yelped, but Abbas was ready. He ducked low, pushing off from the sand, bringing his fists in toward his chin. He slipped beneath the alien, punching up in swift succession, driving the triangular blades of his kataras up into the beast's belly.

It let out that awful, rattling noise, but Abbas could tell that the creature was weak. It was slow, likely hungry, and disoriented.

Abbas was not. As the alien flailed, Abbas drove both knife-points into a seam between its scales and *yanked,* tearing the creature's side open. Its dark blood spilled onto the beach, and it staggered a little ways off before collapsing onto the sand, twitching into stillness.

The soldiers cheered and whistled as Abbas turned back to his general. "*Now* it's dead," he said. "This is the new plan. Yara, you will stay with me. Rabbel, have this ship checked over and then seal it up and tie it to one of the boats." He pointed to the abandoned fishing vessels still scattered along the beach. "Take five of our people with you, and float it back to the Citadel. I want my advisors to look at it. We'll see if we can make it fly again."

"Yes, sir!" Rabbel saluted before turning to the soldiers and picking who would come with him.

Abbas wiped his blades clean on the sand and returned them to their places on his belt. On his way past the alien ship, he stopped to slap the side.

All his life, he had been told that he was nothing. A waste of air. A bastard. Disposable.

Look at me now, he thought with a smile. *I am the King of the Citadel, and my people will do more than survive.*

We will thrive.

We are taking our world back.

27

VERA

VERA WAS WORKING in the garden, running over a list of the supplies they would need to collect, when Len and Guppie emerged from the woods carrying the stained tarp and an empty gas can. They had only made it a few steps when a rumble echoed through the clearing. Vera snatched up her garden fork, while Guppie planted his feet and brought his pistol to bear.

"Is it them?" she asked, trying to spot the source of the noise.

Guppie shook his head. "Sounds like a car."

The pickup truck was parked in the driveway, and Vera was familiar enough with the ATV to tell that an entirely different vehicle was headed their way. They had done their best to prepare for an eventual alien attack, but they had never discussed what would happen if other human survivors showed up.

Vera knew her customers well enough to know Len wasn't the only one who lived secluded in the hills. But since they'd heard nothing from anyone else in the last weeks, she had to assume they either hadn't survived or weren't curious about others.

But maybe that was about to change. It wouldn't be that hard to put two-and-two together and come sniffing around Len's place. And what then? Would they deny aid to newcomers? Or welcome them in, accepting an even bigger drain on their supplies?

A silver SUV appeared between the trees, screeching to a halt alongside the pickup. Pammy Mae swung out of the driver's seat. It had only been a few hours since she'd taken off, but her hair was wild and she looked a good deal worse for wear.

The passenger door opened, and a strange, skinny man emerged. Vera bit the inside of her cheek to keep from laughing outright at the absurdity of his appearance. *When Mummy warned me not to move to the country, this was exactly the type of thing she was worried about: old white men with homemade explosives and tinfoil hats.* Give him a chainsaw, and the trifecta would be complete.

Guppie let out a little cry of surprise. "Well, I'll be dipped. Sean?"

Sean Hawes held out his arms, and the two men hugged, patting one another on the back. "Guppie, you sly old dog! I didn't know you'd made it." He didn't acknowledge the rest of them, and Vera was in no rush to greet him. She'd never liked Sean much, but even so, it was a relief to see another face. There were other survivors out there. They weren't alone.

"What's this nonsense on your noggin?" Guppie reached up to touch the silver cap that Sean had wrapped his head in.

The smaller man shimmied out of reach. "Don't touch that. It's the only reason they haven't got me yet."

Even Guppie, who was predisposed to politeness, was thrown for a loop by that. "You're wearing it for protection?"

Sean nodded and lowered his voice, although Vera had no trouble hearing him even at a distance. "They can get into your head. Read your mind. I tell you, the Clankers are psychic."

"Is that what you call them?" Vera asked.

Sean looked her way at last, and Vera fell back a pace. Physically, Sean looked all right, but there was something in his eyes that put Vera on edge. She'd seen that look from patients who had been pushed to their breaking point, or who'd come into the ER on narcotics. Whatever he'd experienced while hiding in Little Creek had caused him to snap.

"The things that took over? Yeah, we call 'em Clankers. And that one Miss Butter over here fought is the big, bad grandaddy of 'em all, King Clanker." Sean nodded to Pammy, who had retrieved a bag from the back of the SUV and was standing alongside Len, watching the reunion with wary eyes.

"How many other survivors are there?" Guppie asked.

Sean sniffed and rubbed his wrist across his nose. "None that I know of."

"But you said *we*." Guppie's eyebrows pulled together. "Just now."

Sean's jaw tightened. "There were three of us. In the beginning. Walker, my neighbor, but he only lasted a few days. He was diabetic, and he ran out of insulin real quick. An' Jenny, that nice woman from down the street. We got her into the basement with us that first night. After Walker died, she started acting funny. About a week in, she just up and left. Took off her shoes and walked out into the street, then shouted her head off until they came to get her."

Vera covered her mouth with one hand, letting the garden fork drop to the ground. "That's awful. She must have gone into shock."

Sean spat at his feet and tapped one chipped fingernail against the side of his tinfoil hat. "That's what they want you to think. I'm telling you, they can get into your head. Mind-readers, that's what they are. You're lucky their brainwaves don't reach all the way up here. Have you got any foil? Because you're gonna need some of these before the Clankers come calling."

Vera licked her lips and glanced toward Len. Their host hadn't said a word, but judging by his facial expression, he wasn't thrilled about this new development.

"We, uh. We didn't know about the brainwaves, buddy." Guppie caught Vera's eye, and his face pinched slightly, a subtle indication that he wanted her opinion. It was the first time in a long time somebody had treated *her* as an insider and one of their neighbors as the person who couldn't entirely be trusted.

"Pammy, do you mind asking Cooper to bring out some supplies? I'm sure that Mr. Hawes is hungry." Vera adopted the detached professional smile that she used for customers and diffi-cult patients. Pammy scowled, and Vera flicked her eyes toward the house. *We shouldn't let him inside until we know what's going on. We don't know if we can trust him.*

She didn't have psychic brainwaves, as far as she knew, but Pammy nodded and stalked off toward the shipping container.

Guppie ushered Sean over to the weatherbeaten picnic table alongside the garden beds. Vera avoided sitting with her back to the woods, although she'd used the bench for sharpening her tools and cleaning produce. Sean dropped onto the bench with a sigh, and Guppie sat beside him. Uneasy with sitting, Vera hovered behind Guppie instead. Len kept his distance, watching Sean intently from a few yards away.

"What happened out there?" Guppie asked. "You were able to hide in the *basement?*"

"Only because they weren't ready for us yet." Sean reached two fingers beneath the rim of his makeshift hat to scratch at his scalp. "See, the first night, they killed anyone who went outside. A few people aimed for their cars, and a military van came through, but..."

"A military van?" Len took a step closer. "They tried to evacuate the town?"

The whole time Vera had known the man, Len had been tensed and watchful, but his reaction to this new information left him coiled more tightly than ever before. His hands balled into fists, and his thick chest heaved with some barely restrained emotion.

"Only one," Sean said. "And it was driving real crazy. Whoever it was went straight up to Cloverleaf. It didn't stop for anyone else."

"It was my uncle," Pammy said. She emerged from the house carrying a bottle of water and an energy bar; Cooper trotted behind her bearing a spoon in one hand and two cups of Chef Boyardee on the other.

"How do you know that?" Len demanded.

"I went by my house today." Pammy Mae dropped the supplies in front of Sean and slid in on his far side. "She left me a message. I think she got out—out of the town, at least. We have no idea how bad it is everywhere else, but if my uncle knew to come for her, he must know more about what's happening. The base might be prepared."

"Maybe that's where my parents went, too," Cooper said excitedly. He was the only one to sit down with his back to the woods, and Vera was tempted to move him bodily to safety.

Although, if they came for us now, what chance would we stand? Seeing their approach would only mean that we could stare death in the face.

"Maybe," Pammy echoed. She didn't meet Cooper's eyes and instead stared at a fixed point somewhere deep in the woods.

Sean tore open the wrapper of the energy bar with his teeth and ate the contents in two enormous bites. As far as Vera could tell, he barely chewed. When it was gone, he twisted off the cap of the water bottle and chugged it in one long gulp. His Adam's apple bobbed as the last drop disappeared, and the older man let out a breathy sigh. "I didn't see who they took, but the driver wasn't messing around. Me and Walker tried to wave 'em down and just about got run over."

"Walker Mills?" Cooper asked sharply.

Sean looked up at Cooper like he'd just noticed him standing there. His eyes lingered on his green hair. "You knew Walk?"

Cooper nodded. "Mr. Mills and my dad flew together all the time..."

Sean hooted. "I plumb forgot about that! Your daddy flew them big airplanes like Walk did back in the day. The two of them were thick as thieves," he snorted. "Before Home Depot, that is."

Cooper didn't seem to register the insult. "Where is he?"

"Didn't make it. Used to brag about how being a pilot made him so free." Sean rolled his eyes. "Didn't even make it off our block before all hell broke loose."

Cooper looked down, deflated. "It wouldn't have mattered. The airport was gone."

"Everything's gone now," Sean spat.

"But the military van," Vera cut in, turning back to Pammy. "You think you know where they might have gone?"

Pammy nodded. "Keystone. I've been there dozens of times. Mom wrote the name of the base on the inside of our garage door. I'm sure that's where they were going."

"Then we should follow them." Cooper's eyes glinted in the early afternoon sunlight. "Keystone is between here and D.C., right?"

"More or less," Pammy said. "But it's where I'm headed."

"Smart girl." Sean tore off the tin top of one of the cans and dug into his first helping of Beefaroni, smacking his lips with each bite.

"We should start packing." Cooper stood up. "We can load up the truck, and now that we've got the SUV, we can fit even more stuff in with us—"

"No." Len crossed his arms. "I'm not going anywhere."

Cooper gaped at him. "Are you serious? What's your plan, then? Sit around and wait for them to come up the mountain?"

"The plan was to survive. *Alone*." Len scowled around at the group of them. "I'm not kicking anyone out, but I'm not leaving, either. I've spent *years* getting ready for this. I made a *promise* that I was going to stay alive as long as possible. Whoever wants to stay, you're welcome to. If you want to go out there and get yourselves killed because you think the military gives a flying f—"

"This bunker of yours has an expiration date, and you know it." Cooper waved his hand toward the building. "There's no plan for *after*. This is endgame if we follow your advice, Len. There's nothing more than this."

Vera wrapped her arms around her middle and averted her eyes.

"It doesn't matter what your plans are," Sean said. He licked his lips; the canned tomato sauce had stained them bright red, leaving his mouth the color of an open wound. "Miss Butter wasn't wearing her hat. King Clanker's got his eyes on her now."

"*King Clanker*'s eyes are useless," Pammy said. "Something happened to them."

"He doesn't need his own eyes." Sean lowered his voice and pointed his plastic spoon at her. "He's got *everyone else's*. You know most of those critters in town? Those are his. They aren't the ones that came down on the first night. No, sir. Those are new ones. These suckers are multiplying like you can't believe. Put rabbits to shame, yessir," he said with a big hoot and a laugh.

"How do you know that?" Vera demanded. They'd all seen the eggs from her autopsy, but there was no reason to think the gestation period was that accelerated. *He probably just saw some eggs, just like we did, and his paranoid mind went right to the wildest scenario.*

Sean ignored her. "He's watching for you now, Miss Butter. You stood up to him. All of you. Do you know why they left us in the basement? They were saving us for later. All of us survivors are just insurance for the future." He lifted the half-eaten can of noodles. "We're his MREs. When they get peckish, they'll come out here for you lot, and when you killed his soldiers, you moved up the Doomsday Clock."

"I don't know about that." Pammy picked at a loose splinter in the top of the picnic bench. "But it doesn't matter. I'm headed to Keystone either way."

"Me, too." Cooper set his jaw. "Vera? What about you?"

"I..." Vera trailed off. Guppie had saved her life that first night, but she'd already returned the favor. Now her debt lay with Len, who was the only reason any of them had survived this long.

Len didn't need loyalty. The supplies in the bunker were dwindling faster than anyone would like. What he *needed* was a smaller drain on his supplies. Besides, Vera had already promised herself that she was going to find out what had happened to her family. Put that way, there was only one sensible choice.

"I'm going, too," she said aloud. "I'll leave most of the repellent and half the tools. It should only take us a few hours to get to Keystone. If you're willing to give us a day or two of supplies, just in case we have to bunker down for the night somewhere, that would be ideal."

"Well, I'm staying." Guppie shook his head. "I'll figure out how to pull my weight, Len."

"You're fools," Sean said amiably, scraping the last of the sauce out of the can. "But I can understand why you'd want to hide. As for me, I'm leaving, too. Now that King Clanker's seen me, he'll know how I kept him out of my head. I can't risk staying."

Vera heard something like disappointment in his voice. *Did he secretly relish an encounter with this King Clanker?* She wouldn't put it past him.

"If you all want to go, I'll give you enough supplies for the trip," Len said. "But for the record, I'm not going to track you down and bury you when the... the *Clankers* finish what they started." He turned on his heel and headed back to the house, calling over his shoulder. "Guppie, when they're gone, we can talk strategy. I'll pack some things for the rest of you. The longer you stay, the closer it'll be to dark." He slammed the door behind him so hard that the walls rattled, and one of the dogs barked from inside.

"Guess that settles it, then." Pammy got up. "We'll take my mom's car, and we'll stop for the ATV on the way out of town." She and Cooper headed back toward the house. Cooper waved his arms in excitement as they retreated, while Pammy's back stayed rigid and inflexible.

While Sean dug into his last can of supplies, Guppie got up and gestured for Vera to follow him. They walked over to the SUV, outside of Sean's line of sight.

"Are you sure about this?" he asked.

"Are you?"

Guppie placed one palm over his shoulder, where she'd bandaged his wound weeks before. "Listen, Vera, you and I make a pretty good team. Having a doctor around wouldn't hurt."

"A doctor isn't going to be much use this winter when your supplies run low," Vera pointed out.

"We could start planning runs into town. There were more supplies in the gas station. We have options."

"And that's safer?" Vera shook her head. "Cooper's right about the end date on hiding up here. If we make it to Keystone in one piece, we can send help back for you."

"And if you don't?"

"Then you'll have more time to figure out a plan for how to survive up here." She offered him a watery smile. "I don't know if you've noticed this about me, Mr. Martin, but I'm stubborn."

Guppie looked her over, then opened his arms. "I don't know if hugs go against your religion, but I'm giving you one."

Vera rolled her eyes and stepped forward, wrapping her arms around him. "Take care of yourself, Mr. Martin. *Guppie.* And watch out for Len."

"Keep those kids safe," Guppie replied. He sniffed against her ear and patted her back once before pulling away and rubbing at his eyes. "And don't get killed, all right?"

"Same to you." She stepped back. "And try not to go crazy up here."

Guppie pivoted and peered over the top of the car to where Sean was sitting. "No promises. You think he's onto something with those tinfoil hats?"

"Oh, please." Vera waved a hand. "That's the paranoia talking."

It didn't escape her, however, that she'd thought the same thing about people like Len before the sky fell. And look how *that* had turned out.

28

LEN

LEN STOOD BY THE SHELVES, sorting through the items at the front. A few of the MREs were coming up on their expiration date, but Cooper and the others would only need them until they reached Keystone. *Assuming that Keystone isn't overrun.* He pressed his fingertips against the packaging and closed his eyes.

The plan to flee the bunker was a foolish one. Giving away his supplies to the stubborn group was about as productive as tossing them into the trash, as far as Len was concerned.

And feeding yourself only to keep yourself alive for another six months? Or a year? Is that a better use of them?

On impulse, he tossed a handful of meals into the box at his feet. It would last the group a week, maybe more.

Deimos snuffled at his elbow and lifted his tail in a cautious wag. Phobos was more attuned to his training, but Deimos had always been better at picking up on his emotions. When he ignored him, Deimos dragged a wet tongue over his outer elbow.

"I'm fine, Deim. Go lie down."

Deimos lay down at his feet and stared up at him. When he narrowed his eyes, he wagged his tail again.

"Good Lord." He added a few energy bars to the box. "Don't be so sentimental. They stayed for a while, and now they have a new plan. This is the best possible outcome, anyway."

Deimos whined.

"I'm not upset," he insisted as he crouched down to examine the lower shelves. He added two bottles of Pedialyte to the box. "It's just that splitting up is *always* a bad idea. We're better as a group... although I don't know about this new guy."

Deimos rolled on his side to expose his belly.

Len reached over to give him a cursory pat. "We'll be fine without them. And Guppie's staying. Maybe we should plan some fortifications like he suggested. Anyway, I don't care that they're leaving. If they want to get killed, it's on them. I can't stop them."

"No, you can't."

Len flinched as Cooper knelt down on the far side of the bloodhound to scratch his chin.

"You know that you don't have to leave today," Len said. "Sleep on it."

"We were already planning to go. It was never an *if*, but a *when*." Cooper nodded to the box. "Looks like maybe you've given us more supplies than we really need."

Len flicked the box with one finger. "I figure that you're doing me a favor by taking off now. Even if I give you a few extra, I'm saving rations in the long run."

"If you say so." Cooper turned his attention to Deimos. "And who knows, buddy, maybe we're right. If it turns out that there are more survivors out there, maybe we'll be back with the big guns to settle the score."

Len's hands trembled. Cooper might trust the military to come through for them, but he knew better. The thought of a soldier coming to rescue their loved ones from Cloverleaf was nice and all, but Len had too much experience with vans pulling up in the night to assume that they always meant good news.

And yet, Pammy was so certain that her uncle had come to the rescue. So what was he supposed to do with that? Even if the rest of them could find safety at a military base, he knew better.

If they knew enough about the invasion to make it here in time, then they'll know who I am.

He'd seen what had happened to those who'd posted or even speculated about the Steward Message. Or rather, he'd seen them disappear. What would they do with him?

"Good luck." Len got to his feet, lifting the box of supplies along with him. "I mean that." His eyes burned, but he would be damned if he let Cooper see how much all this worried him. "Come on, let's get going. You're burning daylight."

Cooper and Deimos followed him up the stairs. Pammy was waiting at the top with her rifle clutched in both hands.

"This is yours," she said.

"Nah." Len pushed past her. "I've got plenty of supplies. You take it. I'll give you some more ammo, too."

"We're leaving the other ATV," Pammy said.

"Good to know." Len headed out the door, and Phobos leaped up to follow him. The dogs could tell that something was wrong, and they stuck to his heels as he strode out to the SUV. Vera already had the hatchback open and had already stowed an array of long-handled garden implements, the chainsaw, and two packs of insecticide spray cans.

"I left you everything else," Vera said. "For your fortifications. The flamethrower, the repellent, all of it. I hope it makes up for everything."

"You don't owe me jack." Len slid the box in alongside everything else.

Vera laid one hand on his back. "Of course we do."

The kindness and affection in her voice only made Len angrier. He shrugged Vera off. "We're not friends. We're allies, and this is the new tactic. Unless you make it back here eventually, we'll never know who was right."

"So I guess we'd better make it," Vera said. "Until then, good luck."

Screw luck. Len curled his lip back in a sneer and stomped off toward the door of the house. He didn't need to see them off. Watching people leave was a bad omen, anyway.

What they were doing was desperate. It was reckless. It was dumb.

Just like his brother had been.

He didn't need luck. What he needed was a strong drink and for everyone else to leave him alone and stop making him care so damn much.

29

GUPPIE

AS THE SUV PULLED AWAY, Guppie waved them off. As they rounded the bend in the gravel drive, he almost called, *Come back! I've changed my mind!*

Instead, he lifted his hand in a final wave, and turned his back on the departing vehicle. He could understand why everyone else had left, but the only one who had the slightest idea of what was going on was still in the bunker. If Guppie had learned anything in the military, it was to stick close to the guy with insider information. They were the ones who knew when and where to seek cover, and they were more likely than anyone else to make it out alive.

Guppie gathered up the trash from Sean's impromptu meal and returned to the house. Between Sean and the corpse of the Clanker, he hadn't had a chance to eat anything since that morning. He'd grab some lunch, talk to Len, and see what his plans were for fortifying the bunker.

The shepherd lifted its ears when he walked in, and Guppie stopped in his tracks. Len sat at the small kitchen table with his dogs lying at his feet. In one hand was a shot glass. In the other, he held a bottle of amber liquid.

"Whiskey?" Guppie breathed. "You've had *whiskey* here this whole time?"

"Just because I let you all crash here doesn't mean I was obligated to share everything." Len jerked his head toward the cabinets. "Grab a glass, partner. It's just you and me now."

Guppie dumped the trash and retrieved a mug, then sat down on the end table that they'd been using as a makeshift chair. "Listen, Len, I know that you're all about being independent, but like you said, it's just you and me now. If we're going to work together, don't you think it would be fair of you to tell me what you know?"

"*Fair* is a pretty strong word." Len poured a double into Guppie's mug. "Since when is the world fair? Is any of this *fair?*"

"They killed your wife, didn't they?" Guppie wrapped his hand around the mug. "That's why you don't trust the feds?"

Len snorted. "The feds. The government. Hell, the whole system. It doesn't take much to have a healthy distrust of authority." Len tossed back his glass and immediately reached for the bottle again. "But I don't know."

"Meaning...?"

"I don't know if she's dead." Len slammed the bottle back onto the table. He didn't bother with the cap this time. "Is that what you want to ask about? My wife?"

Guppie took a swig of his whiskey. It was the good stuff, with the deep, rich flavors of oak and woodsmoke that didn't burn like hell on the way down.

"Carla was working at NASA." Len spat the words. "In one of the facilities in D.C. She was working on her doctorate. She had a degree in astrophysics and wanted that 'Dr' in front of her name. They had her sign all of these NDAs, so I don't know too much about what she did. They had sent out a probe almost a year before, the *Stark*—some of this she told me, and some of it I've pieced together since. Anyways, they got a transmission back. Something out there sent it." He waved up at the roof. "She was excited about it, at least at first. She loved it there, even if she couldn't talk about it much."

Len fell silent, and they both took another drink.

"Then things changed." Len closed his eyes and the lines in his face deepened. "I think it started a couple months before. They were doing these simulations. She couldn't say much, but they were... *disquieting*, was the word she used. She said they were nothing, but she started acting strange. Nervous. Not paranoid, exactly, at least not at first. She would sit out on the back porch of our condo at night watching the sky. She called it 'problem-solving.'"

Len tapped his glass on the table. "Then one evening I get this text. Some number I've never seen. I mean, it wasn't even a phone number. Just showed up as like 4 random digits. No message, just an audio attachment with a bizarre alphanumeric file name. I was this close"—he pinched his fingers together and squinted through them at Guppie—"to deleting it. I mean, I don't open random attachments. Who does? To this day, I don't know why I did. But I did. And it was Carla. I'd never heard her like that. Ever. She was out of breath like she was running. I could hear voices in the background."

He knocked his knuckles against his forehead, squeezing his eyes even more tightly shut. "I didn't understand. She told me to hide, that she was coming home but her employers might come for me first. She was calm about it. *Frighteningly* calm, but she was talking fast."

"Do you remember what all she told you?" Guppie asked.

"That she'd intercepted a message about aliens, and that the government knew. That they knew they'd be vicious and powerful.

Just like that. Just 'Hey honey, space aliens are real and they're gonna violently invade soon and, you know, be careful.' What do you do with that? She was... scattered. Almost delirious. I thought she'd lost her goddamn mind, but you can tell a lot from a person's voice, you know? Somebody you've known your whole life? She was terrified, but her head was clear."

Len let his eyes drift open and lifted his cup again, but didn't bring it to his lips. "She told me to find a place where the feds wouldn't look for me, and to arm myself. I'm honestly not sure what frightened her more, the threat of *aliens* or the people she worked with. I kept thinking that there was another explanation, but she was so shaken. If you knew Carla, you'd know that wasn't like her. The worst part was, I couldn't ask questions. I couldn't do anything but listen. I replayed it like thirty times, standing there in the living room. Which was stupid. I should have been hiding."

"So she was right?" Guppie cocked his head. "They sent somebody?"

"Yeah, *somebody* is right. Not just cops. Agents. Men in black, as crazy as that sounds. I spotted them too late to run. We had a crawlspace under the porch. I had just enough time to get there and lay completely silent. I was like a corpse. I didn't see what happened. I just knew there was a racket inside."

Len tossed back his second drink. "When they were gone, I finally came out. They trashed her office. Took all her notes, everything. I think that's what convinced me. I tried to get in touch with her colleagues, but their numbers were disconnected. It was like they were all *erased*. And then this message got leaked online... the Steward Message, they called it. People on the internet thought it was a hoax, but I knew. One of the guys she worked with, a real prick it sounded like, was named Steward. Then everything about the file dried up online, and I knew they'd made it disappear. I knew they'd disappear me, too. So I disappeared first."

"Hell in a handbasket." Guppie poured him a third drink, then capped the bottle. "No wonder you're skittish. I assume that's why you didn't go public."

"Come on." Len curled his lip. "Do you think that I could have gone to the media with this? You know how people are. Everyone would think I was on drugs, or crazy. The feds wouldn't have to get involved, because nobody would take me seriously."

Guppie nibbled his bottom lip. Rumors had circulated through Little Creek about the guy building a cabin way out in the woods. A few of the contractors he'd hired had joked about it in O'Toole's bar. They'd made snide comments about how he was off his rocker —or his meds. Nobody had piped up to ask if he knew something the rest of them didn't, and Guppie certainly hadn't assumed that he was operating on insider intel.

"No," he said at last. "We wouldn't."

"Do you know the last thing she said on that message?" Len gulped. *"Promise me you'll survive. I'll find you if I can.* Carla risked everything to warn me. If she'd been able to make it out, she would have tried to save the rest of you. She'd have figured out the right words. Even if she could only convince one rinky-dink, ass-backward little town of rednecks, she'd have tried. She would have wanted me to save as many of you as I could. But what am I supposed to do when people want to leave? There's no hope for them in Keystone. The military doesn't give a rip about their safety. This is foolishness. They're going to be eaten alive."

"Hey." Guppie reached over to squeeze Len's hand. "You already saved them. Maybe you're wrong about this. Maybe they're going to pay it forward and save someone else, and it'll all be on account of you. And Carla. I'm sure she'd be proud."

Len's mouth twitched, and he pulled away. "Maybe so."

Guppie was about to say more when he heard the rumble of

the SUV's wheels in the driveway. He sat up, tilting his head toward the door.

"Sounds like they came to their senses." He let out an involuntary sigh of relief. "That didn't take long."

The shepherd's hackles rose, and his nose twitched. The dog let out a growl so low that the reverb echoed through Guppie's chest. The sound outside grew louder, and Guppie was suddenly aware of the fact that it was coming from more than one direction.

"That's not the SUV." Len lurched to his feet and flung himself toward the door, throwing the heavy bolts across the top and bottom. A moment later something pinged across the roof above them like a hailstorm, accompanied by a growl of what might have been thunder.

Last time Guppie had checked, the sky was clear.

Maybe we should have tried our hand at making a couple of tinfoil hats.

30
COOPER

THEY LET VERA DRIVE.

After the incident on the road that first night, Cooper didn't trust himself behind the wheel. Sean didn't offer, not that anyone would have suggested it.

Cooper didn't like Sean. He didn't know him, admittedly, but he knew *of* him through Walk. Walk was one of the sweetest old guys Cooper had ever met. Every time he came into the Country Duke, he had a smile on his face. Sean ... wasn't that way.

The news about Walk hit Cooper hard. Maybe it was just that Walk reminded him so much of his father. If he hadn't made it out, what were the chances his father had?

He put those thoughts firmly out of his mind. The house had been deserted. His parents were half Walk's age. They'd made it out; he just had to find them. Just like they would find Pammy's family.

Pammy sat in the back seat, watching out the window for the place where she'd left the ATV.

"Here," she said, tapping one finger against the glass. "Pull over."

"Might as well stay in the road," Vera said. "Not like we're going to encounter cross-traffic." She put the car in park and killed the engine.

Sean poked his head up front between the seats. "You know, you use more gas turning the vehicle on and off."

"Noted," Vera said. "But we're also quieter this way."

Pammy slid out of the back seat, and Cooper followed her. "Are you sure that you want to do this?" he asked.

"Don't worry, I'll stay close," Pammy told him. "I don't like having us all in the SUV at once, you know? The more vehicles we have, the more options we have."

And you don't want a repeat of the night Nate died. Neither of them mentioned it when the topic could be avoided, but the horror of that moment was always on Cooper's mind, and he had no doubt that it lingered with Pammy, too.

"I'll stay out front on the road, just in case I need to—" She stopped in her tracks and her mouth fell open.

The ATV stood in front of them, surrounded by fallen branches.

"What's wrong?" Cooper asked.

"I didn't leave it like this." Pammy Mae took a tiny step forward. "It was hidden. I covered it with the branches."

He shrugged. "So they fell off. Come on, we need to keep moving."

"Cooper." Pammy pointed at the ATV. A charred object sat on the seat.

Cooper squinted at it for a moment. It almost looked like a skull, but it wasn't human. "What is it?"

"The head of the Clanker I killed." Pammy backed away. "Cooper. *Run.*"

Something shifted above them, and Cooper raised his eyes to the branches overhead. Dark forms stirred among the leaves, just out of sight. Then came the echoing whine that had followed them out of Little Creek that first night, like a cicada song.

"*Run!*" Pammy screamed. She bolted toward the ATV, kicking the head of the dead Clanker aside. "Get to the car!"

Cooper did as she commanded. Pammy had her shit together, and she didn't need Cooper slowing her down. His feet slipped on leaves as he scrambled toward the road. That horrible, whistling hum filled the air around him, drowning out even the sound of the ATV. It throbbed against his eardrums like another heartbeat.

"Start the engine!" he bellowed as he approached the car. "They're here, they're here, they're he—"

He was reaching for the handle when something struck him, and he fell with a bolt of blinding pain. Cooper wasn't even sure where he'd been hit. Agony radiated out from his lower back, knocking the wind out of him. He rolled over and found himself pinned beneath the legs of one of the Clankers as it raised its serrated proboscis above him.

The back door of the SUV whipped open, smacking the Clanker to one side and passing only inches above Cooper's face.

A pointed, long-handled hoe emerged through the door and struck the creature alongside its torso. As the alien's many legs sought purchase on the ground beneath them, Sean leapt out of the back of the SUV and raked the tip of the hoe across the Clanker's glittering eyes, gouging a rough furrow through its lenses.

"Get the hell out of here!" he spat.

The monster fell back, chittering as it went, and Sean kept advancing, striking the creature again and again with such fury that the beast collapsed under the onslaught. Sean's skinny arms never stopped moving. He battered the Clanker until its thorax split open, letting out one last rattle as it died.

Sean stood over his fallen enemy, waving the hoe above his head and screaming into the woods. "Who else wants a piece of me? Huh? Go tell your alien king that *this is goddamn America!*"

Cooper struggled to his feet and wiped at his face where the Clanker's blood had spattered across his cheeks. "Sean," he croaked. "Can you see her?"

"I don't see a single one of those cowardly little buggers." Sean lifted the hoe about his head with both hands. "Because they know better than to mess with me, don't they?"

"Not the Clankers." Cooper clung to the door of the SUV. "Pammy. Where's Pammy?"

He could just see the ATV from where he stood. Its seat was empty, and other than the SUV's engine, all the sounds around them had died. The ATV was off, and the other Clankers had vanished. As for Pammy Mae, there was no sign of her.

They took the keys. *Somehow, they were smart enough to know to take the keys.* He hadn't heard the ATV come on because it never had.

They knew she would come back for it.

Sean was right. They're after her.

"Come on, boy." Sean pushed him through the open door of the car. "I told you before, King Clanker had his eye on Miss Butter. What the King wants, he gets."

"No," Cooper groaned. He'd told himself that he didn't have to worry about her, that she was the one member of their party who could handle herself. Now, there was no sign of her, not even a smudge in the dirt.

He closed his eyes as tears dripped down his cheeks. *They got her. Just like Nate.*

Once again, I failed.

31

LEN

THIS WAS the moment Len had been waiting for, ever since his wife had told him to get out of the city. He had built the bunker to weather this very storm, and of course it had come right after the one time that Len let his guard down. When was the last time he'd had a drink? Eight months ago? A year?

"Basement," he snapped. "Now."

Phobos bolted for the trapdoor, and Deimos followed, looking back at Len for confirmation.

Something struck the shipping container door from the outside, and the metal buckled against Len's shoulder.

"You've got your gun, right?" His voice sounded as if it was coming from someone else, someone who wasn't the least bit alarmed. He was already taking stock of the room, measuring what they would need to take with them.

The sounds outside continued, but the creatures weren't battering themselves against the metal anymore. It was all too easy to picture them slinking around the walls of the bunker searching for weak points and seams, like foxes taking stock of a chicken coop.

"Gun's right here." Guppie drew his pistol as he backed toward the trapdoor.

Len removed his weight from the shipping container door and took a few cautious steps away. Even with the mayhem of so many unexpected houseguests, he had stuck to his old habits: his protective gear still sat by the door, and he had kept the dogs' control collars charged on the solar battery that powered the bunker. He snatched up everything within reach and did a quick sweep of the interior, painfully aware that every second he spent up there could count against him.

The metal roof above them emitted a grating squeal as a saw-toothed limb punctured the steel. Phobos snarled from the stairwell.

There was no point in prolonging the inevitable. Len rushed toward the stairs and dragged Guppie along in his wake. They stumbled on the top step, and Len reached back to pull the trap door in place. Two long rebar poles braced the reinforced door against the concrete foundation, and Len slammed them into place with his free hand.

"Looks like we might've made the wrong call," Guppie observed. "Should've taken off when we had the chance."

He shook his head and pelted the rest of the way down the stairs. "You seriously think that the folks outside are prepared to deal with something like this? You think Vera is prepared to throw down with an army of aliens? How many guns did they take?"

A note of mania had entered his voice, but Len was powerless to control it. He should have insisted that the others stay. He should've forced them into the basement at gunpoint for their own good. He had known better, and he had still let them go.

"Hey." Guppie said. "Not helpful. You can't spin out on me like that, partner."

That was fair. "Sorry, you're right. We have a plan for this."

"We do?"

The plan. Of course there had been a plan. Ever since the bunker was built, Len had been running through it, looking for weak points and flaws.

"First, close the door." He took a deep breath and forced his voice back to a place of neutrality. "Whether it's the feds or the invaders, stay belowground."

"There's more than that, though, right?" Guppie asked.

When they had taken his wife, Len had forced himself to lie perfectly still in the crawlspace under the porch. He had found himself right over an ants' nest, and thousands of the tiny creatures had taken offense. They had crawled all over him, biting him as they went, desperate to protect their home from a creature too large and too dangerous for their simple minds to comprehend, never guessing that Len knew exactly how angry and violated they felt. Unlike the ants, he had no way to bite back. All he could do was hold his breath, ignoring the stings, and hope like hell that the men above didn't think to look underground.

Two of them had walked out onto the deck, silhouetted by the flashing lights that had surrounded the complex.

Wasn't this one married? one of the men had asked. *There should be a husband around here somewhere?*

Doesn't matter. Even if she warned him, he's a nobody. He won't be trouble for us.

He'd kept every muscle perfectly still, lying stiff as a corpse in the damp earth, powerless to protect the woman he loved, to defend himself, even to swat at the stinging ants that had crawled into his nose and ears. He'd been incapable of making trouble then.

Times had changed.

"Yes," he told Guppie. "I built it to be difficult to get in here. They'll take their time battering down the doors, cutting the power, shutting off every chance at egress. They'll drive us underground, and if they're satisfied that we won't make trouble, they'll leave us alone."

Guppie looked around the bunker.

The lights above them fizzled and died. His companion let out a yelp of alarm, and one of the dogs growled—most likely Phobos, by the sounds of it—but in the darkness, Len felt strangely reassured. This was part of the plan.

He reached for the flashlight on his Kevlar vest and switched it on.

"Do you like dogs?"

Guppie held his hand up to block his eyes from the beam. "Is this a good time to be talking? Shouldn't we be *doing* something?"

Len picked up his go-bag from the unfinished space under the stairs. "Nope. If they just cut the power, that means they're still outside. Battery's on the roof. We'll wait until they come knocking on the door." He pointed the beam of the flashlight to the rebar holding the trap door in place.

Guppie made a little sound of frustration. "And then what?"

"Are you sure I should tell you?" Len scratched Deimos behind the ears. "What if they can hear your brainwaves?"

"Son of a—" Guppie's groan became muffled as he buried his face in his hands. "You've flipped your switch. Gone off the deep end."

"Maybe. Maybe not. What makes you think that Sean Hawes is any crazier than I was when I built this place?"

"Fine. Yeah, I like dogs." Guppie gripped his pistol in one hand and watched the trapdoor.

"Are you familiar with rat terriers?" Len slipped the command collar around Deimos's neck and powered it on. "Little dogs. They make good pets. But even when they aren't trained as working dogs, their instincts get the better of them. Once they hit on a target, their prey drive overrides all of their other instincts." He buckled Phobos's collar in place, too, before sliding his earpiece on. "They'll go after their quarry with such intensity that they'll bury themselves alive. Plenty of them have gotten stuck in burrows and warrens, unable to back out, while their prey uses another exit to get away."

"Hang on." Guppie lifted one hand to stop him. "Are you saying...?"

Len turned his flashlight toward the back wall of the concrete bunker where a gun-safe stood. "Time to find out how strong their prey drive is."

32

GUPPIE

LEN WAS out of his goddamn mind—and had clearly spent too much time alone with his dogs if he was comparing the aliens to terriers. His grin was made all the more unsettling by the strange shadows thrown across his face by the flashlight.

More sounds sifted down from above, although they were muffled by the concrete walls above them.

"Now might be a good time to do whatever you have in mind," Guppie whispered. Now that Sean had put the idea in his head that the Clankers could read their minds, Guppie found himself almost believing it.

But that wouldn't make sense... the one in the gas station didn't know what we were doing. If it had, Vera and I would both be dead. It wouldn't have been distracted by exploding chip bags or my impromptu soda gun, because it would have known that both were harmless.

That didn't rule out the possibility that they could understand human languages, of course, but Guppie doubted that, too. Still, there was no point in taking unnecessary risks.

Len got to his feet and crossed the concrete floor of the bunker until he reached the safe. He spun the dial a few times, and the door swung open, revealing a hole in the concrete behind it. The safe was a few inches deeper than it seemed from the outside.

"Is it set *directly* into the wall?" Guppie whispered.

Len patted his shoulder. "Good luck tearing it off the wall," he whispered back. "Come on, boys." He stepped up into the safe and into the tunnel beyond, waving the dogs forward.

"You're nuts," Guppie hissed as he stepped inside. "How did you afford all this?"

"Carla and I played the stock market and got out at the right time," he whispered back. "And I built in a recession." He pulled the door shut behind them and spun the knob.

The ceiling of the concrete tunnel was low enough that Guppie had to walk hunched over, and even then his head kept brushing the ceiling. If he'd needed further proof that Len was off his gourd, the tunnel proved his point.

I'm glad he's on my side, he thought.

After a few feet, the tunnel sloped sharply upward, giving way to steps. Guppie had to crush himself against the wall so that Len could shimmy his big body past him and mount them first. Eventually, they reached another trapdoor.

"Stay," he told the dogs, and Guppie assumed that the instruction was meant for him, too. He waited until Len opened the door a sliver and peeped through. He turned off the flashlight, allowing the diffused sunlight of the world outside to illuminate his line of sight.

"All right," Len whispered. His voice was barely audible even in the narrow space. "We should have cover for now, but I want to make sure they're all inside before we do anything. Stay quiet."

The dogs seemed to understand this last command. They

followed Len through the manhole cover without making a sound, and Guppie struggled after them, holding his breath.

They were inside a shed, the one where Pammy had stored the ATVs. A stack of lawn implements, battered cardboard boxes, and a lawnmower blocked the manhole cover from view of the door. Pammy probably hadn't even realized it was back here.

A few breaker boxes were set along the back wall, out of easy reach of anyone who might stumble into the shed. A window was set into either shed wall, one facing the bunker, one facing the drive. If he craned his neck, Guppie could see the entirety of the bunker, including the last scuttling form of a Clanker disappearing through a gash in the roof.

"What's to stop them from coming after us?" he whispered. The image of a small dog working its way deeper and deeper into a burrow stuck with him, but once the Clankers heard them start the truck, they would come swarming back out. He wasn't sure how many of them there were this time, but given how much of a racket they had made on the roof, it was safe to say there were at least a dozen of them. Maybe more. Maybe a lot more.

We don't know that we can outrun them.

Len licked his lips. "Do you see any more out here?"

"No." If they left on foot, they might get a head start, although that wouldn't do them much good in the long run. How long would it take for the aliens to realize that the bunker was empty and the quarry had slipped away?

Len stood upright, making a sharp gesture to the dogs as he did. Both of them immediately lay down, watching him as if he were the only creature in the world. Guppie had met a lot of dumb dogs in his day, but if these two were willing to trust Len without question, he reckoned that was probably the thing to do. Not like he had much choice now, anyway.

Len opened a metal box mounted on the back wall. Instead of

the usual series of breakers that Guppie had anticipated, this box revealed nothing more than a light switch. On the top of the face plate, someone had placed a Mr. Yuck sticker. On the bottom, written in Sharpie, was simply the word *NO*.

"Ready?" Len asked.

He didn't have the faintest idea what he was supposed to be ready *for*, but it didn't matter. He didn't give him time to answer. He flipped the switch upward and flattened himself against the wall.

Nothing happened.

Guppie peered around, hoping for a better view. Maybe he had released some kind of chemical weapon? Or somehow activated a remote lock that would seal the door to the basement of the bunker? The dogs didn't move a muscle.

After what felt like an eternity, Guppie turned to Len with a question on his lips. Len's mouth was moving, but no sound was coming out.

Three, he mouthed. *Two. One…*

With a crack louder than any thunder, the world blew apart. The window facing the house blew inward, sending a shower of broken glass spinning through the interior. Guppie lifted his hands over his head and dropped into a crouch as the tools in front of him shifted.

For the first few seconds, everything seemed to be moving toward him. Then the floor slanted away, and the boxes and lawn implements slid forward. The dogs' nails scrabbled against the shifting boards, and Guppie fell forward onto his knees, still trying to protect his head and the back of his neck. His ears rang, and at first he thought he was going blind until he realized that a tremendous puff of dust and dirt had been flung through the shattered window. He coughed a few times before he was able to pull the hem of his T-shirt up over his nose and mouth.

It seemed to take an awfully long time for the dust to settle, and even then, Guppie didn't move. He kept waiting for the roof above him to collapse.

When it didn't, he opened one eye. A terrible silence had settled over the property, the sort of extreme stillness that followed a shelling or the detonation of a bomb.

"What in the hell happened?" His voice came out raw and ragged, but at least it proved to him that he hadn't gone deaf.

One of the dogs whimpered, and Guppie looked up to see Len moving toward the door of the shed.

"Watch out for the glass," he said. "And keep your gun handy."

The bloodhound looked as shaken as Guppie felt, but between the four of them, there wasn't a single scratch. His legs wobbled beneath him as he rose to his feet and followed Len out the door.

Stepping through outside was like emerging on foreign soil. There was nothing left of the bunker, not even rubble. The earth had swallowed it whole.

"How...?" he rasped.

"I built the bunker over a sinkhole." Len descended along a new decline alongside what was left of the garden beds. "I figured I wouldn't need as many explosives to collapse the structure if there was a cavern underneath."

"And you rigged that all up to a *light switch in the shed*?" Guppie peered over the edge of the hole. Chunks of concrete were visible beneath, mixed in with limestone and the twisted carcass of the shipping container. All of it was slowly sinking beneath the water table.

"Yeah, well, I worked with what I had. I couldn't very well commission someone to build me something fancier." Len scanned the ruins.

"Sociopath," Guppie mumbled.

Len turned his back on the ruined bunker and clasped

Guppie's shoulder. "I'm pretty sure you have to be a sociopath to survive past the end of the world." With that, he climbed back up the slope to the uneven ground where the pickup sat.

What does that say about me? Guppie wondered, but it didn't really bear thinking about.

"Len?" He hurried after him. "What now? What's the plan?"

Len had always been fierce to the point of being mildly terrifying, but something in his demeanor has shifted. He was touched, like Sean was touched.

"I can't speak for you," he said, "but I left them alone. I played nice, and still, those bastards came for me in my house. Now, I'm coming for theirs."

BEYOND LITTLE CREEK

Lake Spivey
Jonesboro, Georgia

———

Celia Morris lay on the covered dock on the shores of Lake Spivey, unable to move. In the beginning, she had struggled against the strange foamy substance that held her in place. As time passed, however, she had begun to drift. The wooden slats no longer dug so painfully into her back; her flesh had softened, eaten away by the caustic substance, and Celia had begun to ooze between them.

At first, Celia and Wilson had hidden in the attic of their Jonesboro home. They'd been able to bring enough supplies along that, by Wilson's calculations, they could survive for one hundred and twenty-six days before they'd need to go out again. When he'd explained this to Celia, she had nodded and clutched her knees to her chest and bitten her tongue.

One hundred and twenty-six days.

Food was not going to be the problem.

At first, their biggest problem had been the aliens. They had huddled in the corner of the attic, biding their time while the infrastructure of Atlanta's suburbs collapsed around them. Wilson had clutched his Bible to his chest and uttered prayers for their deliverance. He was convinced that the invasion was a sign.

Celia wasn't so sure. If this truly was the end of days, shouldn't it all be over quickly? Wouldn't the world come unmade in six days, returning to the silence of the void on the seventh, unmade in the order that it had been created?

When the floods began, Wilson thought it was another sign. "Like Noah in his Ark!" he hissed to Celia.

Celia stared up at the rafters in silence while the storm pounded on their new metal roof. It had come with a lifetime guarantee.

Doesn't need to last much longer, she thought wryly. *We're getting there.*

The storms were followed by a heat wave. The heat in the attic had been more than uncomfortable—they had left Celia desperate for water and choking on the stench of their homemade latrine. Those had been the worst days of her life.

And then Wilson had died.

That was what broke her, in the end. She'd lasted four days in that infernal heat with what was left of her husband. It was his heart that had killed him, Celia was certain. It wasn't his first heart attack. She'd recognized the signs.

That was when she'd known that this wasn't the Lord's work. The truth became obvious as she lay in the attic, sweating, aching, and bereft. Celia had already died.

She was already in Hell.

Trapped in the foam prison made by the demons that had overrun the city, Celia stirred. She wasn't sure how long she had been there. It had been a long time since she could open her eyes, even to tell if there was daylight outside. Now, when she tried to blink, she could *feel* her eyelids move, but the slow decay of her body had already taken her sight. Celia was being digested alive.

Like Jonah in the belly of the whale. That was what Wilson would have said.

Something stirred outside her makeshift cell, and a moment later, she was pierced by a terrible, relentless pain. Celia moaned as she was lifted up; patches of wet, swollen skin sloughed off of her as she was carried away. It seemed to her that she could hear water lapping at the shore of the lake, but she'd heard water for some time. When she was a girl, she'd held a seashell to her ear and listened to the sound of the waves trapped inside. *No, Ceelie, it's only the pulse of your own heartbeat echoed back to you,* her mother had explained.

Celia was tired. She'd been tired for a long time. By the time she'd crawled out of the attic, she'd already given up. She wanted to get back to Wilson. He'd found a way to escape, and he'd left her behind.

She was going to get him back.

The creature carrying Celia tipped her forward, letting her slide beneath the waters of Lake Spivey. She couldn't feel the cold; she couldn't feel much anymore, only a brief whisper of terror when the water filled her nose and mouth.

I'm coming, Wilson, she thought. *I'm coming.*

A hundred little mouths engulfed her.

Dying didn't take as long as she'd feared it would.

33

VERA

SEAN BUNDLED Cooper into the back seat while Vera tried to figure out what the hell had just happened. Once again, the aliens had come for them, and once again, she had frozen up.

"Drive," Sean ordered. His tinfoil hat was slightly askew, and there were flecks of white spittle in the corners of his mouth. "Put the pedal to the metal, darlin'."

Vera Khan never had been, and never would be, anyone's *darlin'*, but this clearly was not the time to belabor the point. She started the engine and laid on the gas.

"We gotta find her," Cooper said.

Vera shook her head. "I'm sorry, but she's gone." How exactly that had happened, Vera still couldn't quite work out.

"No no *no!*" Cooper pummeled his fist against the back of the passenger seat. "They weren't *hunting*, Vera. They took her. They left a warning. They took the keys."

"King Clanker doesn't mess around," Sean hooted.

"What are you talking about with this *King Clanker* business?"

Vera asked. It was a straight shot down the road, and she kept her eyes on the treeline, watching for some sign of the creatures that had attacked them. There had been more than one, but in the chaos, she couldn't say with any certainty *how* many had fallen upon them.

"I told you... he's the boss. He tells all the other Clankers what to do with his *psychic energy!*" Sean swirled one finger around his temple. "They aren't puppets, exactly, but he pushes them here and there, tells them where to go and who to hunt and what to do when they catch us."

"Like a general," Vera murmured.

Cooper nodded. "They're not acting on instinct, Vera. They're smarter than we thought, and they're after Pammy."

"And they got her," Vera insisted. "This doesn't change the plan, Cooper. If anything, it only makes it more urgent. We have to get to Keystone before they catch up with us—"

A deep rumble echoed in her ears, and the ground shook beneath them. Vera almost swerved off the road in alarm.

"What was that?" Sean bellowed.

Cooper swung around in his seat, peering out the hatchback window. "Oh, *no.*"

"What?" In the rearview mirrors, Vera watched as a plume of dust and smoke rose from the mountain behind them.

"The bunker." Cooper's voice wobbled. "The bunker's *gone*, V."

They couldn't see the site through the trees, but Cooper was right. The cloud of dust was certainly coming from behind them, from the side of the mountain where they had left their allies.

Guppie. Vera gripped the wheel in a chokehold. *Oh, Len.* The Clankers must have arrived at the bunker around the same time as they'd pulled up to the ATV.

Out of their little group of five, only two were left.

That only made it *more* important that they look for someplace safe to land. They owed it to the people they'd left behind.

"Vera." Cooper sat back down and stared at her in the mirror. "We have to find Pammy. I'm not leaving without her."

Vera immediately switched on the vehicle's child locks; they had just reached the paved route, and she didn't put it past the young man to bail if he got an answer he didn't like. "I hear what you're saying, Cooper, but you need to listen to me. That's not how these things work. They're... bugs or crustaceans or something. They don't plan ahead. Pammy's dead. I'm sorry."

"Dammit, you're not listening!" Cooper exclaimed, at the same time that Sean shouted, "*Look out!*"

Vera hadn't been paying enough attention to the road. She'd been too worried about Cooper's response to the attack and hadn't noticed the makeshift barrier that now barred the road. An assortment of cars, some of them on their sides, covered the road.

She bit off a curse out of old habit and spun the wheel. The SUV spun and came to a stop only a few feet from the vehicles.

Cooper leaned forward between the seats. "I don't remember this being here."

"It wasn't," Sean said. "When Miss Butter brought me up this way, the road was clear."

"Funny." Cooper shot Vera a sidelong glance. "It's almost like they boxed us in. But what kind of *bug* would be smart enough to do that?"

Vera swiveled in her seat to examine the wall of vehicles. "Think we could move them?"

"Yeah, if we went out in the open and made ourselves into Clanker-bait!" Cooper exclaimed. "It's obvious that they put them here to block our path."

"They're not for us," Sean said. "They just wanted Miss..."

Vera held up both hands and pressed her palms to the wheel.

"I get it! I get it. Will the two of you just *knock it off* for *one second.*" She threw the SUV into reverse and spun the SUV around, almost clipping the guard rail in the process.

She took the county highway in the opposite direction, toward town. She didn't like getting so close to Little Creek, not knowing what was hiding out among the buildings. At least she could drive at a steady clip. On their way down the mountain, they passed a wrecked Jeep that had been crushed against the rail, with its canopy torn asunder.

"Where are you going?" Cooper asked.

"We're *going* to Keystone, and from there, I'm going to D.C. If you want to rally the troops and come back with help, good for you. But I can't do this, Cooper. *We* can't do this. The three of us can't succeed where Pammy and the others failed. They were the fighters. They were the tacticians. You and me? We're the peace-makers. The planners." Vera lifted one hand from the wheel to gesture sharply to the back seat. "And I'm not going to speak for you, but for my part, I don't trust Mr. Tinfoil Hat back there in a firefight."

"Hey, now." Sean crossed his arms. "You, of all people, should understand where I'm coming from with the head coverings."

Vera snorted. "You've got to be—"

"*Look out!*" Sean and Cooper screamed in tandem, but this time Vera had seen the barricade well in advance. A row of cars was lined up, blocking the road at the far end of town. She braked in plenty of time to stop. Unfortunately, that left them out in the open with no way to get around the obstacle.

"Dammit," Vera breathed. "What do we do now?"

"We can't run," Cooper said. He leaned between the seats. "Don't you get it? They're after us. They're not going to let us get out of Little Creek."

"Maybe we could take one of the side streets and go around

the back way..." she began, but even as the words left her lips, she glanced up the road to her left and saw the downed power line; beyond it lay a pile of rubble.

"We'll have to abandon the car," Cooper said.

Vera squeezed her eyes shut. They couldn't even retreat to the bunker: there was no way out now but forward, and they had no one to rely on but themselves. No one was coming for them.

And what if Pammy's Keystone theory was wrong? What if the base had been overrun in the last few weeks? What if every city and every town on Earth had toppled?

What if they were the last three humans left alive?

"Hey." Cooper's hand closed over her shoulder. "Vera. Deep breaths, okay? Look at me. I've got an idea."

"Okay." Her voice came out as a squeak. "Hit me."

Cooper pointed up ahead. "The Country Duke is just up the road, on the far side of the blockade. If you can get me up there, I can wrangle a piece of heavy equipment, and we'll come back this way. I'll move the vehicles out of the way, clear the road, and you can head out for Keystone, okay?"

Vera nodded. She didn't like the fact that Cooper left his own future plans out of the description, but she'd take it for now. "We leave the SUV, then?"

Cooper nodded. "But we take the keys."

"And we're just going to go out there with our fists raised?" Sean demanded.

"Nah." Cooper hooked his thumb toward the back. "We're gonna be armed."

WHEN VERA HAD ANNOUNCED her plan to move to the country, her mother had launched a protest campaign in an attempt to dissuade her. This had consisted of family movie nights featuring horror movies set in small towns, long-winded discussions about the dangers of rural life, and dozens of links to true-crime articles and podcasts sent via both text *and* email.

You never meet chainsaw-wielding maniacs in D.C., her mother had said, to which Vera had replied, *That's right, Mummy, only politicians.*

Never in her wildest dreams had Vera imagined that *she* would become the chainsaw-wielding maniac, but as they prepared to set out for the Country Duke, she hoisted the saw in both hands.

"Are we ready?" Sean asked. He was holding a can of Raid in each hand, and had two more tied to his belt among his homemade tin can bombs.

"Born ready." Cooper brandished a long-handled garden mattock. "I'll take the lead. Sean, you take the rear. Vera, if we run into trouble, fire up the saw."

Vera nodded and wrapped one hand around the starting cord.

"All right." Cooper jerked his head toward the sidewalk. "This way."

Walking too close to the buildings left Vera on edge. She kept waiting for something to scuttle out through the broken windows above them, or appear over the tops of the buildings. The fact that she couldn't *see* anything didn't help. They were here, in town, *somewhere.*

"I don't like this," she hissed. "Where did they go?"

"Maybe most of them were up at the bunker," Cooper suggested. "And the rest took Pammy."

"Took her where?" Vera asked.

"To their castle," Sean said. "Their castle on the hill."

Vera shook her head and looked down at her feet. Sean and his madman riddles were driving her up a wall, but he was still on their side, and she'd dealt with enough cases in the ER to know that he probably wasn't *trying* to yank her chain...

Sometimes, it bothered Vera that she couldn't just come out and say what she was thinking, but in this particular instance, the desire to quash her annoyance saved her life. She saw the shadow moving behind her just in time, and although she couldn't have said *what* she had noticed, she knew without a doubt who—or rather, *what*—had cast it.

Vera sidestepped just as four spear-like forelimbs struck the pavement at her feet. A shadow was visible, moving below the grate of the storm drain beneath them, while the spidery limbs emerged from the opening at street-level.

"They're in the sewer!" she bellowed. With that, she fired up the chainsaw.

Cooper reacted instantly; he swung the gardening mattock down in an arc, with the fork side first, and caught the Clanker right behind its head. The beast's rattle was audible even over the roar of the chainsaw. Cooper jerked the Clanker, hard, yanking it out of the storm drain and into the open air. It flailed and jabbed at them. This one was longer and skinnier than S-001, but it boasted half again as many limbs, all of which were longer. Vera was *fairly* confident that they had an extra joint, but she didn't stop to wonder about intraspecies dimorphism. Instead, she raised the chainsaw, and with a bellow that would have given her mother the vapors, she brought it down on the beast's peaked spinal column. Black ichor spilled from the gouge in its exoskeleton and clung to the chain, which shot upward and flecked against Vera's face and chest.

The chain cleared the belly of the Clanker, which broke in two. Its limbs still skidded on the sidewalk, but Sean was already on top of it, spraying insecticide into the open wounds. The ichor fizzed and bubbled on contact, and the creature shuddered.

Vera let the chainsaw die in time to hear the insecticide cans fizzle while Sean hollered, "I said die, you ugly egg-laying sonofabitch!"

Vera's heart pounded in triumph, and she bared her teeth at Cooper in what was supposed to be a smile but felt more like a snarl. "Thanks."

"No problem." Cooper straightened up and rested the handle of the mattock on his shoulder. "Who says we're not combat-ready?"

Before Vera could respond, a low rumble emanated from the sewer beneath them, the echo of a dozen or more creatures converging in the depths.

Vera squared her shoulders and lifted the chainsaw again. "Ready for another round?" she asked Cooper.

Sean's empty cans of pesticide pinged off the cement behind her. "No time for that. Hit the decks, kids."

Vera turned her head toward him. "What—?"

Sean shoved between them and dropped a tin can through the opening of the storm vent.

Vera dropped the chainsaw and followed it to the ground, landing so hard that she knocked the breath out of her lungs. She wrapped her arms over her head and held her breath.

The blast wasn't as loud as she'd expected, and it certainly didn't compare with the size of the explosion that had rocked the mountainside earlier. It *was,* however, enough to lift the metal grate a quarter inch in the air. This was followed by a shower of roofing nails that clattered to the ground and chimed against the steel grate.

By the time Vera sat up, Sean was already on his feet.

"That won't slow 'em down much," he said. "And now they know exactly where we are. Got to keep moving, kids!" He took off down the sidewalk toward the Country Duke with his sandals flapping loudly against the pavement.

Cooper righted himself, and Vera retrieved the chainsaw. She made sure that the SUV keys were still in her pocket before jogging after them.

34

COOPER

SEAN WAS skinny as a rail and mad as a hatter, but when he set his mind to it, the man could run. Cooper was soon out of breath. Then again, Cooper was regularly out of breath.

"We should have trained with Guppie more," he told Vera.

"I didn't see the point." Vera's expression hardened. "I figured if the survival of the human race depended on my ability to do cardio for any length of time, we might as well accept our fate."

Cooper hadn't spent a lot of time one-on-one with Vera. On the surface, they had the least in common: he didn't know the first thing about horticulture, and *she* didn't seem like the type who was big on video games or equipment repair. Their paths had rarely crossed, even in a town the size of Little Creek.

On another level, however, Cooper was confident that they had plenty in common. They were both outsiders who would never quite fit in, no matter how hard they tried.

Sean had already reached the parking lot of the Country Duke, and by the time Cooper's feet hit the tarmac, Sean was tugging at the handles of the double doors.

"It's locked," he shouted.

Cooper caught up to him, pulling his keyring out of his pocket. "We'll go around back. I've got an employee key." It was a good thing his boss had never gotten around to installing the security upgrade; most of the other Country Dukes had upgraded to a digital keypad and alarm system, but the power was down so often that it didn't seem worth the hassle, and anyway, nobody ever tried to break in.

Vera caught up with them, and Cooper led them to the employee entrance. All of the windows and doors were intact, as far as he could see. The lights were off, but there were enough windows at the front and back of the box store that even in the deeper recesses of the store, they could still see fairly well.

As they walked down the aisle of goat and rabbit feed along the back wall, Cooper wrinkled his nose. "Do you smell that?" he asked in a stage-whisper.

"Spoiled feed?" Vera asked.

Sean shook his head and patted one of the bags. "Naw. The stuff they put in feed now, a bag like this'll keep for a year or more, unless it gets wet. That isn't spoiled grain, anyhow."

Cooper shuffled sideways until he could see up the aisle. "It almost smells like..."

"Ba-*brawk!*" Something white leapt off the shelf toward Cooper, flapping its wings in his face.

"Aurgh!" Cooper lifted his arms to fend off his attacker. When he looked up again, he saw a small white rooster standing on the floor in front of him with its feathers puffed out and its long comb flapping.

Vera let out a snort-laugh. When Cooper turned to glare, she covered her mouth, but she wasn't able to stifle her mirth entirely.

Chick season had been wrapping up when the world ended, and the manager had marked the last Silkies down to a dollar the day before the party in the woods; they'd already been feathering out. Apparently they'd been old enough to survive the loss of power, and had the run of the store ever since.

"Don't worry, mister." Cooper held up his free hand to ward off the irritable bantam. "I'm not gonna bother you."

A few curious clucks echoed around the store from the tops of shelves where the other birds had come to rest.

"Here. I've got a peace offering." Cooper dug the tines of the mattock fork into the nearest bag of feed and tore it open. As the pellets tumbled to the ground, the rooster stopped posturing and hurried over to investigate. Cooper tore open a few more bags, although he knew from experience that chickens could peck holes in the feed bags without *too* much trouble.

"Where are they getting water?" Vera asked as three hens came down to join the pint-sized roo.

"Probably from the buckets we put out to catch spills when the roof floods." Cooper knelt down to stroke one of the hens. It was nice to think that, even though the town had been practically razed, signs of life were still popping up here and there. The aliens wouldn't wipe out everything.

Sean licked his lips and reached for a chicken. "We could take one for later..."

Cooper held up the mattock to block his way. "Nope. We've got food in the car, and a plan for escape. Leave them be."

"Soft-hearted," Sean murmured, but when Vera caught his eye, she nodded her approval.

"Come on," Cooper said, getting to his feet. "Let's go back to the shop and see what we can snag."

Sean gazed longingly at the hens for a moment before he allowed himself to be led away. As they passed by one of the rain buckets, Cooper glanced inside. It was more than half-full. If he left one of the doors propped open, the chickens could leave if and when their supplies dried up.

A hundred years from now, there might be a wild bantam population in the woods of Little Creek and the Crag's Head Gamelands.

The other option—that the chickens, like their human counterparts, would be picked off by their otherworldly enemy—flitted through his mind, but Cooper pushed it aside. If he let himself think like that, there would be no point in anything. If he didn't allow room for doubt, then he could force himself to keep moving.

He was alive.

His parents were alive.

The chickens would survive.

And Pammy... she was alive, too, although with every passing moment, he knew that the likelihood of finding her in time was shrinking.

Better find her soon, then.

As far as excavators went, the one kept in-stock at the Little Creek Country Duke wasn't the biggest on the market, but as Cooper's father would have said, it was nothing to shake a stick at. Instead of tires, it ran on heavy treads, and even at rest the hydraulic arm reached well past the roof of the shop.

Prior to his presumed death, his boss, Dick Ansel, had taken great pride in the oversized equipment, although he'd never sold the one they kept on the lot. Most of the small farms in the area didn't require anything that heavy, and the bigger ones—mostly aggregate farms bought out over the years by larger companies—custom-ordered their equipment directly from the manufacturers for a lower price.

You're never gonna sell that hunka junk, Bobby, the mechanic who'd trained Cooper, often complained.

Probably not, Dick had agreed, *but man, don't it catch the eye?*

If Dick were still alive to appreciate the fact that his pride and joy would be used in the fight against Earth's enemies, it would have done him proud.

"You sure you know how to drive this thing?" Sean asked, staring up at the cab. "Sure is a big'un."

"Have a little faith. If I can fly an airplane, I think I can drive an excavator." Cooper hauled himself up into the Caterpillar.

Sean snorted. "So you're a pilot like your old man, eh?"

"Nope. But I took some lessons with Mr. Mills."

"Figures. Just proves how crazy Walk was," he grumbled as he followed. "But that was Walk. He was a softie, too."

Cooper turned the starter on the Cat, and it rumbled to life. "Trust me, I know my way around heavy equipment, Mr. Hawes. Other than video games, it's about all I've been doing for the past four years."

"Video games, for cryin' out loud! All that shootin' and stabbin' and fighting aliens and zombies seemed like a load of nonsense. And I guess I was right, 'cuz when the aliens came, it didn't do you a lick of good, did it? Let's hope you drive better'n you shoot."

"You haven't *seen* me shoot," Cooper said as Vera piled in behind him.

"My point exactly," Sean said. "If you could, you'd have a gun. That girl's better equipped to fight the King than you are."

"If you're talking about Pammy, she does *everything* better than I do," Cooper observed. "And probably better than you."

He drove back toward the barricade, keeping the Cat slow and steady. It took him three tries to figure out how to maneuver the arm properly, but when he got it, he was able to shift the blockade aside one car at a time. When the road was clear, he pulled the Cat aside to make room for the SUV to drive through.

"You made that look easy," Vera said as Cooper opened the door.

"Hey, look at me," Cooper said. "I did something right for once."

"Don't sell yourself short. It's not the first time."

The SUV was right where they'd left it. They approached with caution, giving the storm drains a wide berth, but there was nothing hiding under the vehicle waiting to attack, and the keys were still safely in Vera's pocket.

"I guess your bomb gave them a run for their money," Vera told Sean.

Sean hooked his thumbs through the belt loops of his cargo shorts. "They've been working so far."

Vera tossed the chainsaw onto the passenger seat and climbed in, but to Cooper's surprise, Sean didn't reach for the back door.

"Are the two of you coming?" Vera asked.

Cooper shook his head. "I told you my plan. I'm going to take the Cat and look for the Clanker nest."

Vera groaned. "Come on, Cooper. We've had two lucky breaks in a row. Let's take advantage of it. Len would want us to."

"Maybe that's what Len would *want*, but it's not what he would do." Cooper backed away a step. "He could have hidden out in his bunker that night, and we'd all be dead by now. He had a way to stay safe, and he risked everything on the off-chance that he could save a few more lives."

"Pammy isn't—" Vera began again.

"Even if Pammy's dead, I'm not leaving until I know for sure. And if she is... if she is, I'm gonna take down the King." Cooper lifted his chin.

The night of the invasion, Cooper had learned what kind of man he was when faced with danger he didn't understand. He was the guy who ran when he didn't think winning was in the cards.

Not now. He couldn't go back in time, but he could prove to *himself* that he was the kind of man who stuck by his convictions.

Vera's eyes swept over him, and she sighed. "What about you, Sean?"

"I was fixing to come to Keystone with you, but I figure if some chubby kid with green hair and permanent marker on his nails has the balls to stand up to the King, shoot, I can't leave now." Sean scratched his chin. "Besides, there's nothing left for me out there. I might as well tell that bugger to stick it where the sun don't shine."

Vera pressed her lips together in a thin line.

"Hey." Cooper took a step forward and laid his hand on her arm, squeezing gently. "I understand that you don't want to stay, and I'm not trying to change your mind. Go to Keystone. We'll catch up if we can."

"Why do people *always* think it's a good idea to split up in situations like these!" Vera exclaimed. "You don't even know where you're *going*."

"Sure we do." Sean bobbed his head. "The nest."

"And where is that, exactly?"

He turned away from them and pointed one knobby finger up the hill toward where the gabled roof of Heartland County High School peered over the horizon.

"The school is his castle, and the town is his fiefdom," Sean intoned.

Cooper gritted his teeth. Pammy Mae was in there, assuming that she was still alive. That figured. High school had been the bane of his existence; it stood to reason that an army of gut-sucking aliens would gravitate toward that area. "Then that's where we're going."

Vera hesitated for a long moment, and Cooper wasn't sure if she was worried about them, or simply reluctant to head out on her own.

"Take care, Vera," Cooper said. "Have a safe drive, okay? And if you see my parents, tell them that I love them."

"Will do," she said. "Be careful, Coop."

She closed the door behind her, and Cooper waited until she started the engine before turning back toward the Cat.

"Nice lady," Sean said as the SUV pulled away. "Kinda makes me wish I had given her shop a chance. I always figured she was just here to gather intel for when the Arabs took over the States."

Cooper rolled his eyes and bit back a groan. Still, being with Sean was better than being alone, and even if he wasn't Cooper's first choice of ally, he seemed to know more about the Clankers than anyone else alive... not that there was a huge sample to draw from.

Cooper fired up the Caterpillar and set out toward the north side of town, hoping against all reason that Sean was right.

35

PAMMY MAE

PAMMY MAE WOKE with her cheek pressed against a cold surface and an unfamiliar damp substance pressed against her lips.

Ew, she thought vaguely, *am I drooling in my sleep? Nasty...*

Gradually, she became more and more aware of her surroundings. She was lying on a flat, cool substance—concrete, perhaps?—with her belly pressed against the floor and her arms at her sides. Judging by the crick in her neck, she had been there a long time.

She tried to move her arms, but they wouldn't budge. Something was holding them in place. When she tried to open the eye closest to the floor, the liquid stung her eyeball; the other lid would not move at all. The damp sensation covered her whole body, not just her mouth, and whatever it was seemed to be responsible for holding her in place.

The last thing she remembered, she had been in the woods. The keys to the ATV were gone, and the aliens had dropped down from the trees... and that was all. Anything after that was a blur.

That first night, when Sam had been pulling his *Take us to your leader* routine, the aliens had reduced him to jelly in a matter of seconds. Her last conscious thought had been that she wouldn't survive the day, and she'd never make it to Keystone.

And yet, here she was, alive and kicking. Or at least, attempting to kick. Her legs were no more mobile than her arms.

She didn't waste time wondering if this was some strange version of the afterlife. Her momma had drilled it into her head from an early age that there were only two places she could go after death: 'up,' or 'down.' She wasn't comfortable, so this definitely wasn't Heaven, and given the absence of Hellfire, she was confident that she hadn't gone 'down' either.

Robbed of mobility and sight, Pammy was forced to rely on her other senses. When she listened intently, she could make out a fizzy pop, like freshly-poured soda in a wide-mouth glass. Beyond that, there were echoes of things moving around outside of whatever bubble she currently inhabited. They reminded her of sound traveling over water.

Or the natatorium.

The pool building had been constructed in Heartland County High only a few years beforehand, when she was still in middle school. Pammy's mother and her friends had complained about the rise in zoning taxes, but the kids loved it.

The longer she listened, the more certain she became. She'd wondered where the Clankers had made their nest, and during her rounds, the high school had seemed like the obvious choice. Now, she wondered if the Clankers had been observing her from a distance with the same intensity that she'd observed *them*. If so, it certainly explained how they'd gotten the jump on her.

Experimentally, Pammy opened her mouth. Since her face was pressed against the floor, the wet substance hadn't been able to seal her chin in place. As her lips parted, a foamy, bitter liquid dribbled in. The instant it hit her tongue, the liquid went flat.

The taste was enough to make Pammy gag, but since it was the only movement she could make, and the alternative was lying there and waiting for the Clankers to return, she spat out what remained in her mouth and tried it again. Within seconds, she found it easier to breathe, and before long she was able to open her eyes.

A white substance, like carbonated shaving cream, filled her whole field of vision. Pammy sucked in another mouthful and spat it out, leaving the foam even thinner. Now she could see dark shapes moving around, but she couldn't make them out clearly.

Careful, now. If you expose yourself too much, they'll realize you've come to, and they'll come back for you.

She took her time, pausing between each mouthful of the sticky substance. At last, a small window opened up, letting her see out into the natatorium.

In hindsight, she wished she'd stayed blind.

The room was bristling with Clankers. Their leggy black bodies lined the pool deck and the walls, and something stirred in the water not far from where Pammy lay. Other white, foamy lumps filled every corner of the room: the other citizens of Little Creek, presumably.

I've got to get them out of here, Pammy thought. She tried to move, but the foam held her fast. Now that she could see it from the outside, she realized that the lumps reminded her of something. *Spittlebugs.* A few times a year, Jerry Peterson had waged war on juvenile froghoppers, claiming that they damaged his ornamental grasses, and the residents of Cloverleaf had watched in amusement as he applied a mixture of hot peppers, garlic, and liquid soap to the little foamy outcroppings formed by the insects. Pammy had always thought they were cute, although the name was off-putting, and she wasn't a fan of the sudsy messes they made in the grass.

Now, she could appreciate the fact that the bugs had at least been *small*. Most times, Pammy didn't mind insects, so long as they weren't scions of an alien race sent to exterminate her entire species.

As she watched, one of the aliens approached the pool. It leaned its thorax over the water and extended the joints of its abdomen. Pammy watched as the tip of its thorax spread open, and dozens of the jelly-like eggs emerged, slipping beneath the surface of the pool only to bob back up.

The chlorine from the pool must have evaporated weeks ago. The chemical smell she remembered from gym classes of years gone by had been replaced with a muggy, swampy odor. From her current angle, Pammy couldn't get a good view of what lay in the depths, but judging by how many eggs had been inside the one Vera had sliced open, she could guess.

The Clanker's ovipositor closed, its thorax tightened, and it shook itself like a dog after a swim. Then it ambled over to the nearest lump and drove its front legs into the foamy prison.

Pammy flinched, imagining the person inside, but the figure that the Clanker dragged free was in no position to complain. The body was so badly decayed, Pammy couldn't recognize who it had been before, or even what gender they had been. The alien dragged the body over to the side of the pool, leaving a wet trail across the pool deck where the feet trailed on the concrete. Then, with a mighty heave, it flung the body into the water.

For a moment, the body floated. It bobbed once as something from below tugged it. A few seconds later, it bobbed again. Soon it was shuddering, as hundreds of unseen mouths took bites out of the remains. In less than a minute, what was left of the person sank into the deep end.

Sean said that they keep us the same way we store MREs. The spittle surrounding her was simply the bioorganic equivalent of foil-lined packaging.

The Clanker went about its business, passing within inches of Pammy's face. It didn't come for her, but the horror of the moment left her stomach churning. As bad as the corpse's fate had been, Pammy was more concerned with how it had ended up in that horrible state. Had the person been dead when they were captured? Had they died in the foam? Or had some corrosive chemical in the spittle slowly eaten them alive?

It was in my mouth, Pammy thought in disgust.

All the same, she'd learned an important lesson. The Clankers had taken her to their lair, on what they thought was their home turf. Technically, they were right. But Pammy knew the high school layout by heart, and now she knew the location of the alien hatchery.

I hope that's worth something to me before I'm dead.

BY THE SECOND hour of spitting, Pammy's mouth was finally going dry. She was giving serious consideration to using another body fluid to help free her, but so far the notion was still too disgusting to take seriously.

Even though it could keep you alive?

Yeah, she thought, it might. But a girl had to have standards.

Instead of kicking her arms and legs at random and exhausting herself, Pammy adopted a new tactic. She flexed her muscles for a few seconds at a time, doing her best to make small, controlled movements. Her progress was slow, but bubble by bubble, the alien spittle gave way, until it was possible for her to wiggle her shoulders.

Her skin was tingling, which didn't seem like a good sign. On the other hand, the Clankers around her hadn't moved much since the one had laid her eggs. They seemed almost... dormant. Sleepy. Did bugs sleep?

As tempting as it was to make a break for it, Pammy forced herself to keep working on her mobility. If she took off before she was ready, and got stuck mid-escape, it wouldn't matter what the aliens were doing.

She had almost made enough room to roll over when the Clankers around her began to move again, and Pammy immediately forced herself to lie still. She squeezed her eyes shut in frustration.

I wasted my chance. The aliens were waking up, and soon feeding time would come around again, and they would see that Pammy's eyes were visible through the foam, and it would all be over. Her escape attempt would be voided.

Pammy was so lost in lamenting her fate that she didn't register the aliens' response at first. They had begun to rattle again, and their combative thrum had a different quality than it did just before they attacked. If anything, the way they raised their forelimbs like threatened spiders seemed almost defensive. They surrounded the pool, not watching where they stepped; one of them put its feet right on top of Pammy, and its limbs sank through the foam to her level, jabbing her in the ribs as the creature crawled over her. Pammy held her breath in case they could hear her breathing.

She needn't have bothered. The aliens were all focused on the far corner of the natatorium.

Pammy held her breath. Only then could she hear it: an echoing drone outside the building. As the sound outside got louder, Pammy realized that it was mechanical in nature, too deep and too consistent to resemble the call of the Clankers.

She raised her eyes to the roof, following the Clankers' line of sight. Something was coming, and she could only hope that it was on her side.

They knew it was coming before I could hear it, she thought.

For the last few weeks, she assumed that the creatures 'spoke' to each other using that call. But what if sound wasn't the point? What if they could feel the vibrations in the air or the ground?

It would go a long way to explaining why Sean thought that they were psychic. If she was right, that meant one more fact about the Clankers that she could understand... and exploit.

All she had to do was live long enough to figure out how to use it against them.

36

VERA

VERA DROVE SLOWLY, watching the Caterpillar in the rearview mirror. She was no stranger to leaving people behind, but her choice to escape D.C. had stemmed from her desire to move *toward* the future she wanted, not away from the one she feared. She hadn't *abandoned* her parents. She'd simply moved on.

To some extent, that was her intent as she drove past the Country Duke: to move *toward* a future in Keystone, and eventually return to D.C. This time, however, it felt a whole lot more like running away.

She couldn't bring herself to really lay on the gas, which was one reason it took almost a quarter of a mile for the alert icon to pop up on the SUV's dash. "What now?" Vera groaned, squinting at the image. If the oil needed to be changed, it could wait, but if the fuel gauge was low she'd have to find someplace to pull off and use the gas can *while* watching her own back.

It was a circle with a wiggly line beneath it. *Tire pressure.*

Her heart sank. Now that she was aware that something was

wrong, she could tell that the car was handling poorly. She was riding the rim on at least one wheel. Maybe more than one.

She stopped the SUV, but left the engine idling as she opened the door. It didn't take a mechanical genius to figure out the problem. Small silver circles dotted the front driver's side tire.

Roofing nails, she thought grimly. *Just like the ones Sean used in his homebrew bomb.*

All four tires were flat. She'd thought they were lucky that nothing followed them to the Country Duke. Getting the car back had been so easy—*too* easy. And it wasn't like aliens needed to use nails to do the job.

They'd wanted to send her a message.

Sean was right. The Clankers weren't just insects.

Vera slammed the door, closed her eyes, and pressed her forehead to the steering wheel. If the Clankers had done this, they were probably following her. It was possible to ride the rims for a while, until she was well out of sight of the town.

And then what? Hope that you can make it all the way to Keystone on four flat tires? Risk breaking down along the way, in unfamiliar territory?

You're alone, Vera. There's no one to ask for help. You can't leave it up to someone else to decide what to do.

Vera's lip quivered as she lifted her eyes to the rearview mirror. A single dark shape moved in the road behind her. Even the way the aliens walked was different from beast to beast. They'd had plenty of time to study humans, and no doubt knew all about their weaknesses.

As it approached, Vera glared at it. Her dismay hardened into resolve. This was *her* town, too, no matter what anybody said. Sure, she was a newcomer, but she worked hard to make space for herself, and she'd *done* it.

Now, that life was over, and she had no way to pick up the pieces. The Clankers were to blame for that.

How does that make you feel, Vera? she asked herself.

Makes me angry, she answered. *Actually, now that I think about it, it makes me mad as hell.*

She spun the steering wheel to the left until she felt it bang against the stop and then mashed down on the gas.

The SUV hesitated for a moment; then she heard metal grinding and her theory about riding on rims was confirmed. She didn't care. If anything, it made the SUV that much easier to spin around.

By the time she was turned around and facing the Clanker, she could see that the beast was approaching the car directly. Maybe it didn't understand what she was doing. Maybe it just didn't care. Either way, she quickly picked up speed, aiming to ram it.

Just as the Clanker looked like it was going to disappear under the hood, it pounced. One of its forelegs speared the hood as the rest of it rotated over.

She barely realized what was happening before another foreleg came down on the roof of the SUV and punctured through it like it was aluminum foil.

Vera just managed to dive sideway onto the passenger seat as the alien appendage stabbed into the headrest.

The underbelly of the creature was splayed across the windshield, with the proboscis unfolded and open against the glass.

Something banged hard against the side of her face and sliced into her cheek. It was the chainsaw bouncing around in the passenger seat.

She snatched it up and yanked the ripcord in one motion.

The sound of it inside the SUV cabin was deafening. She swung it upward, but the car was veering wildly now and her momentum threw her forward and she sent the tip of the chainsaw into the front windshield.

It might have been shatterproof, but it wasn't chainsaw-proof. As it juddered into the glass, the whole front windshield seemed to buckle and fall inward, chunks of shattered glass bouncing off the chainsaw and pelting her face and upper body.

She kept pulling in a wide arc with all the strength her upper body could muster. Fueled by adrenaline and righteous anger, she started to scream incomprehensibly. She waved the saw so wildly it was a miracle she didn't take her own arm off in the process.

The saw finally swung all the way over above the steering wheel, and it smacked right into the soft underbelly of the Clanker sprawled across the space where the windshield had been. The chain juddered again, this time against the beast's exoskeleton for a moment, before finding traction.

A stream of the alien's dark, oozy insides was flung back in a stripe across her face. She closed her eyes just in time to avoid the blowback, but her mouth—still open in a scream—wasn't so lucky. The insides were bitter, with a faintly meaty flavor that should have turned her stomach.

It didn't. For the first time in her life, Vera experienced blood-lust, and the rancid tang of the Clanker only spurred her on.

The beast made a deep, reverberating sound and pulled back away from her and down the hood. The chainsaw, wet with Clanker blood, slipped out of her grasp and went dead still sticking out of its underside. A mass of meat and ligaments hung out of the exoskeleton around it.

Vera was back to sitting upright now and the bloody steering wheel was in her hands. She slammed on the brakes and the front of the SUV dipped down hard as the Clanker went sliding off the hood and tumbled over the front grille.

She screamed again and crammed her foot back on the gas.

She waited to see a foreleg come swinging up again on the hood, but the damage from the chainsaw must have been enough. The Clanker slipped under the SUV and she felt the left front side of the vehicle leap up into the air. That was followed a moment later by the back left doing the same and she was flung forward violently into the seatbelt — which she only in that moment became aware she was wearing.

She slammed on the brakes and looked behind her at the still form of the smashed Clanker in the middle of the street.

"Have you had enough?" she screamed. "Or do you want more? Because believe me, you sonofabitch, there's more where that came from!" The sound of the curse leaving her own lips was enough to startle a wild burst of laughter from her.

This was what happened to Sean. He cracked, just like you're cracking. Vera could almost feel her rational, reasonable self peeling back as she shed it like an old skin. But what was the point of thinking rationally when the whole world was spun on its head?

After waiting to see if there was any other movement, either from the Clanker or in the surrounding trees, she collapsed forward on the sticky steering wheel, breathing hard.

"Is that all you've got for me, King Clanker?" she screamed.

When nothing filtered back to her but the echo of her own voice, Vera sat back. She reached down to the door and found one of the water bottles Len had given them only a couple hours before. Taking a deep swig, she considered her options.

It was getting late. Even this time of year, she only had a few more hours of light. If she left now, she almost certainly wouldn't be able to reach Keystone before nightfall... assuming that the SUV was still up to the task.

And then what? Head to D.C. alone, and look for her family? What would she say when she found them? *Yes, Mummy, that's right, I left a child to face the alien hoard on his own. Well, no, he wasn't a little kid... just a young man who wanted to find his family, but he wanted to save his friend first, so I sent him off alone with a corn-fed Good Ol' Boy and saved my sorry hide. Yes, Mummy, I recall my oaths. "I will remember that I remain a member of society, with special obligations to all my fellow human beings, those sound of mind and body as well as the infirm."*

As she sipped from the bottle of water, Vera's eyes were drawn up the hill, where the roofline of the high school was still visible.

She still had every intention of going home... but she wasn't going there without Cooper. She should never have left him in the first place. Maybe when the aliens punctured her tires, they had done her a favor.

Little Creek might be done with her, but Vera couldn't say the same. Her friends needed help, and Vera was going to make sure that they got it.

Pammy Mae's backpack still sat on the floor of the passenger seat. She filled the pack with the rest of the insecticide, the bottled water, and their emergency medical kit. She tucked a pair of gardening shears in the back flap, point-down, wrapped in one of Pammy's discarded shirts to keep the blades from puncturing the bag.

Vera briefly considered bringing the chainsaw as well, but she wasn't interested in going back to the dead Clanker and she wasn't sure how much fuel it had left anyway. Instead, she hefted a fiber-glass-handled, pointed gardening shovel out of the back. Leaving the door ajar, she rested the handle against her shoulder, pulled the book bag into place, and set out toward the school.

37

GUPPIE

GUPPIE SAT in the bed of the truck as Len drove toward town. Most of the supplies that Vera had left them had been set in the shed, and Len had rooted through them before their departure. He'd tossed objects into the bed, seemingly without rhyme or reason, and Guppie had watched, still numb from everything that had happened earlier.

Len was out of his mind. And yet—here was the part Guppie struggled with—he had been *right*. One thing was certain: Guppie wasn't going to doubt him again.

The bloodhound sat in the cab with Len, but the shepherd was in the back with Guppie, watching him with clever, mistrustful eyes. The critter seemed to think that *Guppie* was responsible for the explosion earlier.

The woods were strangely quiet as the truck rattled down the gravel service road. Perhaps it was the shock of the explosion, and the sensation of having dodged fate yet again, but Guppie was feeling particularly introspective as they rattled along. His eyes drifted over the mountain laurels and low-lying evergreens nestled among the canopy of upright oaks and meandering maples, entwined with creepers. Rocky outcroppings littered the slopes, the bones of the mountain breaking free of their mossy flesh, peppered with ferns, milkweed, barberry, and wild garlic. Guppie had lived most of his life in the midst of this casual, half-wild beauty. Aside from the 'skeeters and the ticks, the West Virginia wilds boasted a kind of quiet ruggedness.

It'll all be like this when we're gone, he thought. *The whole town will return to the woods.* The aliens might be dead set on destroying the human inhabitants of the town, but they were unlikely to stop and weed dandelions from between the cracks in the sidewalk.

Guppie was still staring out into the woods when he spotted a familiar vehicle: Pammy Mae's ATV, still standing amid the brush. He frowned—it didn't seem like the kid to leave it behind, but maybe Vera had talked some sense into her. The idea of her riding out in the open left him anxious and twitchy.

"These kids deserve better," he told Phobos. "You know, Sean and I always used to gripe about how the kids these days were too soft and didn't take things seriously, but I guess Pammy showed us. Even Cooper isn't what I thought he was."

Phobos pricked his ears and sat up, tilting his head to one side. A questioning whine emanated from his throat.

Guppie twisted around to look down the hill toward town. The lowest houses along the road weren't visible, but the trees were thinning out this low on the slope. He squinted, gripping the butt of his pistol with his free hand.

"What is it, boy?" he whispered.

He expected to see a cluster of Clankers headed their way, but as far as he could tell, there was nothing. Then his eyes re-focused a little, picking out a bright-yellow box in the distance, chugging away up the slope on the north side of town.

"Well, I'll be dipped," he mumbled. "Where did they get an excavator?" No wonder they'd left the ATV behind. They'd traded up.

He pried open the back window separating the cab from the bed. "I take it you're seeing this?" he asked Len.

The shepherd growled and shifted closer to Guppie, ready to defend its owner from any perceived threat, but Len said, "*Down!*" in an authoritative voice that would have done a sergeant major proud, and the dog immediately dropped against the rubber liner of the truck bed.

"Yeah, I see it," he responded, turning onto the county highway leading toward town. "I'm assuming it's one of ours."

"We following 'em, then?" Guppie asked.

Len nodded. "Pammy figured that they might have holed up in there."

Guppie cocked his head. "I don't remember her mentioning that."

"We talked without you a few times," Len said. "Just one-on-one."

"If she had intel, it seems like she should have shared it with all of us. I thought the plan was to make decisions as a group."

Len's eyes flickered away from him in the rearview mirror.

"Hey." Guppie squinted at him. "What else did you talk about in these cozy little chats? Anything else I should know?"

"We... we may have discussed whether it was wise to kill one. When we agreed to go after the one that Vera cut up, Pammy expressed some concern that we might be painting a target on our backs."

Guppie groaned. Time had slipped away from him—Pammy's foray into town had come only the day before. He hadn't put two and two together, but it made sense in hindsight. She'd kicked the hornets' nest, and the Clankers had responded.

"We needed more information," Len said. The defensive note in his voice caused Deimos to raise his head.

"I agree," Guppie said, resting his elbow on the sliding track of the window. "But in the future, I hope we can trust each other a little more. I'm not thrilled about the fact that I've spent the last few weeks sleeping over a stash of C4 without knowing it, and given that this alien autopsy thing blew up in our faces, too... I'd like some warning, next time."

Len opened his mouth to argue, but Guppie held up his hands.

"It was your bunker. I get it. Your home turf. But we're all on our own now. So what do you say to the idea that we work together from now on? As equals."

Len's eyes bounced between his reflection and the road. Guppie could understand where he was coming from; after he'd been discharged, he hadn't trusted anyone. He'd walked on eggshells around people for *years*. He'd driven away every woman who'd been willing to give a relationship with him a shot, because he didn't *trust* people anymore. He'd needed to be in control, because letting his guard down—even the smallest fraction—had been so terrifying that he couldn't face the prospect.

So he got it. But he also knew it didn't work, not anymore at least.

"Hey." He leaned closer, until he risked falling through the little window. "If we were in peacetime, we could take it slow. Test the limits of our comfort zones. But this is war, Len. I'm not one of your dogs. If we're going to survive this, we've got to work together."

Guppie knew exactly how hard it was for Len to say, "Okay. I promise. And when we get to the nest, I'll run my plan by you before we try it, okay?"

Guppie nodded, and his mouth curled up at the corners. "So you've already got a plan, then?"

He nodded. "It's gonna sound crazy."

Guppie slapped the edge of the window as they descended toward the high school. "Far as I can tell, crazy's the only thing keeping us alive."

38

COOPER

"YEE-EE-EE-HAW!" Sean drummed his palms against the dashboard of the Cat. "Now this right here is what I'm *talkin' about!* Give her more gas!"

Cooper shook his head, but Sean's enthusiasm was surprisingly infectious. It was like running a raid in an MMORPG with someone who was desperate for the boss-specific gear drop and had spent the last few weeks struggling without a guild to back him up.

Over the years, Cooper had entertained many fantasies about destroying his high school, although he'd never figured out one that suited him. Despite the taunts and teasing he'd received from his classmates over the years, and his teacher's wishy-washy, BS responses, he didn't want to *hurt* anyone. If anything, he wanted to tear down the school brick by brick with his bare hands. The building on the hill was the symbol of all his past failures: the bullying, the low grades, the fact that he'd never been able to get out of this town... He'd wanted it out of his view. Out of his *life*.

It had never occurred to him to bring the Cat.

"Where do we start?" he bellowed to Sean over the roar of the engine.

Sean cackled and threw his hands in the air. "Wherever you want! You have the power, boy. Even if he can get in your head, I *dare* King Clanker to come after you now!"

Cooper bared his teeth in a vicious grin. "Sorry," he murmured to the old building. "I have to do this. For the good of humanity."

He started with the principal's office, where he'd been sent for 'instigating the fight' where Lyle Compton gave him a black eye. He raised the arm of the excavator, angled the bucket so that the tines faced down, and brought it crashing into the roof over the office. As the bricks collapsed inward around the fresh, gaping hole, a little of his anger uncoiled. After all, Principal Struble was gone. Lyle Compton was gone.

Are you really going to spend the rest of your life angry at ghosts?

He swung for the counselor's office next, where Ms. O'Malley had, on more than one occasion, suggested that Cooper 'just try to fit in.' As if he was the problem, and conforming was the solution.

As he worked his way down the building, his reasons for crushing the walls of the building changed. Some of his best memories of being a teenager centered around the drama club. Cooper bared his teeth as he brought the hydraulic arm of the excavator down on the auditorium; there was no way he was letting the Clankers have *that* space of their own. Same with the band room.

Now, the gym? Let the Clankers have the gym. Blood-sucking alien scum would have fit right in with the jocks.

Except for Nate...

Cooper's hands trembled as he rotated the cab toward the natatorium. He lifted the arm, but before he could bring it crashing through the wall of the poolhouse, Sean threw himself over the wheel.

"No!" he said. "That's where they nest. If Miss Butter isn't bug food by now, she's in there."

Cooper powered down the Cat, letting it idle as he turned to Sean. "You think?"

Sean nodded. "At night, you can see 'em crawling on the roof. Keeping guard. And besides, I've *seen* it."

"Seen it?" Cooper echoed. "You mean, you've been inside?"

Sean licked his lips. "Listen, boy-o. I know you think I'm cracked as a copper kettle, and I understand why... but I'm telling you, the Clankers can get in my head, and the connection goes both ways. I've seen 'em inside there, fillin' the pool with their foul eggs, keeping their food half-alive until it's time to feed their young. That's what happened to Jenny: they took her away and kept her fresh until it was her time."

Cooper watched his fellow passenger warily. That frightening, fierce intensity had come back into Sean's expression. The dude was out of his gourd.

I'm trapped in a twenty-ton piece of equipment with a madman, he thought.

On the other hand, Sean had survived in the confines of Little Creek for weeks. Cooper's eyes flicked toward the natatorium; shadows moved inside, although there was too much condensation on the glass to tell for sure what was in there.

"Let's say you're right," he murmured. "Can King Clanker read your mind right now?"

"Hard to say." Sean shrugged. "The hat helps."

"And what would happen if you took the hat off? Would he come for us right now?" Cooper frowned up at the battered tinfoil cap.

"Oh, this baby stays." Sean patted the blunted foil tip at the top of his head. "She's with me until the end, until I'm ready to tap into their hivemind. That's my big move. My checkmate." He grinned, revealing his uneven, yellowed teeth.

Cooper gulped and leaned back against the door. "Okay. Understood. So, uh, what happens in the meantime? Sounds like you're saying that if I wreck the nat, any hope of getting Pammy back is gone."

Sean's gaze shifted toward the window behind Cooper's shoulder. "Looks like the cavalry has arrived."

Cooper turned his head to see what Sean was talking about, and his eyes widened. A tiny figure was making her way across the parking lot on foot, gripping the handle of a shovel in both hands. Her face was partly obscured beneath a splatter of black gore, and her clothes were soaked with what had to be alien blood, but there was no mistaking her silhouette.

"Vera?" Cooper made sure that the Cat was in park before opening the door and climbing down to ground level.

"Hey!" Sean called from above him, brandishing the mattock. "You forgot your weapon!"

Cooper nodded to show that he'd heard and jogged over to Vera. "You came back."

"They screwed up my *tires!*" she said, as if the widespread destruction of the world as they knew it took a backseat to this offense. "I've had it. So what's the plan?"

Cooper opened his mouth to answer, but the screech of tires on the road distracted him. They both turned to the parking lot entrance just in time to see the familiar, battered pickup screech into the lot.

"Hey!" Guppie waved at them from the back seat and jumped out before the engine even stopped. "You're not dead!"

Cooper stared at him. "Neither are you!"

Guppie thumped him on the back and said, "We're hardy souls." He then turned to Len, who was just swinging out of the truck. He had a pair of binoculars in hand; when he met Cooper's eye, he nodded, then went back to surveying the area in front of the school.

"We just thinned out a lot of the local Clanker population," Guppie said proudly.

Len seemed less impressed. "That won't slow them long. We need to move."

"Uh." Cooper sucked his teeth and shot Vera a sideways glance. "We think Pammy's inside. In there." He gestured to the natatorium.

Len lifted the binoculars to his eyes and leaned back against the truck. After fiddling with the settings for a moment, he let out a low whistle. "Place is crawling with them, huh?"

"I guess." Cooper almost added what Sean had told him before, but he swallowed the words. Cooper wasn't sure how to communicate Sean's certainty and urgency without seeming a little strange himself.

They could grill Sean about his theory later, all of them together. Once they got Pammy back.

Len sniffed and lowered his binoculars. "We got a plan of attack?"

Cooper shook his head. "Can't very well keep smashing my way in, I guess. If she's still alive, she could be crushed."

Len licked his lips as he tucked the binoculars into the front pocket of his vest. "I've got a suggestion. Guppie said that I need to trust you all more, so I'll tell you what I'm thinking... but it's going to take all of us working together. As a *team*."

He didn't strike Cooper as being particularly thrilled about the idea.

"Does it have to do with terriers?" Guppie asked, lifting one eyebrow significantly.

"Not exactly." Len gestured to the truck bed, and the hodgepodge of supplies he'd brought along from the bunker. "Have any of you ever heard of a mosquito fogger?"

39

LEN

LEN STOOD outside the gaping hole in the wall of the battered high school, staring into the darkness beyond. Concrete dust was still rising from the rubble, and the ground was littered with broken bricks. Phobos and Deimos stood at either side.

Sean, Vera, and Guppie waited behind him, with their arms full of supplies. Len checked them over one last time before lifting his walkie-talkie.

"Are you ready, Coop?" he asked.

His voice crackled back to him. "Sure am. I'm on the southwest corner of the nat. Tell me when to go."

"Whenever you're ready. Remember, Cooper: just like snipping the corner of a frosting bag. You want to control the flow."

He chuckled into the mic. "The most surprising part about all of this is the fact that you know anything about cake decorating."

"I'm a man of many layers." Len paused. "Get it? Layers?"

"Mhmm. How about we leave the dad-jokes to Guppie?" The engine grated through the speaker. "Hang tight. I'm going in. Operation: Cake-tip is underway."

On the far side of the building, the hydraulic arm squealed, and the building shook as Cooper dug the bucket into the top corner of the natatorium. The mic whined, and then Cooper's voice returned. "All right, Len. We're good. I'll wait for your signal... oh, hell, they're already coming through. *Go go gogogo!*"

Len clipped the walkie to his waist and gestured for the trio to follow him. "Come on," he told them, mostly for the dogs' benefit. "Time to hunt."

He'd worried that the day's exertions were too much already, but Phobos and Deimos both leapt into action. They scrambled into the school, with Deimos baying as they went, leaving their two-legged counterparts to bring up the rear.

Cooper had given them a rough idea of the school's layout. *One left, and you'll reach the hall; the nat entrance is the big door at the next left.* Simple enough, and they only had to make it to the first intersection before Len could stop worrying about the rest of the crew.

There were Clankers in the hall, but before Len was in range, Phobos slid on the linoleum tile until he was beneath one. From there, he lunged upward, clamping his jaws around the Clanker's undercarriage and tugging it downward. Deimos, usually the most passive of the two, came up under its neck, clamped the beast's neck in its jaws, and twisted.

Clean. Efficient. Len had never been more proud.

The four humans skidded into the intersection of the corridor, and Len whistled to bring the dogs back to his side. He'd borrowed Vera's gardening shears, and the pistol he'd loaned Guppie was back at his waist. It was a much better weapon than a rifle in these tight quarters. Sean dumped the boxes of powdered insecticide onto the ground in a heap. The last of the gas went on top of the powder, turning it into a highly flammable sludge. When Len nodded, Vera lifted the hose of the backpack portable agricultural flamer she'd brought with them that first night, and sent a small gout of fire toward the boxes of insecticide.

As a foul-smelling smoke rose from the boxes, Len caught Guppie's eye. He nodded once before powering up the leafblower Pammy had brought back from her mom's place.

Len hadn't been sure that it would work, but as Guppie aimed the blower above the acrid flames, the cloud of insecticide swept through the halls. Len pulled the hem of his shirt over his nose as the trio disappeared behind him and whistled for the dogs. Before the worst of the smoke could reach them, he yanked open the doors leading in the direction of the natatorium.

He didn't expect that the insecticidal fog would stop a truly determined Clanker from taking the wrong exit, but he hoped that it would funnel them toward the hole Cooper had made in the roof. The fewer Clankers headed his way, the easier his recon mission would be.

The chamber on the far side of the doors looked out on the pool, but to get inside, he'd have to take either the girl's or boy's locker room entrance. The dogs looked to him for confirmation, but Len took a moment to peer through the foggy glass surrounding the pool.

True to his word, Cooper had opened one corner of the roof, and Clankers had swarmed the opening. To Len's dismay, however, there were still plenty more to go. The lower part of the window sported so much condensation that he couldn't see the floor or the pool properly. There was no telling how many more Clankers waited just out of sight.

He retrieved his walkie. "You still holding the fort, Cooper?"

Cooper's voice was tense as he replied, "I'm trying."

The building shuddered; presumably, he was using the arm to

grind the escaping Clankers to a paste. It was tempting to wait him out, but by the sounds of it, things weren't going as smoothly as he hoped.

"I'm inside," he said into the mouthpiece. "I'll let you know when we're clear."

The boys' locker room door was jammed shut, which made the decision about where to go a lot easier. Brandishing the shears with one hand, Len stepped through into the girl's locker room.

The smell that hit him as he stepped inside was enough to startle him into gagging. Wet bits of clothing and soft human bones lay strewn about on the floor. He had seen what happened when the adult Clankers fed, and at least these remains weren't as... *meaty.* Still, the smell of wet decay left him gasping.

The dogs picked their way between the bones. Deimos snuffled them curiously, but Phobos kept his eyes moving, braced for another strike. Len could still hear the Cat from in here, but it was muted, as if it were operating half a mile away and not directly outside this building. He tiptoed over to the far door and tapped it with his toe. It was set on a two-way pivot hinge, so that it could be pushed open from either side.

"Stay close," he told the dogs, and shouldered his way through the door.

He was greeted by a burst of echoing sound that seemed to come from all directions: the squeal of hydraulics, the song of Clankers, and the crunch of falling bricks. Len stared into the chaos for a moment before realizing, just in time, that his arrival had not gone unnoticed.

Phobos tackled the incoming Clanker; its body was so low to the ground that Len was able to drive his foot down on its back before digging the tips of the shears into its segmented eyes. Leaving the shears open, he forced them down the length of the

Clanker, splitting it open almost as neatly as Vera had sliced into her autopsy subject.

Before the thing even stopped moving, Len had moved onto his next prey. He opened the shears a little too wide, only to realize that the pivot-pin holding the arms of the shears together was made to come apart. Presumably, they'd made them this way so that the shears could be sharpened more easily, but as far as Len was concerned, he'd just gone from having one pair of shears to having two long-handled knives.

He grinned as he hurled himself toward the neck of the Clanker, driving one blade in from the front of its belly and one in from its back. When he pushed them apart, his hands met on the creature's far side, while the points crossed inches from his nose.

Interesting. He'd have to watch out or risk skewering himself.

He rolled to the side, avoiding the sharp edges of the blades, as one of the Clankers whipped its tongue at him. The tongue missed by a hair's breadth, but Len tripped on a white, bubbly lump on the floor as he stumbled away, and fell back into the foam. Whatever it was was wet and slippery beneath his palm, like old wet leaves in the garden bed when he turned over the soil in the spring. The smell hit him a second later.

It was a body.

Len's gorge rose as he rolled to the side and tried to find his footing. Through the hole he'd left in the foam, he could make out a pale floral pattern. Whoever it was had been wearing their pajamas when they died.

Len rose to one knee and flipped the blade around so that the point aimed behind him, and swung his arm back, right into the side of the Clanker that had approached him from the back. It struggled so hard that it pulled the blade out of his grasp, but Phobos leapt on the Clanker before it could strike, finishing what Len had started.

"Good boy," he panted as he struggled to his feet and pulled the blade out of the thrashing alien's back. In these close quarters, his bulky size was an impediment, but at least the aliens were just as challenged. Phobos waved his tail once as he came to his side, falling into formation.

Len had lost track of Deimos, and he spun in a circle, trying to figure out where he'd gone.

"Here, boy!" he called.

His words echoed around the pool deck as he rotated on the spot, but there was no sign of him.

No. Not Deimos. He was his baby, his big dumb sweetie, the one who worried about his happiness as much as his health. He sniffed once and wiped his eyes on his sleeve before realizing that the foamy residue that had covered the body on the floor still clung to him. He spun once more, for good measure, just to be sure.

If he hadn't, the raised proboscis of the Clanker behind him would have severed his spine in one blow. Instead, it struck him in the shoulder blade, carrying Len to the ground with such force that his face cracked against the concrete. He tasted blood, and he heard as much as felt one of the bones in his cheek give way.

Above him, Phobos howled, but Len's eyes fluttered shut. Pain radiated out from his face in waves. When he tried to get one hand under him to push himself up, the Clanker drove one spearlike leg through his shoulder. Len struggled as it dragged him forward, scraping his injured face against the rough concrete of the pool deck, until it lifted him up so that his leg dangled off the ground. He swatted weakly at the foot protruding from the front of his shoulder; his weight worked against him, widening the hole as he hung there helplessly.

Phobos tried to help him, but out of the corner of his eyes he saw the Clanker swat him away. He heard him yelp, and Phobos didn't come back to his rescue.

Only then, with his toes six inches off the ground, did Len see what awaited him in the pool. Clusters of black Clanker eggs floated on the surface, and a layer of algae was taking hold at the edges of the water, but in the middle—where their constant surfacing kept the algae layer at bay—unfamiliar shapes roiled *en masse*. They might have passed for tadpoles, but as one passed near the surface, he realized that they were shaped more like dragonfly nymphs or caddisfly larvae, each the size of a large Chihuahua. He gagged again as the Clanker lifted him above the surface of the water.

The bones in the locker room: they were all that remained of the prey that the Clankers fed their young. Len struggled as the toes of his boots brushed the surface of the water. The larvae gathered beneath him, extending their mouths toward him, straining upward in search of their next meal...

Len's eyes rolled to one side as something moved along the edge of the pool deck. It almost looked like Pammy, albeit a worse-for-wear version of Pammy, wielding a long pool net. Deimos was at her side, baying as they ran.

Ghosts, he thought. *I'm seeing ghosts. Next, it'll be Carla...*

The ghost of Pammy Mae lifted the pool net over head like an oversized lacrosse stick and swung it down in an arc against the back of the Clanker that held Len.

Perhaps she wasn't a ghost, because the Clanker fell back, rattling as it retreated. It lowered its foreleg in the process and Len slipped off. He fell to the tiles right in front of the alien breeding pool.

Pammy Mae tried to bring the pool net down on the creature again, but it swatted it away with one of its sharp forelegs and sent her sprawling into the pool maintenance closet that abutted the guys' locker room.

The Clanker then hesitated, watching for movement from

Pammy and seemingly unsure of which prey it wanted to go after first, her or Len.

It chose Len and came darting straight for him.

Good, he thought. *Come and get this.*

The shoulder he'd been speared through was also the side where the pistol he'd taken back from Guppie hung at his waist. When he'd been unceremoniously dumped on the ground, he was in such a heap that reaching over and grabbing it with his good arm was easy enough.

Now he swung the pistol up and fired point-blank into the Clanker's descending proboscis.

He fired until he heard the gun clicking, and had just enough time to be angry with himself for spending all his ammo in one kill, when the collapsed Clanker's forward momentum smashed into his face, which already felt like it had been run over with sandpaper.

The impact sent Len over the lip and into the alien breeding pool.

For a moment, he floated there, weightless and limp. *Pammy was alive.* Cooper had been right.

That was something. In all this mess, the fact that one of them had survived a direct attack made it seem like there was a light at the end of the tunnel.

A light. People always talked about a light. His Muslim grandmother and aunties had always made it seem like the angel of death would take his soul away on a beam of heavenly sunlight. His Protestant mother, who had left the church behind before Len was born, and uncle weren't so sure. Carla had been an outright atheist.

Synapses firing in the brain, Carla had scoffed. *There's a scientific explanation for everything, Len, and don't let anyone tell you otherwise.*

Whatever the explanation, Len saw it now: a distant glimmer at the edges of his consciousness.

Len's eyes snapped open.

Screw that.

There was no chlorine sting in the waters of the pool, although the water was stagnant and foul. The larvae reached for him, extending half-formed legs and puckered, tubular mouths.

His left arm was no good, so Len had to rely on his legs. He kicked hard toward the surface, extending his right hand toward the lip of the pool. His wrist brushed against one of the larvae. Its flesh was soft and pliant, and its legs were almost gentle as they latched onto his wrist. There was very little pain as the mouth speared his forearm.

At least at first.

He didn't try to shake it off. Hundreds more were reaching for him, slicing into his wet clothes. His heavy vest was pulling him down, dragging him under toward the cool blue floor of the pool beneath.

He needed air desperately. The hole in his shoulder burned, and he had no sense of how far away from the surface he was. A long time seemed to have passed.

Even as he thought it, his finger broke the surface and scrabbled at the edge of the pool.

With another kick, he brought his head above the water. His good elbow looped over the edge of the pool, and he tried to pull himself out. There were too many nymphs, all fighting to get a taste of him. He snarled as he kicked, dislodging a few more. The one in his arm wriggled free and plopped back into the water with a small splash.

A furry brown face appeared over the lip of the pool. Phobos barked once, then grabbed the back of his jacket and pulled.

He tried to help him, but ended up flopping around like a

dying fish. As he lost ground, Len went limp, trusting the dog with his whole weight as he hauled him back to safety.

Len lay face-down on the pool deck, choking on rancid pool water. He hissed when his injured cheek brushed the floor.

"Good boy," he said, as his vision went dark.

There were no lights this time to guide his way.

BEYOND LITTLE CREEK

The Hi'aiti'ihi People
Humaitá National Forest, Brazil

——————

There were only ten of them, as there had been for some time. Several rainy seasons before, the oldest woman in their tribe had died. A few months after, a boy was born; he took a portion of the old woman's name, and the balance was restored.

They did not mark time. None of them marked their ages by any calendar. What was not present did not require a name, because there was no reason to speak of it.

The shaman was sitting with the other women beside the river, scraping the scales off of the fish they had caught earlier that morning, when the men returned. Their expressions were troubled, and she searched among them, wondering if one of them had not survived the hunt.

All were present. More importantly, they had brought game

with them, although the shaman had never seen its like before. It was larger than a panther, shinier than a leaf after a fresh rain, and it made a sound like old bones clacking together. It was dead.

The eldest of the men laid the creature on the ground, and the tribe gathered around, examining it without touching it. The elder had its blood upon him, and the shaman gestured toward the river.

"Wash your hands," she told him, "and do not let the water you have touched flow downstream."

While he obeyed, the shaman examined the dead animal. She had many words for what it was *like, but not*, and yet she could not say what it *was*.

"Is it Igagai?" one of the men asked.

"No," the shaman said.

"Is it a beetle?" one of the women asked.

"It is not," the shaman replied.

Of their group, the shaman was not the oldest. She had not come into her power over time, the way the elder had come into his. Since she was small, she had been able to walk between the overlapping worlds of the body and the spirit, between *ibiisi* and *abaisi*, between people and not-people. This creature was an *abaisi* of some kind, but that was all she could say with certainty.

The elder returned and squatted down in the circle of nine that surrounded the shaman and the *abaisi*. "What shall we do with it? Should we eat it, or not?"

The shaman considered this for a long moment, although she could not have said *how* long, because the only time was now. In the *now* when she made her decision, she lifted one of the stones from the riverbank, grasped it tightly in both hands, and crushed the *abaisi*'s head. There was power within it: not just the physical power provided by ordinary meat, but spiritual power, too.

The shaman dipped her fingers into the creature's battered carcass. She lifted a small bite to her lips and let it slide between her fingers until it rested on her tongue. The tribe watched in silent interest, waiting to see what would happen next.

The shaman did not swallow. She waited, letting the meat settle in her mouth. It did not taste good, but she did not spit it out.

Her vision flickered, and the shaman closed her eyes. She saw the stars, but from the outside of the sky, and more of the creatures, *many* more, in a gathering greater than that of all the tribes their band had ever encountered combined. They came from a realm beyond that of Igagai, filling the night...

The shaman spat out the bite of meat and rushed to the river. She washed her hands first, then used them to scoop up mouthful after mouthful of water, spitting it back out, desperate to wash the remnants of the *abaisi* off of her tongue.

"Burn it," she told the elder. "If you find more, kill them."

The members of her tribe looked at one another with questioning glances.

"They are not of our realm," she explained. "They have come from somewhere else. They do not belong here."

This was enough of an explanation for the tribe. The elder lit a fire while the others piled brush over the creature. Even the smallest boy helped.

Before long, the creature was nothing but charred shells and ash, and the tribe had moved on to the daily business of living. They forgot about the *abaisi,* because it was no longer present.

Only the shaman remembered. Even though all time was *now,* the visions she had seen in the not-now stayed with her. A change was coming, and a time when her wisdom would be needed more than arrows, when her spiritual strength would be more necessary than the elder's knowledge of hunting.

For the first time in her life, the not-knowing terrified her.

40

PAMMY MAE

"LEN!" Pammy wasn't sure if she'd been knocked out or not, but she found herself in a sitting position with her back against a supply cabinet and the pool net lying broken next to her.

She got up on wobbly legs and rushed to her friend's side. He collapsed onto all fours next to Phobos, who was whining in dismay. Len was barely breathing, and the larvae of the Clankers still clung to him.

Even as she watched, the juveniles detached. Apparently they weren't the biggest fans of being left in the open air. They released Len and half-crawled, half-rolled back toward the edge of the pool, toppling over the edge like quivering sacks of gelatin.

The dogs crowded in, and Deimos licked Pammy's cheek. It was lucky that the bloodhound had honed in on Pammy's scent when he had, and doubly fortunate that he'd been able to pull her free of her own sudsy prison. If he'd only done it a minute earlier, she might have been able to keep Len from being turned into a Clanker kebab. Then again, if he'd waited much longer to find her — or Pammy'd had the kinds of exposed wounds that

Len had — she might have just been gnawed down to a nub by now.

Len lay perfectly still, but when Pammy pressed her fingers to his throat, she could make out a pulse. He was breathing shallowly, too, which meant that Pammy didn't have to give him CPR—lucky, since Pammy had never quite gotten the hang of it in the yearly first aid course offered by the school.

"Sorry if this hurts," she said before rolling Len onto his back. She was just about to hook her elbows under Len's shoulders and drag him back toward the locker room doors in a fireman's carry when his eyes popped open. Or rather, his one eye did. The other was completely swollen shut.

She turned his head and he coughed up what seemed like half a gallon of water and muck, then got to his knees.

"What happened?"

"We were just leaving," she said. She helped him to his feet, but he leaned hard on her and she had to pull his arm over her shoulder to support him properly.

They had only made it halfway across the distance before Pammy paused.

"What is it?" Len said, sensing her hesitation.

The last of the Clankers had swarmed out through the hole in the corner of the building, but Pammy found herself staring at the pool, where a whole new generation of Clankers waited to spawn.

"I have to do something," she said. She helped Len over so he could lean against the wall. "I'll be right back."

Len chuckled hoarsely as he slid down to a seated position. "I'm not going anywhere."

"Wait here," she told the dogs, as if she really needed to. They weren't going to be leaving Len's side now. "Stay."

She ran back to the pool maintenance closet that abutted the guy's locker room. Inside, she found several drums marked with hazard symbols stacked on one side. On the other was a stack of five-gallon buckets labeled *Chlorine Tablets*. Pammy peered at the label, trying to make sense of the contents, until a laminated sign on the wall caught her eye.

Ten tabs per cleaning cycle, it read. *Add chlorine last!*

She turned back to the label on the buckets. Apparently, each bucket contained approximately ten, the perfect amount for whoever had been in charge of pool maintenance in the pre-invasion days.

Pammy lifted four bucket handles, two in each hand, and hurried back toward the pool.

The lids were childproof, but Pammy found one of the discarded blades from the gardening shears that Len had used in his fight against the Clankers, and used it to pry off the lids one by one. When she was finished, she carried the buckets to the edge of the pool and stared down at the young Clankers.

They were clearly dismayed by the fact that their most recent meal had not only fought back, but somehow escaped in the process. They gathered beneath her with their little legs flailing against the surface of the pool until bubbles formed.

Pammy grinned down at them, and her distorted reflection leered back up at her.

"Feeding time," she told them.

If she hadn't been watching her reflection, she wouldn't have seen the Clanker coming. This one didn't rattle. It moved silently, legs raised, staying low to the ground.

"Look out!" Len cried, but his warning was too little too late and he was a dozen steps away and barely able to move.

Pammy whirled to face her attacker, but her hands were empty. The broken pool net lay fifteen feet away; the discarded blade she'd used to pry open the lids was just out of reach. There was no way she was going to reach it in time, but she'd die before she gave up. She lunged toward the blade, hitting the concrete on her belly as she snatched at the handle.

As her fingers closed over the grip, a terrible *crack* echoed through the natatorium. *It got me,* she thought wildly. *It already got me, and I just can't feel it yet.*

Pammy rolled onto her back, gripping the handle of the blade in both hands. The Clanker was writhing, staggering weakly to one side. A huge chunk of its plated exoskeleton was missing.

Deimos stood over Pammy, the fur along his spine bristling, teeth bared. Viscous Clanker-blood dripped from his jaws, and matted the fur of his neck and chest. A low growl echoed through him, so deep that she felt it more than heard it. When the Clanker thrashed toward them, he mirrored its movements, keeping his body between Pammy and the alien. If she hadn't known the dog, Pammy would have been terrified. He was usually the calm one. The sweet one.

And he'd just saved her life. *Again.*

Pammy sat up, watching as the Clanker stumbled into the water. Apparently, the Clanker-fry didn't have any compunctions about cannibalism. As the beast sank, its young descended on it, dragging it below the surface.

It did not rise again.

"Good boy," Pammy said, laying one hand on Deimos's shoulder. The dog instantly relaxed, turning to her and licking her cheek with his huge wet tongue. "The next time we find food, I'm gonna give you, like, a million dog treats."

Behind them, Phobos whined. He'd taken up a similar defensive posture next to Len, but like his owner, it was obvious that the shepherd was hurting. Pammy had never had a dog of her own, and if she had, she'd have gone for something small and cute. A companion animal. A lapdog. Guard dogs had scared her.

That felt like a lifetime ago.

Len shook his head and said, "Let's finish this, huh?"

Pammy rolled to her feet and patted Deimos once more for good measure. "Let's."

Pammy grabbed the blade– no more getting caught weapon-less — and returned to the edge of the pool where the fry had already finished their feeding frenzy and were ready for more. One by one, she upended every bucket of chlorine tabs into the pool.

She stood there and watched as the nymphs bit into the tablet packaging. No doubt dumping chlorine straight into the water wasn't the usual protocol, but this was a special occasion. She watched as the larvae shuddered and flailed, kicking up human bones and the freshly-scoured remains of their own kind. As the chemicals spread through the water, the nymphs writhed, trying to climb out of the water in order to escape the toxic substance, then dropping back in to escape the open air. There was nowhere for them to run. No matter what choice they made, they were doomed.

Now they know how we feel.

Pammy watched until the surface of the pool turned calm again, with no movement in the water to mar her reflection. Gradually, the bodies of the Clanker-fry bobbed to the surface, belly-up and limp-legged.

Pammy Mae flipped their corpses the bird before turning on her heel, retrieving Len, and kicking her way through the girls' locker-room door.

41

GUPPIE

AS THE POISONOUS smoke from their chemical fire wafted down the hall toward the natatorium, Guppie peered into the gray cloud, hoping for any sign of Len. The flames were burning down, but the miasma it had left behind lingered. He'd abandoned use of the leafblower and set the equipment aside in exchange for the gardening mattock he'd borrowed from Cooper.

To his left, Vera clutched the handle of her gardening spade in one hand and the hose of the agricultural flamer in the other. Sean was behind them, wielding his spray cans. He'd dropped into a crouch, facing the opposite direction.

"What are you doing?" Guppie asked, looking over his shoulder at his old friend.

"Making sure they don't flank us." Sean shook the spray cans for good measure. "King Clanker is tricky. They might be headed where Len wants 'em to go, but I don't think he'll leave so easily. Gotta watch in every direction. You never know where they'll come from next."

Well, I don't think they'll be coming from the direction of the pool, so long as Len was right about how toxic this stuff is to them...

Of course, there was no telling what cocktail of chemicals would make an alien sick. Which was why, even though Guppie trusted Len's instincts, he was still armed.

He was still watching the smoke in the direction that Len had disappeared when Sean shouted, *"He's here!"*

Guppie whirled on the spot, squinting into the dark hallway where Sean was pointing. He couldn't see a thing. "Where?" he asked.

"I can't spot him yet." Sean kept pointing. "But I know it. He's *close.*"

Guppie suppressed a sigh. "Look, buddy, I know that you've got a thing about this one particular Clanker, but don't you think..."

"Above you!" Vera cried.

Guppie looked up to see a Clanker drop from the ceiling toward him. He had just enough time to brace the handle of the mattock against the floor and duck.

Any other Clanker would have been speared on the implement, but Sean had been right: this Clanker was the biggest of them all. It landed with its legs fully extended, with its underbelly just brushing the tip of the mattock.

"*Crap,*" Guppie mumbled.

He and the Clanker moved at the same time. As Guppie hefted the tool and swung the forked end upward, the Clanker charged forward so that it was behind him. His swing threw him off-balance, and Guppie stumbled, just missing the proboscis as it snapped over its head.

He turned to follow the Clanker, but its myriad legs meant that its movements were nimbler than his. While he spun like a top, the Clanker took a few lazy jabs at him with its forearms.

"Spit him like a goose!" Sean bellowed. "Give him the heave-ho!"

Guppie grunted and spun again. "Darn thing won't hold still..."

He finally managed to get himself facing it and took a few jabs of his own, but the Clanker danced out of his reach, like a boxer might... a boxer who was top of his weight class and confident that he was going to win the match.

A burst of fire caught Guppie's eye as Vera joined the fray, brandishing the hose of the ag flamer. The Clanker stumbled back, and Guppie swung for its legs.

The beast reached the wall and began to back up, gripping the whitewashed cinderblocks with its pointed feet as it hinged its spinal column backward.

Vera grinned in triumph as she set jet after jet of flame toward the King.

Her smile dropped abruptly away when the flame died and didn't ignite again.

"Oh, hell," she breathed. "I'm out of fuel..."

"Get back!" Guppie exclaimed.

Vera turned and fled, and the Clanker rattled in triumph as it descended on them again.

In Guppie's peripherals, Vera wriggled out of the flamer pack and lifted the shovel in both hands. The Clanker, either annoyed that she had made a fool of him or singling her out as the weakest of the pack, charged directly toward her.

"No!" Guppie bellowed. "You leave her alone!" He lifted the mattock over his head, prepared to bring it down like he was chopping wood.

The Clanker paused, and two of its limbs flicked out to the side. That was the only word for it: *flicked*. Like Guppie was a pog, or a mosquito, an insignificant object not worthy of the Clanker's full attention.

The legs caught him square in the chest with such force that Guppie was thrown off his feet. His head smacked against the loose bricks left by Cooper's incursion with the excavator.

"Guppie!" Vera screamed.

I'm coming, he tried to say. *I won't let it hurt you. I will defend you against all enemies, foreign and domestic...*

But Guppie's battle now was against the darkness creeping into the edges of his vision. *No,* he screamed at himself. *You will not pass out.*

But he would have. He was sure of it. Vera and the Clanker had already vanished from his vision, and he'd all but lost the battle when a piercing sound brought him back from the edge of unconsciousness like a splash of cold water.

It was the incongruous sound of boisterous laughter.

42

VERA

SEAN WAS LAUGHING DELIRIOUSLY. Even in his most insane moments, Vera hadn't heard him sound this demented.

Vera, meanwhile, was petrified. She whimpered as she took a step back from the creature that Sean had called King Clanker. The beast truly *was* enormous, but now that she saw it in person, she recognized it.

This is the one from the gas station. The chemical burns to its many eyes were her first clue, but any doubts that remained were banished by the sight of its splintered front leg. She had broken it off as it groped for her through the storage room door back in the gas station on that first night.

They'd had nearly a month to come to grips with everything that had happened, but now that she was facing the Clanker again, the terror of that night left her rooted to the spot. The creature moseyed forward, taking its time, one foreleg raised and the battered stump flailing at the same angle but a whole joint short. Its proboscis opened and closed again, as if that creature was licking its lips. Any minute now, that tongue would come flying out toward her...

"Aw, Your Highness, you don't scare me." Sean swaggered forward; his flip-flops slipped in the rubble, but he kept his beady eyes fixed on the King. "You know who I am, don't you?"

The Clanker's whole body twisted to one side, like a dog cocking its head.

"That's right." Sean's lip curled. "You know me. I'm your worst nightmare. You hate me even more than Miss Butter."

"Sean!" Vera hissed. "What are you doing?"

"Don't mind us, little lady." Sean crossed his arms and tapped the gnarly toes of one foot against a cracked brick. "Ol' Foreign Royalty and I are having words. See, I know him, and he knows me, an' he knows I'm gonna be the death of him. Isn't that right?"

Vera took another step back. Was Sean trying to buy her time? If she ran, the Clanker would be on her in an instant, and there was no way she was going to leave Guppie behind...

The Clanker lunged toward her, but with one smooth motion, Sean ripped off his tinfoil hat and sent it spinning away down the hall. He raised his hands in front of him like a wizard out of one of the many bad BBC specials from Vera's childhood. The tin cans that were tied to a sagging belt that encircled his waist shook like maracas.

"No!" he intoned. "You will not harm her!"

To Vera's surprise, the Clanker whirled back to him.

"I have tasted Clanker flesh!" Sean howled. "When Walker and I saw what you'd done to this town, how you'd sucked out its very soul, we returned the favor! I know how you think, Your Highness." He tapped one fingernail to his liver-spotted temple. "And I'm telling you what I know: this is it. Death has come for you."

The Clanker shuddered and let out a low whistle as its legs

worked over the tile. It was fixated on Sean. *It almost seems agitated.*

"That's right, I ate one of your little cronies, and you know what I think?" Sean sneered. "Your people taste like *sh—*"

He was cut off as the Clanker darted for him, but Sean danced aside with more agility than Vera had given him credit for.

"Ha!" he cackled. "Truth hurts, don't it. You're my white whale, Your Highness, and I'm your Ahab. Does it make the hunting harder, now that Miss Butter got your tongue?"

The enormous Clanker lunged again. Its back was to Vera now, and she raised the shovel. The blade had a decent point on it, and if she could drive it between King Clanker's plates, she might be able to kill it. She'd just have to be fast enough that he didn't have time to prepare.

Sean caught her eye and shook his head once—so even if he was out of his mind, he had a plan of some kind.

The Clanker paused in its pursuit of the old man, but before it could change its mind about its intended prey, Sean spread his arms and narrowed his eyes.

"Come get me, you foul-tasting old bug. You want revenge for your kinsman? Well, so do I! Come get me!"

The Clanker pounced. Vera expected Sean to jump out of the way, but the old man held his ground. The Clanker speared him with its forelimb, forcing him off his feet until it pinned him to the wall.

Sean laughed. "I told you!" he shouted. "I told you this was it for us! I spit on your grave, King Clanker, I—"

Vera watched in horror as the Clanker's proboscis descended, slicing Sean open from his collarbone to his pelvis in a single strike. It sliced open his belt of tin cans and it came apart in his hands.

He was cackling when it happened, and he launched the belt

flying over Vera's head as the creature dug its mouth into his still-warm belly. Sean caught Vera's eye and mouthed, *Now*.

She came in swinging, driving the shovel between two of the Clanker's plates and forcing them apart. The upper plate came free with a sound like skin being peeled off a raw chicken, and King Clanker let out a terrible noise. It dropped Sean and tried to spin around toward her, but Vera never stopped moving, stabbing the shovel into the Clanker's meat with blow after blow after blow. When the blade of the shovel broke off, she stabbed him with the handle instead.

But it wasn't enough. She knew that. She'd exposed a weak point, but the Clanker was just too big for her to exploit it.

She'd failed. *I'm sorry, Sean. You deserved better.*

"Move!" screamed Guppie from behind her. She was so startled, both by the fact that he was awake and the fact that his booming voice was so full of urgency, that she jumped backwards and almost stumbled over.

Guppie was holding one of the tin cans from Sean's belt in his outstretched arm. She saw the spark on the top of it and realized Sean must have somehow lit it with the grill lighter hung around his neck in the moments before the Clanker struck.

The tin can disappeared into the meaty, bloody guts of the creature that Vera had opened up with her shovel, along with Guppie's arm all the way up to his elbow.

"Move!" Guppie screamed again as he yanked his arm back out and spun around just as King Clanker ripped its forelimb out of Sean and whipped it around to slice Guppie in half.

A moment before it did, the creature's entire exoskeleton bulged outward, quivering and straining, before it finally ripped open and exploded outward, sending a powerful blast of heat and shrapnel flying through the air. Vera was lucky to have fallen backward, and Guppie to have his back to the blast when it happened.

As it was, scattered pieces of Clanker blood and guts fell all over Vera and the walls behind her. What was left of King Clanker toppled over and lay motionless, spurting dark fluid on the ground.

Vera was too stunned to move for a moment. She just stared at the mangled pile of alien anatomy, her mind wandering back to the autopsy she'd performed. Had that only been a day ago?

She finally came to her senses and crawled over to Guppie, who was even more soaked in Clanker blood than she was.

"You OK?" he croaked to Vera, as if *she* were the one that had just put a homemade bomb in the belly of a beast.

She nodded, and he fell back and closed his eyes. She patted his shoulder and gave him a once over, but she didn't see anything that looked like a major injury.

Guppie crawled past her to the other side of the room. She turned and followed.

Sean lay face up. Somehow, he was still breathing, though Vera knew that wouldn't last long. The damage was catastrophic. The only reason he was successfully holding his insides *in*, as far as Vera could tell, was that he was on the ground on his back and gravity was helping him. If he made any kind of move, he was likely to, perhaps literally, fall apart.

"I'm sorry," she whispered, to Guppie as much as Sean.

I will remember that I remain a member of society, with special obligations to all my fellow human beings, those sound of mind and body as well as the infirm.

She had judged Sean in life. She had doubted his intentions. She had called him crazy and infantile and deluded. And yes, he'd been all of those things, but they'd still had a duty to one another as neighbors. As townsfolk. As *people*.

"Oh, Sean," Guppie croaked out. "Oh, Sean."

Sean's eyes tracked to Guppie. When he spoke, blood seeped from the corners of his blood-stained lips. "So soft, Guppie. You're so soft." He managed a half-laugh, half-cough, then drew in a ragged breath. "Bud's ranch."

"Don't talk, buddy."

Sean's expression barely changed as he drew in another breath. A few flecks of Clanker-blood had flicked against his eyes, but he didn't blink them away.

"Bud's ranch," he repeated. "That's where Walk's plane is."

Vera froze. *What is he saying?*

Guppie opened his mouth, but nothing came out. He was, for once, at a loss for words.

"It was never at the airport," Sean wheezed. "He didn't trust 'em not to gouge him with hangar fees."

Sean managed to smile, which was probably a mistake. He winced. "Don't look at me like that. By the time I knew the kid could fly it, I had my eye on the King. That had to come first. But now... but now..."

His eyes rolled back and his expression went blank. His jaw had gone slack.

Vera couldn't breathe. She couldn't move.

Something snuffled at her elbow, and Vera looked up to see Deimos examining her with droopy, sorrowful eyes. He licked her face, lapping up one of the tears she hadn't realized she'd shed.

"Vera? Guppie?" a woman's voice asked. "Are you okay?"

Pammy Mae stood behind her, with Len's limp form leaning heavily against her. Len's whole face was swollen and bruised, and blood caked a wound in his shoulder.

Vera shook her head, but it was Guppie who spoke. His voice was suddenly strong and urgent. "Where's Cooper?"

43

PAMMY MAE

PAMMY COULDN'T MAKE sense of what she was seeing. Dark blood and flecks of Clanker meat and shell were scattered everywhere. There was a bloody stump of a Clanker in the middle of the room. Guppie and Vera were crowded around the prone, clearly dead body of Sean.

Pammy couldn't bring herself to look at Sean's face. Knowing that people were gone, or watching the cars pile up behind her on the service road, was one thing. But staring into his eyes, acknowledging the mess he'd left behind, made her remember things she'd rather forget...

...*Cooper's parents ... the crunch of Nate's spine...*

...and imagine things she'd tried to put out of her mind. Like her mother.

"Where's Cooper?" Guppie repeated urgently. As he levered himself off the ground, he let out a groan. "Oh, heck, my back..."

Vera seemed to come back to her senses. She came over and carefully pulled the walkie-talkie off Len's belt. "Cooper, we're coming out. Do you read me?"

Only static emanated from the speakers.

"Dammit," Guppie said.

Even as he spoke, a dull rattle sounded from the shadowed depths of the corridor.

There was no time to worry about Cooper. *We have to move.*

"How do we get out of here?" Pammy asked. "Have you got a ride, or...?"

"The truck." Guppie waved one hand toward the gap in the wall. "Pickup's outside."

"Great." Pammy spun Len toward the exit. Vera turned and helped Guppie hobble outside.

Guppie stumbled as Vera steered him out to the parking lot. She seemed to be filled with renewed energy and all but sprinted to the truck with Guppie struggling to keep up. Pammy was slower with Len leaning into her. The dogs stayed close behind.

After Guppie had pulled himself up over the tailgate, he helped her heave Len into the bed, careful not to let his injured head smack against the lining.

"Hold something over the wound in his shoulder," Vera said. "Try to staunch the bleeding."

Guppie nodded, and Vera yanked open the driver's side door of the truck while Pammy helped Phobos up onto the tailgate. The dog was limping, but in spite of his injuries, he lay down beside Len, taking up his position of loyal guard. Deimos made the jump on his own. Pammy slammed the tailgate after them.

"Keys, keys, keys..." Vera mumbled, and Guppie reached into his pocket and tossed them up into the cab as Pammy lifted one leg into the passenger side door.

"*Pammy!*" The voice was so soft, she almost didn't hear it. She froze and turned her head toward the wreckage of the natatorium.

An enormous yellow excavator stood at the far corner of the building. Dozens of Clankers swarmed over it, like ants defending their nest. Plenty more of them were dead, squished on the grass or smeared onto the side of the wall, but that didn't help the kid trapped inside. Cooper's face was pressed to the glass, and he was *smiling* at her.

Like he was happy that she'd made it, even though he was stuck.

Pammy turned back to the truck. She still had the lone blade from Len's gardening shears, but as far as she could tell that was the only weapon that was left.

It wasn't as if she could fight the Clankers with just that.

Cooper was on his own. He wasn't her responsibility. Staying could cost her life, and probably wouldn't save his.

... you owe him...

No, it was crazy. Pammy wasn't going to entertain the idea. *You lied to him about his parents. Whatever else you think... you* owe *him.*

On impulse, Pammy jabbed her finger at the CD player between the seats. Guppie's truck had to be almost as old as he was. Who even *used* CDs anymore?

A disc popped out, and Pammy squinted at the label. There was nothing printed on it, but in tidy marker, someone had written the words, *Bada** Mix For Uncle Gup,* asterisks and all. Good enough. She pushed it back into place.

"Vera." Pammy turned to the wild-eyed woman in the driver's seat. "I need you to do me a favor. When I say go, turn up the radio to max. Circle the lot for as long as you can. If I don't make it back to you before the Clankers catch up, just drive. Got it?"

Vera opened her mouth, but instead of arguing, she nodded.

"Give me one second. Wait for my signal!" Pammy slammed the truck door and backtracked to where Guppie sat.

"Give me your shirt," she told him.

Guppie frowned. "I... what?"

"Gimme your shirt." Pammy was already pulling her own ragged button-down over her head to reveal the tank beneath. Guppie shrugged and peeled off his own sweaty, grimy t-shirt. Pammy nodded in approval as he shoved the shirt into her hands. "Dang, Guppie. Who knew you had a six-pack?" She let out a bark of laughter as she jogged backwards, wrapping one shirt around each fist like a makeshift boxing glove. Then she slipped her right hand through and grabbed the long-handled gardening blade. She swung it experimentally once and then nodded to Vera as she passed.

Here goes nothing. Time to test the theory that the Clankers responded to sound waves and audio as much as anything else.

The muffler on the pickup had seen better days, but the radio worked just fine. Pammy grinned to herself as Gretchen Wilson's *Redneck Woman* blared through the speaker. Guppie's kin didn't disappoint.

The Clankers were still swarming the excavator, but when Vera threw the truck into drive, some of them turned to focus on the pickup with the radio blaring. Pammy raised her shoulders and braced her arms, just like Ms. Pennington had shown them in their Self-Defense for Pure Girls during church camp the summer before freshman year.

Aim for your assailant's weakest points. Use their own momentum against them. Hit where it hurts. Stay close. Don't try to win.

As she closed the distance between them she gestured sharply to Cooper. "Get out of there! They'll follow the noise!"

A few of the Clankers crawled off the excavator and headed for the truck. Pammy sucked in a relieved sigh as one scurried past her without so much as looking her way. They were like bees protecting a hive, or swarming ants: they wanted to defend their young, and the loudest equipment presented the biggest threat.

Not all of them ignored her. When one of the Clankers detoured in her direction, she dropped to the tarmac in a forward roll, dodging the Clanker's front legs and landing on her feet beneath it. She stuck the landing, bringing her arms up hard and slamming the gardening blade straight up into the creature's belly.

The exoskeleton cracked under the pressure, and she plunged her wrapped fists in three more times in rapid succession, puncturing clear through to its meaty underbelly with the blade, while the shirts protected her hands from the splintered shell. The Clanker let out a rattle as she spun out from under it with little grace, expecting another attack while she was vulnerable.

But it never came.

It seemed the Clankers no longer showed any interest in attacking in coordination, or even attacking her at all. It was as if their strings had been cut. Whatever single-minded intelligence had driven them before was gone.

Because we killed their King? That had been Sean's theory, and their panicked chaos only seemed to support his notion about what made the Clankers tick.

The next time Pammy looked up, Cooper was rotating the Cat. It seemed to have registered to him that, since they were no longer inside, there was no reason to leave the natatorium intact. He sent the hydraulic arm crashing through the side of the building, raising a cloud of dust and sending bricks flying every which way.

The majority of the swarming Clankers, already in distress, suddenly abandoned their pursuit of the truck and hurried back to the building once more. They were as rattled as she'd ever seen Clankers.

It occurred to her that if she was giving credence to Sean, then she should also consider another of the crazy things he said, specifically that the Clankers reproduced so fast they made rabbits look lazy. Maybe these were all ... new ones? It would explain the confusion.

But surely there were still some of the original ones from the first night around. They wouldn't have a problem if King Clanker was dead.

Pammy leapt into a toe touch as she dodged another of the aliens — *Who knew four years of cheer practice would pay off during the alien Armageddon?* — and punched down into its back when she landed, her blade crashing down into the harder exoskeleton on the back. Not that it mattered, because the alien didn't slow down to even engage her.

She'd almost reached the Cat when the door swung open and Cooper scrambled out. He almost fell in his haste to escape, but he bounced back to his feet when he hit the grass and lit out for her position at a run.

"Keep up!" she shouted above the cacophony of Clanker-song, engines, and Kenny Chesney's *Summertime* blaring from the truck speakers.

In all her life, Pammy had never run so fast. Vera was already headed toward the parking lot exit, and Pammy adjusted course so that their paths would cross.

They were about fifteen feet away when a Clanker reared up between them and the truck. It was big, and Pammy didn't have trouble believing this was a first-night alien. Pammy would have run smack into it if Cooper hadn't caught the back of her shirt in time to pull her back. Pammy raised her blade as the Clanker prepared to strike, but a series of loud *pops* sounded off from the area of the truck. The Clanker writhed before toppling forward with bullet holes in the back of its upper body.

Guppie was kneeling in the truck, an old bolt-action sniper rifle at his shoulder, paler than the butter sculptures at the annual county fair with a pained expression on his face that suggested his back wasn't any better than before.

"We had a *gun?*" Pammy demanded, indignant.

"Len told me where he stashed it in the back of the cab," Guppie said with a shrug. "You never asked before you decided to take off like Wonder Woman."

Pammy shook her head as Cooper shoved her forward.

Cooper managed to reach the truck first, hauling the door open. Pammy vaulted into the front seat and hurled herself over the console into the bucket seats in the back. Cooper climbed in after her, and even before the door was closed behind him, Vera peeled away.

Cooper jammed his thumb at the radio and killed the music.

"Pammy!" he yelped. "That was amazing! You were all... *wham! Pow!*" He lifted his hands in front of him and jabbed at the air.

"Yeah, great." She tore the shredded shirts off her fists and glanced back toward the school. "Just put the pedal to the metal, Vera. Any minute now, those bugs are gonna find..."

A high-pitched screech cut her off, growing in volume by the second until she thought her eardrums would burst. The Clankers' usual call was low and booming, but the pitch and frequency of this screech was agonizing. From the back of the truck, the dogs yelped. Cooper stuck his fingers in his ears, and Vera worked her jaw.

The Clankers were screaming.

"*Faster,*" Pammy said, but she couldn't hear her own voice over the din. She pressed her palms to her ears and swiveled all the way around. Clankers poured forth from the hole in the wall of the natatorium. As she watched, they climbed the excavator *en masse* and pulled off the doors, streaming through the console that Cooper had abandoned.

They don't need a King to lead them now, she thought. Pammy Mae knew exactly how fierce mothers could be. The aliens had been frantic to defend the nest, and now that they knew their nymphs were dead, they had nothing left to lose. Even when Vera laid on the gas, the Clankers nearly kept pace with them.

Pammy spun around to face the console. Her eyes lit on the fuel gauge, and her stomach plummeted.

"We've got less than a quarter tank," she said, raising her voice loud enough to be heard over the shrill of the aliens.

At least we destroyed their nest, she thought grimly, but that was cold comfort. Before long, the last residents of Little Creek would be gone for good.

"That's plenty!" Guppie yelled up to the cab from the back.

Pammy spun around. "What?"

There was a twinkle in Guppie's eye that had absolutely no place in the back of the pickup.

"That's plenty," he repeated. "To get the hell out of Little Creek."

44

COOPER

AS THEY APPROACHED MAIN STREET, Guppie stuck his head through the truck slider. "We're going to Bud Lopez' ranch out on Route 119."

Cooper exchanged a look with Pammy.

"What's out there?" Pammy asked.

"Nothing much. Just Walker Mill's airplane."

"What?" blurted out Cooper.

"Turn right here," Guppie told Vera.

She whipped the wheel to the right. They sailed around the corner so fast that Cooper hit the door, and Pammy Mae let out a yelp from the back seat as she overbalanced.

"Where do I go from here?" Vera demanded.

"Back up the mountain. You can't miss the big signs for his place. You'll turn left into it."

Cooper was still trying to wrap his mind around what Guppie had just said. "How do you know that's where Walk parked his Cessna? I thought it burned with the rest of the planes at Heartland County Municipal."

In fact, he'd dreamed of coming across another plane, but without knowing where one might be, that was a needle in a haystack. He knew there were homebuilts around — *hillbillies love flying bicycles*, Walk liked to say — but unlike his dad, he didn't know a lot of pilots in the area.

"Sean told me," Guppie said.

Sean? "He didn't say anything to me."

"The crazy bastard was fixated on that King Clanker. He kept it to himself because I'm guessing he thought he'd lose his shot."

"That sounds about right," Pammy said. "So you know how to fly?"

The question was directed at Guppie, but he shook his head and pointed at Cooper.

Pammy looked over at him in surprise. "You? Nate said you blew your dad off when he offered to pay for lessons for you."

"Yeah, I did." He shrugged. What else was there to say? Walk had let his license lapse and his dad had his pulled. But Walk had kept his plane and dared the government to do something about it. He'd taken Cooper up and given him private lessons just because he liked his dad. Then Cooper had decided he didn't want anything to do with it and stopped.

"I mean, I've never flown *solo*," he admitted. "But I practiced a lot of takeoffs and touch and go's and I can fly visually just fine."

Vera glanced back at him. "When was the last time you actually flew?"

"I dunno. Eight years ago?"

Pammy guffawed and Vera jerked her eyes to the rearview mirror.

"I've played a lot of flight simulator since then."

Guppie reached through the truck slider and slapped Cooper's shoulder. "It's like riding a bike. It'll all come back."

Cooper turned away from Pammy and tried to ignore her

staring at him. Her accusations from that first night rang in his ears. *You've been useless all night, Cooper. Nothing you've done has helped even slightly.*

Hopefully this plan wouldn't get them all killed... although, if it did, there would be no one to hold him accountable.

The sun was creeping toward the horizon as the pickup climbed the mountain for the last time. Cooper's heart was pounding so fast it could have powered the engine on its own.

"There it is," Guppie said, pointing at a big overhanging sign that said *La Tierra Verde Rancho.*

Vera turned in, and Cooper's teeth rattled as they sped over the rocky gravel road that led into the ranch proper.

The ranch was enormous, and Cooper knew that the Lopez family spent the summers up in New York. He suspected that Walk had the place to himself whenever he wanted to take his plane up.

Cooper scanned for the telltale signs of an airstrip...

"There!" Cooper shouted. The windsock was the giveaway, fluttering lightly in the breeze. Below it, the ground had been graded down for a dirt taxiway to a narrow grass strip. It was plenty long, at least.

"There's the hangar," Guppie said, pointing to a pair of connected tin roof sheds at the far end of the dirt taxiway.

As soon as the truck juddered to a stop, Cooper kicked the door ajar and launched out.

It took an agonizingly long time for all of them to get out of the truck: Vera clutching a battered backpack; Guppie carrying Len's limp body in both arms; the dogs limping after them; and Pammy Mae bringing up the rear, walking backwards and watching the woods on either side of the grass strip.

Cooper was dimly aware of shadows moving around them, closing in as he pulled the big hanger doors open.

His heart sank when he looked in. "That's not his plane."

Guppie hobbled past. "Let's not get picky, Cooper." He carried the sniper rifle around his neck and had his eyes along the treeline like Pammy.

"I mean, this won't do. This is a Cessna 152. Not a 172."

"So?"

"So it's not a four-seater. It's a *two*-seater!"

The Cessna 152, like the 172, had a high-wing design with a wide fuselage that sat on tricycle-style landing gear. But for all their similarities, it was the differences that were going to get them killed. It was smaller, older, and lower-powered.

"It'll be tight," Guppie said. He'd already opened the passenger door and was looking inside. "But there's enough room if three of us squeeze in the cargo space in back."

"No," Cooper said. "You don't understand. It can't carry that much weight. It's made for two people, maybe three with minimal gear."

"We'll figure it out," Pammy said. She yanked the chocks away from the wheels. "We need to ditch weight, right? So what can we take off this thing?"

"The doors will come off," Guppie offered. "I've seen these things fly without doors at all. Hell, you shoulda seen half the helos we flew back in the day."

"And we don't exactly need two seats, do we?" Vera offered. She was already examining the base of the co-pilot's seat. "Damned if I know how to get it out, though."

"It's probably pin-linkage," Guppie said as he went running for a toolbox. "We need to hurry. You heard those Clankers howling. They're angry and they're chasing us."

Cooper shook his head. "It won't be enough. We'll have to leave the dogs and even—"

"We aren't leaving the damn dogs," Pammy snapped. Guppie

tossed her a hammer and she ripped the shear-hinge off the passenger door with one swing and wrestled it off the fuselage with no finesse whatsoever.

Pammy lifted Phobos up the side of the plane until the dog was able to jump in, then tried to pick Deimos up.

"He saved my life," she insisted. "We're not leaving them." In the end she crouched down and let the big dog use her as a step-stool until he, too, was safely inside.

Guppie used a punch and hammer to make quick work of the pilot-side door. By the time that Cooper made it into the left-hand chair, Pammy and Guppie had already detached the co-pilot's seat. Guppie tossed it clear and he and Pammy jumped in.

This is insane. At least he had a seatbelt. There was nothing more than a foot-high lip to keep the rest of them from falling out of the plane on either side.

Cooper tried to quiet his mind. He could hear Walk telling him to just follow the checklists and he'd be fine. *Shortcuts are what kill most pilots, not a lack of skill.*

Cooper reached under his seat and found the laminated checklist in a clipboard, right next to the logbook.

He found the headset hanging on the control column and put it on.

"What are you doing?" Pammy exploded from his right. With the seat gone, she was sitting awkwardly on her knees with Deimos in front of her. "Are you going to call the tower for clearance?"

"Right," Cooper mumbled, pulling the headset back off. "It's just on the checklist."

"Screw the checklist."

"Look, if I miss something, we'll be dead, OK?"

Guppie suddenly pitched forward from where he'd been squeezed next to Vera and Len.

"We're gonna be dead anyway if we don't take off quick." He pointed and they all turned to look.

While there were trees around the ranch house and the airstrip, there was nothing but open corn fields looking back the way they'd come.

Cooper could just see the squiggling lines of movement all rushing in their direction. It wouldn't be long before the first of them had reached the edge of the runway.

Cooper flashed back to a science program he'd watched on TV as a kid where they'd inserted a tiny camera into an ant farm. As an eight-year-old, he'd cried because the ants looked so big.

Man, I was a dumb kid. Didn't know how lucky I had it.

Pammy turned to him. "Cooper…"

He took a deep breath. "Right."

No checklist. Just memory. You can do this. *What really matters?* In his mind, he skipped past a dozen different steps to the big ones. *Fuel. Flaps. Thrust.*

He reached down and slapped the fuel shutoff valve to the on position and opened the throttle. Then he grabbed the fuel primer and gave it four quick pumps.

"Here goes nothing."

He flipped the master switch and the gyros all came to life on the instrument panel. He said a silent prayer and glanced at the fuel gauge. Half-full. *That'll do.*

He took another deep breath and cranked the ignition over.

And cranked it. And cranked it.

For an agonizing few seconds, nothing happened.

Then the engine caught, and the propeller came to life.

"Yes!" he shouted.

The plane instantly jerked forward and to the left and the left wingtip almost smashed into the hangar door as the plane roared out.

"Shit!" He'd forgotten to set the parking brake.

Not that it mattered now. He mashed down with the foot petals to turn the nose wheel and nearly put the other wing in the dirt when he overcompensated. It was hard to tip over a tricycle plane, but he was doing his best.

Finally it bounced back upright and straightened out.

Cooper took a second to get his bearings when Guppie shouted, "Here they come!"

Cooper glanced over, but Pammy was right in his face. "Go, go, go!"

He shoved the throttle all the way in, spun the flaps to ten degrees, and pointed the plane down the center of the grass airstrip.

From the backseat, Guppie fired his rifle and the sound almost made Cooper lose control of the plane again.

"Does this thing go any faster?" Guppie shouted over the sound of the engine. "I thought we were taking off, not Sunday driving."

"I told you, we're overweight. It's going to take a second—"

Guppie's gun went off again and a spent cartridge bounced off Cooper's shoulder. He risked another glance and immediately wished he hadn't. The nearest Clanker was less than a hundred feet away. He could see their glassy eyes reflecting evening sunlight back at him.

He turned forward and looked down at the instrument panel.

40 knots.

41 knots.

42 knots.

Too slow still.

"Look out!" Vera shouted.

Cooper glanced up and his heart stopped.

A Clanker was standing in the middle of the runway.

He instinctively yanked back on the yoke and the little plane sprang into the air. He had no idea if a Clanker could jump or not.

In the end, it didn't matter. The bottom of the propeller sheared right through the top half of the Clanker. It must have turned upward in an attempt to attack them. The long tongue was shredded and the front of its proboscis ripped right off.

The plane was nowhere near ready for liftoff, though. It drifted back down and the big, low-pressure tires absorbed the impact as they settled back on the grass airstrip.

At this point, the runway was starting to curve downward off the back slope of the mountain. Cooper hoped this would finally give them the momentum they needed to get airborne, although that would do little to help him hold level flight, let alone climb, with an overloaded plane.

Some alarm sounded in the back of his mind. Even too slow for liftoff, the plane was too sluggish. *What am I missing, Walk? What is the shortcut that's going to kill me?*

Trim! He'd forgotten to set trim!

Cooper frantically looked down and found the trim wheel. He spun it to the takeoff position.

He glanced back at the airspeed indicator.

55 knots.

Barely fast enough, and still too slow for an overweight plane. But getting there. Just another few seconds...

"Cooper!" Pammy shouted. She was pointing out the front windshield.

He looked up to find trees looming up ahead of them.

He was out of airstrip.

He pulled up on the yoke and felt the plane straining to gain altitude.

"Pull up, pull up, pull up!" Pammy shouted.

But he couldn't, not like she wanted. If he did, he'd take away too much speed. He had to feather it to keep gaining altitude without losing speed.

"This will be close!" he shouted as the tops of the trees stubbornly refused to dip below the windshield.

If I only graze them, we might still be OK...

He only saw the Clanker in the trees because he was looking right at the treetops.

It was a big one, maybe as big as King Clanker. It was definitely one that had come with the first wave.

It tensed for a moment, and the tree it was in quivered.

Cooper watched in horror, unable to do anything at all about it.

Just as it pounced, Guppie's rifle barrel stuck out the open side of the cabin where the door had been and discharged.

The sound was so loud that Cooper was momentarily deafened.

The glistening eyes in the center of the creature deformed and splattered open where the bullet hit. But the creature's forward momentum carried it toward the plane.

Guppie fired again and hit it once more right in the proboscis. It ripped clean through the alien and exploded out the back, tearing off exoskeleton as it went.

The Clanker banged against the side of the plane, then bounced off and toppled down to the trees below.

Cooper fought to hold the plane in flight. He desperately watched his instrument panel. *RPM. Oil Pressure. Temperature. Fuel.*

Everything held in the green. The Clanker hadn't done any damage.

Behind him, Guppie let out a mad cackle that would have made Sean proud. "Hot damn, kid, you did it!" he shouted as he slapped Cooper on the shoulder.

Cooper barely felt it. The plane was still desperately struggling for altitude and airspeed. It was a fine line and Cooper had to straddle it, or they were dead.

If there had been so much as a hill in their way, they would have crashed. But luckily they were going east, and it was basically downhill from Little Creek all the way to the Atlantic.

He spotted the interstate. Since they were flying so low, it was hard to miss. He turned and began following it. It would take them all the way to Keystone.

He finally started to relax and felt his hunched shoulders lower. He was drenched in sweat.

He glanced behind him to see that Vera was also hunched over, tending to Len, who appeared to have passed out.

Pammy leaned over and raised her voice. "Nice work," she said and nudged his arm. "I mean it. We'd be toast if it wasn't for you."

Cooper stared straight ahead. "I knew we'd make it. I *knew* it."

He didn't feel that way at all, or hadn't until moments ago, but it was nice to say it aloud. It made it seem like it had been true all along. He turned to Pammy and smiled. He was weirdly giddy. "And I *knew* you were alive. Didn't I, Vera? Didn't I tell you?"

"Sure did," Vera muttered from the back, not looking up from her work. The dogs sniffed around her, examining Len with deep concern.

A strange expression passed over Pammy's face. "Is that why you came to the school? For me?"

Cooper nodded.

"Well, and because Len wanted to punch King Clanker in the balls for indirectly blowing up the bunker with roughly a quarter ton of C-4," Guppie added. "Long story."

Pammy blinked a few times. Cooper thought she might be fighting back tears. "I... thank you. I didn't realize."

"You'd have done the same for me. You *did* do the same."

Cooper nudged her with his shoulder. "We make a good team, don't we? And now we're going to Keystone, where we'll hopefully find your mom, and my parents, and some people who have a plan to fight the Clankers."

Pammy bit her lip and frowned at the ground. "Yeah. Hopefully."

45

LEN

PAIN PIERCED the veil that surrounded Len, and he twitched. He wanted to raise his hand to fend off the source of the pain, but his limbs were like lead.

"Len?" Vera's voice was gentle in her ear.

Len opened one eye. The other seemed to be stuck; try as he might, he couldn't part the lids.

"Where...?" he grunted.

Vera laid one hand on his good shoulder. "We got out."

Len's eye roamed around him. They were in a cramped space. The walls were curved, but there was an enormous amount of air and noise whipping around them. The only illumination came from the flashlight that Guppie held, pointed almost directly at his face.

"Bright," he grumbled.

"Sorry." Guppie lowered the beam. "Vera was trying to figure out what to do about your..." He circled his own eye with one finger.

"Here, Len. This might hurt, but I'll try to be gentle." Vera picked up a white plastic pack and crunched it between her hands, then extended it toward Len's cheek. "It's an instant cold pack, so it should help with the swelling..."

She pressed it gently against Len's eye, and the pain deepened. Len groaned and shifted away from her.

"Sorry, sorry." Vera pulled the pack away. "I'm afraid that your orbital bones have taken a beating. I'm hoping I can take a closer look when we get to Keystone."

"Keystone?" Len repeated. His mouth was bone-dry. "Are we...? How?" Moving his jaw had gotten more difficult, and the terrain of his mouth was different. *How hard did I hit the ground, exactly?*

"Cooper thinks we'll be there in a couple of hours." Vera fiddled with the pack again.

Len shuddered and turned his head, trying to get a better view of their surroundings. Cooper sat in the only seat in what he realized now was a small airplane, his hands at the controls. Pammy was uncomfortably on her knees next to him. There were, he realized, no doors. That was the cause of the wind and noise.

The dogs lay beside Len, who had his head on Vera's lap, along with somehow Guppie squeezed in. He was reminded of an old movie about a family driving across country in a station wagon. Deimos was snuffling in his sleep, and Phobos was lying on his side, snoring gently.

"They're okay?" he asked.

Vera nodded. "As far as I can tell. They've taken a beating, but all of us have. I don't see anything wrong with them that a few days of rest won't cure. Here, Pammy, hand me the water, and we'll try again with the cold pack."

Pammy obediently reached into the pack lying beside her and

produced a bottle of water. Vera lay the pack across her leg, cracked the lid of the bottle, and slid one arm beneath Len's head. "You're going to have to sit up a little. Let me help."

Len did his best to help, but Vera's efforts were the main reason that he managed to struggle upright. He leaned against her shoulder and opened his mouth so that Vera could offer small sips from the bottle, mouthful by mouthful, until it was empty.

"Enough for now," Len rasped. He was still thirsty, but the effort of staying upright was too great, even with Vera holding him. "Where's Sean?"

Vera lowered him back to the floor. "Gone."

Len let his eye fall shut. "And we found an airplane?"

"That's about the size of it. Your idea to storm the school was good..."

"Not good enough."

"Hey," Guppie said. "We killed a bunch of the bastards — we damn near took out an entire brood — and we got King Clanker. That's something."

"And now we're headed to Keystone," Vera added. "None of us would be here right now if it weren't for you."

They were talking to him like this should be *good* news, but in a choice between a Clanker nest and the military, Len figured it was just about a toss-up. At least with the Clankers, he didn't have to wonder about their motives.

"You should get some rest." Vera patted Len's arm. "I've done everything I can for now, and when we get to Keystone, I'll take a look at that eye. Okay? In the meantime, I'm going to lay this cold pack on your face as gently as possible. Too much swelling could put pressure on the eyeball itself..."

Len nodded his agreement and braced for the weight of the cool compress.

He'd done what Carla asked. He'd survived the invasion. Now all he had to do was survive the Army, and figure out if his wife was still alive somewhere.

We've made it out of the frying pan, he thought grimly, *and now it's time to throw ourselves onto the fire.*

EPILOGUE

———

"DR. BONAPARTE, DR. STEWARD, DR. NOLTE."

Carla turned as the lab door opened and three men in military uniforms stepped through.

The man with the most stars and bars on his uniform nodded curtly to each of them. Carla still couldn't keep their ranks straight, and the man before them was unfamiliar. The researchers and the Army guys tended to steer clear of one another. "I'm going to have to ask you to come with me."

Stew, still leaning back, opened his arms wide. "Actually, we aren't doctors. We were doctoral candidates when you guys kidnapped us. Remember? Also, we're still on break."

The officer's lips pressed into a thin line, and Stew sighed. "Fine."

The three of them got to their feet, although Stew grumbled under his breath as they followed their escort down the sterile, army-gray halls of the survival outpost. Carla kept her head down, but as always, she stayed watchful. If there was a way to break out of the place, she was going to find it one of these days.

Where's Len right now? she wondered. As far as she knew, he'd had time to prepare for first contact.

Sweet Len... whenever she thought of him, the first image that sprang to mind was of him standing at the altar at their wedding. He was so handsome. During their first dance, he'd gazed down into her smiling face and told her, *I can't wait to see what you'll be like as a mother.*

She'd rolled her eyes and kissed him once, to the cheers of their guests. *Let's start with a dog and go from there.*

Carla's lips curled up involuntarily at the memory. Then her eyes refocused on the halls of the underground outpost. Len was always a fighter, but honestly... what were the odds that he'd made it this long?

Low. But that wasn't going to stop her from hoping.

Their escort led them to a reinforced steel door, where the officer knocked twice.

"Name and rank?" a voice on the far side asked.

"This is General Greene. I have our research team in tow."

Carla and Nathan exchanged a skeptical glance, and Stew crossed his arms.

The door unlocked and swung inward. They were on a solar generator, but in an effort to conserve power, they used personnel security protocols rather than keycards and scanners. In Carla's opinion, it gave the whole place a very Cold War, cloak-and-dagger vibe that would have been amusing if this wasn't her *life*.

The General ushered them into the room, while his cronies took up the rear. Carla waited for Stew to take the first step, but

Stew shook his head, bowing low and extending his arms to the open door.

"You first, Carla."

Carla went first, taking slow, measured steps. It wouldn't shock her to learn that she'd been deemed disposable and that the General had brought them here to kill them without making too much of a fuss. The room inside reminded her of their old lab, with a bank of computers along one wall. In the middle of the room stood a round dais, and on that...

Carla had yet to lay eyes on a *homoptera invadendae* firsthand. She'd seen the footage, of course. There was no mistaking the creature. It writhed when it saw her and let out a rumbling growl, then flung itself toward her.

Carla dropped into a crouch and raised her arms protectively.

"There, there," the General said. "At ease."

Carla didn't blink as the creature bashed itself against the glass that surrounded it. She slowly dropped her arms.

The dais formed the base of what amounted to a high-tech terrarium. The creature threw its segmented body against the glasslike substance again and again, still making that low, echoing noise.

"Holy *hell*." Stew stepped into the lab and his jaw dropped. "Look at the bastard. He's a big one, isn't he?"

"Which means it's probably a female," Nathan added.

The rest of them hung back, but Stew walked right up to the glass and laid both palms against it. The creature drummed its legs against the material, then jabbed its wickedly serrated proboscis against the glass.

"Hungry, huh?" The mocking lilt in Steward's voice set Carla's teeth on edge.

"This is your new assignment," Greene informed them. "You know more than anyone else in this facility about these beasties,

based on what you were able to discern from the message you
intercepted, and we're looking for more information. A way to
fight back. Do whatever—"

"Oh, *now* you want to fight back," Stew snapped.

Greene didn't miss a beat. "Shocking as it may seem, there is
more going on than you are privy to."

"It must not be going great," Nathan noted.

"We're planning for every contingency, doctor."

"Not a doc-tooor," Stew sang.

Carla felt sick and her voice shook as she spoke. "Just to be
clear, there's more of a plan than just hiding until this all magically
blows over?"

"There's a broader plan," Greene agreed.

"Which is?"

"Classified."

Stew looked like he might have an aneurysm. "What a
load of—"

"As I was saying," Greene interjected. "Do whatever you want
with this one; we can always get you more. I believe Mr. Nolte had
a background in biology, and our host here, Dr. Sharma, is an
accomplished entomologist."

Greene gestured to the woman holding the door open, the one
who had apparently let them in. She appeared to be in her early
sixties, with heavy glasses, silver hair, and no trace of mirth in her
gaze.

"If you need anything, you can reach us over the network chat
on the computers," Greene said. "We'll do what we can to support
you, within reason."

Stew offered him a lopsided salute. "Heard and under-sterd,
mon capitan."

One of these days, Stew's attitude was going to earn him a
bullet in the head, but today was apparently not that day; Greene

nodded to his men, and the three of them retreated. Sharma closed the door firmly in their wake.

Stew grinned at their new companion. "So, Dr. *Shawarma*, what's your deal?"

Sharma flipped him the bird. "I've heard about you, Jeremy Steward. Watch your mouth with me if you don't want to end up as bug food." She turned on her heel and withdrew to the computer bank. Settling into one of the chairs, she informed them, "This one's mine. As long as you're helping, we'll get along, but if you're going to pull any *boys-will-be-boys* antics, get out of my face and don't waste my time."

Stew snorted and punched Nathan's shoulder. "I like her already."

As the others claimed their computer stations and sat down, Carla looked again at the alien, which had calmed down and was watching them with uncanny intensity.

The *invadendae* might be the enemy of humanity, but Carla wasn't convinced that they were her biggest problem.

Three weeks ago, as the invasion began and no coordinated response seemed imminent, the three of them had sat in their bunks and wondered what the military knew that they didn't.

She saw now that it was the other way around. It was what the military *didn't* know. They clearly didn't know what was coming until the last moment. The plan to save the government had been hastily executed. If there was a 'broader plan,' she was willing to bet it was being orchestrated by the same group that had conspired to bury the warning message in the first place. That was treason against the entire human race as far as she was concerned.

She still had no idea who that group was specifically—or why they had done it. But she was getting closer to finding out.

Yeah, she thought, staring at the glass enclosure. *This just might be the perfect opportunity to get revenge on the monsters who destroyed my world.*

————

FIND OUT
WHAT HAPPENS
NEXT!

Click here to read
UPRISING
(Heartland Aliens Book 2)

GET FREE BOOKS!

Building a relationship with readers is my favorite thing about writing.

My regular newsletter, *The Reader Crew,* is the best way to stay up-to-date on new releases, special offers, and all kinds of cool stuff about science fiction past and present.

Just for joining the fun, I'll send you 3 free books.

Join The Reader Crew (it's free) today!

—*Joshua James*

ALSO BY JOSHUA JAMES

Saturn's Legacy Series (4 books)

Gunn & Salvo Series (7 books so far)

Box sets

Lucky's Marines (Books 1-9)

Lucky's Mercs (Books 1-4)

The Lost Starship (Books 1-3)

With Scott Bartlett:

Relentless Box Set: The Complete Fleet Ops Trilogy

With Daniel Young:

Oblivion (Books 1-9)

Outcast Starship (Books 1-9)

Legacy of War (Books 1-3)

Heritage of War (ongoing)

Stars Dark (Books 1-8)

————

Click here to read
UPRISING
(Heartland Aliens Book 2)